Blood Slaves

Blood Slaves

Markus Redmond

KENSINGTON PUBLISHING CORP.

kensingtonbooks.com

DAFINA BOOKS are published by
Kensington Publishing Corp.
900 Third Ave.
New York, NY 10022

All Kensington Titles, Imprints, and Distributed Lines are available at special quantity discounts for bulk purchases for sales promotions, premiums, fund-raising, and educational or institutional use. Special book excerpts or customized printings can also be created to fit specific needs. For details, write or phone the office of the Kensington special sales manager: Kensington Publishing Corp, 900 Third Ave., New York, NY 10022, Attn: Special Sales Department, Phone: 1-800-221-2647.

The DAFINA logo is a trademark of Kensington Publishing Corp.

ISBN: 978-1-4967-5316-8
First Kensington Hardcover Edition: August 2025

ISBN: 978-1-4967-5318-2 (ebook)

10 9 8 7 6 5 4 3 2 1

Printed in the United States of America

Library of Congress Control Number: 2024944353

Interior design by Leah Marsh. Map design by Cassandra Farrin, North American map courtesy of Kaldari and Halava/Wikimedia Commons. Adinkra symbols: drutska/Adobe Stock; blood spatters: grumpybox/Adobe Stock; fleur de lis: Alvara Cabrera/The Noun Project; flames: Jonas/The Noun Project, kareemov1000/The Noun Project, iejank/The Noun Project.

The authorized representative in the EU for product safety and compliance
is eucomply OU, Parnu mnt 139b-14, Apt 123
Tallinn, Berlin 11317, hello@eucompliancepartner.com

In thanks to Herschell & Thelma for the past, Jeremy, for the gleaming future, and Isis, the sweetest Strawberry, for my eternal present.

Please note the following trigger/content warnings:

Blood and gore

Violence, nudity, murder, maulings

Treatment of slaves, including beatings; torture; emotional, psychological, and physical abuse; sexual abuse, including rape; child abuse, including pedophilia; cultural abuse; racism, including racist slurs, hate speech, and systemic racism

This is not a story about slavery.

This is a story about a slave.

Gives me freedom or gives me death!

—Akwasi Nwosu, aka "Charlie," 1710

DEAR READER,

First and foremost, thank you for choosing *Blood Slaves*. There is certainly no shortage of wonderful books to choose from, so I sincerely hope you enjoy this wild and bloody ride! Especially since, technically, it wasn't supposed to happen.

You see, I didn't intend to write *Blood Slaves* initially—I just wanted to write a badass vampire book. That's exactly what I was in the middle of writing in May 2020, right before George Floyd was murdered. Suddenly, I felt stunted. I got lost in the news footage, the villainous video of him dying under the knee of Derek Chauvin, the police officer's hands stuffed in his pockets, sunglasses above his forehead, causal as you please.

Then came the protests, the outrage that drove people from their homes in multitudes to decry the senseless murder of a Black man by the police in the middle of a pandemic, when both the science and medical communities were begging us to stay home to "stop the spread."

I was outraged, too.

By the outrage.

George Floyd's murder was tragic, yes, but by no means a new or unique occurrence. Countless Black men and women have had their lives snuffed out by police officers who then faced little to no consequences. It happened while a Black man was in the Oval Office. It happened during the Civil Rights Movement in the 1960s. It's been happening since the era of slavery in colonial America. In fact, modern law enforcement has its roots in the slave patrol. Founded in South Carolina in 1704, its purpose was to "empower" the white population by organizing groups of armed men to monitor the movements of enslaved Black people, especially those who escaped or were viewed as defiant, and enforce discipline.

In other words: hunt down Black people.

So, in the spring of 2020, 401 years after the first enslaved Africans were brought to these shores by the colonists, yet another Black man was murdered by police. But all the indignation felt disingenuous. People were fed up with wearing masks, and this man's murder provided the perfect, righteous excuse to finally get out of the house. It all made me feel as though no one thought of George Floyd as a person. Just a reason to do or say whatever it was they felt like doing or saying.

That reminded me of all the times I'd felt less than a person because my skin was different than the people I was dealing with. The degrading auditions I went to as an actor for roles labeled "Thug #4" when I had worked for years, meticulously, to hone my craft.

The time I was pulled over by police, my heart pounding in my throat, taken to the police station and held, while officers took pictures with me to show their kids, then made me write "Doogie" as my employer on the police report.

All of this over a taillight that had gone out.

Standing in that police station, surrounded by white men with badges, and guns, and power, who got a kick out of "booking the Black guy on that TV show," I knew what the consequence would be for me if I didn't go along with the humiliation. That if I was going to make it out of the situation unscathed, they were going to have to think of me as one of the "good ones."

And that thought made me angry.

Now, listen. I understand this pales in comparison to people who have had to pay for their skin color with their lives. But all the same, I was left feeling powerless—until I went back to my vampire book.

Vampires. I started wishing I could be one. An all-powerful, immortal being. How easy it would be to take revenge against those who had oppressed me and others who had been maltreated with that kind of power. How quickly scores could be settled, even ones that were centuries old. So much could be changed. So many wrongs could be righted. The kind of power that could change culture, society. History.

So, I abandoned the vampire story I was writing and embarked on a new and very different one. On July 8, 2020, forty-four days after the murder of George Floyd, I started writing *Blood Slaves*. No notes, no outline, just raw, furious words. Each one I wrote gave me my power back, made me feel like a whole person again. Worthy. Forty-four days later, I had a finished first draft.

Now, we're here.

My hope for you, dear reader, is to realize that, like the Ramangans of this saga, your power resides within you, that it is yours, and that it is always there for you. All you have to do is claim it. Trust it. Embrace it. When we stand firmly in our power in the spirit of good, it only grows. And because we feel powerful, we can recognize and respect the power in everyone else and see all as individuals deserving of their hopes and dreams without explanation or justification. Existence should be the only prerequisite for giving and getting common decency, no matter what color skin you were born with.

I wish to thank both my agent Jennifer Chevais and the good people at Kensington Publishing, my editor Leticia Gomez in particular, who felt all the things I am hoping you will feel, for championing this story, and getting it out into the world and your hands. And don't worry, it's still the badass vampire book I started out wanting to write.

Welcome to the rebellion.

Sincerely,
Markus Redmond

The New World
ca. 1710

18 years since they's put me on that ship

Western
Sea

Parts
un

We are but things of
death stealing life.

One

1407, THE FINAL YEAR OF THE RAMANGA

othing was more delectable to his ears than the screams of terrified humans. Fear made blood rich with flavor.

And Rafazi was famished.

Through his red-tinted vision, he chased the fleeing people of the Ouahaza village. This was a favorite game of his kind: They would use their inhuman speed to whip the fear of their prey into a frenzy, blurring past them with the promise of violence before pouncing. It made the blood so much better when they finally fed.

Rafazi spotted a young man in the distance, running away with all his might. His filthy appearance told him the human farmed the land. The smell of his blood was intoxicating. Rafazi thrust himself forward, and within seconds, the farmhand's throat was in his grasp. The young man screamed at Rafazi, and he laughed in delight. He knew he looked monstrous; his eyes glowed bright red, made even brighter by his engorged and extended brow. The veins in his dark face were transparent, making the blood coursing through them visible.

The man's screams became whimpers when Rafazi opened his mouth, revealing it to be full of sharp, jagged teeth; the upper row framed by two longer, razor-sharp fangs. Rafazi dug the thick talons shooting out from the ends of his fingers into the sides of the farmhand's neck, just enough to extract a sampling of blood. Rafazi ran his tongue across his talons, savoring the blood coating them, no longer listening to the farmhand's screams.

Taking a moment to look across the village, now left in utter chaos by his brothers and sisters of the Blood, Rafazi reveled in what he'd become.

Four centuries ago, he'd been a small and broken man of fifty living in the Ukami village in the Kingdom of Nri, harvesting grapes for a callous winemaker who paid him meagerly. Then *She* changed everything. She was the most beautiful woman to ever bless his eyes. Her dark skin was rich and without blemish, Her hair lush and wild; Her voluptuousness took away his power of speech. He'd hardly believed it when She'd merely spoken to him.

She had been obviously wealthy and worldly, everything he wasn't.

She was also dead.

Despite no longer drawing breath, She was far more alive than he'd ever been. Once the stunningly beautiful woman made him what She was, She left him in the care of others of their kind, then promptly disappeared. He would see Her every hundred years or so, whenever She felt a need. It was rumored She enjoyed spending time in the Kingdom of England, but he had no way of knowing for sure.

Regardless, he remained ever faithful in his devotion to Her, and rightfully so. Because of Her, the eternal power of the great Gamab's blood, a greatness only Alkebulan's divinity could provide, rushed through his veins. In death, She gave him life. She made him part of the Tribe, a community, a place of belonging.

Though the Kingdom of Ghana was the tribe's home, they traveled far and wide into parts of Europa and even Anatolia. They pillaged and plundered their way through foreign lands, taking what they wanted and devouring anyone who tried to stop them. They experienced fine art, language, culture.

Above all else, however, was the congregation of power She made him a part of. In his former life, Rafazi was weak, stepped on, looked over. But his new tribe possessed power beyond human possibility. And now, so did he. Never again would he have to suffer humiliation or degradation at the hands of another.

He'd been reborn. He was free.

Some of the others in the tribe would grant the Blood to outsiders for the right amount of gold, but Rafazi never did. He never saw the point in creating responsibility for himself beyond the fulfillment of all his earthly desires for the price of forever feasting on the glory of blood. His bloodlust was his second master after Her.

Rafazi sank his teeth and fangs into the farmhand's neck, and fresh, warm life entered his mouth. He gulped it down heartily.

So deeply engrossed was he in his own satiation, it took the rallying cry of one of his own to alert him to the danger upon them. Warriors brandishing blades of silver had charged into the village. Rafazi watched with trepidation as blood and blades flew. Having drained the farmhand he'd been feeding from, he discarded the body and backed away.

"A coward in life, a coward in death, eh, Rafazi?"

A surge passed through him at the sound of Her voice. He turned and blinked as though his eyes deceived him. The One who made him, the One he secretly pined after for centuries, stood before him, as beautiful as ever. Her skin, the deep rich color of brown scapolite, enthralled him now as much as it had at their first encounter, as did the red glow of Her eyes. He'd learned many languages in his travels—another perk of the Blood—including the one She spoke to him in now. He remembered Her telling him on Her last visit it was one of Her favorites.

"While your brothers and sisters meet their doom, you run and hide," She noted.

"No," he said, racking his brain for an excuse his Maker would find pleasing. "I was . . ."

"You were worried for yourself. I made you, Rafazi. I know your blood. You cannot lie to me. And I have never faulted your selfish nature." She paused. "But there is a plague coming."

"A plague?" he scoffed. "What plague can harm us? We are above human illness."

"And yet their tainted blood poisons us. This is no mere fever, famine, or pestilence. I have never seen an affliction like it. Though death comes slowly for the humans who carry it, drinking from one who does leads us to our immediate destruction. Whosoever drinks from any human infected by it will be rendered into an immobile stupor, leaving the senses dulled and powerless against warriors wishing to separate our heads from our bodies. I fear it is a plague beyond this world's making."

"By what force?" Rafazi asked her.

"I do not know. It is beyond the power of man. It could be the work of the gods."

"Are we not gods above men?"

"You fool! We have been granted this power by the gift of Gamab's blood. Could it not be taken away if we are deemed unworthy of it?"

The distress in Her voice shook Rafazi to his core. Never had he seen Her as he did now: frightened and tainted by remorse.

4

"For century after century, we have exacted nothing but our own pleasure at the expense of our own ancestors," She mused, even as battle cries filled the air behind them. "There is not one among us who was not born human, yet we devour our past and use mortal blood to sustain our future."

"But this is the fate of our kind. Their blood is what sustains us," Rafazi argued.

"We are but things of death stealing life. As I stole yours."

"My life was no life."

"And yet, it was yours, and I stole it away from you. I decided your fate. I did not have the right. This plague has come as a reminder: We are not gods, Rafazi. Still, so long as we exist, we must protect ourselves."

"How? If we cannot feed, we cannot fight off their silver, and we will perish!"

"Which is why you must instead partake of the beasts, as the humans do, to sustain yourself. It is rumored some infect themselves with the plague to prey upon us. You must alert your brothers and sisters not to drink from any human until this plague passes, and you must join their numbers in a display of fierceness, and strike fear in the hearts of those who continue to hunt us!"

Rafazi knew himself. With his inhuman strength and speed, avoiding silver blades was possible, so long as he had sufficient blood, and the best kind was human. Though he had battled against humans in the past, he did not prefer to. He was not one to lead others into war; and despite the remorse his Maker expressed for their nature in light of this plague, Rafazi was not ready to depart his existence.

As a human, he'd been terrified of death. Having survived it, he was even more determined to hold onto his existence, right or wrong. He was still haunted by the short moments of black he was engulfed in before being reborn, and he'd vowed never to see such darkness ever again.

He reveled in the velvety softness of Her hand against his cheek and closed his eyes in rapture as She drew closer. His lips parted and quivered with his desire for Her. He desperately wanted to hold Her, kiss Her, but he didn't dare.

"Tell them," She whispered. "Perhaps there is a way our might can serve this earth, but only if we survive, by the blood of Gamab."

"By the blood of Gamab," he whispered back, but he could already feel the wind from Her blur speeding away. "Jenue," he breathed devotedly as She disappeared.

A guttural scream turned his attention back to the battle, where Rotina, the leader of their tribal band, was ripping the head off a warrior who had slashed her with his blade. As the other warriors came for her, she flipped the head she held and cradled it against her as she sprouted large, fleshy red wings from her back. Her wingspan was so great the warriors were sent to the ground when she flapped them and rose into the air, causing them to cry out in terror.

Rafazi saw her grimace in pain from the gaping gash in her side, but Rotina was the eldest and strongest among them. Had she not been able to escape the pursuing blades, she would have been done for, but once she could ingest the blood from the warrior's head she carried, she would heal and lay waste to them all. Once the battle was over, he would share his Maker's news with Rotina.

She would know what to do.

Rotina suddenly seized up in midair, and the head she'd been drinking from tumbled from her grasp. Her wings flailed wildly, and her red eyes went black before her head slumped, and she stopped moving. Stiff and lifeless, she slammed to the earth below. The warriors rushed to her, slicing her to pieces with their blades. He now knew the warriors' blood carried the plague.

Rafazi reared back in horror as others of his tribe who were feeding on both the villagers and warriors succumbed to a similar fate, right before being decapitated. There was nothing left for him to do but save himself.

If he could.

There was no way to know if the farmhand was infected. Stricken with dread, Rafazi used the speed of his blur to disappear into the night.

IN THE FOLLOWING MONTHS, more and more of his brethren and sistren fell victim to those afflicted with the plague and the warriors who came afterward. Rafazi abandoned his tribe, choosing to pass for human. He fashioned a beige, thick flax fiber cloak, stitching plates of metal in it to protect him from the deadly rays of the sun.

With the plague spreading, no human blood was safe, and he grew weaker. The temptation of blood was too great to stay among the humans for long, so he took refuge underground, feeding on whatever creatures he could find to sustain himself, but it was never enough. Whenever he surfaced, it seemed warriors weren't far behind.

Without being able to replenish his strength to fight back, Rafazi fled to the sea, swimming as far as the Isle of Fogo to bury himself. The molten rock flowing underneath the island's surface threatened to end his existence, and he contemplated letting it before the desperate need for survival overtook him, and he swam back to the mainland.

For the next three centuries he remained on the move, growing weaker with each passing year, becoming a shell of the being he once was, surfacing in the wilderness at night to search for the blood of lesser beasts, then retreating below the earth's surface before the rise of the sun. He received no visit from his Maker and presumed Her dead, as he did all his kind.

She had been right. They were paying for their hubris. He was truly alone in the world now, with no knowledge of whether the plague still cursed the living. But in its absence, human blood ruled his every thought.

One day, a rumbling above piqued his curiosity, and he could hear screams, both of fright and anger. The scent of horses was abnormally strong, as was the odor of blood—so much blood.

Human blood.

Rafazi's eyes flashed red with hunger, and sensing night's fall, he surfaced, unable to resist the pull of what he had denied himself for so long and was, finally, ready to perish for the taste of. The power once seen in faces like his own was replaced with fear of the enraged pale faces he saw ransacking the village he stumbled upon. The pale-faced men were rounding up the villagers, putting them in chains, and setting huts on fire.

Those who fought back were met with swords, wasting their life blood to water the land they called home. Rafazi rolled out of the path of a charging horse, clutching his cloak closely in fear as he tumbled. He was weak and delirious with hunger. And though the living before him seemed healthy enough, so had the humans he had watched his kind feed from before their tainted blood sent his brothers and sisters to their doom.

"I found another over here!" A man with pale skin sat atop the charging horse, which now hovered over Rafazi as the man called out to his companions. Rafazi knew his blur would be no match against the horses the pale-faced men rode. Having grown too weak to hunt larger animals, his diet had consisted of insects and rodents for years.

He was quickly surrounded and pulled to his feet by a band of raiders in red coats who locked his wrists in iron cuffs. He so desperately wanted to plunge his teeth and fangs into any one of them, but he was outnumbered. He was sure doing so would result in lethal retaliation.

"Thought you could hide from us, did you?" one of the pale-skinned men remarked before shoving Rafazi face-first into the dirt.

"If he's too feeble to walk, he's too feeble to work," Rafazi heard the man on the horse say. Looking over his shoulder, he found the barrel of a miniature cannon pointed at him. It was unlike anything he'd ever seen, but he was well aware of his weak state and his will to remain in existence. So, slowly, he pushed himself to his feet.

"I can walk," he said, taking in the shock spreading across the pale men's faces.

"Where did you learn to speak our language?" one of them asked.

"I have traveled." His simple response elicited a round of hearty laughter from the men as they pulled him toward other chained prisoners.

"Well then, you're about to do a lot more."

Two

1710, Province of Carolina

They ran for their lives. Their legs ached, their chests heaved, and their lungs burned, but they pressed on.

"C'mon, Willie! We ain't gots much longer now!"

Willie pushed his brawny frame forward, the sweat on his brow proof of his effort, but still he lagged behind Charlie's longer, leaner physique.

"Y'done say that two times! I's runnin' fast as my legs'll carry me!" Willie panted, pushing himself harder to catch up.

Willie and Charlie. These were not the names either man was born with, but the monikers they were assigned because their white captors were unwilling to pronounce their real names. They were the names they had met each other by on the Barrow Plantation where Willie had been enslaved for the past seven years. Charlie had been traded to the plantation last year. Willie had heard the whispers about Charlie's past: his capture after trying to escape the last plantation he was on, his obstinate attitude, his tendency to fake illnesses to avoid work, his murmurings of running away.

Charlie was, in many ways, Willie's opposite.

Willie had been a slave for eighteen years, two years longer than he had been free and more than half his life. He knew of the severe punishments reserved for those who tried to flee.

Unlike Charlie, Willie did his best not to provoke the overseers of the Barrow Plantation, but his efforts to keep quiet and productive did not stop the Barrow Plantation's chief overseer, Monroe, from tormenting Willie every chance he got.

Enduring cruelty was a reality of life for Willie. But when Monroe had grabbed Willie's basket of rice stalks, tossed them across the wet paddy, declared he hadn't met his daily harvest requirement, and used the falsehood as justification to punch him repeatedly while the other overseers held him down, Willie started listening to Charlie's whispers.

"We's can be free," Charlie had breathed in Willie's ear as the slaves shuffled off the rice paddy after the incident. "You think these whip-crackers care 'bout ol' meek Willie? 'He work so good and don't kick up no fuss,' but what good it done you? You ain't gonna win. Ain't none of us gonna win. You gots to *take* freedom, Willie. Ain't nobody gonna *gives* it to you. I say, gives me freedom or gives me death!"

Freedom. What had been a way of life for Willie in his younger years was now something he ran through the wilderness in the dead of night for as an adult. As if he were stealing it instead of it having been stolen *from* him. For a brief moment, under the light of the moon and stars, Willie felt as if he were a boy again, running wild in the night with the other boys to see who among them was the fastest. The urgency in Charlie's voice, however, reminded him of the greater purpose of this run. As did the ache in his expanding lungs with each step forward he took, fighting to keep pace with Charlie.

"Don't stop, Willie!" Charlie called back. "We's cain't stop!

We's gots to get past them red oak trees up yonder, and we's home free!"

Willie's nose scrunched up from the pungent smell of red oak hanging in the air. The path to sweet freedom was through the sour odor of those trees. The irony was not lost on him. It seemed somehow fitting.

"What gonna be waitin' for us up North? If we ain't nothin' but niggers down here, what we's gonna be up there?"

An all too familiar sound echoed through the night air, stopping both men cold.

"Bloodhounds!" Willie hissed as quietly as he could. The vicious barking of multiple dogs was getting closer. "We's gonna get caught! I *knows* it!"

"No, we's ain't!"

Willie and Charlie darted through the woods at top speed. Willie ran with a specific desperation, one he felt in his veins. It was the same desperation that had surged through his being when he ran toward his burning home in his native village in the Kingdom of Ghana, intent on rescuing his mother and sister. The same desperation he had felt burning through him when he was stopped short of reaching them by the white raiders who pulled him farther and farther away from them. The same desperation in his father's eyes before they widened in death as a ruthless raider's blade entered his back and pierced through his chest, drenching his agya in blood.

The fast clomps of horse hooves stomping through the woods joined the evil cacophony of the barking bloodhounds. Willie fell farther behind Charlie as they plunged deeper into the wilderness.

"We's done for, Charlie," Willie whined breathlessly. "We's cain't outrun no steeds! If'n we go back now and . . ."

"You hush up with that go back talk!" Charlie cried out. "I ain't never goin' back! Keep goin', Willie! We's gonna make it! Don't stop!"

Charlie swerved to the right. A bloodhound broke from the pack and chased after him.

"Charlie!" Willie hollered.

A second bloodhound leapt onto Charlie's back, tackling him to the muddy earth, its jaws snapping ferociously. The pack moved in, and within moments, the mud turned red as the dogs feasted on the slave.

Willie had heard of slaves having their toes cut off for running—or worse, of slaves disappearing in the middle of the night, never to be heard from again—while the overseers congratulated themselves for "teachin' that nigger a lesson." He'd seen the wounds and welts of those who had been savagely beaten within inches of their lives for trying to run. But he had never, with his own eyes, witnessed the brutality these dogs were commanded to perpetrate on one human being by another.

Charlie's screams were reduced to horrifying gurgles as the bloodhounds ate the life from him. Willie's knees wobbled, and the sick in his stomach built as one of the bloodhounds turned to him, snarling, its snout reddened by Charlie's blood.

Willie forced his legs forward again, and the hound chased after him, its barks ringing in his ears. His heart was beating so hard and fast in his chest it pained him, but his fear fueled him.

And then a sharp whistle cut through the air.

Willie skidded to a stop in the dirt as Monroe Washington, the chief overseer of the Barrow Plantation, angled his horse in front of him, blocking his path. The slight white man with his thinning brown hair sneered down at Willie with a face full of angry wrinkles. His cheek bulged with his ever-present ball of chewing tobacco in his mouth, and his lips and chin were stained with residue from years of constant spittle. His vengeful face was the one Willie saw more than any other, but still he winced at the sight of the man. The abruptness of stopping, mixed with the fear pulsating through him, caused Willie to double over and empty his stomach.

"Aw, now! That ain't no way to greet me, boy!" Monroe raised his foot and kicked Willie in the face. Willie fell to the ground hard, cradling his bloodied nose as four other horses, all ridden by field overseers from the plantation, encircled him.

"Well, well, well." The words slithered lazily from Monroe's lips. "Did y'all decide to go out for a midnight stroll?" Monroe spat a glob of brown spittle into Willie's eye while the other overseers laughed. Monroe smiled at Willie's humiliation as the slave attempted to wipe away the spittle but was stopped by a whip lashing across his chest. Willie looked up to find the handle of a leather whip in Monroe's hand.

"Don't you wipe it away," the chief overseer barked. "Hell, dark as you is, ain't like you can see it!" Monroe cackled, and the other overseers followed suit. "I'm a might surprised to find you out here, Willie boy. Ain't like you to be ornery like this one here."

Willie ran the tips of his fingers along the fresh welt forming across his chest and winced from the pain. Charlie's gurgling could no longer be heard, and Willie's vision blurred with tears.

"Don't you start cryin' yet, nigger," Monroe taunted him. "I ain't even got started. Tie him up!"

Two of the overseers quickly dismounted and moved toward Willie, who, in his desperation, leapt to his feet and made a break for it. The overseers were right on his heels and tackled the slave to the wet earth, punching and kicking him before one planted his knee on the back of Willie's neck, forcing his face into the muddy ground. Willie worked his face back and forth in the mud, struggling to find an air passage while the other overseer tied his wrists behind his back.

"It's your lucky night, boy," Willie heard Monroe say as rough hands yanked him to his feet by a tuft of his hair. The foul stench of Monroe's tobacco filled Willie's nostrils, and his stomach churned again. "Your master wants you alive, unlike your buddy there. Now, let's pay last respects."

Monroe dismounted from his horse and yanked Willie toward Charlie's remains as the bloodhounds, their mission accomplished, circled the leftovers of their meal. Willie struggled against Monroe's grip, and the overseer pulled a second weapon from his waistband in response, a flintlock pistol sword—a simple hand pistol with a long, thick, sharp blade attached at the bottom of its barrel. With one hand clasped around the back of Willie's neck, Monroe placed the blade at Willie's throat, paralyzing the slave where he stood.

"Now you quit all that fussin' and fightin', or you're liable to get yourself cut somethin' awful," Monroe hissed in Willie's ear. "You gonna stand there like a good lil' nigger's s'posed to and look at your dumb, dead nigger friend, so's it can be a lesson to you 'bout what happens when you decide to go stealin' what ain't yours."

In a simple, involuntary act of defiance, Willie shut his eyes.

"Open up them eyes of yours, boy!" Willie heard Monroe's words a second before pain rang through his head as the overseer bashed him in the temple with the butt of his pistol. Willie heard the hammer of the gun click. "I said, open 'em!" The threat of Monroe's demand opened Willie's eyes, forcing him to bear witness to the carnage of Charlie's body.

Willie trembled at the sight: Charlie's dead eyes were open wide with terror from the attack. His body was ripped and mangled, the work of the bloodhounds that even now continued to tear lazily at Charlie's dead flesh.

Willie's eyes burned, but there was something else beginning to rumble inside him, something he hadn't felt since he was torn from his family nearly two decades ago.

"Well, boys, looks like we ain't gotta feed the dogs tonight!" The overseers once again laughed at Monroe's words while

Willie's whole body shuddered. "Well, go on," Monroe told Willie. "Pay your respects."

What was there to say? This man, Charlie, who wanted nothing more than to live his own life, no longer had one.

"Nothin'?" Monroe snickered. "Fine. I'll go. Here lies one dead nigger." Monroe spat tobacco residue onto Charlie's corpse. "Good riddance." The overseer turned to Willie again. "Now, I know you niggers is savage and can't understand this, but civilized folk pay last respects to their fallen. I'm givin' you one last chance to be civilized." Willie's jaw tightened, but he felt the rumbling inside him swell. "No?" Monroe asked. "All right, but don't say I ain't give you the chance. Tie his black ass up behind me," Monroe instructed the overseers as he walked to his horse. "It's time to take him back and teach him a lesson of his own. Ain't nothin' better than beatin' a good nigger gone bad."

Willie took one last look at Charlie. "You free now," he muttered under his breath to the dead man as the overseers pulled him away. Willie felt his inner being detach. His childhood had been filled with men and women of strength and vigor, dignity, and grace. They were people he had looked up to, who looked like him. Never did he imagine he would see those proud people suffer such atrocities at the hands of Europeans, nor did he think others of their own kind would aid in this heinous endeavor.

Looking back at Charlie's corpse, Willie imagined what the man's life would have been if he had never been brought to the shores of this New World. What would have become of Charlie had none of this ever happened? He wondered if there would have been more dignity in Charlie's death.

As the overseers tied him to the back of Monroe's horse, Willie could only look back over his shoulder at Charlie, left for dead in the woods without a second thought. Willie's breath came faster, and the rumbling within him continued to grow.

His fists clenched as his thoughts flashed back to watching his family die in his native village.

But it was of no matter.

In this world, Willie's thoughts didn't count for a damn thing.

Three

THE BARROW PLANTATION

James Barrow walked through the grand foyer of Barrow Manor with his twelve-year-old son Thomas in the wee hours. While young Thomas was yawning and rubbing his eyes as he tried to keep step with his father, all six feet, three inches, and three hundred and fifteen pounds of Big Jim—as he liked to be called—was alert as he marveled at the magnificence of his home.

Barrow Manor was the premier symbol of James Barrow's wealth and was as well-known throughout the Carolina Province as the Governor's Palace, partly because of the entertaining the mistress of the house, Big Jim's wife, Charity Barrow, liked to do.

But even she was unaware of the full grandeur of Barrow Manor. She, like anyone privileged enough to have stepped within its walls, knew of the manor's pure calcite marble flooring tiles from Italy, the curved double staircase in the entryway inspired by palaces Big Jim had seen in France, and the pearl-white façade that seduced the eyes of all who looked upon on it. But what few knew of was the maze of hidden walkways leading to hidden rooms behind the walls. They got little use, but Big Jim liked knowing they were there, savoring the fact he possessed space he did not have to share. At twelve thousand square feet, Barrow Manor was fit for a king.

Which was exactly how Big Jim saw himself. And every king needed to teach his prince the ways of the kingdom.

"This will all be yours one day, my boy," Big Jim said to his sleepy son. "You've got a birthday coming up. You'll be a man soon, so it's time you start to understand what goes into making this good life."

Big Jim led Thomas under the ornate crystal candle chandeliers imported from Paris in the entryway and out the front door into the crisp, early morning air, making their way across the expansive property toward the rice and cotton fields. The Barrow Plantation sat on the most desirable plot of land in all of Lakeside, Carolina. Its six thousand acres bordered a huge lake, which made for productive rice fields. On their own, the rice paddies generated a substantial fortune, but combined with the cotton fields, the plantation made Big Jim the wealthiest landowner in the province.

"Mind where you step, son," Big Jim cautioned Thomas. "Don't want to get those shoes dirty." The landowner was dressed in an elegant gray suit with a silk cravat imported from England, detailed with silver embroidery in an elaborate floral design. His son wore a smaller version of the same suit, and they wore matching black leather shoes with silver buckles. Big Jim forewent the traditional three-point hat, proud of his full head of salt and pepper hair at the age of sixty. As a man of means, he believed in always looking wealthy and was raising his son to do the same. It kept Big Jim from remembering the destitution of his past.

"Now then. This first lesson is about property," Big Jim began. "Everything you see in our manor and on this land, with the exception of your kinfolk, is property. Property I own. The fields, the livestock, the stalls, buildings in the kitchen yard, the overseer houses, the horses . . ."

"The niggers?" Thomas asked.

"*Especially* the niggers. But they're pieces of property capable of forgetting they are property. When they do forget, it takes a forceful hand to restore order."

"Are you going to whoop one, Daddy?"

"No, son. I own this land and everything on it. I do not concern myself with the doling out of discipline. I mandate it to the overseers to carry out."

"Are the overseers property, too?"

"Well, no," Big Jim chuckled. "They are white men. There is a difference between what you own and those who work for you. But not much." As he winked at the boy, Big Jim smiled at the glimmer in his son's eyes. It was the look of admiration he saw in the gaze of others, but it meant more to see it from his son. Having young Thomas's respect was important to Big Jim—and expected—but his son's reverence was even more desirable. It was something he had longed to feel toward his own father but never could.

Big Jim's father had inherited a thousand acres of the land Big Jim now called his own, but his father had cared more for the drink than his family and had built nothing to leave to his son.

Many had offered to buy the land, and a sale would have gone a long way toward his family's comfort, but Big Jim's father refused every time. He'd been an angry and stubborn man, unwilling to yield to anyone for anything. The land was his, he would proclaim, and if he wanted to do nothing with it, he had every right in this New World. His pride kept his family in poverty, and Big Jim despised his father for it.

Every now and again, at the constant insistence of Big Jim's mother, and when his father could bother to scrounge up enough money, the senior Barrow would try his hand at growing cash crops: sugar, tobacco, coffee. But he'd failed at each one, cursing the land as barren, never recognizing it was ripe for rice. The younger Jim watched other families prosper, acquiring wealth with their crops, along with slaves to grow their wealth, while he lived in squalor. He grew to be as angry and stubborn as his father, and aimed his ire directly at the senior Barrow, which increased the familial strife.

The one thing the Barrow men did agree on was their worthiness of wealth. It was clear to them both theirs was the master race. There was no other explanation for the easy conquering of the Africans and Indians. The world was their birthright, and yet his father continually failed to seize it for himself and his family.

Big Jim would *not* make the same mistake.

Once the elder Barrow had finally drunk himself to death, Big Jim vowed to build a legacy, one of wealth and stature, something he could proudly hand down to a son of his own. He set about learning of the best crops his land could produce. He bought the biggest and strongest slaves he could find to cultivate the land. He reinvested his earnings into purchasing and cultivating more of the land surrounding those original, seemingly barren acres passed down to him. *His* determination, *his* savvy, *his* grit had turned the land into the six-thousand-acre empire of success everyone in the province knew today as the Barrow Plantation. Big Jim was going to leave this empire, *his* empire, to his son, and he would be damned if some slave was going to put even one penny of it in jeopardy.

Thomas jumped as the sound of a whip cracked across the fields. Big Jim put an arm around his son as they surveyed the scene of Monroe whipping Willie, whose wrists were chained high up on a large wooden post. The slave twisted to and fro, his face a grimace of pain, his back having been whipped so severely that large chunks of his skin were gone, and his raw flesh pulsed as it began to blister.

"That slave must've done something awful, Daddy."

"He did." Big Jim smiled at his son. "Slaves are the one kind of property capable of stealing from you. Because if they run, they're stealing. Do you know why?"

"Because you own them."

"Quite right. Always hold on to what's yours. Don't let anybody take it from you, you hear?"

Thomas nodded, and Big Jim ruffled the boy's hair before moving to Monroe, who stood behind Willie, a leather cat-o'-nine-tails whip in his hand, sweat on his brow, and a smile on his face. He was surrounded by the other field overseers in Big Jim's employ, and four bloodhounds milled about lazily. As a precautionary measure, the other field overseers carried their long rifles at the ready, in case the chained-up Negro made any sudden moves.

Monroe turned a smile in Big Jim's direction, and the plantation owner scowled at his chief overseer's brown-stained teeth, littered with bits of tobacco.

"What you think, boss?" Monroe asked.

"I think you should close your mouth," Big Jim huffed. Monroe was a creature he had never understood. For a white man, he was nearly as uncivilized as the slaves. If it wasn't for his efficiency in the fields and his knack for sales, Big Jim would have been happy to never lay eyes on Monroe again. "There are finer ways of enjoying the pleasures of tobacco than gnawing away at it like a wild goat."

"I meant this here nigger that done run, boss," Monroe replied like a scolded child. "You want me to whip him some more?"

Big Jim moved closer to the wooden post to face Willie, his face scrunching up from the smell of urine soaking the crotch of the slave's pants. He chuckled as Willie twisted in pain against his restraints. Clocking the tears running through the mud covering Willie's face, Big Jim removed a handkerchief from his pocket. Instead of offering it to Willie, he used it to polish the exquisite ring he wore on his middle right finger: a perfectly round, two-carat ruby in a gold setting. Big Jim relished the gem's finely cut edges; he'd been told upon sale the jewel was mined in Persia.

"I understand my puppies ate up your good-for-nothing friend, and I suppose you're feeling some kind of way about it," Big Jim said to the sobbing slave, "but y'all tried to steal from me. Now, Monroe tells me you're of more value on the field than your dead friend, so I will assume you were led astray on account of your feeble mind. With the distraction of him gone, I reckon you will be back on the straight and narrow now. Right, Willie?"

Willie answered in heaving sobs. As far as Big Jim was concerned, heaving sobs were not an answer. A slave not answering his master was obstinance. And obstinance was not something Big Jim was willing to tolerate.

"Have you gone deaf, boy? I asked you a question." When there was no reply from Willie for a second time, save for his breathless sobbing, Big Jim nodded to Monroe. "Get the board."

"Well, hot damn!" Monroe moved to a small metal table nearby and grabbed a long, thin wooden board cut full of holes. With familiar ease, he slammed the board, hard and fast, onto Willie's shredded back. As the slave hollered in agony, blisters on his back began to rise through the holes of the wooden board, causing it to stick to Willie's flesh. Monroe once again raised the whip and struck Willie's back, bursting the new blisters as Willie cried out.

Big Jim studied Willie's torment-filled face before giving Monroe a second purposeful nod. Monroe returned the board to the table and picked up a bowl filled with salt and pepper. He threw handfuls onto the raw, torn flesh of Willie's back. The slave screamed in torture as his back bubbled and pulsed. When Willie slumped limply in the chains, defeated and barely able to gather breath, Big Jim waved Monroe back.

"Now," Big Jim addressed Willie once more, "I'll ask again. With the distraction gone, you will return to the straight and narrow. Right, *Willie?*"

Willie's response this time was labored huffing, so Big Jim gave Monroe a third nod. Two more handfuls of salt and pepper landed on Willie's ruptured back. The slave hollered out in agony again, and Big Jim passed the time by giving his ring another wipe with his handkerchief until Willie's screams settled into whimpers. "Have you forgotten the name I gave you, boy?" Big Jim asked him with a calm voice.

"Willie . . ." It was barely audible, but Big Jim nodded. There was a fine line to be straddled here. A dead slave was a wasted investment.

"And you will return to the straight and narrow, now, won't you?"

"Yes . . . sir . . ."

"Good. You remember this pain the next time you think about stealing from me, Willie," Big Jim said. "And to be clear, your running is the same as you stealing from me because I own you, and I would hate to have to take your toes to keep you put, you hear?"

"Yes, sir," Willie croaked out weakly.

Big Jim's dark eyes narrowed, and his voice dropped an entire octave, going from soothing to ominous in an instant without ever losing its calm, as he got right in Willie's face. "I am your *god* now. And don't you forget it, boy. Because I am the only god you've got."

The slave blinked, and his head flopped down. Big Jim slapped Willie's drooping face twice. No response.

"I'd say he's had enough now," Big Jim told Monroe with a smile. "Wake him up and make sure he gets an early start today. He's got double the workload since his buddy took his leave from us." Big Jim headed back for the manor with Thomas, leaving Monroe and the overseers to clean up the messy business.

Four

TOIL AND TROUBLE

Gertie paced through the tall grass under an oak tree on the western edge of the Barrow property. Her soft thicket of curly black hair rustled in the night breeze as she wrung her hands, her dark skin glimmering in the moon's silvery glow. She hadn't seen Willie since the overseers had called the slaves off the rice paddy hours ago.

This place, secluded from the crude cabins of slave village, had become dear to her; it was where she and Willie found comfort in each other, however fleeting, away from the brutality of their lives.

But the survival of their comfort depended on secrecy. Marriages and families among slaves were not recognized in the colonies and were often broken up in the trades between plantations. Were they to be found out, their master might sell one of them off out of spite. Though they did not dare define the relationship, their affinity for one another had grown.

It was here Willie had brought her after Monroe had hollered mercilessly at her—even though Gertie had no idea what she had done wrong—and took his whip to her on the paddy in front of everyone. As she had sobbed, she told him of her home in Mauritania, where she was born twenty-nine years prior, of her family and how they had all died on a slave ship before it reached the colonies, leaving her alone in a foreign land. He told her of the burning of his family home and the murders of his kin in Ghana. They became the closest thing either one of them had to family.

Willie and Gertie began stealing away together at night in the tall weeds and the taller grass, sharing intimate moments. She told herself their time together was never anything more than a welcome respite from their daily reality. She had to. She couldn't allow herself the agony of anything more.

And yet here she stood, waiting. She had come to depend on their stolen time together, even yearned for it. Leaning against a tree, Gertie realized she was standing now exactly where Willie had stood, his fists clenched, his eyes wet with tears, as she calmly rubbed his back, massaging in the notion that things could get better if they simply did good.

It was a fanciful notion, yes, but it was something she lived by: The reward for doing good was more good. It had not yet come to pass since she had been taken from her homeland, but it was a principle she continued to hold on to. It had to mean *something*.

In this special place, there were no consequences to their having wishes and desires. Here, she was free to indulge her hopes—escaping the cruelty of the plantation, making a life of their own, building a house, growing their own food, raising a family, two girls and a boy. It calmed her mind to do so, but perhaps it was no longer enough for Willie.

Gertie knew he suffered from Monroe's unrelenting abuse, but she also knew his commitment to keeping his head low. It was a trait she took pride in having encouraged in him. Willie spoke little of the beliefs he was raised on, but the pantheon of gods and Pangool of Gertie's homeland was vast. The ideology of them all, including the Pangool, who were created by Roog, the supreme being and creator god, to help and guide humans, was predicated on the idea that good and evil were not finite but rather solely dependent on the actions of the individual and the impact those actions had on humanity, family, friends, neighbors, strangers, even enemies.

Doing good begat good and made a person, spirit, or deity, good. The same was true for evil.

The people who ruled this New World did not seem to share the same belief, not from anything Gertie had witnessed. They held little regard for the majesty of women, another mystery of her enslavement. Even their own women were treated as little more than flesh factories to produce more offspring. Born into a matrilineal society in her native village, Gertie had no problem sharing her thoughts with the other enslaved men, including Willie, when she deemed it necessary, though she'd quickly learned white men had no use for her wisdom. Willie's ability to hear her when she spoke was what drew her to him. They didn't agree on everything, but on the big things they had been of the same mind, especially when it came to running away.

At least, she'd thought they'd been of the same mind.

The ferocious nature of the slave patrol was well-known, and while freedom was a beautiful thought, she had helped Willie realize running would mean certain death. Seeing Willie in the company of Charlie for the past few days had given Gertie cause for concern. She knew anger lived inside Willie, and she knew where it could lead if left unchecked. She had come to care for him now; she saw it as her duty to keep the torments plaguing him at bay.

Had she failed him?

Her body lurched forward as a sickly churning in her stomach began. Wrapping her arms around her belly, she closed her eyes and breathed through the ache. This was the third time in a week she had experienced this sensation, one she silently cursed as she vomited. The action left her lightheaded, so she didn't trust her ears when she heard a groan in the distance. But it sounded again, and Gertie moved back toward the cabins.

In the middle of slave village, she found him, on his hands and knees, barely able to move. She ran to him in the darkness, his back wounds still oozing blood, pus streaming down onto the back of his pants. Unbridled tears fell down her face at the violence perpetrated against him. Still on his knees, Willie managed to straighten himself as Gertie knelt to face him.

"Willie! What they done to you?"

"They done killed Charlie," Willie said in a weak whisper. "Hounds tore him limb from limb."

Hounds. Charlie had run. And Willie went with him. Gertie pulled him in close, cradling his head over her shoulder, careful not to touch his back. Her jaw clenched, she tempered the tears streaming down her cheeks as she kept a gentle touch on Willie's head and neck. Not wanting him to see the thunder on her face, she blinked back her tears until she could feel the heat in her cheeks subside. "C'mon," she said. "I's get you to the sick house."

Gingerly, she helped Willie to his feet and led him into a small wooden cabin, which served as a miniature infirmary. She guided Willie to a small, rickety bed, creaking and moaning as she laid him face down on it. She gathered a clean blade and a jar filled with a mixture of red wine and honey. Her stomach turned again at the sight of his back. It took great effort to keep her hands from shaking.

It was obvious they were no longer of the same mind when it came to running. He could have been killed just as easily as Charlie had been. He knew he was the closest thing she had to family. Perhaps the thought escaped him before he followed Charlie into the wilderness.

Perhaps he hadn't thought at all.

As gently as she could, Gertie cut the shredded skin away on Willie's back with the blade before applying the honey and red wine mixture. She worked in silence while Willie gasped and winced. It was better this way. She had nothing good to say to him this night, and he was in no state to hear any of the things racing through her mind.

"I know it hurt," she decided to say instead. "I's sorry. I reckon y'done had your share of pain tonight." She wiped away her tears with her forearm. Her fingers quaked, and she heard the tremble in her voice. She was sure Willie had, too.

"I ain't means to put burden on you this a'way," he said. "I's sorry."

Gertie dropped her head and stifled her sobs. She bit the inside of her cheek to keep even the slightest whimper from escaping her lips. "Ain't a one of us don't dream of freedom," she said with as stable a voice as she could muster. "Cain't nobody blame you for it. 'Sides, we ain't make no promises to one 'nother. We cain't no way." Collecting herself, Gertie went back to work on Willie's back. She swallowed and hoped both the rumble in her stomach and the ache in her heart would go away.

WILLIE DID HIS BEST to ignore the roiling in his stomach but feared he wouldn't be able to for much longer. The small cabin he occupied was fit for three people, but seven cots were crammed inside with barely any room for much else.

The tremendous pain Willie was suffering from made the prospect of relieving the mounting pressure in his bowels unbearable. The thought of moving was bad enough without factoring in the trek out to the trench. In his current condition, he didn't feel he would be able to handle the stink, which meant taking a shovel and digging a hole to empty his insides. He clenched to contain his flatulence before pushing himself up from his cot as quietly as he could.

Willie moved slowly through the grass. Every step brought him agony. His escape plan with Charlie revealed the folly of running in brutal fashion, and he cursed himself for ignoring Gertie. She could be relentless in her pronouncements, and sometimes a bit domineering, but there was always caring in the sound of her voice, so the silence with which she had tended to him had been as painful as his wounds.

His reasons for running would be of no use to her, and though he had grown fond of her, he couldn't allow himself to admit, let alone feel, love. In the New World, love was futile. The ache in his heart over how he'd disappointed Gertie remained, but there was nothing he could do to fix it.

As he shoveled over the hole he'd dug for his waste after having relieved himself, Willie found movement a bit easier. He spun around when a nearby rustling in the grass startled him, and he fell to his knees from the effort, wincing in anguish. It was darkest here, near the edge of the property. He moved cautiously, his eyes wide and alert when he heard the rustling again. Using the shovel to pull himself up to his feet, Willie glanced toward the forest and stopped, unable to move from the sight before him: Two small, round sources of red light shone from deeper in the grass.

Eyes.

The glowing red eyes began to pulse, and Willie's hands shook. Whatever possessed those red eyes, if you could call them that, made no attempt to attack him, but the threat of danger lurked ominously. Palpable. He peered back into the red fixed upon him, contemplating a step forward, when he realized he was unable to move. He pinched his thigh roughly, and the sensation of hurt told him his legs still worked. He seemed to be paralyzed in his mind alone.

It occurred to him he could become the master of his mind.

"What you be?" Willie asked.

The sound of his vocal cords coming to life surprised him as a sense of bravery returned to him. The red disappeared, and the sound of rustling returned, until it faded as well. Willie blinked and searched the distance but found nothing except darkness. He was delirious with pain from Monroe's lashing. Perhaps it was causing him to see things.

UNDER THE HOT CAROLINA sun, Willie toiled in the lush, green rice fields with other Barrow Plantation slaves. They were young and old; some were children, some were pregnant women, some were elderly, but they all worked the same—hard and long, under the watch of overseers who prowled through the fields on horseback, long rifles slung menacingly over their shoulders, whips holstered on their belts along with small leather pouches containing small horns of gunpowder and lead balls.

The summer sun showed them no mercy, and between the blood and pus from the still-fresh lashing wounds, and the sweat from his exertion, Willie's thin and dirty white shirt stuck to his back in excruciating fashion. He sloshed through the soaked paddy, the water covering his feet providing little relief from the heat.

"It's powerful hot, and I know you's in pain. You gots to bear it," he heard Gertie whisper to him. The tremble in her voice remained, the same as he had heard last night when she'd dressed his wounds. He turned to take her in. The white cloth covering she wore over her lustrous hair made her alluring features even more pronounced, but the pain she carried was all over her face. The urge to explain himself to her consumed him, but the rice paddy was no place for such a conversation. Even if they were in a place where they could speak, he feared he didn't have the words to make her understand why he ran. Still, he had to say something to her.

"I's powerful grateful for what y'done for my back," Willie told her quietly as an overseer rode past behind them.

"It's a blessin' you's still got a back, runnin' like y'done," was Gertie's reply once the overseer passed. Her words stung Willie. They were thick with her hurt, hurt he didn't know how to address. They had spoken of the futility of running, but there was a fire building within him, especially after being forced to witness Charlie's murder, and he feared it would never recede.

Gertie would not return his gaze. She quickened the pace of her work, and Willie turned away. "Why you's run and leaves me behind? Where you's get the gumption?" The crack in Gertie's voice as she hissed her question cut through Willie's core. He had no words of comfort, but she deserved a response.

"I couldn't takes no more . . . Wasn't my aim to leaves you behind." Willie could feel her eyes on him now, waiting patiently for him to continue while his fear began to twist and bubble up inside him. The penalty for getting caught talking in the fields was the whip, and Willie's back couldn't take another flogging. Not this soon anyway. His thoughts were interrupted by the frantic whispering of Gertie, who could no longer wait for an answer to her question.

"I's truly sorry for what happen to Charlie," Gertie murmured as quickly, quietly, and purposefully as she could. Willie could sense she was building up to something and gathering her courage as she went. "But what you's thinkin'? Ain't like they ain't got slaves up North. You end up like Charlie, where that leaves me?"

"Gertie . . ."

"I knows we ain't got claim to one 'nother, and we's both got burdens hard to bear, and I knows you ain't knows when you run, but I gots powerful scared . . ."

"Gertie, I's sorry, but what is you . . ."

"I ain't had my blood," Gertie blurted out in a hushed whisper.

The words stopped time for Willie. Her words caused him to drop the rice stalks he had gathered in his hands.

"We's gonna have a baby?" Saying the words made Willie shudder.

"Shh!" Gertie hissed. Willie turned to find a few other slaves sneaking looks at them. "Monroe find them stalks at your feet 'stead of in your hands, he gonna finish what he started on your back!"

Willie swallowed back a shout. He could feel his lips stretching into a smile, his heart dancing inside his chest. A baby! A baby meant a family. He turned back around, his eyes catching Gertie's, and her face grew soft.

"Well now. What we talkin' 'bout?"

Willie's heart dropped at the sound of Monroe's voice. He gritted his teeth and kept his head low. He could see Monroe's shoes, so he knew the chief overseer had dismounted his horse to interrogate them.

"Ain't no talkin', boss," he heard Gertie say. She, too, kept her eyes low and fixed on the rice paddy and her work. "Just workin'."

Following her example, Willie quickly gathered up the stalks of rice he'd dropped, placed them in his basket, and continued with his harvesting. He tried his best to stop his hands from shaking as he did so.

Though elation had flooded his mind upon first hearing Gertie's words, it quickly gave way to grief. He was about to become a father to a child, a symbol of hope, new beginnings, possibility. But there would be nothing new for this forthcoming life. His child would be born into a life of slavery, a life he risked his own to escape, simply to be viciously returned to captivity, merely another piece of property. He'd heard whispers in slave village of womenfolk who had taken cotton root bark when they found out they were with child; others had secretly smothered their offspring at birth. He wondered if Gertie had considered either of these options and found himself blinking back tears at the thought.

"How's that hot sun treatin' you, Willie?"

Willie squinted up at Monroe as the overseer took out his water canteen and shifted his weight so as not to block the sun from Willie's face. Willie leaned toward Monroe's shadow, and Monroe moved again, keeping himself from serving as a shield from the sun. Wiping the sweat from his brow, the slave glared at the overseer, who allowed the water in the canteen to spill over his face and down his front before shaking the canteen, making a show of it being empty.

"Woo-wee! That hit the spot, I'll tell you what!" Monroe exclaimed, wearing his satiation with a proud smile on his face. "Now, in another hour or so, y'all will get a taste of what I feel. Just a taste now; there's a lot of y'all and ain't but one bucket. So, y'all be nice! Now keep them eyes in your head, and keep up the good work there, Willie!"

Monroe leaned down and slapped him on the back as hard as he could, and a roar of agony escaped Willie as he doubled over. Blind with pain, he shut his eyes and dug his fists into the muddy paddy, his arms shaking as his back throbbed. It was bad enough that this was the life he'd been dealt, but now he had subjected another soul to the same horrible fate. His shoulders quivered with shame as he opened his eyes. The initial surge of pain in his back began to subside, and he raised his head to find Monroe crouching in front of him with a stained-tooth snarl. "You wouldn't be down there restin', now, would you?" Monroe asked.

"No, sir," Willie said as he pushed himself up and got back to work.

Five

LAST OF THE RAMANGA TRIBE

illie took his place in a line leading to Irene, a young house slave of twenty years with silky black pigtails and much lighter skin than the field slaves. Sitting on a small wooden chair underneath a large umbrella, she repeatedly filled a tiny cup with water from an oversized bucket for the sweaty slaves waiting. The crew of overseers, including Monroe, surrounded her, ensuring things moved along in an orderly fashion, while they drank from their own personal canteens.

Irene was pretty and never had a bad word to say about Big Jim, the plantation, the overseers, or any white folks. Willie surmised Big Jim put her smiling face in front of them on hot summer days like this one to keep the men docile. If so, it was an effective strategy. Nearly all the men on the paddy and from the cotton fields found their smiles upon Irene's appearance.

Willie shook his head at the lustful yearnings the two slaves in line ahead of him had for her: Minor, a tall, bulky man with a perpetually irritated grimace who was a few years Willie's junior, and Derby, who was a hair younger than Minor. Broad shouldered yet lean, Derby was fond of forsaking his shirt, leaving his chiseled physique on display. This led to his popularity among the women, while stories of his passionate exploits brought him admiration among the men. So far, Gertie had not been taken by Derby's charms, but Willie secretly worried if he was enough to keep her from doing so.

"There's less water today 'cause two of y'all thought runnin' was a good idea, and both of them found out the hard way it wasn't," Monroe called out to the slaves. "So, some of y'all ain't gonna get no water this time 'round, and y'all can thank Willie and Charlie. Well, just Willie, seein' as how Charlie ain't no longer with us." Monroe's cackle was duplicated by the other overseers. As the line inched closer to Irene, one of Willie's hands balled into a fist before two smaller, softer hands covered it.

"You ain't to blame for what happen to Charlie," he heard Gertie mumble behind him, carefully keeping her subtle gesture out of the overseers' sight. Willie breathed as he opened his hand and allowed her fingers to intertwine with his.

"And while y'all are at it," Monroe continued, "maybe talk a lil' sense into Willie. Remind him how good he got it, how good y'all all got it. Y'all wouldn't be nowhere 'cept for your master's kindness and generosity. Wouldn't kill none of y'all to show some gratitude."

"A lil' gratitude go a long way, Willie," Irene said to him, her eyes betraying her smile as he finally stood before her for his share of water. "Massa's good to us all. You should 'pologize for what you done and work even harder to make amends for what you tried to take 'way from him."

Willie nodded respectfully as he took his drink under Monroe's watchful eye and returned Irene's smile as he handed the cup back to her. Despite how others felt about them, Willie carried no resentment toward the house slaves. As far as he was concerned, it didn't matter where they were on the plantation—none of their lives were their own. They were all slaves. "You tell Massa I's happy to 'pologize for my wrong." Willie never looked at Monroe as he headed back onto the field.

THE SKY HAD TURNED a dark orange, and a gentle breeze blew across the paddy as the slaves were called off the fields for the night. Willie helped Gertie up from her knees and immediately regretted doing so. He couldn't afford to call any additional attention to himself or Gertie, especially now, but he couldn't help himself.

"I ain't gonna crumble to nothin'," she chuckled to Willie. "I still gots power to walk on my own."

"You ain't the only one walkin' no more," Willie said, his voice thick with concern. She smiled, and Willie reveled in the warmth of it.

"It gonna be all right," she said softly. "Somehow, it gonna be all right."

"What we got here?"

The sound of Monroe's voice snatched the warmth away.

Willie's jaw tightened as he and Gertie kept walking in silence, and Monroe followed close behind like some sort of evil chaperone. "What's all this here whisperin' y'all been doin' at each other all day?"

"Ain't no whisperin', boss. The heat done got to Gertie this here day," Willie said plainly, hoping to put a quick end to the intrusion. "I's just makin' sure she get on her way all right, is all."

"Seem to me she can get along on her own. 'Less that caboose of hers done got too big to carry. Eh, Gertie? Master been feedin' you too good?"

The smack sounded along with Gertie's yelp and Monroe's cackle, telling Willie the overseer had slapped Gertie's bottom.

The lecherous smirk on the overseer's face along with the tip of his tongue sticking out the corner of his mouth made Willie move Gertie to his other side, away from Monroe, as calmly as he could, but he could feel his blood begin to boil.

"Don't that beat all," Monroe drawled. "And here I thought niggers was ignorant to chivalry."

Willie and Gertie locked eyes for the briefest of moments, and she blinked to him in gratitude.

"She gonna have to move her fat ass on her own tonight, boy, 'cause you comin' with me." Monroe grabbed hold of Willie's collar and yanked him away from Gertie, every step taking him farther away from the woman who carried his only family within her.

THE FAINT STENCH OF feces floated through the evening air as Willie and Monroe approached the back of Barrow Manor. Two house slaves moved a large collection of chamber pots onto the back porch of the manor before retreating into the house.

The clanking of metal pulled Willie's attention away from the porch and onto a lone slave, a short, slight figure covered in filth who emerged from the horse stables and made his way toward the porch. Dark and sickly, he wore a thick flax cloak over his head, shielding his form from the elements. The clanking sound and the foul stench both grew stronger as the figure passed in front of Willie and Monroe.

"That there's Shit Boy," Monroe said, waving a hand in front of his nose. "He dumps all the shit. Animal shit, your master's shit. He cleans out the stalls and the chamber pots, too. We leave him out here on his own 'cause he smell like shit, so don't nobody wanna be 'round him no way. But tonight, he gonna get a lil' help from you."

Willie knew better than to object. This was another torment Monroe designed specifically for him. He had learned to expect such unpleasantries in the company of the overseer. What he couldn't make sense of was the faraway look Monroe seemed to have in his eyes now.

"Used to have me a little farm of my own." The tone of Monroe's voice was startling. It was as if he were speaking to Willie as a fellow human being, and the sound was as foreign to Willie as English had been when he'd first heard it nearly two decades ago.

"Small little patch sat over yonder 'til your master bought it up from me to make it a part of all this here. Wasn't much, but it was mine. Had me a nigger, too. Looked just like you. Nigger cost me my land, my wife . . ." Monroe stopped himself, and Willie could see the loathing in his eyes. "I hate all y'all niggers," Monroe spat out. "Especially you, Willie. If you weren't somebody else's property, I'd rid this world of you. I hate you standin' here breathin' the same air as me when you ain't even a full human person. Now get. And don't be late on the field in the mornin' on account of this, you hear? If you one second late, I'll beat you 'til the black falls right off you."

I hate you, too, Willie thought as Monroe left. How satisfying it would be to relieve Monroe of his pistol blade and whip and stand toe to toe with him in a fair fight. Willie had no doubt he would crush the overseer, but doing so would cost him his life, such as it was—and now his wretched life had created another.

The thought pained him. The life he had helped create could not be protected or honored unless . . . unless he could find the courage to make a better existence. Maybe he could find another route to run with Gertie before she got too far along, one he could convince her was worth traveling. Perhaps there was a place far away from the South *and* the North, a place like they had always dreamed of where they could be all alone in a house of their own making, grow their own food, raise their children. What kind of man, father, would he be if he didn't at least try to make a better life for his own flesh and blood?

"Woo-wee! You stank somethin' powerful awful, Shit Boy! Take yourself 'way from here now, before your stank get up in Massa's nose! Don't you come no closer now!" The house slave's chastisement of the figure called "Shit Boy" pulled Willie from his thoughts. She placed two more chamber pots on the back porch, her face scrunched in disgust as she made a show of keeping her distance from "Shit Boy."

"Hey now!" Willie called out as the house slave rushed back inside. He fought the urge to react to the smell as he made his way closer to the figure. "Monroe done told me to c'mon out here and helps you."

The filthy slave turned to Willie, his eyes an unexpected bright red under the cover of his cloak.

Willie blinked. He had been worked hard in the sun all day on little sleep while still recovering from the beating Monroe had given him, and maybe the stress of what he was going to do about Gertie's news was beginning to take hold. He blinked again, rubbing his eyes with the heels of his palms. When he opened them, the filthy slave's eyes once again looked normal to Willie, and he released a breath in relief.

The filthy slave examined Willie for an intense moment before cracking with laughter. "Monroe must hate you," he said, his voice weak and raspy. "You know what they call me?"

"I don't reckon I feels right callin' you that. They calls me Willie."

The filthy slave nodded before grabbing two of the chamber pots and handing them to Willie, who recoiled from being so close to human waste. Grabbing two more chamber pots, he walked away from the manor, leaving Willie to follow. "Why does Monroe hate you, Willie?"

"He say it's 'cause I's breathin' the same air as him. I reckon we's all breathin' the same air, so it don't make no sense to me," Willie said. The filthy slave remained silent, which further piqued Willie's curiosity. "Ain't never seen you before."

"I'm not meant to be seen."

"What y'done to get this here nasty work?"

"I asked for it."

"Why?"

"To be left alone." The filthy slave stopped and turned back to Willie, who was taken aback by his pointed, abrupt response. Willie wanted to converse with the man, make him feel more human than he'd seen him be treated. He never suspected his words could be irksome. "It's better for everyone if I'm left alone."

The words loomed like an eerie warning to Willie as the two of them arrived at a long, open trench. It was a place Willie knew all too well as it had been the only option for slaves to relieve themselves until some of them took up the task of digging one closer to the cabins in slave village. A swarm of flies buzzed all around the open trench filled with animal and human waste, and Willie stood back as the filthy slave emptied the chamber pots he was carrying into the trench.

"Empty those pots in here. I'll get water from the well to clean them out with." The filthy slave headed off toward the well on the other side of a barn.

DARKNESS OVERTOOK THE SKY faster than Willie thought it would. As he finished emptying the last of the chamber pots into the trench, he wondered what was taking "Shit Boy" so long to come back. It had been a long day, and he was tired. He wanted to take to the lake to wash the stench from himself, get back to Gertie, and, hopefully, get enough rest to be useful on the field in the morning. Being useful would keep Monroe at a distance, at least for a little while.

Willie walked past the barn on his way to the well and found the doors open. The filthy slave's thick flax cloak was discarded on the ground at its entrance. Willie was a well-muscled man, but he found the cloak to be heavier than he imagined when he went to pick it up. He was sure the hard, broken surfaces he could feel between the fabric were made of metal.

How could this slave have walked with such ease with this weighty cloak on his back? Why wear it in the first place? It was surely extremely hot to wear in the sun. Then, he heard a rustling from inside the barn. It gave Willie pause, but his curiosity rose as the rustling grew louder. Cautiously, he took a step forward and peered inside the barn. In the darkness, he could make out a large stack of hay at the other end of the barn—moving.

Something was inside of it.

Slowly, Willie moved deeper into the barn, keeping his eyes focused on the moving haystack as the light from the moon lessened with each step. The rustling from the hay grew frantic, and Willie's muscles tensed with a sense of danger. Calling to mind his thoughts on courage earlier, he rushed toward the shaking stack and pulled handfuls of the hay away.

He was taken aback by the sight that greeted him.

"Shit Boy" was staring back at him, panic clear on his features, but his face . . . It was no longer human. His eyes were wide and an even brighter red than Willie remembered. He blinked in disbelief as those red eyes took on a glow. The filthy slave's brow was engorged and extended over his eyes, making their red color even more intense. The veins in his face were visible through his dark skin—as was the blood coursing through them.

His mouth gaped open, revealing sharp, jagged teeth, the upper row of which was framed by two longer razor-sharp fangs, coated in blood. At the ends of his fingers were thick, pointed nails akin to talons, which held the carcass of a rat ripped in half. Willie stumbled back as he and the slave locked eyes with each other.

"I did not intend for you to find me," the filthy slave said calmly. "But find me you have."

He tossed the dead rat away and pulled another from beneath the hay. "You wanted to know why I wish to be left alone. Now you know."

The slave ripped the rat he held in half with his talons, then drank its blood as if drinking from a tiny water cup. Once he had ingested the blood, his dull and sickly skin began to look richer. He seemed more alert, more energized. More alive.

The entire display left Willie frozen, and he was struck with the realization of who, or what, he'd seen in the grass in the dead of the night. The filthy slave stood and stretched as if he had awakened from a long slumber before he faced Willie, a soft smile on his strange features. "Don't be afraid," the slave said to Willie.

"You was what I seen . . ." Willie's voice trembled.

"I was. Your scent drew me."

His scent? Willie couldn't make sense of the filthy slave's words, but the fear within him had been awakened. "What you's gonna do to me?"

"Do? To you?" the filthy slave chuckled. "The size of you! Could I harm you? Even if I wanted to?" Willie took him in with wide eyes. He hadn't taken notice of it before, but his voice was clear, his speech clean and precise, the way the white folks spoke. This realization, coupled with the change in his appearance, made him seem like a different person to Willie—if what he was could be considered a person. "I mean you no harm." The filthy slave stepped closer to Willie and inhaled deeply, causing Willie to take a step back.

"What is you?"

"Nothing anyone would believe if you told them."

The words struck Willie as a subtle threat. They also rang true.

"I am Rafazi, the last of my kind," the filthy slave said. "The last of the Ramanga Tribe."

The statement quelled Willie's fright immediately. He laughed in disbelief as if a huge weight had been lifted. "The Ramanga Tribe?" Willie's relief was such he'd begun to guffaw.

"Our name has elicited many things through the centuries," the slave who called himself Rafazi said, "but never laughter."

"Ain't no Ramanga Tribe!" Willie laughed. "They's just a story folks tell they young'uns back home to keep 'em in line. Ramanga ain't nothin' but myth, legend."

"Legend, yes. But we were no myth."

Willie knew he should be frightened of the man before him, but he was overtaken with nervous laughter once again. "I's s'posed to believe you is Ramanga?"

"I am of Ramangan blood, yes."

"So, you gots the strength of ten men, and the speed of the wind, and you can bend minds? You?"

"You forgot about the iron teeth, the eating of nail clippings from the fingers of nobles, and the immortality." Rafazi smiled, and Willie shook his head. "The bit about the teeth and the nails were made up to mock us, but the rest is all very true."

"Workin' in this here shit for so long done got to you," Willie said, hoping to escape the absurdity of the conversation he'd found himself in.

"Perhaps it has. And yet, my eyes glow red, the veins in my face can be seen through my skin, my talons are as sharp as blades, my mouth is filled with jagged teeth and sharp fangs, and the blood of rats has reinvigorated me. Do you not believe your own eyes?"

"The heat done made me see things . . ."

"It may have, but it did not keep you from seeing the truth of who I am. We ruled the night for centuries. Our numbers were small, but we were powerful. Feared by all from Wagadou to the Kingdom of Nri."

46

"I remembers hearin' the elders talk 'bout the Wagadou Empire in my home village. They say it fell five hundred years ago," Willie reasoned, secretly surprised to still find himself in this conversation.

"I am over seven hundred years old," Rafazi said, "but my existence has become unbearably burdensome of late."

Willie felt lightheaded. He could not deny what he had seen. He could simply leave the barn, but he could not shake the feeling that he did not want to.

Could Rafazi be bending his mind?

"It has been centuries since I've tasted the blood of a human," Rafazi began, and dread began to overtake Willie. "Will you gift me the taste of yours?"

"No!" Willie took a step back, stabilizing his footing. The impulse to run grew strong.

"I can prove I am who I say I am, Willie. Allow me your blood and watch how it restores my power. A small bit of it, and you will see a difference."

It had been a trying day. Rafazi was small, frail, and yes, he had changed form after drinking the blood of rats, and he claimed to be the last surviving member of a mythical, centuries old African tribe. But it had also been horrendously hot all day. Willie thought perhaps he was delirious from the heat and stench. Maybe, Willie supposed, he had passed out under the sun hours ago, and this was all a strange dream brought on by heat, pain, and exhaustion.

Perhaps Rafazi wasn't even real. This thought calmed him.

He was dreaming.

"Please, one taste. Please!"

In his dream, the man calling himself Rafazi was shaking with need, pleading with eyes of bright, glowing red. Willie smiled to himself. He had given much more blood unwillingly to Monroe when he was awake than the amount Rafazi was asking for.

So, Willie raised his arm.

It was a dream, after all.

Tears of gratitude filled Rafazi's red eyes. Rafazi stepped forward and opened his mouth, and from this closer vantage point, Willie noticed the sharp fangs were coated in a thin sheen of moisture. Grabbing hold of Willie's arm, Rafazi whispered a *Thank you* before he bit into it. Willie winced from the bite at first, but soon, a small rush of euphoria surged through him—first through his arm, then throughout his entire body as Rafazi drank his blood.

Willie had no idea how long Rafazi had been drinking before Willie's knees buckled beneath him. He tried to pull his arm away from Rafazi, but Rafazi clung to it, his grip tightening, strengthening.

"Stop!" Willie tried again to dislodge his arm from Rafazi's clenched jaw, but Rafazi grabbed Willie's side and held him in place. Willie could not fathom why he was unable to break free from Rafazi's grasp, but terror filled his throat when he realized he was incapable of doing so. "Rafazi!"

Reluctantly, Rafazi pulled his mouth off Willie's arm with a satisfied look on his transformed face. Willie stumbled back a bit as he ran his fingers over the puncture wounds in his skin.

"Your blood is a miracle!" Rafazi smiled. "It is the best I have ever tasted!"

As he gathered his bearings, Willie's eyes returned to Rafazi, and he was shocked once again. Rafazi's form was human once more, and he looked like a new man. The richness of his dark skin had fully returned, and he seemed younger, more vibrant, and far healthier.

"Do you still doubt me?" Rafazi asked Willie, full of vigor. "How shall I demonstrate my power to you? What do you think would happen if I punched you?"

Rafazi may have looked much better, but Willie still saw a man much smaller than he was. This was indeed a dream.

"Do it and finds out!" Willie chuckled.

He then silently cursed himself for dreaming the action of Rafazi punching him in the stomach so hard he was sent flying through the open barn doors. As Willie caught his breath and pulled himself together, he realized he was at least twenty feet away from the barn.

A mysterious blur came charging out of the barn and headed straight for Willie. His heart raced as he struggled to sit up and move out of the blur's path before it reached him, but it stopped abruptly. When the blur became clear, it was a grinning Rafazi. He showed no signs of exertion, only exhilaration.

"Blood, glorious blood, free of the plague!" Rafazi exclaimed with glee. "And your blood . . . In all my years, I've never tasted any other like it!"

Rafazi took off in a haze of speed, leaving Willie alone on the ground, his breath coming in heavy pants. He winced at the real pain in his gut as one thing became abundantly clear.

He was *not* dreaming.

Aren't you tired of it? The constant fear? The brutality?

Six

HUMANITY, INTERRUPTED

"Don't just lie there! Move around!"

Irene flinched at the unexpected sound of Big Jim's voice. He usually remained quiet during his invasions, never requiring anything of her except to lie still with her legs spread. It was made clear to Irene when she was bought that all her other duties came second to this: enduring his bloated, naked frame atop her; his sweat dripping into her eyes; his sour, scalding breath suffocating her; the ache of her ribs from his weight repeatedly slamming down on her until he lifted his fat hips and spilled his seed onto her stomach—a courtesy she was grateful for.

The room in which he chose to commit his crime was the tiny room Irene slept in alone. Though it doubled as a storage closet, containing sacks of rice and a bale of harvested cotton, she didn't have to sleep overcrowded as the other house slaves in the manor did, a fact she knew ostracized her from them.

Big Jim had been grunting his exertion for ten minutes before his words pulled her gaze away from the small open window that provided the only ventilation in the room, made stuffier by Big Jim's sweaty presence. Irene could see a sliver of the moon through the window, the only light the space saw in the wee hours. If she stared at it hard enough, she could pretend she was floating up to it, far away from this place, from this ghastly man. But it only worked when he kept quiet.

"How you wants me to move, Massa?" Irene asked. She had learned early on the value of submissiveness in her dealings with Big Jim.

With his eyes shut tight, he sped up his thrusting. "Shut up," he huffed, pumping himself until he came to an abrupt halt. Irene could feel him soften, but he hadn't spilled his seed inside her. She struggled to breathe until he removed himself from atop her frame. He began dressing himself with a frown. Irene wasn't sure what to do; he had never left before achieving release. Irene, wanting to be helpful, found and handed him his shirt. He snatched it away.

"The slave that run the other night," she began tentatively. "I told him to 'pologize to you like you told me to. He say he would." Irene smiled like a child seeking approval from a parent.

"Might as well be fucking my wife," Big Jim said, ignoring her words, his voice hard, before he abruptly left Irene alone in the room. Once she was sure he'd gone, she bent over the edge of the small bed she had been afforded and retched.

WILLIE SAT ON THE front steps of a slave village cabin with Gertie by his side. Since she'd taken off her cloth hair covering and folded it in her lap, her curly mane hung free. Willie thought she was a beautiful sight to behold.

A rare spirit of frivolity had taken hold of slave village this night; though, at intervals, several among them kept watch at the village's entrance for curious overseers who might take offense to their enjoyment.

Folks had gathered outside their cabins, and some danced around small pit fires while others played joyful tribal sounds from handmade instruments. One old man played along on a crudely made violin, stomping his foot, and grinning with a mouth only half full of teeth. A group of child slaves danced together inside a ring drawn in the dirt, clapping their hands rhythmically as they sang a song:

My ol' mistress promise me
'Fore she die she'll set me free
Now she dead 'n gone t' hell
I hope dat devil will burn her well!

Ever since Willie had been enslaved in this New World, he'd heard the words "devil" and "hell" used by white folks in reference to some unseen, nefarious figure, and the place in which it resided. He assumed their devil was in opposition to the god he'd heard them speak of with reverence, and their hell someplace akin to the Underworld, but constructed for the punishment of those who had done evil during their lives. Perhaps they spoke of the place because they anticipated going there. He doubted the children had any more than a rudimentary understanding of the words when they worked them into their song—despite theirs being the first generation largely born into servitude to the white folks—but the sentiment of their rhyme was felt by the young and old alike in slave village.

"My, my, Miss Gertie. Ain't you a sight to see."

Willie felt his neck stiffen at Derby's appearance. He remained shirtless, and his rugged abdomen seemed to glisten in the moonlight, either from water or sweat, Willie couldn't tell which. He was careful not to react, but he watched Gertie cautiously as she looked up at the young man.

"Is you tryin' to charm me, Derby?" she asked in a dry tone, and Willie felt his shoulders relax a bit.

"Ain't know I hads to try," Derby said, flashing his smile. Gertie was already shaking her head.

"Get 'way, boy," Gertie chuckled. "I's too tired for your foolishness." Derby never lost his smile as he nodded and moved along, and Willie's warm smile found Gertie.

"I s'posin' I ain't even here," he playfully huffed. "Derby ain't say word one to me."

"And he ain't never gonna," Gertie said. "He ain't got no use for what's 'tween your legs. You just be glad *I* ain't say nothin' to him." As she laughed, Willie ran a hand up the back of her neck, pulled her in close, and kissed her. He felt her fingers wrap around his arm that was holding her, and he extended their kiss. "'Sides," Gertie chuckled as they softly ended their kiss, "look here."

Derby hadn't gotten more than a few feet away from them before he was besieged by admirers. His arms went around two of the women seeking his attention, and the three disappeared between two cabins. Willie and Gertie regarded each other with raised eyebrows at the incident before cracking with laughter so strong it caused them to lean against one another. There was little joy to be found on the plantation, but watching Gertie rebuff Derby was as close to bliss as Willie could get.

Tussy passed around two jugs of wine, and everyone took turns drinking. She was a hefty slave nearing sixty years who wore a bonnet to hide her thinning hair and the scars on her face from years of abuse. She smirked at Willie and Gertie, both of whom returned the look with smiles. It felt good to smile. This wasn't exactly a celebration as much as a rare opportunity to do something other than toil for the Barrow Plantation. It was a rare chance to breathe and smile—to steal some joy.

To feel, if just for the moment, human.

"To Charlie," Tussy toasted, raising a jug as everyone gave her their attention. "And every soul got snatched before him." The slaves nodded in solemn agreement as she took a sip from a jug before passing it to Gertie. "And to the ones still here."

Gertie shrugged her shoulders and gave a quick giggle as she took the jug of wine. She turned to find Willie smiling at her, and she passed the jug to him. "Don't reckon I should partake of this here," she told him in a quiet tone.

"Why not?" Willie asked.

"Look at Ol' Fuddle over there."

Barely six feet from where they sat, a short, rotund slave with an empty jug in his hand stumbled back and forth as children tapped him on the back before running off giggling. With each tap, Fuddle spun with a little less stability and a bit more aggravation until he fell flat on his face. They all laughed at the sight.

"If'n the drink make big Ol' Fuddle stagger 'round so," Gertie smiled, "it cain't be too good for this here lil' one growin' in my belly." She leaned against Willie again, and he allowed himself to revel in the feel of her. It was exactly the distraction he needed after the events four nights ago with Rafazi.

Willie hadn't told anyone what he'd seen, not even Gertie. They would think him a fool. There was no longer any doubt Rafazi's claim was true, but Willie simply could not handle the existence of a Ramangan on top of everything else. He had served his punishment, he was back in the rice fields, and there was no reason he would need to see or speak of Rafazi ever again. He was sure the slave had run far, far away with his incredible speed.

A young slave girl no older than fourteen years—Fanna, he had heard the others call her—danced alongside an elderly man around the fire. It was rumored Fanna had been a solitary purchase, arriving on these shores without any family, something Willie related to. The elderly man and Fanna laughed together;

Fanna's dimples puckered in her cheeks. He hadn't heard Fanna speak since she'd arrived on the plantation, but the smile on her face now spoke volumes.

"Look at her," Gertie said to Willie. "A joyful child she must've been." Gertie's smile faded as she rubbed a hand over her still-flat belly. Willie placed his hand over hers, and his brow furrowed.

"What I done?" he whispered. "I's scared for you ev'ry day. For you, for me. Now I done doomed a child."

"We's done this here together," Gertie said, her consoling hand cupping his cheek, "and we's cain't change it. You don't wants to change it, do you?"

"No," Willie said determinedly. "This here child gots a right to life, but not this here one. What hope a child have in this here world? Be born, toil, die. And if'n the child grow and decide to be free, he end up like Charlie . . ."

"You ain't end up like Charlie." Gertie took his hands in hers. "You's scared as I be. I knows a man ain't s'posed to claim his fright, but fright keep us 'live. It keep this here baby 'live, too."

"But that ain't no way," Willie grumbled. "I's powerful scared when I run, but I done it. I done it 'cause I's so tired of bein' afraid. Ain't you?"

"I is," Gertie agreed, her eyes glossy. "But there gots to be a better way. And we owes it to this here child to find it. I's so sick of this worry."

"Then don't worry none this night." Willie stood and she stood with him, clutching her head covering as he led her away from the cabin. Together, they crept around the back of slave village and rushed to their special spot in the tall grass under the tall oak tree.

With the sounds of the slaves' merriment still in the air behind them, Willie and Gertie kissed deeply. She sank into him, pressing her sensual, supple form against his. The feel of her was the closest thing to bliss he knew; it was refuge he found in her arms in these brief, stolen moments, and he had come to need it as much as he needed air to breathe.

With Gertie in his arms, Willie gently dropped to his knees and laid her in the grass. They kissed again, slower this time, as Willie ran a hand softly over her belly. Gertie closed her hands over his and kept them there, her eyes wet.

"What happen to Charlie ain't the only end," he told her. "He used to always say, 'Gives me freedom or gives me death.'"

"And death is what he got," Gertie whimpered. "I don't wants to die to be free. I don't wants this lil' one to die, and I don't wants you doin' nothin' gonna take you 'way from us . . ."

"I don't knows much 'bout this here New World, but I knows it's big. There gots to be a way, Gertie, and I's gonna find it, a way we's all three can be free. Maybe it ain't up North, maybe it's somewhere else, but I aims to find it for us and take us there."

"No, Willie. This world ain't gonna give us no say. Only value we got is what we's can do. Massa done set up them breedin' rooms, and sometimes, them overseers have they way with the women. If'n Massa gonna want them chilren raised, maybe I could be they's mammy. Maybe if'n he agree, our lil' one could live a might better . . ."

"So you's can raise him to get sold? No, Gertie. The world cain't stay this way forever. We ain't s'posed to live like this here. We gots a right to freedom sure as we's born. Now, I ain't runnin' 'til I finds us a way to be free, all three of us, but I's gonna find a way to get us far from this place. I promise you. 'Til then, this here child will know love."

It was the first time he had ever said the word, in any context, to Gertie.

Love.

It felt criminal to even utter the word, but it was what he felt, as complicated as it was, for her and his unborn child.

"Love?" she asked with a shaky voice.

Willie caressed her cheek with a soft smile and nodded. "We's gots to have love for one 'nother before we can pass it to this child . . ."

"I might already do." Gertie pulled him in close and gently removed the shirt from his still-healing back. "Promise me," she breathed as she ran her hands against his hard, broad chest, gingerly fingering the scar there from the welt Monroe had given him with his whip. It didn't deter Gertie; her eyes were slits of passion. "Promise me you ain't gonna do nothin' to take you 'way from me . . ."

"I promise." Willie nuzzled into her neck, wrapping his arms around her as his arousal grew.

"I's so afraid for what gonna become of our lil' one," she whispered. "Free me from it for a short while . . ."

The comfort they found in their passion for one another took over, and they surrendered themselves to it. Gertie lowered Willie's pants and gasped with desire.

"You gives me that worry," Willie moaned into her lips as he entered her. The explosion of pleasure made this comfort they indulged in blossom into something more, something deeper. He released the worry and uncertainty, and allowed himself to get lost in Gertie, her feel, her scent, her touch, the generous curvature of her frame. Her moaning in his ear caused him to pant her name. So lost was he in his ardor, the sound of his name being whispered seemed a world away. The persistent hiss finally registered, and he found Tussy standing over them.

"Tussy!" Gertie exclaimed as she fumbled with her dress, pulling it down over her legs as Willie reluctantly climbed away from her on his belly while lifting his pants over himself.

"Willie, the overseers is comin'," Tussy spoke quickly and quietly, "and they's drunk! You 'member what happen last time they's drunk and come down here. I knows it ain't right, but the only face keep Monroe from leerin' at the womenfolk when he in this state is yours!"

Gertie was shoving her hair underneath her cloth covering. "Willie, I don't wanna be . . ."

"Hush now. Ain't gonna be. You just stay here and keep yourself hid." Pulling his shirt over himself, Willie followed Tussy back to the slave village where the slaves were already milling about nervously. Fires were being put out, and women and children were being hurried into cabins. The music and merriment had stopped.

"Get any wine left put 'way before Monroe see it," Willie told Tussy.

"Mind yourself now," Tussy responded. "You cain't take a beatin' for all of us, not after what Monroe already done to your back."

Monroe was leading two overseers, drinking from open bottles of whiskey, into the middle of slave village, stumbling and laughing as they moved forward, their eyes bright and glossy, their rifles hanging loosely from their shoulders. With Monroe was Butch, a bald, dirty man with a middle so thick he seemed as wide as he was tall, and Amos, a blond thirty-year-old, who ran his hands through his hair far more often than was necessary.

The slaves who hadn't made it to shelter before the arrival of the overseers were frozen in place. Amos approached a group of children who were still standing in the dance ring and started to clap his hands and stomp his feet, devoid of any rhythm. He hovered over them with menacing glee.

"What the hell you lil' niggers doin'? Stompin' 'round to that jungle music? How 'bout I stomp your lil' black asses into the ground?" Amos pushed them all out of the circle and kicked the dirt to erase it as the children ran to hide behind their elders.

"Was y'all makin' merry?" Monroe asked in a voice made shaky with drink.

"Looks like, boss," Butch answered, taking a long pull from his bottle and spitting the spirit onto one of the burning fires, causing the flames to flare. Frightful screams from those who were closest to it rang out as Butch moved to Tussy, yanking the jug she had been about to hide out of her hand and taking a swig before calling back to Monroe. "And they stole wine to do it."

"Your mistress gave you wine for healin' means," Monroe fussed. "You drinkin' it is stealin'!"

"We ain't stole nothin', sir," Tussy said. "This here wine we's done made ourselves from savin' up grapes when Massa was kind enough to give us some."

"Them grapes was for *eatin'*, so it's still *stealin'*," Monroe snapped. "What we gonna do 'bout this?" Monroe turned an angry eye to Willie, who had stepped forward slow and steady, placing himself between the overseer and Tussy.

"We's sorry, sir," Willie offered evenly. "Weren't our place. You go on return that wine to Massa. We's bein' too loud. We's gon' to bed." Willie walked Tussy back toward the cabins, and the rest of the slaves slowly started to walk away.

Amos kept a lecherous eye on a young slave girl, no more than twelve, who'd been lingering alone in the middle of the village. As he drunkenly stumbled toward her, Willie clocked the rifles all the overseers still carried. He had no move to make. As the overseer reached the girl, something flashed across the clearing, something no one could make out, and in an instant, the girl was gone. Amos stood dumbfounded, as did everyone else. He spun around in confusion.

"Where the hell she go?"

The overseer redirected himself toward another young slave girl, this time Fanna. Amos took two steps in her direction before his brow scrunched in confusion as Fanna disappeared in the same fashion the first girl did. Amos spun around in anger.

"What kind of nigger voodoo y'all tryin' to play on me, huh?" he yelled, pulling his rifle off his shoulder and swinging it around, looking for someone to aim at, igniting the slaves' panic. They ran for their cabins, which caused Butch and Monroe to pull their guns.

"Search them cabins!" Monroe hollered. "Find the girls and take them to the breedin' rooms!"

With wicked smiles, Butch and Amos rushed for the cabins, knocking down anyone in their path. Willie noticed Fanna sitting on the ground a few feet away from him, her hands shaking, looking as confused as everyone else. Amos spotted her as well and made a beeline for her, grabbing her by the hair and dragging her to her feet.

"How the hell you get away from me like you did? Huh?" Amos barked.

There was only one explanation, Willie realized.

Rafazi.

And if he could move fast enough to rescue one girl, maybe he could save them all.

Monroe put the blade of his pistol sword to Willie's neck. "What the hell is goin' on 'round here, boy?"

"Nothin'. I swear," Willie said as calmly as he could, hearing the accusation in the chief overseer's voice. "We's all been drinkin'. We needs to go on to bed. I's powerful tired, boss."

"I ain't drunk! Now, you up to somethin', I know it!"

"Ain't up to nothin'. No, sir."

"You callin' me a liar, boy? Last time a nigger called me a liar, I sliced his neck from ear to ear with this here blade. Said he wasn't defilin' my wife, but I knew he was." Monroe's voice cracked as he continued. "Caught them in my barn. My wife, just a-bouncin' on top of him, hollerin' and carryin' on like she ain't never done for me!" His speech continued to slur, and his blade-holding hand shook, the fire reflecting off the blade, keeping Willie on edge and in place. "I slit his throat and that nigger-lovin' whore's, too! Filthy nigger made me kill my wife and lose my farm! And you know what? Every time I see your ugly face, I see him."

Willie said nothing but kept his eye on the cabins while Monroe held him in check. The pleas and screams of the slaves echoed in the night along with the shouting of Amos and Butch and the sounds of the cabins being ransacked.

"Where the lil' slave girl you sweet on?" Monroe asked Willie.

"Ain't sweet on nobody, sir. I's here to work."

"I ain't blind!" Monroe shouted before he called out to Amos, who had a kicking and screaming Fanna over his shoulder. "Amos! Find the girl with the cloth coverin' on her head and take her to the breedin' rooms!" Amos nodded and moved along, and Monroe hissed in Willie's ear. "I'm gonna fuck your slave girl, and you gonna watch me do it."

Willie's blood went hot with rage, but one twitch of Monroe's blade could spell instant death for him, and he was paralyzed by the promise he'd made to Gertie, by his own desire to live, by his fear. But it wasn't fear making his blood boil. This was something else, something deeper.

Something stronger.

"Lookie what I found me hidin' in the bushes!" Butch cackled as he stepped out from behind a cabin, yanking Gertie's mane back and forth, causing her to stumble as she cried out.

"Well, well, well. What do we have here?"

The sound of Big Jim's booming voice eviscerated Willie. His presence and the hungry look on the plantation owner's face as he stared at Gertie meant things were about to get worse. Willie forced his eyes away from Gertie so Big Jim would not read his affection for her, but the grin on the slave owner's face told him it was too late. Big Jim moved close to Willie, and the slave dropped his head.

"Willie," Big Jim spoke softly with a smirk, "you aren't afraid of me, are you?" Willie kept his head down. He had suffered for not answering his owner before, but this time he couldn't. His voice would convey too much. "My house girl says you got something you want to say to me. Well? I'm listening, boy."

Willie racked his brain for a response good enough to keep the mother of his child from danger. But before he could say anything, Butch approached them with a struggling Gertie in his grasp.

"Don't you worry, Willie," he heard Big Jim say. "I've come upon the perfect way for you to apologize to me."

Seven

THE BREEDING ROOMS

illie fought the urge to swallow as Monroe's blade scraped against his throat as he was led into one of the breeding rooms. They were adjoining open air cabins at the edge of slave village, reserved for slaves to make more slaves. It was a relatively new business venture of Big Jim's to further supplement his already considerable income. But this night, one of the rooms would serve as live theater for the perverse entertainment of the plantation owner and his overseers.

"Woo-wee! I can't wait to fuck me a nigger bitch!" Butch hollered at the top of his lungs in drunken excitement. He groped at his crotch as he watched Amos rub himself against a sobbing Fanna. Having already been tied to one of the bedposts, Gertie stood, alternated between shutting her eyes and looking at Willie, while Big Jim openly ogled her.

Do something! Willie's mind churned, searching for something he *could* do, any action he could take, anything to survive, to stop this from happening.

"Willie here's sweet on this one," he heard Monroe mutter to Big Jim.

"Any fool can see that," came the slave owner's response.

"Well, I was hopin' I could teach him a lesson by takin' her tonight for myself."

"Take? There is nothing here for you to take. Anything you might have been able to call your own you lost long ago," Big Jim sneered at Monroe. "Everything you see here belongs to me. Including you."

Willie was acutely aware of the anger Big Jim's answer stirred in Monroe as the hand holding the blade at his throat began to shake again, and its edge nicked Willie's skin. He winced as his head involuntarily jerked back from the blade and he felt the trickle of blood the blade's small cut released. His eyes followed the slave owner making his way over to Gertie. She flinched at his presence, and the reaction made Big Jim smile. Gertie's breathing increased as he ran a fat hand down her arm, his ruby ring scraping across her skin.

"Are you wet yet?" Big Jim whispered, but her turning away from him and shutting her eyes did not stop Gertie's tears from flowing down her cheeks. Big Jim leaned down and ran his tongue up the side of her face. Gertie tightened her lips in a failed attempt to stifle her sobs, and Big Jim chuckled, then sighed. "Mighty white of you to offer your little slave girl in apology," he said to Willie as he roughly grabbed at Gertie's breasts. "Thank you kindly!"

Big Jim's laughter made Willie ball up his fists in anger, and he had to bite down on his inner cheek to temper his growing rage. Anything he did in retaliation would be met with swift and brutal, perhaps deadly, force. But Rafazi . . . With Gertie being mercilessly mauled and Monroe's blade at his throat, he wished Rafazi would return with his speed and strength.

Rafazi. Willie began willing his thoughts to reach the Ramangan. *Where are you?*

"You see?" Monroe hissed, pulling Willie from his thoughts. "She loves it. I bet she can't wait to take her master's white cock. And once she does, she'll forget all about what you got between your legs!"

"Like your wife forget what you got when she stray from you?" Willie hadn't intended to say the words out loud, but witnessing Gertie's molestation put cracks in the promise he'd made to her in the tall grass. This abuse she was suffering was not purely her own; the child she carried was also being victimized. His child. And the new feeling got stronger. It threatened to overwhelm the fear he'd grown accustomed to living with. Monroe punched Willie hard before grabbing him by the neck and slamming his back against the wall.

"How's your back feelin', nigger? Huh?" Monroe growled as Willie grimaced in pain. "Want me to open up them wounds for you? Just say the word!"

"Enough!" Big Jim's bellow brought all the activity in the room to an abrupt halt. "Monroe, you are ruining the atmosphere in here!" Monroe stepped back, and Willie tried to think of a way to somehow use this brief halt in the turmoil to his advantage. His eyes darted back and forth for any workable opening. "Get these niggers on the beds," Big Jim ordered as he began to untie Gertie. "I'm good and ready for a little something dirty."

Big Jim threw Gertie on one bed and removed his breeches, while Amos shoved Fanna onto the other bed by her neck.

"You can be awake or asleep for this, but you gonna get my cock wet one way or another," Amos told Fanna as he climbed over her on the bed. Fanna kicked her legs at his torso as he wrestled against her. Willie's eyes shifted back and forth between the girl and Big Jim hovering over Gertie on the other bed, his breathing ragged. His fear had slipped. It was anger surging through him now.

"What you think you gonna do, huh?" Monroe taunted, having read Willie's expression. "Think you gonna be some kinda hero?"

Amos yelped out as Fanna got ahold of his arm and bit it. The overseer yanked his limb free before backhanding the girl so hard she fell back on the bed unconscious. He finished off the rest of his whiskey bottle and threw it on the ground, but before he could remove his pants, the mysterious blur returned, appearing and disappearing again in an instant, taking Fanna with it.

This time, however, the blur had been noticeably slower. This time, it was much more obvious to everyone something had entered the room, and it put Big Jim and the overseers on high alert. Their sexual assaults were momentarily forsaken for their guns while Big Jim quickly pulled up his breeches.

"What in the hell?" he asked.

"Been happenin' since we got out here, boss," Butch answered. "We think it's some kind of nigger voodoo shit."

"Nonsense. Some of these slaves are so damn fast you have to keep your eyes on them at all times."

"I ain't never known one to be this fast, boss."

"You're drunk, is all. Hush up!"

The white men began scanning the room so as not to miss anything. Willie's eyes met Gertie's, and she shook her head, to which he could only blink in apology to her. His rage had found opportunity.

He wouldn't get another chance.

Willie lunged for Monroe's pistol sword at the exact moment the blur returned to the room, but it had gotten even slower, slow enough for Willie to register it as Rafazi, who raced past Big Jim and picked up Gertie. Willie struggled against Monroe for the weapon as Butch swung the butt of his rifle at the blur. He missed Rafazi but struck Gertie in the head hard enough for Rafazi to lose balance and drop her.

"Gertie!" With an involuntary impulse, Willie released Monroe's gun, shoved him to the ground with ease, and leapt across the beds to get to her.

"Gertie!" Willie cradled her in his arms as she rubbed her head, wincing and groaning. Her eyes opened and immediately went wide. "Willie . . . !"

He spun to find Butch pointing his rifle down at them. Amos had pinned Rafazi against the wall, his rifle held tight against Rafazi's chest. Willie reared back as Monroe barreled toward him, his pistol sword pointed at Willie's head.

"You ain't fit to live, boy!" Spittle dripped from Monroe's bottom lip as he screamed at Willie, his arm slashing down. But Big Jim caught his arm before the blade could make contact. Shaking his head at Monroe, the plantation owner shoved the overseer away.

"I will not have you ruin my night, Monroe," he said before turning to Willie and Gertie with a twisted smile. "This night has been exciting, and it's going to be fun fucking your dirty slut right in front of you, boy."

Willie's nostrils flared and his hands shook, but Gertie grabbed hold of him, moving to her knees and forcing his head to hers until their brows touched.

"I's already with child," Gertie whimpered so softly Willie could barely hear her. "They's can only sully me so much. Don't you break your promise again."

It was all the time they had.

"Get those clothes off her, and get her back up on the bed," Big Jim ordered as he stripped down entirely, and Butch snatched her up onto her feet. Tearing the dress from her, he took as many liberties as he could, his hands groping at her naked flesh. Gertie stood and shook in silence, tears rolling down her cheeks.

"Yeah, you go on and cry," Big Jim said with a smirk. "Let it all out, sugar. I was too good to Irene. I need to feel the pain coming off you!" Pushing her onto the bed, he roughly spread Gertie's legs and climbed between them. Gertie turned her wet eyes to Willie as he was dragged to his feet by Monroe, who had the barrel of his pistol against Willie's temple.

"What you want us to do with this here stinky one, boss?" Amos asked, digging his rifle barrel into Rafazi's chest.

"You and Butch lock him up in a cage, put him in the field, and leave him there as a warning for the others," Big Jim said, never taking his eyes off Gertie. "Monroe, you keep Ol' Willie right here where he can see all the action!"

Amos cracked the butt of his rifle across Rafazi's head, sending him to the ground, then hauled him out of the cabin by the collar with Butch in tow, with Gertie's wailing ringing around the room as Big Jim slammed himself into her. The louder she cried, the harder and faster Big Jim pumped his hips. But she kept her eyes on Willie.

And Monroe, holding Willie at gunpoint, made sure he kept his eyes on the desecration of Gertie and their child.

Eight

A Seed Planted

Willie's sobs were as heavy in his chest as Gertie had become in his arms. Big Jim's repeated assaults had left her unconscious, at which point he discarded her and left the room.

Willie was gutted. He had let this happen to her. The mother of his child. If he still had a child. Big Jim had been so rough with Gertie, Willie wondered if the trauma had injured the baby growing inside her. Gingerly, he wrapped her ripped dress around her nakedness as best he could before picking her up.

What kind of father could he be after this? Monroe was right. Willie wasn't fit to live. When he arrived at her cabin, he found the other slaves waiting for them. They silently made way for Willie as he placed Gertie gently on her cot. It did his broken heart a measure of good to see Fanna safe in another cot, even if she was still unconscious from her ordeal.

"What happen, Willie?" Fuddle asked him, fully sober after the evening's events. "I mean, I knows what done happen, but what happen with Fanna? Somethin' powerful fast come through here—ain't none of us seen it exactly, not enough to rightly know what it be—but when it gone, Fanna was lyin' on this here cot."

Willie's head and heart were too heavy to offer any explanation. "Well, she safe now."

"Ain't none of us is safe." Tussy's words were met by murmurs of agreement from the others as she stepped forward. "Now, I don't know what done happen, but Fuddle speak true. Somethin' come through here, somethin' not of this world."

"Had a stank to it," Fuddle added as the murmurs grew a bit louder.

Rafazi's words echoed in Willie's head: *Nothing anyone would believe if you told them.*

"The same somethin' snatched that child outta Amos reach the first time. Cain't no gust of wind carry no child." Tussy eyed Willie closely. "What you know 'bout it?"

"What there be to know, Tussy? Whatever it be, it be on our side. It save Fanna. It tried to save Gertie, I seen it try."

"Yeah, but it ain't." The suspicion Tussy gave voice to was on the faces of the others, and the weight in Willie's head got heavier. "I been duckin' the whip since they brung me here, and that been bad enough," Tussy continued. "But if'n I gots to start duckin' whatever this here is y'done brung down on us . . ."

"I ain't brung nothin' down, Tussy."

"I seen you, Willie! When wickedness come and swoop up Fanna the first time, I seen you wasn't surprised, plain as day. I seen you, seen your eyes. Like you's willed it so. Fanna safe for now, but what darkness y'done brung us, Willie? What you brung back here after you run off with Charlie?"

Willie had neither the time nor inclination to entertain accusations. "I done told you, now . . ."

"You ain't told me nothin'! Two of you run off, only one come back breathin'."

"The hounds took him, Tussy! You been known that! You think I's to blame for Charlie? Come on, now." Willie was tired, and Tussy keeping at him when Gertie was so hurt, blaming him, was making it hard for him to keep his head up.

"I don't rightly know what to think with what all happen in this cabin, but I knows this here: Evil be real! And if it come to your aid somehow, some way, well then, some price need to be paid to keep it from turnin' on you. On us! What evil got to be done to keep whatever this be from turnin' on us?"

Willie examined the faces of Tussy and the others, and the unspoken message was clear. He wasn't welcome here, not tonight. Something they could not make sense of had made its presence felt, scared them, and their glares told Willie they held him responsible for it.

Perhaps he was. The truth would make him a fool in their eyes, or worse. There was nothing left for him to say. So, he left the cabin and walked out into the night, his head swimming in turmoil. Gertie was unconscious, Rafazi was in iron, and Willie was beginning to believe all of it was his fault.

And then, like a loud whisper floating across the night directly into his ears, Willie heard his name.

Willie . . .

He spun around, listening to the wind. The gentle roll of the lake. The scurry of critters in the fields. The chirp of crickets. But no voices. He shook off the sound of the voice before he heard it again.

Willie . . .

It might not have been real, but he felt compelled to follow the sound. He kept hearing his name as he followed the voice, until he found himself on the rice paddy, and in the distance, saw Rafazi sitting cross-legged in an iron cage.

From up close, Willie could see how badly the man had been beaten by the overseers before they locked him up. His whole face was swollen. He was bloodied, and iron shackles bruised his wrists and ankles where he'd been fettered.

But he was also wearing a smile.

"It worked! I wasn't sure I was strong enough, especially after what they'd done to me." Rafazi coughed up blood before spitting it out, along with a loose tooth.

"What you's talkin' 'bout? What worked?"

"Me calling you. You heard me calling your name, didn't you?"

Willie could only shake his head. "Ain't possible . . ."

"When I'm at full strength, you'd be amazed at what I can do. But right now, I need your help. The sun will be up soon. I need to get out of this cage, or I'll meet my end."

"Yeah, you right. Massa may kill you yet."

"The sun would take me before he wakes."

"What you mean?"

"Without my cloak, I can't survive the sunlight. I need you to get me out of this cage."

"You say you's Ramanga. The legend say Ramangas is immortal."

"Immortality doesn't mean invincibility, Willie. The price for immortality, my abilities, power, is blood. Without more of it, I won't have enough strength to break these bars, and the sun will take me."

"What you mean, take you?"

"It will burn me to ash."

"So, you *can* die?"

"In actuality, I am already dead. But if I'm not careful, yes, my existence can be ended."

"So, then what happen if'n you get outta this here cage? The sun still gonna rise."

74

"I'll retrieve my cloak, then burrow underground until nightfall."

"You's gonna bury youself? How you survive?"

"I don't need to breathe, Willie. Listen, I would love to explain all of this to you, but there's no time. I need to get out of this cage right now, and to do that, I need more blood."

"I's go find you a critter . . ."

"No. I need human blood. Your blood."

Willie stepped back from the cage. Had Tussy been right? Had he brought even more wickedness into the lives of the slaves? Was Rafazi a creature of evil?

"I can see the fight within you," Rafazi said. "It's the curse of humanity. Inherited logic versus the truth before you."

"What truth?"

"You have nothing to look forward to in this life, Willie. You are a slave. Your life is not your own. It has been stolen from you. The child in Gertie's belly already belongs to your master."

"How you know?"

"Her blood, Willie. When I picked her up, I could smell two distinct scents, two people."

"I's powerful grateful for what you tried to do for Gertie . . ."

"Aren't you tired of it? The constant fear? The brutality? Monroe? Big Jim? All of it? Don't you want revenge for what they've done to Gertie? To you?"

Logic was losing to truth. Every word Rafazi spoke filled Willie with something more than anger, more than revenge.

Purpose.

Could he truly have it?

"Don't you want to know power? Have it to wield as your own?" Rafazi continued. "Don't you want your child to know freedom? Don't *you* want to know it again?"

"Yes!"

"Then give me your blood!"

As the final wall of reluctance crumbled inside him, Willie thrust his arm between the bars of the cage, and Rafazi's face distorted, as it had nights earlier. He sank his fangs deep into Willie's flesh. The familiar surge of pleasure passed through Willie, and he was reminded of his first encounter with Rafazi, whose red eyes had begun to glow. Willie winced from the vigorous sucking and tried to dislodge himself from Rafazi's jaw as he grew lightheaded.

Just a bit more . . .

Willie's vision went hazy at hearing the voice in his head, but seconds later, Rafazi released his arm. Willie fell to the damp earth and rubbed his eyes, trying to regain his focus. When he sat up, Rafazi had torn the bars from the cage and had effortlessly tossed them into the rice field. Rafazi stepped out of his former confines, breaking the irons on his hands and legs with his bare hands as he did so.

When Willie's faculties had fully returned, Rafazi stood majestically before him. His bruises and wounds were gone, and he still had the face of a monster. Willie could feel his heartbeat in his throat.

"What is you?" Willie knew he had asked the question before—he even knew the answer—but the shock of what he had witnessed, seeing Rafazi's true power with his own eyes, it simply did not seem real. It couldn't be. A smile spread across Rafazi's face.

"I think you know." Rafazi helped Willie to his feet and placed a hand on his shoulder as his features once again became human.

"Thank you, Willie. I've allowed myself to be weak for too long, hiding in the dark from humans in misery; it made me forget my power. After you gifted me your blood the first time, I could have run off, but, alone, it would have been more of the same for me. And you probably would have taken the blame and paid for my departure with your life. I couldn't abide that.

I've been alone for a long time, Willie, and I want a brother again. I want him to be you. Let me make you. We will free ourselves and every slave on this plantation, and on every other plantation. These whip-crackers have no right to do what they've done, but we can make them pay. We can make them bow to us and make the colonies ours. *We* will be the masters. This I promise you."

Witnessing the effect his blood had on Rafazi with a clear head made one truth abundantly clear to Willie: If he were to have any chance of finding real freedom, of sparing his un-born child from a life of malicious bondage, it was in Rafazi's promise.

Willie found his smile. "How we's do it?"

Some of them are even
the folly of a weak white
man and a filthy Negress.

Nine

IRENE'S LAMENT

"Mornin', y'all!"

Carrying a small silver teapot, Irene made her way through the grand salon room at a hastened clip. Two house slaves, both women with complexions comparable to Irene's, refused to respond to the young woman's greeting and instead chose to glare at her as they went about their dusting.

It was behavior she'd grown accustomed to as Big Jim afforded her small luxuries above the other house slaves, such as the discarded linen petticoat of Missus Charity Barrow, which Irene had tailored herself to fit her form. The rest of the house slaves' clothes were made of "Negro cloth," a linsey-woolsey fabric so coarse it often irritated the skin. It was barely a step above what the field slaves were given to wear.

"If you don't mind my askin', why y'all in here dustin'? Y'all usually have breakfast duty with me." Irene kept her voice light and pleasant.

"Massa say let you work on your own," one of the house slaves blurted out. "I reckon he wanna see if you good for anythin' 'cept layin' on your back!"

The house slaves cackled. Irene didn't expect kindness from them, but the constant ridicule magnified her loneliness in this place. "High yella whore!" one of them called out behind her, but she pushed past it like she did every day, headed for the dining room, and prepared herself for the contempt of the Barrows.

A sumptuous breakfast consisting of various items lay before them: hasty pudding with bacon, cornmeal porridge with molasses, butter rice, hoe cakes with maple syrup, assorted rolls, and pastries. Big Jim and Thomas enjoyed beer—a pint for the father, a small glass for the son—with their meals, while Big Jim's wife and his daughter, Virginia, waited for their tea to be served.

"More tea, ma'am?"

"Don't ask stupid questions. Land o' Goshen, it has taken you forever to do anything today!" Charity snapped.

"Forgive me, Missus. I ain't mean to forget the tea. I's workin' on my own today, and . . ."

"Stop your confounded gibberish, and do your job!"

As she filled Charity Barrow's cup, Irene could feel the tall and lean forty-year-old woman's cold glare. She was careful not to meet her mistress's gaze, but Charity made no effort to hide her hatred for Irene, something Irene attributed to Big Jim having no interest in hiding his nightly assaults of her. Part of her carried sympathy for the woman: They were both being abused by the same man.

"Give me tea! Hurry up!" Virginia Barrow thrust her teacup directly into Irene's face, smacking it into her nose. It was more humiliating than it was painful, but Irene endured it quietly. Virginia was nineteen years old and took after her father physically: large, corpulent, and imposing.

"Look at what you've done! You tainted my cup with your dirty half-nigger face, and now I can't drink out of it!" Virginia threw the porcelain cup to the floor with an insolent pout. Irene's lips tightened, but she was happy the thick carpet had cushioned the cup, keeping it from breaking and her from hunting for shards of porcelain under the table.

She cast her eyes at Big Jim. The last time Virginia threw a tantrum, it was because she hadn't liked the way her flounder had been prepared. "It's disgusting! I may as well be eating lobster," she had yelled at Irene in a tirade. She'd picked up her plate and had been about to throw it at Irene when Big Jim's voice had intervened. "Take it away, Irene," he'd said. "I will not feed ungrateful children at my table."

It wasn't exactly in defense of her, but it had saved her work. This time, he did not meet Irene's gaze, choosing instead to keep his focus on the latest edition of *The New Atalantis*.

"What are you staring at, you stupid Negress?" Virginia growled. "Get me another cup!"

"Yes, ma'am. Forgive me."

"Pour my molasses first!" Irene obeyed Thomas's order and did her best to ignore his lecherous stare. Even at his tender age, the boy had a destructive streak his father explained away as "mischievous." More than a few of his "pranks" played on the house slaves had resulted in broken bones or worse. A well-placed set of marbles left in the cookhouse had caused one of the cooks to slip and bang her face on a hot stove, scalding the right side of her face and severely damaging her eye.

Thomas had no remorse or sympathy and took to calling the disfigured slave "Ol' Patchy," thanks to the patch she wore over her injured eye. With the onset of puberty, the boy had taken to groping the women house slaves every chance he got. Irene was no exception.

"A little more," Thomas ordered. She could feel his eyes lingering on her form instead of his plate. She ended the episode by hurriedly setting the small porcelain pitcher of molasses down and moving to the head of the table where Big Jim sat. She offered him a smile, but he never looked up from his book to see it.

"Would you like another pint of ale, Massa?"

His response was an irritated huff. She searched her mind for how she could have displeased him. Perhaps it was Willie's fault. Maybe, even after using the exact words Big Jim had told her to, Willie still hadn't apologized for running. At a loss, she moved away from Big Jim, which put her in closer proximity to Charity. She then noticed something rare in the room, and it sent a jolt of unease through her: Charity was smiling.

"I trust you'll be ready to receive the governor and the Callowhills for lunch this afternoon, James?" Charity asked.

"I thought the Callowhills were moving to the North."

"They are, but they are still our friends, and they are coming for lunch this afternoon."

"Why would any self-respecting Southerner move to the North?"

"I don't want to have to be around Penelope!" Thomas complained.

"Thomas!" Charity exclaimed. "Penelope and her parents will be guests in our house, and you will treat them as such. You will also be on your best behavior in front of Governor Collins. It is an honor to have him in our home."

"The honor is his for getting to step foot in my house," Big Jim muttered as Charity turned to Irene.

"And you shall be flawless in your service to them. Do you understand?"

"Yes, ma'am." Irene nodded obediently, but it wasn't enough. Charity pinched her arm roughly, twisting the skin until Irene released a small yelp of pain.

"Do you understand me?"

"Yes, ma'am!"

Charity delivered a few more moments of pain before releasing Irene. "Well? What are you standing around for, you stupid girl? Go get things in order for this afternoon! Now!"

Irene nodded and started out of the room, halting when a black shoe smacked her on the back of her head. She turned to find Thomas holding its match.

"And shine my shoes!" Thomas threw the second shoe at Irene, who ducked out of its path before picking up the pair.

"And hurry up with my tea!" Virginia griped. "Don't we have more niggers? Why are you the only one serving us?"

"Because Irene has had it too easy in this house." Big Jim closed his book and glared at Irene.

"A direct result of your behavior toward the girl," Charity said, keeping her head down as her smile grew a bit wider.

"Nevertheless, I've decided she will have to work harder to earn her keep. I had Clarence delegate the rest of the breakfast staff to other chores so I could gauge her work performance. It was abysmal. I doubt she will be of any use to Clarence when the guests arrive."

"Then who will serve them, James?" Charity asked. "Granted, this one is atrocious, but she and Clarence are the most presentable slaves we have for company."

"Clarence!" Big Jim bellowed, and a lanky house slave of forty-some years—in a faded, but neat, black wool livery suit and with an expression of perpetual panic on his face—immediately entered the room.

Clarence was the driver of the house slaves, the one in charge. He used a crisp, white handkerchief to wipe the sweat from his brow; there always seemed to be sweat on his brow. He was lighter in complexion than the field slaves, but still darker than Irene.

"Forgives my tardiness, boss," Clarence apologized with a slight bow. "Just my nigger nature, I reckon. I won't keeps you waitin' again."

Irene couldn't stop her eyes from rolling.

"You and Irene will be serving lunch today," Big Jim said.

"To the Callowhills and Massa Collins, yes, sir. I got them kitchen yard niggers whippin' up somethin' powerful scrumptious for y'all."

"I've watched Irene's service this morning. I don't think she'll be enough help to you this afternoon."

Irene's eyes went wide as Clarence smacked her on the back of the head. She narrowed her gaze at him as he reprimanded her. "Lazy nigger! You coulda shown Massa how much you 'preciate all he done for you, but what you go do? I's sorry 'bout her, boss. You would think the white blood in her would rise to your biddin'."

"I want you to get the one called Gertie to help."

Irene and Clarence looked at each other in confusion.

"Gertie, boss? From the field?" Clarence asked.

"From the field?" Charity protested. "Have you lost your wits, James? I will not have field niggers in my house!"

"Well, when you get a house of your own, you can decide. Until then, *I* will decide who does and does not set foot in *my* house, and I say, get Gertie."

"You don't like overseers in this house, let alone field slaves," Charity pressed. "Now you've got a specific one in mind?"

"Why her, Massa?" Irene asked.

"How dare you question me? How dare any of you question me?! Am I supposed to answer to women and niggers now? In my own house?" Everyone flinched as he raised his voice, but no one more than Irene as he zeroed in on her.

"If you must know," he seethed, "as disappointing as you've been lately, a field slave can't be any worse. She might even be better at doing the job to her master's satisfaction. Who knows? As useless as you've become, I may not end up needing you at all." His threat could not have been any clearer to Irene. "Now, Clarence, you bring that field nigger in here, clean her up, and get her ready. And Irene? You make sure you don't foul up. Not for another second. You hear?"

IRENE RUSHED ACROSS THE kitchen yard. Time was short: She still had to get herself and Gertie ready to serve lunch, but she'd forgotten to fetch butter from the milk house. Moments alone like this plagued her. Navigating the insults, assaults, and abuses in the path of her duties kept her mind occupied. However, when left alone, she never knew if her thoughts would become simply rageful or deathly ruinous. Between the two, she always prayed for the rage. Viciously violent imaginings of using brute force to destroy her tormentors were far better than the overwhelming despair living deep inside her ever since she'd been torn from her mother and sold off.

Thankfully for her, rage had taken hold, and Clarence was being eviscerated in her mind. It was clear he saw himself above the rest of the slaves, especially those who worked in the fields. Irene wasn't blind to the pressure Clarence was under. He was responsible for everything every house slave did, and anything their master disapproved of would get Clarence punished worse than the offending slave.

She knew Clarence was frantic about Shit Boy's current slacking and had begun helping with the cleaning of the chamber pots to keep Big Jim from noticing. But she had grown to hate his kowtowing, the way he groveled incessantly before the Barrows, speaking worse than he knew how to in their presence, berating the other slaves to make himself seem better, more subservient, as if it was a good thing.

It never worked. The Barrows never hid their disdain for him, and yet, he never let up. As if somehow, if he rebuked his own people long enough, he would be seen and treated as a white man.

Maybe his behavior would change if she planted Clarence's

head in the mud, stabbed a dagger through his skull, and twisted it until he learned to be a little more respectful to his own people, to her.

She'd held the thought ever since he had asked her to clean the guns and knives in one of Big Jim's weapons closets. The plantation owner had four such closets scattered throughout the main level of the house, though she never saw the man use any weapon. Perhaps she could sneak one away and use it on Clarence to straighten out his thinking.

After all, the man who'd sullied her mother was white, so she was genetically closer to what Clarence wished he could be than he was. Shouldn't he at least show the white blood running through her veins more respect?

As she got closer to the milk house, she realized she could hear the rhythmic creaking of a wooden chair tapping against a wall, along with panting. She wondered which of the slaves had paired off to quelch their desires.

On more than one occasion, she had stumbled upon the field slave called Derby "dipping his stick"—as she had heard some of the women say—in another field slave; sometimes his physical companion was one of the house slaves. There were rumors he had designs on her, but she paid them no mind. After enduring the violations perpetrated upon her by Big Jim, Irene would have been content to never see another male member again.

Slowing her pace and moving against the back wall of the milk house, she saw her assumption had been wrong. As she peeked around the corner, she found Clarence tied to a wooden chair that was knocking against the wall with every hunch of Charity Barrow's hips. The mistress of the house sat astride him, pumping her hips up and down, her skirts hiked up in her hands. Her eyes were closed in carnal rapture; his were wide open with what looked to Irene like a cross between panic and pain.

"Please, Miss Charity," she heard him plead with labored breath. "We's gonna get caught out here in the open like this here!"

"Shh," came their mistress's reply. "You keep your nigger cock hard until white mama gets what she needs."

Irene cursed. She recognized the look on Clarence's face. It was a mirror of her own each time the master of the house climbed atop her. Watching the two of them, she was grateful Barrow never saw fit to restrain her the way Clarence was now.

The notion of a man being violated in this way had never occurred to her, but witnessing it proved to be as gruesome to her as what she was made to endure. Everything about Clarence made sense to her now. His two-faced attitude, his generally unpleasant posturing, the constant sweat on his brow.

She didn't like it, but she understood survival took many forms.

"Miss Charity," she heard Clarence huff as their mistress rocked back and forth at a faster pace, causing the chair to slam louder against the wall, so much so, Irene ventured another peek. "I's gotta get ev'rythin' together for the lunch. I need to get that field Negress tidied up, and there ain't gonna be enough time . . ."

"We've got time, you filthy nigger." Her pants were coming hot and quick now, and her hips rolled continuously as she dropped her skirts and threw her arms around her house slave's neck. "Big, dirty black savages . . . strong, filthy niggers . . ."

Irene covered her mouth and stifled a gasp as Charity spasmed and shook as she orgasmed over Clarence while he grunted and squirmed with his impending, involuntary ejaculation.

"Miss Charity!" Clarence's exclamation made her hop off his lap, revealing his twitching member. Clarence shut his eyes tight and shuddered as it spewed forth. Charity giggled at the sight. Irene was both relieved and mortified for him—relieved his ordeal was over, mortified for what he had endured. She wondered how long this had been going on.

"Look at the mess you made," she heard Charity snicker. Irene ducked behind the wall again, keeping herself hidden.

"I's sorry, Missus."

"Clean yourself up and hurry. I will not have you embarrassing me at this luncheon."

"Yes, Missus."

Charity quickly untied the rope holding Clarence to the chair and ran off. Irene decided not to go into the milk house until Clarence had pulled himself together and rushed back toward the manor. It would delay her, and she knew she would be chided severely for her lack of time management. But this time, she was prepared to take it. She knew Clarence needed to chastise her. It was the only way he had of righting the wrong done to him.

Ten

OUT OF THE MOUTHS OF BABES

Clarence, in a newer and freshly pressed livery suit, and Irene and Gertie, both clothed in formal but modest servant dresses, stood ready to serve the Barrows, the Callowhills, and Governor Abraham Collins, appointed by the Crown to preside over the Province of Carolina, in the grand salon room of the manor.

Irene thought the governor a rather oafish man, and his appearance was a bit comical to her, especially for a man of prominence: His shape resembled a giant pear with legs. His smallest feature was his head; the rest of him seemed to balloon out below it. But he, like the rest of the white folks, ignored their servers, conversing among themselves, though Irene withstood the quick glimpses of hatred from the women in the room and the lustful glances of the men—except for Big Jim. His hungry peeks were reserved for Gertie.

The field slave's mane of soft hair had been released from

its cloth covering at Big Jim's behest, and she seemed to fidget with it as well as her servant dress.

"Settle yourself," Irene whispered to Gertie.

"I's cain't," came the reply. "This here dress too soft. It don't feel right, and I . . ." Her words trailed off when her eyes found Big Jim. It was clear to Irene how nervous she was to be in his presence, maybe even scared. "I ain't s'posed to be here." Gertie eyed the veritable feast: An array of baked breads, biscuits, and pastries were being served along with sliced meats—ham, chicken, and turkey. Fresh vegetables and fruits were also available, as was ale, tea, and milk. Fine plates and crystal glasses had been set out to serve it all on.

Irene wondered if Gertie had ever seen so much food in her life or if she even had any inkling of what any of it tasted like. She knew the field slaves were given corn mush to survive, and here poor Gertie was being forced to serve from a buffet capable of feeding all the field slaves until they were full.

"Your home is exquisite as always, James," Abraham said, running his fingers over the cloth covering the table where the food sat. It was thick and luxurious with intricate tapestry. "Is this new napery?"

"Yes, it is, Governor. Arrived on shipment last week from Turkey," Big Jim said proudly.

"Goodness! All the way from Turkey? It must have cost a fortune," remarked Anna Callowhill, a proper redheaded woman of high social standing. Irene thought she heard a tinge of envy in her voice.

"Then it's a good thing I'm rich!" Big Jim laughed at his comment, and the white folks politely laughed along with him. So did Clarence.

"You's right, boss! You's the richest man in all of Carolina!"

Subtly, Irene shook her head at Clarence as the entire room paused. Big Jim's glare sent Clarence's eyes to his shoes.

"Looks like I might be in the market for new slaves as well." The laughter in the room returned. "Slaves can be a tricky commodity," Big Jim added. "Sometimes, they forget their place and engage themselves in behaviors disrespectful to the good fortune they've been afforded by us."

The plantation owner's statement sent a shiver up Irene's spine. Clarence nudged Gertie and nodded toward the plates. Gertie turned to her with eyes as wide as saucers. "Do what I do," she whispered to Gertie. The field slave's hands shook, and Irene took them in her own, looking to Gertie as kindly as she could. Gertie cast her eyes downward, and Irene turned to find Big Jim leering at her, licking his lips as he inhaled a biscuit.

"Frankly, I find slavery to be a kindness to the nigger population," he was saying. Kindness? Irene's experience being enslaved was a great many things, but she had never once found it to be kind. She noticed Clarence's face was fixed in a permanent smile, as if he hadn't heard Big Jim's words at all.

"They are nothing but savage animals by nature, prone to primal urges," Big Jim continued, and Irene watched his eyes shift again to Gertie. She recognized the look in his eyes as she remembered his words to her, how disappointing she was, how useless she'd become, how Gertie would be better at satisfying him. Gertie specifically. She heard the field slave's breathing increase, saw the pure terror in her eyes. A flicker of terror caused Irene's own hands to shake. Her master's threat to her was becoming more real by the second.

"Having them here, putting them to good work, letting them know about the Good Lord instead of whatever filthy pagan animal they worshipped before—it's a far better life than running around naked in the mud or whatever else they did in the jungle. Their savage nature comes out sometimes, but beating it back is us doing the Lord's work for their own good."

Irene was confused. She had heard of, and even learned bits and pieces about, the white Christian god from older slaves.

The master and mistress from her first plantation never made any effort to teach her anything about their religion, and neither had anyone on the Barrow Plantation. Still, considering Big Jim's marriage and her limited knowledge, Irene was fairly certain his god would not have been thrilled with his nightly visits to her room.

With a smile on her face, Anna clapped her hands together and raised them above her head. "Amen, Mister Barrow," she said, and Big Jim returned her smile.

"Well, I consider myself honored to have the approval of someone with such piety, Madam Callowhill."

As the two shared a laugh, Irene noticed Anna's husband, Robert Callowhill, rolling his eyes.

"Those Quakers up north seem very confused on the matter, if you ask me," Big Jim concluded.

"Not every Northerner is a Quaker, James," Robert spoke up politely. Irene was sure being half Big Jim's size and at least ten years younger accounted for the politeness in Robert's tone. "Not even in Pennsylvania."

Anna and her daughter, Penelope Callowhill, who wore her red hair in pigtails and whom Irene pegged to be of thirteen years, stared at Robert as if he was out of his mind.

"You'll have to forgive my husband," Anna huffed with a nervous laugh and a genuinely mean side-eye at Robert. "His business travels have increased as of late, especially with this impeding threat of a move to Pennsylvania. I fear he has not had occasion to frequent the Lord's House as much as he should."

"I suspect the extended exposure to Northerners and their wayward thinking doesn't help," Big Jim chimed in, and Robert squirmed under the gaze of the room.

"Are you opposed to slavery, Robert?" Abraham asked with a mouthful of food. Irene wondered how he was able to keep such an amount in his tiny mouth.

"Why, no . . . I simply don't see the need to punish them without cause. They should be kept in good health to be of use, should they not?" The hesitation in Robert's voice piqued Irene's curiosity as he spoke. "I'm sure you didn't invite us all here to discuss the virtues of slavery, James. As you well know, I own slaves myself, and I am certainly not a Quaker."

"Good. Because those heathens signed a petition against slavery damn near the minute they arrived on these shores. In Pennsylvania, mind you," Big Jim said. "Downright disgraceful."

Irene closed her eyes for a moment and wished some of these Quakers her master spoke of would come and rescue her.

"Heathens might be pushing it," Robert said in response to Big Jim.

"Careful, Robert," the governor teased as he washed his mouthful down with a gulp of ale. "Disagreeing with James can be unwise."

"Quite right," Big Jim said without an ounce of jest. "Truthfully, I don't think heathen is word enough. They take the Good Book and twist it around for their own purposes. I've come to regard you as a good Southern man, Robert, and I cannot bring myself to understand why you would want to move to Pennsylvania, of all places."

"We're not moving yet. There's still much business to be finalized first."

"But Mister Barrow is right, Father," Penelope spoke up, which appeared to take everyone but Robert by surprise.

"You will forgive me. Our Penelope is unduly opinionated," Robert explained.

"She also doesn't seem to know her place. Looks like the North is already having an adverse effect on your family, and you haven't even taken up residence there yet," Big Jim warned.

"But I agree with you, Mister Barrow," Penelope said, unfazed. "I've told my father I wish for us to stay here in Carolina where folks understand God wants us to have slaves. It says so right there in Ephesians: 'Slaves, be obedient to them that are your masters according to the flesh, with fear and trembling, in singleness of your heart, as unto Christ.'"

"The passage reads 'servants,' honey," Robert corrected his daughter.

"What's the difference?" Anna interjected in defense of Penelope. "She is right, and so is Mister Barrow. Niggers need to be put to hard work and ruled by the whip because they are complete savages!" Anna looked directly at Clarence as her voice grew increasingly agitated. It made Irene nervous, but Clarence never lost his smile. Anna stared at him hard, as if demanding some sort of response. Charity gave him a slight nod of permission.

"Yes, ma'am," Clarence said to Anna with his ever-present smile as he refreshed her tea. "We is *savages*."

"I was attacked by one." Anna's admission was met with shock by Abraham and the Barrows, and with another subtle eye roll from her husband. "I was in my garden, tending to my roses. I turned around and there, standing behind me at the edge of the garden, was the biggest, blackest, ugliest nigger I had ever seen."

"Was he one of your own?" Charity asked, leaning forward, seemingly enthralled.

"Oh, I don't know. I don't make it my business to learn the slaves. Ideally, I like them out of sight and out of mind. We leave the tending of them to our overseer, Samuel Knudsen, a fine Christian man despite his station, strong in faith, spirit, and body." A husky note entered the woman's voice when she said the word "body," something Irene found curious. "Anyway, this particular nigger had startled me terribly. I could smell his rancid stench all the way across the garden. I ordered him to leave my garden at once, but he ran up and grabbed me from behind, and I could feel his . . . pushing up against the back of me. I was sure he was going to force himself on me."

"Goodness!" Charity exclaimed, shifting in her seat awkwardly, rhythmically.

"I screamed and screamed for help, but my husband, I suppose, had fallen deaf."

"I was away on business the day you say it happened, Anna. What could I have possibly done?" But Robert's words were ignored.

"Thank goodness for Samuel. He arrived in the nick of time. He tore me free, killed the nigger, and buried him in the woods where he belonged. Samuel saved my life that day. Such a blessing he is."

"Goodness!" Charity repeated, her cheeks flush. "Such an ordeal!"

"I've explained to my wife the incident would never have happened had Samuel been doing his job," Robert interjected, "but she insists on painting him the hero."

"Well, *you* didn't save me, Robert!"

"As I have said, on numerous occasions, I was in Pennsylvania on business when it happened, Anna. And as I've seen no evidence of the incident, I'm not entirely sure it happened at all! A good slave may have been murdered for nothing for all I know!"

"There are no good slaves, Robert," Anna said with a sigh. "There are useful ones and the rest. And quite honestly, what's the point of them living if they cannot be useful to their masters and mistresses? Especially if they have ill intent?"

Irene fought to keep herself from shaking. She was screaming inside. *And we is the savages?!* She caught Clarence chiding her with his eyes, behind his frozen smile, as if he knew what she was thinking. He turned away from her, and Irene noticed Charity staring intently at him as she crossed her legs. Irene watched him avoid the woman's gaze and present a plate of food to Penelope while Big Jim leaned back in his seat, enjoying the chaos he'd incited.

"The point is," Anna continued, "they are nothing but savage animals prone to forgetting their place, as Mister Barrow said."

"Only if they're not taken in hand," Big Jim offered. "I had two who got it in their heads to run away. I had my overseer open up the back of one after my hounds ate the life out of the other one. After a little extra incentive, the one still drawing breath is much better behaved." Irene caught the subtle wink he gave to Gertie, who looked as if she might burst into tears.

"But it's not the field slaves you have to worry about," Anna commented. "It's the house niggers."

Clarence's fake smile began to crack.

"My mother is right," Penelope chimed in, and Robert flushed red.

"That is quite enough, Penelope."

"Nonsense. I believe I would enjoy hearing from young Penelope. Out of the mouths of babes, as the Good Book says. Wouldn't you agree, Governor?" asked Big Jim.

"I should like to hear what she will say next on the matter," Abraham said, siding with Big Jim. "Speak, child."

Penelope sat up straighter as Anna looked at her daughter with pride, and Robert visibly braced himself. Irene braced herself as well. She noticed Clarence was having an increasingly harder time holding on to his artificial smile.

"The house niggers are worse," Penelope began, nodding toward Gertie. "At least the field slaves, like this one here, are usually separate from the house, where they belong. But the house slaves, especially the light ones, like her"—Penelope pointed at Irene directly, who had no idea what to do with all the eyes on her—"they get to thinking they've got privilege. They get to work and live in the house; even overseers aren't allowed in the house. Sometimes, they even travel with the family. My mama says some of them are even the folly of a weak white man and a filthy Negress. Those ones especially, they get to thinking maybe they're as good as white and should be treated as if they *were* white."

Penelope looked Irene directly in the eye as she continued pointedly. "But you are not white. One drop of nigger blood in you makes you a nigger. Any white blood you have is forever tainted. So, you should never forget to be grateful for the work your master gives you to do, every lick of it. You have no other value than doing the work you're assigned to do. If you can't do it, you should be fed to the hounds."

Blood rushed to Irene's face. This young girl could not have been born spouting such hatred. She had to have learned it as sure as she learned to speak, and still the words spewed forth with such assuredness as if they were her own.

The anger racing through Irene now was palpable, but she could not pinpoint its exact source. Perhaps it spawned from the girl's words; maybe it was the freedom with which she was allowed to speak them. Or perhaps it was the white woman bragging about a Negro man being murdered on her behalf because she had accused him of attempting to grab her, when she, Irene, was assaulted nightly by a white man who faced no consequence for his actions at all. Even the white woman's husband questioned the validity of her story, but still, a man, a Negro at that, a human being, was executed, and no white person involved suffered any repercussions.

Irene was under no delusions. Despite the white blood of the overseer who had defiled her mother coursing through her veins, she was nothing but a Negro and a slave. It was all she would ever be.

"Well, well. What say you, Governor?" Big Jim asked.

"I dare say she may well be wise beyond her years," came the answer.

"Tell me, young Penelope, how did you come to acquire such wisdom?" Big Jim asked her. The young girl turned a cautious eye toward her father, but Anna intercepted the look.

"Go ahead, child," she told Penelope. "Speak freely and true."

"Yes, Mother. Well, Mister Barrow, I do know the Christian thing to do is to respect your elders, but I cannot lie in the presence of the Lord."

"Well, we aren't in church now," Robert said sternly, but Penelope glared back at him without ever batting an eye.

"Those who walk in the Light are always in the presence of the Lord, Daddy," she said as Anna sneered at her husband. Irene could feel her hands begin to tremble. Big Jim's own children had been sitting and eating quietly, as they often did at the many engagements like this she had served. Yet the more venom this Penelope child spewed, the more opportunity she was given to do so. Irene was beginning to think it was further punishment she was made to endure for displeasing Big Jim, and it was as vicious as any strike she'd ever been dealt.

"You see, Mister Barrow," Penelope continued, "my father is not present to raise me in the ways of the Lord like a father should, so I often rely on my mother for guidance to teach me what a good Christian girl should be."

"But surely you must long for a father's leadership."

"Yes, sir. Mister Knudsen is kind enough to offer his insight to me on occasion."

"Mister Knudsen," Robert scoffed. "The man is my overseer, yet she reveres him more than her own father!"

"Samuel may be of low station, but he comes from loyal stock," Anna said. "His father served Robert's father, and he too was a righteous man and the best nigger-breaker the province has ever seen!" The pride in Anna's voice made Irene shudder. "Truth be told, and you will forgive me, Robert, but taking into account what constitutes a man, Samuel has the advantage over my husband, I am sad to say."

"Why? Because he is of larger stock than me?"

"Considerably." Anna's eyes fluttered at the utterance. "He is strong, yes, but also courageous. He protects me when you won't. He is knowledgeable in his tasks and in the Lord."

"And it is my work which feeds his belly! Mine! He does not deserve the respect of my daughter over me. Is there not a passage in the Bible saying to honor thy father?"

"I do not aim to disrespect you, Father," Penelope said calmly, "but the Good Book is clear, and while you sometimes question it, Mister Knudsen is staunch in his faith, as is Mother. Forgive me, Daddy, but truth be told, thanks to my studies with Mother, I have come to regard Mister Knudsen in the way a daughter regards a father."

"But *I* am your father. You take another man's words to heart over mine?"

"'If any man come to me, and hate not his father, and mother, and wife, and children, and brethren, and sisters, yea, and his own life also, he cannot be my disciple.' Mister Knudsen says the Lord means we must always choose Him, even over our family. We must love what he loves and hate what he hates, and God hates niggers, Daddy. You don't, but God does. He cursed them with blackness because they are born of sin. One need only read of the Curse of Ham in Genesis. They are but beasts of the fields, dirt walking upright, and should surely be put to death if they refuse to be obedient to their masters. It is the law of God. Mother and Mister Knudsen taught me right from the Bible, and I am sorry, but I cannot take your word, or anyone else's, over the Lord's."

Robert was left speechless, his mouth agape in shock, and for the first time in her life, Irene felt as if she had some semblance of what the white man was going through. He looked crestfallen, mortified by the words of his own daughter. There was a despondency in him she recognized because it was something she had come to live with. Taking in the talk around her, she felt gutted, nauseous, and, given the look on Big Jim's face as he turned to her, in danger.

"Quite right, Penelope," her master said, never taking his eyes off her. "A useless nigger might as well be a dead nigger."

Eleven

BETWEEN DEATH AND VENGEANCE

Irene ran past the fields of the Barrow Plantation toward the lake at the far eastern edge of the property, sobbing heavily. She did not believe she could run and not be caught, and though light-skinned, she wasn't light enough to be mistaken for white. She'd always heard men refer to her as pretty, but it served her no real purpose that she saw, except for the one she served under Big Jim.

After his comment at lunch, she worried he might be planning to kill her. So, Irene stood at the edge of the water and thought of her mother, Cecilia. Her rage had run out, and she fell to her knees, surrendering to her despair. She looked up to the stars and wailed out in sheer agony before collapsing.

"Forgive me, Mama," she whispered. And then she allowed herself to tumble forward into the lake.

She closed her eyes as the water engulfed her. The peace she had sought reached out to her—then it was abruptly disturbed by vigorous splashing. Had one of the overseers seen her? If she was caught, she would be beaten, which she found absurd. Hands lodged under her armpits and dragged her to the surface. She struggled against them, but the hands were stronger. Air entered her lungs, and Irene coughed. As she caught her breath and her vision cleared, she saw an equally drenched Willie and a bone-dry Shit Boy standing above her in the moonlit darkness.

"Willie . . . ?"

"What you's thinkin', Irene?" Willie asked. She sat up, and Shit Boy moved to her, supporting her. She eyed him with familiarity.

"Shit Boy?"

"Or Rafazi," he said matter-of-factly.

"Your name Rafazi?" she asked. He nodded, and Irene shook her head. Of course he had a name. Shit Boy was no proper name for a man. She cursed herself for ever having used it. Still, his appearance was puzzling. She'd never seen him look so . . . alive. "What happen to you? You looks different, and you don't smell of shit. Where you been?"

"Is you all right, Irene?" Willie interjected. "What happen? Rafazi heard splashin' and carryin' on . . ."

Irene didn't want to tell them the truth. "I's fine. But what y'all doin' way out here at this hour?"

"What was you doin'?" Willie got quiet. "Was you tryin' to . . . ?"

Irene dropped her head as her tears returned. "Massa only brought me here to have his way with me. Now he tired of me. He don't like any real work I do, so he brought Gertie to the manor to help serve his guests."

"So that's why Clarence come snatch her up . . ."

"Massa say a useless nigger a dead nigger," Irene sobbed, "and he tell me I's useless. He aims to kill me, and I don't wanna end up like Charlie. I ain't got control of much, but I can control how I die. And if'n I gotta die, I reckon I'ma be the one doing the killin'."

Rafazi's eyes danced as he smiled at Willie.

"What you smilin' 'bout?" Irene asked him, wiping her eyes.

"I think you should do some killing, too. Just not of yourself."

"Rafazi . . ." Willie shook his head.

"What?" Irene inquired.

"Isn't it funny how these whip-crackers came to this land in search of freedom for themselves, only to take it away from us?" Rafazi asked sardonically.

Irene took note of how clear Rafazi's speech was. She had never noticed it before. Everything about him now was puzzling to her.

"Well, maybe not exactly funny," he amended.

"It's powerful dangerous for you to be out here, Irene," Willie warned, drawing her focus back to him. "Massa find you out your place, he'll have your hide."

"He drunk from ale," she said, "out cold by now, I's sure. This my only chance to be free."

"What if it wasn't?" Rafazi asked.

"Rafazi!"

"We're going to need others, Willie! She could help us!"

"Help you what?" Irene asked, looking between them. "What y'all up to?"

"I'm special," Rafazi said, "and I can make us all special. Special enough to take revenge against the overseers and the master and claim our freedom."

"Special how?" Irene asked. Rafazi looked at Willie, who threw his hands in the air. "What is goin' on?" she insisted.

"Remember now, you asked me, all right? Don't get scared."

And then Rafazi . . . changed. She could not believe her eyes as his turned a glowing red. She watched his brow engorge and the veins in his face fill and pulse with blood. Irene felt a tremble rumble through her body, and instinctively, she moved closer to Willie for safety. Some part of her noticed he seemed unaffected by Rafazi's transformation.

"Don't you worry, none," she heard Willie say. "He ain't gonna hurt you." When Rafazi bared his wet and dripping fangs, Irene screamed until Willie quickly covered her mouth. "Shh! It's all right, it's all right," Willie whispered to her before hissing at Rafazi. "That's enough, now! She done seen what she need to!"

Rafazi reverted to normal, and Irene felt Willie rubbing her back reassuringly as she shook in fright. "Hush now," Willie soothed her. "He ain't gonna do you no harm. He the last of the Ramanga Tribe."

Having been born in the New World, Irene had no idea what the Ramanga Tribe was, where the tribe came from, nor which country her own mother hailed from. Willie smiled, and she figured he must have read the confusion in her expression.

"Hundreds of years ago, back on the Gold Coast and across the west, the Ramanga Tribe was feared. They was powerful, immortal, and they fed off . . ." Willie stopped short of saying the words outright, searching for a softer approach.

"Blood," Rafazi filled in. "We . . . I feed on human blood." Irene blinked in horror. "Not yours!" Rafazi quickly told her. "But you could help us."

Gathering her breath back, she spoke slowly. "Help you how?"

"I can make you, Willie, and every slave here who wants to be powerful, like me, but I need to feed on someone, drain them, so I can reach my full strength."

"So, what you wants me to do?"

"Wait. You understand what he askin'?" Willie asked her. "He want you to help find somebody so's he can kill 'em."

"Someone white and oppressive. I don't want to drain any of our people. I don't even want to feed on our people," he said. Willie glared at him. "Not anymore," he amended.

"Anymore?" Irene asked.

"The point is, I want to turn our people and take revenge against these whip-crackers for all the harm they've done to us."

Revenge. The word rang in Irene's ears like the chime of Barrow's grandfather clock. She felt her despair dissolve, and she began to feel powerful. Hearing the word filled her with something she felt deeply, though she didn't have a name for it.

She would later learn it was purpose.

"When?"

"What?" Willie asked, his voice full of surprise.

"You wants me to find somebody by tomorrow mornin'?"

"Tomorrow night," Rafazi told Irene. "I'll need to steer clear of the overseers until then."

"Okay," Irene said plainly.

"Okay? Irene, is you sure? You understand what he askin'?"

"Yes, Willie. Rafazi want revenge. That's what I want, too."

All her life she had been bottling her rage, stuffing it down to survive, when what she wanted to do was exact justice by her own hand. Now, she was being given the chance to do so. Her eyes were not deceiving her. The path itself wasn't precisely clear, but Rafazi had been.

"I was sunk so far down I was gonna kill myself," Irene told them, her back straightening. "Now, Rafazi, he a monster, but so is *every* white man and woman I done ever met. My father, my first massa, this here massa, them overseers, that evil little girl come here for lunch today, all of them. But Rafazi a monster on our side. If'n it's 'tween death by my own hand or death fightin' with a monster on my side, I choose fightin'."

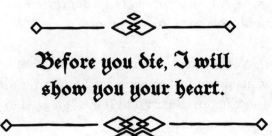

Before you die, I will
show you your heart.

Twelve

AN UNBELIEVABLE TRUTH

"ow's that eye feel, Willie boy? Makin' you feel like tellin' me what happened to that cage? Where that lil' nigger done run to?"

Willie was sweating profusely. His back wounds burned in the sweltering heat, the water in the marsh sloshing around his feet felt as if it had been brought to a slow boil, and now, there was an intense sting in his left eye from the blow Monroe had just delivered with the butt of his pistol. Willie had fallen to his hands and knees on the paddy, heavy huffs of angry air pushing through his nostrils. He had to take Monroe's abuse in stride. A plan was beginning to take shape. He had to strengthen his resolve. It was a matter of time now.

"Now, I know you know what happened, and I know you had a hand in it! How the hell you do it, huh?" Monroe hissed. "Tell me!"

"I ain't done nothin', sir," Willie said slowly, swallowing back his temper. It was only a matter of time, he reminded himself.

As long as he could keep his wits about him and his temper in check, it was all just a matter of time.

GERTIE COULD FEEL WILLIE'S eyes on her as they worked, but she couldn't bring herself to return his look. She had purposefully positioned herself on the paddy so her back would be to him. She did not want to blame him for what had happened, but she kept playing it over in her mind: Big Jim hovering over her in the breeding room, and her catching Willie's eye and shaking her head no, no. In the only way available to her at the time, she had told him *not* to attack Monroe.

He saw her, blinked in recognition, and still, he had charged for Monroe.

She didn't remember what had happened next, though she'd had the sensation of being suspended in midair and moving at an incredible speed for a brief second while being engulfed in the smell of excrement before a blow to the head had sent her to the ground.

She'd been groggy from the blow, but she was sure she'd never before seen the short, rebellious slave who had been pinned to the wall by an overseer's gun. And he'd seemed too small and frail to have had the strength to pick her up.

What bothered her most about the ordeal was Willie. She had been victimized because of Monroe's wrath toward Willie. And even though he couldn't have stopped what had happened, his actions had made it worse. At least she was back on the paddy. Being in Barrow Manor felt wrong—the soft clothes, the food she could not touch, the wicked words spoken, Big Jim's lingering gaze. Working the field again felt like a twisted type of freedom, but she still wasn't free from hostility.

"You think you protectin' him, don't you?" Gertie heard Monroe growl behind her.

She remembered Big Jim ordering the small slave to be locked in a cage on the fields, but when she was summoned off the paddy by Clarence yesterday morning, she'd only seen a broken cage. It had been dismantled somehow; its pieces scattered in the field. She'd assumed the small slave had been locked up somewhere else.

"You think I'm stupid, boy?" Monroe snarled.

"If'n you think I done broke that cage apart way it was, I don't rightly know what to think." A few slaves working near her turned to look back at Willie, his comment of subtle defiance having visibly stunned them, but Gertie did not. She hung her head. His promise to her seemed to be moving further and further from his mind. The next thing she heard was the disgusting sound of Monroe spitting, a thump, then Willie's groan, and the shuffling and sloshing of feet in the marsh.

"You sassin' me, boy?"

"I ain't done it! I cain't!"

"Well, the lil' piece of shit locked up in it sure couldn't have done it! Now, I don't know how you done it, but I know you had somethin' to do with it! Now, where is he?"

The clanking of metal made Gertie's hands shake.

"Don't you dare."

Derby was next to her, working diligently. He wasn't even looking at her, but Gertie could feel the intense rumble he directed at her. "Don't you dare turn 'round," he said in a low growl. "I know you's feelin' some kinda way for Willie, but he done dug his own grave back talkin' at Monroe. Don't you join him."

His concern was so genuine it made it hard for her to keep focusing on her work as tears welled in her eyes.

"There ain't no way he could've done it, boss," she heard Butch say to Monroe. "Me and Amos had us a helluva time draggin' it out here to lock that stank nigger up. I don't know what could've broken the cage, but ain't no nigger alive strong enough to tear apart iron."

Behind her back, Gertie could tell Monroe wasn't even acknowledging Butch. "I went out with the slave patrol myself last night," Monroe said, his voice menacing, "and we ain't seen hide nor hair of that shit nigger. Now we gonna have to go out again with the hounds. You sayin' *nothin'* ain't gonna *save* him. We will find him, and them hounds are gonna chew him up just like they done Charlie. All you doin' now is rackin' up the amount of time I'm gonna put the whip to you when I get back. I know you know what happened, Willie, and I know you know where that lil' nigger done went to, and you will tell me true even if I have to beat it out of you bit by filthy bit!"

Gertie shut her eyes and once again fought the urge to look back at Willie. Derby was right. She couldn't risk it. She could only hope he would think of her and the baby with his response.

"If'n you truly think I can break iron," she heard Willie say with labored breath, "what make you think I cain't break you?"

Her eyes darted open at his words.

They were the clearest expression of defiance she had ever heard him speak. A full day out of sight, and he had forsaken his promise to her. She turned in time to see a furious Monroe slam the butt of his pistol into Willie's swelling left eye as hard as he could.

GERTIE STOOD MIXING WINE and honey in the sick house, while Tussy gingerly tended to Willie's wounded eye. Swollen red and purple, with pus and blood oozing from it after Monroe's vicious attack, Willie could not keep himself from grunting in pain when it was touched. Try as she might, Gertie couldn't help but stare at Willie in sympathy. Still, the tension between them was palpable.

"I don't rightly know how y'all gonna do anythin' for that baby comin' if'n y'all cain't even talk to one 'nother." At Gertie's look of stunned surprise, Tussy huffed. "Child, please. We's sleep in the same cabin. You think I ain't known you ain't had your blood? Ain't heard you retchin' in the grass? The way you keep givin' po' Willie the evil eye ev'ry time you do choose to look at him, anybody got sense enough to look can tell he the one done put you in the family way."

"Tussy . . ."

"Oh, hush up, girl. I ain't got nothin' to tell nobody. Ev'rybody gonna know soon enough any ol' way. But I'll say this here. What Massa done to you was awful, Gertie, but Willie ain't done it. Now, I were powerful afraid of what happen for my own reasons, but they done passed now 'cause I knows Willie good. Anythin' he do, right or wrong, he do for you.

"I don't rightly know what happen with the lil' slave Monroe yellin' 'bout, but he run, and Willie coulda run with him, but he here. So, whatever y'all got 'tween you, rid yourself from it. Po' child gonna need ev'rythin' he can get from both y'all 'til Massa decide his fate. Y'all gonna need one 'nother. Y'all better get y'all's minds straight."

"Thank you, Tussy," Gertie whispered. There was nothing else to say. She knew Tussy was right, but it would not be so easy to follow her suggestion.

Tussy sighed wearily and shook her head. "Mmm hmm," was all she muttered when she left the cabin. Once she was gone, so was the buffer, and the tension between Gertie and Willie escalated. Despite her burning emotions, Gertie decided to look up at him. Gently, she raised her fingertips to Willie's damaged eye as he closed them both.

"Look powerful painful," she said softly.

"Feel like my eye 'bout to fall clean outta my head. Gots me a headache somethin' awful."

Wordlessly, Gertie began tending to Willie's eye, using a cloth to lightly dampen the wound with the wine and honey mixture.

"Ain't seen you all day yesterday," Willie said. Her jaw tightened. She did not want to discuss anything having to do with Big Jim or the incident. Not now. Not yet. Maybe never. "Gertie . . ."

"You ain't gots to say nothin'." Gertie was quick to stop him.

"I's sorry."

"Sayin' sorry mean you coulda done somethin' to stop it and didn't. But you couldn't." She searched his face, waiting for him to acknowledge his fault. When he didn't, she threw the cloth at him. "Why you try to stop it, Willie?" she yelled at him. "You promise me!" She placed a hand on her belly. "You promise us!"

"I ain't break no promise, Gertie."

"I hear you do it, clear as day!"

"Do what?"

"You taunt Monroe 'bout his wife. I heard you! I look you dead in the eye and shake my head no!" Gertie pushed through the sobs coming from deep inside her now. "I shook my head, 'cause I seen your eyes, Willie. I seen in your eyes you wanna put a hurtin' on Monroe, put him down. And I knows you was angry enough to forget your promise to me and our child, so I look you clean in the eye and shake my head, and you up and attack him anyway! You steady thinkin' 'bout how angry you is, but they done me way they done 'cause Monroe hate *you*! You ain't think of me or the baby!"

"*All* I's thinkin' 'bout was you and the baby!" Willie raised his voice as Gertie stepped away from him. "I gots to stand there and watch that ol' whip-cracker put hands on you . . . !"

"You cain't win, Willie! We's ain't gonna win that a'way!"

"I had to *try*! Had to do *somethin'*! What kind of man, what kind of father I be if'n I ain't raise a finger to protect my kin?"

"A live one!" Gertie's knees buckled as she bent over and allowed herself to cry hard, barely able to catch her breath. "If'n it weren't for that strange slave come runnin', Monroe woulda killed you. *Killed* you, Willie. And my baby's daddy would be dead! Dead! I cain't . . ." Gertie broke down again, and Willie moved to her, reaching his arms out to embrace her, but she slapped them away. "No! If'n you cain't hold your anger and keep your promise, then I . . . Ooh, I's so mad, Willie! I's so mad 'bout ev'rythin', and I cain't be mad with this here child in me. Ain't no good for either one of us . . ."

"Gertie, I's sorry, but put a gun to a man's head, and there be damage before you even pull the trigger. I will keeps my promise."

"No, you won't, Willie. You mouth off at him on the field today, that's why you's eye all swole up now!"

"Gertie, he tell me I broke up a iron cage with my bare hands!"

"Was he right?"

"What? Gertie, ain't no way no man can break out a iron cage with they bare hands, now!"

"That slave come runnin' in . . . Ain't no way a man as slight as him coulda done it."

"Ain't no way a man could move as fast as he done, but he done it!"

"What is you sayin', Willie?"

Willie's mouth opened and closed without him saying a word. He looked away from her, but the guilt in his eyes did not escape her notice.

"What you ain't tellin' me?" Gertie asked him.

"You ain't gonna believe a word I say."

"You ain't say nothin' yet!" Gertie could feel her nostrils flaring, her heart racing. She could barely breathe. She was as angry as she was sad and confused.

"Rafazi," Willie sighed wearily.

"Who Rafazi?"

"The slave who come runnin' and tried to save you."

"So, you knows him?"

"When Monroe put me on shit duty after me and Charlie run, Rafazi the one I was helpin'."

"So, how he know to come? Did you know . . . ?"

"No! I reckon he come lookin' for me and seen what happen, and seen I ain't have no chance to do nothin', but he could, on account of . . ."

"On account of what, Willie?"

His deep breath terrified her. She didn't want to know what he was going to say if it caused him this much anxiety. And yet, she *needed* to know.

"On account him bein' Ramangan. He the last one left."

Gertie's furious tears returned. "Now you gonna outright *lie* to me?"

"Ain't no lie! Ramanga is true, Gertie, I swear. I seen it with my own eyes. Rafazi, he change, Gertie. His eyes go red, he get fast and strong, faster and stronger than anythin' you ever seen. Strong enough to break apart iron."

Gertie shook her head. She could no longer look him in the eye. "So, what you's reckon he come lookin' for you for?"

"Blood. I gives him some of mine the first night, and I reckon he want more."

Angry sobs exploded from Gertie. Everyone in every country on the Gold Coast knew the legend of Ramanga was nothin' more than a myth. Instead of telling her the truth, like a man should, he was feeding her lies.

"I tell you true, Gertie! He broke out the cage hisself! I seen him do it. He called me, tooks blood from my arm, and soon as he turn, he rip that cage apart. I swear!"

"Then where he go after?" Gertie humored him through her tears.

"I don't rightly know. But he bury hisself underground the

night Massa defiled you. He told me the last night he talk at me."

If Willie could go on in this fashion to her, Gertie wondered if she could continue to feel for him the way she did. She wondered if what she felt for him had already changed. "Uh-huh. Then tell me this here: If'n he so all-powerful, why he ain't leave, run 'way fast like you say he can and never come back?"

"'Cause he got a plan."

"A plan for what?"

"For us. All of us. He gonna make us like he is, and we gonna use his power to gets free."

It was enough. Gertie held up a hand, stopping Willie from speaking. Her tears never stopped coming as she shut her eyes. Everything she thought she knew about him, none of it was true.

"Look at me, Gertie," she heard him plead. "Look at me, now. I's tellin' you true! You know I is. Y'done say it yourself. You say ain't no way a man as slight as him coulda done what he done. If'n I's lyin', how he pick you up and try to save you? How he move so fast? How you think Fanna got free?"

Gertie's heart sank. He was no longer the Willie she knew. Not after this. She backed away from him. "If'n you cain't talk at me true, don't you talk at me at all."

"I s'posin' you's the only one can talk true."

"What?" She felt herself glaring at him now.

"You heard me. You always think you's right all the time, 'bout ev'rythin'."

"I's right 'bout this here!"

"No, Gertie. You ain't. You wrong as wrong can be."

There was no point in saying anything more. Wiping away her tears angrily, she stormed out of the sick house. She could still hear him calling out to her, but she could no longer stomach the sight of him.

"You gonna walk on? Just 'cause you's wrong?"

"I ain't wrong!" she yelled back without ever stopping her stride.

"What if'n you is? What if'n I's the one right this time? What if'n I's the one speakin' true? Huh? What then? What if'n the legend true? I say I's gonna find a way for us, and I done found it, Gertie! Why I say something so powerful crazy if'n it weren't true?"

She covered her ears and pushed her legs faster. She wanted to be as far away from him as she could get.

Thirteen

RAFAZI'S TASK

Thomas Barrow was following Irene around the second story of the manor. She was busy changing bedsheets when she became aware of heavy breathing behind her every time she bent forward across a bed. Upon turning, she would catch the youngest Barrow rushing out of the doorway with his hand firmly planted in his trousers.

Rafazi's task of finding someone to kill had never left her mind. At long last, a plan to end the villainy she lived under was being put in place, and she was going to be a part of it! The waiting was the hardest part. Though she didn't fully understand what Rafazi was, she knew he fed on human blood, which meant two things: He was powerful and could instill fear. She could already picture her abusers trembling in fear at her feet.

Especially the Barrows.

The thought of consuming blood was particularly appealing to her. She reasoned it was worth being able to tear Big Jim limb from limb. It was possible she could become powerful enough to rescue her mother—or avenge her. Suffice it to say, despair had not reared its ugly self in Irene's head since she'd seen the creature inside Rafazi. However, she remained filled with rage, and, knowing what she knew, grew more eager to act on it. But first, Rafazi's demand had to be met.

As far as Irene was concerned, someone offered up for death should be someone unfit to live, a criteria Thomas fit well. He wasn't much of anything as a boy, and Irene figured he would grow up to be a perverted menace—or even worse. It would be cutting a despicable life short before it could inflict the same amount of damage his father had.

It didn't take her long to figure out Thomas's pattern of stalking her. She made quick work of changing the linens in the master bedchamber then hurriedly rolled under the bed. From this vantage point, she watched Thomas's shoes appear in the doorway and pause. They shuffled from side to side before backing into the hallway and disappearing. As he snuck along the corridor, peeking into the rooms, searching for her, Irene crept up quietly behind him.

"Good mornin', Massa Thomas."

Thomas yelped as he spun to find Irene standing behind him. Smiling helped conceal the conspiratorial chuckle she had to swallow as the boy caught his breath.

"Why did you sneak up on me?"

"I 'pologize. I hear your Daddy say you's is thirteen years old now."

"I'm a man now."

"You sure is. I done seen it right away," Irene purred, looking at him coyly. She watched his eyes wander as she purposely shifted her hips.

"You did?"

"Sure, I did. 'Cause I been watchin' you watch me all mornin', Massa Thomas. You like lookin' at Irene?" She heard the syrup in her own voice and had to force herself not to roll her eyes as the boy nodded eagerly. "You wanna see *more* of Irene?" Thomas nodded again, and Irene's smile grew sweeter. "Then you come meets me in the kitchen yard behind the milk house after midnight tonight, and I show you more."

Thomas nodded.

This is gonna be too easy, Irene thought.

THE SUN HAD BEGUN its retreat from the sky as Irene hurried along the rice fields looking for Willie to let him know so he could alert Rafazi. She couldn't *wait* to rebel.

"You lost, girl?"

She was so focused on her search that Butch's horse blocking her path was a surprise. "What's a house nigger doin' out here in the fields? You thinkin' of changin' jobs?"

The proper response to him would have been to avert her eyes and politely apologize, but Irene didn't feel like it. Soon enough, the overseer would be among those weeping at the feet of Rafazi's power. Her power. What hold did he truly have on her? Even if he did decide to harm her, perhaps it would free her from Barrow's nighttime visits. For the time being, spotting Willie in the field, she made subtle motions with her head to him before looking up at Butch.

"Is you deaf, girl?"

"No," Irene said flatly, staring Butch in the eye. "I's just tellin' whoever need tellin' there gonna be fresh white milk behind the milk house at midnight." She raised her voice with each word she spoke and was weathering the odd looks she was getting, especially the one from Butch as his brow furrowed darkly.

"What kind of nonsense are you speakin', girl?" Butch demanded. "Ain't up to you if these here niggers get fresh milk or not. What the hell else milk gonna be but white? And where the hell else milk gonna be if it ain't in the milk house?"

"Like I said. I's tellin' whoever need tellin'." Irene was aware of her tone and the potential consequences of using it with someone like Butch, someone white, male, and in a position of power, but knowing she had arranged for a bloodthirsty monster bent on revenge to gain his maximum power took the threat out of the overseer's presence.

"Who do you think you talkin' to, huh? You address me as sir, and you mind your goddamn manners when you do it."

"Like you done said, *sir*, I's a house nigger. You out here in the field. You reckon you can do somethin' to me without your massa's blessin'?" She registered the wide stares and shaking heads of the field workers, including Willie's, but she didn't care. Part of her wanted the overseer to retaliate; it would make killing him later all the more enjoyable.

Butch snatched the whip from his belt holster and swung it hard, slashing her cheek with such force it sent her to the ground whimpering in pain. Her fingers drew back blood from the large gash on her cheek.

"What a clumsy lil' niglet you be!" Butch was laughing loudly at her as she stood up. The sting of his attack burned and made her eyes water. But inside she was livid. And glad. "I'ma have to tell your master to keep you inside to keep you from hurtin' yourself. If I was you, I'd mind my tongue. Be a shame if you was to fall again. Now get on outta here, now!" Irene scowled up at Butch. "And I'd put them eyes back in your head if I was you."

Her eyes found Willie's once again, and he gave her a single nod. The searing pain in her cheek caused her lips to tighten, but she was pleased. A gash across the cheek was a small price to pay; it could be tended to with cotton cloth, honey, ointment. What was important was the plan, and she had set it in motion.

The pain was worth it.

WILLIE SCURRIED ACROSS THE rice paddy as near to midnight as he could tell, crouching as he went. Approaching the northern edge of the field, he could see the two overseer houses. They stood side by side, single story miniature versions of the main manor, with similar white columns and rocking chairs on both porches looming over the only path out of slave village heading toward the main house. He needed to make it past them unscathed so he could meet up with Rafazi and Irene behind the milk house.

Both houses were dark, but Amos walked out onto one of the porches and into the night air, lighting a short roll of twisted tobacco leaves wrapped in paper with a small piece of tinder wood. Willie dropped to his belly as Amos inhaled and blew a stream of smoke in his general direction. With his left eye swollen shut, Willie watched with his right eye the orange glow of the tobacco stick turn away from him, but he wasn't sure he could trust his right eye alone. Still, he had to make his move.

Willie pushed himself across the wet field as quietly as possible on his toes and elbows when something suddenly grabbed his wrist and pulled—fast. He slid across the paddy, water whipping around him with incredible force. A gush of wind passed over him as he closed his good eye. Seconds passed before he was abruptly stopped.

When he opened his right eye, he was in the kitchen yard a few feet away from the milk house. Rafazi stood before him, his flax fiber cloak slung over his shoulder.

"So, your eye paid the price for my escape," Rafazi said in a hushed tone. "Thank you, Willie. I will make it right."

Willie's fight with Gertie echoed in his mind. Rafazi's plan had to work.

"You okay, Willie?" Rafazi asked.

"I don't rightly know. I don't know nothin' 'cept I's ready to be free." Willie took a step toward the milk house, but Rafazi stopped him.

"Hey. You seem troubled."

"This here life ain't nothin' *but* trouble. Gertie finally talk at me. What they done to her . . ."

"I know."

"I try tellin' her 'bout you, 'bout what you is. You's right. She ain't believe a word."

"You can't blame her, Willie. After the plague wiped us out, we became a myth to many."

"What plague?"

"Hundreds of years ago, an awful sick ripped through the west of Africa and beyond. It was unlike any other plague known to man, and none of us knew its origin. Some believed it came from the gods themselves. It killed humans slowly, but those of us who fed on the afflicted fell into a terrible slumber immediately. Our senses deadened; our bodies went stiff. Those who hunted us would chop off our heads to end us. The one who made me believed it was punishment for all we had done. *Things of death stealing life*, She called us. She asked me to warn the others of what was coming, but I went into hiding instead and swore off human blood for centuries, desperate to cling to my existence. I didn't know the plague had truly passed until I tasted your blood. I had been weak and alone for so long, I was resigned to leave this world by way of your blood. Imagine my surprise when it restored me."

"So, with this here plague gone, cain't nothin' else hurt you but the sun?" Willie asked.

"Like I told you before, immortality doesn't mean invincibility. I won't age my way to death like a human, but there are things I must be careful to avoid, and the sun is one of them."

Willie's fervor decreased. He'd had visions of becoming an all-powerful creature capable of anything, but now the finality of death was still, apparently, possible. "That cloak shield you from the sun?"

Rafazi nodded. "There are other ways I could perish. Like from a stake made from the wood of a willow tree driven through the heart, being beheaded, or being embedded with silver. A cut by silver is poison to my kind; it slows us down and impedes the wounds from healing rapidly. Silver makes us vulnerable. Too much of it will mark a torturous end. If the white folks here discover this weakness, our battle will be far greater."

Willie clocked Rafazi's eyes as he spoke of the metal and silently began weighing the alternatives he was faced with, wondering if joining Rafazi would be enough to gain freedom.

It dawned on him that if they were to be victorious, many more would need to be convinced to become like Rafazi— Ramangan. "You's more human than I thought."

"In a manner of speaking. But Willie, there's one other thing . . ."

Whatever Rafazi was about to say could be said later, as Willie waved him silent when he spotted Irene walking toward the milk house with a short white man whose features Willie couldn't make out in the dark. He and Rafazi moved to the back of the milk house slowly, coming up behind Irene and the target.

"He look small. He gonna be enough to fill you up?" Willie asked Rafazi in a whisper.

"We'll find out."

As they got closer, they could hear Irene's conversation. The short man seemed hesitant to follow her. "What happened to your face?" they heard him ask her.

"Had me a lil' accident, is all. C'mon," Irene replied.

"What kind of accident? Your cheek is bloody."

"I reckon it ain't Irene's face you plannin' to get your hands on." The short man's head scanned the length of her body, ogling her in the darkness. He rubbed his hands together and followed behind Irene. "C'mon. I done picked you special."

"Yeah? For what?"

"For dyin'." Irene quickly grabbed the short white man and spun him around to face Willie and Rafazi.

"Field niggers!" the short white man hollered before Irene covered his mouth with a dirty rag and wrapped her other arm around his neck as he struggled against her. Up close, it was clear to Willie the short white man wasn't a man at all. Willie's brow crinkled with confusion.

"Ain't that Massa's boy?"

"Sure is," Irene smiled. "I know Rafazi say he need a white man to drain to get to full power, and this here ain't exactly a man, but he white and full of blood, and he a nasty lil' thing. Don't deserve to grow up, him bein' the way he is."

"It would definitely send a message," Rafazi agreed as Thomas's eyes darted back and forth between Willie and Rafazi while he fought to break free from Irene's grasp. "What happened to your face?" Rafazi asked Irene.

"One of them ol' overseers slashed me across the face with his whip."

"'Cause you talk outta turn," Willie hissed at Irene.

"So what?" she snapped back. "He gonna be dead anyway!"

"Will you hush up?" Willie ran a hand across his brow in frustration. There was entirely too much talk in the presence of Barrow's boy, who, with one word to his father, could bring their scheme to a grinding halt.

"He'll have to do," Rafazi said with a shrug, but Willie blocked his path.

"You cain't drain Massa's boy!"

"Why not?"

Irene yelped in pain as Thomas pinched her arm and freed his mouth from the rag long enough to shout, "You niggers are dead! When my Daddy finds out . . . !" Irene got the rag around Thomas's mouth again and tightened her grip around his neck while Willie turned to Rafazi.

"That's why!" Willie spat lowly. "Biggest thing we got goin' for us is them not knowin' we's comin', and we done already lost it!"

"Oh. Good point," Rafazi conceded.

Willie kicked the dirt at his feet. He couldn't believe they were sunk before they even got started. "You chokin' the life outta him ain't no better!" he snapped at Irene.

"Well, what we do with him now?" Irene asked.

Rafazi quickly transformed, and Thomas screamed into Irene's rag at the sight.

"You cain't drain him, Rafazi!" Willie warned.

"I won't drain him, but he's already here, and I've only got a day before I start getting weak again." With glowing red pupils, Rafazi leaned down until he was at Thomas's eye level. His eyes began to pulse, and the boy's muffled screams immediately trailed off. "You are in no danger," Rafazi said in a slow and concise tone. "You will stay quiet, lean your head to the side, and let me drink some of your blood." Thomas wordlessly followed Rafazi's instructions.

"So, you *can* bend minds," Willie whispered.

"I'll take a bit of blood and make him forget he was ever even out here." Rafazi bared his jagged teeth and fangs, and Willie saw they were as wet as when he showed them to Irene for the first time. Rafazi bit into Thomas's neck, and the young boy's eyes rolled to the back of his head as his blood raced through the veins visible in Rafazi's face. Willie looked around, making sure they were still alone. If they got caught, they would be done for.

"Okay, Rafazi," Willie said. "You done took more than a bit now. We's cain't get caught out here with Massa's child."

Despite Willie's words, Rafazi fed a bit longer before releasing Thomas, who then lightheadedly stumbled away from them. The Ramangan grabbed the boy by the arms and once again trained his red, pulsing eyes on Thomas's. "You will go back to the manor and sleep. You will remember nothing of this night." Thomas nodded and began to calmly walk back toward the manor. Rafazi's face returned to its human form, and he wiped the excess blood from his lips.

"Amazin'!" Irene exclaimed.

"Hush now!" Willie cautioned her before turning to Rafazi. "You good now?"

"For the moment. It's still not enough for full strength. But you thinking of the element of surprise, definitely the kind of thing a leader thinks of."

"Is the boy gonna forget what he seen? What he gonna make of them marks on his neck when he wake?" Willie asked, shrugging off Rafazi's comment about him being a leader.

"I didn't go deep, just to the fangs. And with the extra dose of venom, there was hardly any pain. There will be a little redness; he'll probably think he got bit by a bug. He'll forget. But bending his mind weakened me. I need more blood."

"Well, how much more blood you need?" Irene asked, thrusting her arm forward. "You can have some of mine!"

"No, Irene. I'm not feeding on any of our people."

"But you feed on Willie, ain't you?"

"His blood is different. Like I've never tasted. It's special."

"Well, then takes more of his now," Irene insisted. "I wants to be what you is!"

"I won't be the one to turn you. Willie will."

"What you mean?" Willie asked, surprised.

"I'm no leader, Willie. When the Ramanga Tribe was strong, I only satisfied whatever selfish whim consumed me at the time.

When our numbers dwindled, I became a deserter. I cared only about my own survival. The last time I saw my Maker, She thought there might be a way our power could serve the people of this earth if we could survive the plague, and I believe this is it. It may be why I survived. The Blood was thrust upon me, but you, you are choosing the Blood to be liberated, a notion I would never have had the courage to entertain. Between your gumption and the incredible power in your human blood, you are the one meant to lead this revolution."

"What is y'all doin' out here this time of night?"

The new voice prevented Willie from even contemplating Rafazi's words. All it did was heighten his anxiety, which intensified immediately at the sight of Gertie running up to them. "Gertie . . ."

But she walked right past Willie, her eyes on Rafazi. She stared at him in silence, studying him. "You's him. You was there when they . . . You's small. How you picks me up so fast like y'done?"

Rafazi looked to Willie, who moved in front of Gertie. And once again, she ignored him, stepping around him and closer to Rafazi.

"Why you gots blood on your chin?" Rafazi gave his chin a quick wipe and licked the surplus blood from his fingers. Gertie sucked her teeth and moved to Irene, grabbing her face. "And who done dress this wound?" Irene winced as Gertie twisted her face back and forth, inspecting the cloth dressing. "You 'bout to bleed through this here cloth. You get what you ask for talkin' at the overseer like y'done. What you doin' out here, Irene? What is all y'all doin' out here?"

"Gertie," Willie said, "you don't wants no part of this here."

"Why not?"

Willie was slow to answer. He had already told her the truth, and she had already decided he was a liar.

"Mmm hmm. Ain't got nothin' to say?" Gertie scowled at him.

"Now, wait," Willie said as calmly as he could. "I need to say this here to you, Gertie. I knows you don't approve, but this here is the right way. It be the *only* way—"

"Well, whatever goin' on 'bout to get found out," Gertie said, cutting him off, "'cause Butch is comin' this a'way!"

Willie burned. He stared at Gertie with hard eyes, and she stared right back in a battle of wills.

"Why would he be coming out here?" Rafazi asked.

"'Cause of Irene talkin' milk house midnight nonsense in the field today! Got me 'spicious, too," Gertie told him.

"Enough, now!" Willie said. "We ain't got time for this! Gertie, you needs to . . ."

"She needs to what?"

Willie shut his eyes and sighed in defeat at the sound of a fifth voice.

Butch was approaching with a snarl, his rifle at the ready. "You niggers been actin' fishy all day. And when I seen Ol' Gertie runnin' her fat ass 'cross the field, I knew somethin' was amiss. I see Irene here is lookin' to fall down again." Butch then zeroed in on Rafazi. "And *you*! You know how much trouble you in, boy? Monroe been out with the hounds and slave catchers lookin' for you. Wait 'til I tell him you been here all along, wastin' his time!"

"Well, here I am," Rafazi said with a calm smile.

"How 'bout you tell me who got you out of that cage, for starters?"

"Instead of telling you, why don't I show you?" Rafazi moved forward.

Butch pointed his rifle at Rafazi. "You come any closer, and I will kill you where you stand, boy!"

Willie raised his hands and stepped forward. He had no idea if Rafazi's fractured immortality could withstand a direct gunshot. His power was real enough to create the freedom Willie desperately wanted, but only if Rafazi remained upright.

"Please, boss," he said to Butch. "Ain't no needin' for this here . . ."

As it turned out, it was all the distraction Rafazi needed.

When Butch turned his rifle on Willie, Rafazi transformed once again and lunged for the overseer. Gertie squealed in terror, and Willie grabbed her, burying her face in his chest.

"Don't look," he whispered to her. "It gonna be over soon."

Rafazi yanked the rifle out of Butch's grip, throwing it to the ground so hard the weapon broke apart. He became a blur, spinning around the overseer before kicking him hard behind both knees and knocking him to the ground. With Butch's knees in the dirt, Rafazi stopped behind Butch, clenching his hands on either side of the man's head in a vise-like grip. Slowly, the Ramangan tilted the overseer's head back so they could look into each other's eyes.

"I want the *slave* who took your life to be the last thing you see," Rafazi hissed before pushing Butch's head to the side and drinking deeply from his neck. While Rafazi's feedings thus far had been oddly gentle, this attack was savage, torturous by design. Willie did not see the same euphoria in Butch's eyes he remembered feeling. There was no wetness on Rafazi's teeth.

Rafazi meant for this feeding to hurt.

To kill.

The Ramangan was tearing into this man's skin with all his jagged teeth, and the response was a scream of agony Rafazi silenced by clamping down on Butch's neck as he fed, tearing his vocal cords, his mouth coated in the overseer's blood. Whatever Rafazi didn't drink cascaded from Butch's body in a crimson waterfall.

And for the first time, Willie saw the actual cost freedom would demand if he stood with Rafazi.

Gertie pushed against his chest, and he loosened his hold on her. Her mouth agape, Gertie's eyes filled with tears as she watched Rafazi dig his thick, sharp talons into Butch's chest, causing more blood to spurt forth. Willie did nothing to prevent her from viewing the carnage. After this night, Willie would no longer try to shield her from it, nor would he be able to stop it.

This was the start of a bloody revolution.

Willie could hear Rafazi gulping. After what seemed like an eternity, Rafazi pulled away from the overseer's neck, his face and hands wet and red. "Before you die, I will show you your heart."

Butch opened his mouth, but there was nothing but silence. Rafazi thrust his fist deep into the overseer's back from behind, punching through the bones of his ribcage. The crack rang in the other slaves' ears like a death knell, and when Rafazi's fist exited Butch's chest, it held a still-beating heart.

Dying embers flashed in the overseer's eyes as he looked down at his own organ. Rafazi pulled his arm back through the hole he'd created in Butch and examined the heart with not so much as a shrug while Butch's body fell forward, lifeless.

"Not as black as I thought it would've been." Rafazi raised the heart high over his open mouth. He squeezed and drank down its remaining blood before crushing it in his fist. He dropped the squashed heart onto Butch's dead body and stretched with renewed vigor as he returned to his human form. Willie took him in, confident and virile, smiling in contentment—and lurid with blood.

He wondered how long it would be before he himself wore a similar look.

"Well," the Ramangan said, "I say we get started."

Fourteen

A First Taste

The sight of Butch in a grotesque, lifeless heap on the ground brought on a churning Gertie could feel rising in her stomach after having witnessed the absolute horror of his death.

His *murder*.

She held onto Willie as she released the bile. As unfathomable as it was, Willie had told her the truth in the sick house. When she could stand on her own power, she stepped away from him. Despite his honesty, it was still something he had kept from her.

She glared at Rafazi now, still lapping away at his fingers as if they were covered in honey. He was a murderous, evil monster—just as in the tales of the Ramanga. How he had convinced Willie he was anything more than a monster was beyond her. In her mind, she cursed them both before chastising herself for not having guided Willie better. Her heart still beat for him, but she feared she had lost him to Rafazi's villainy.

"How long you been known this here?" Gertie asked Willie when she could control her own breathing again.

"I done told you," Willie said. "When Monroe make me help Rafazi with shit duty, he show his true self to me in the barn."

"Why you ain't tell nobody when it happen? Why you ain't tell *me*?"

"I ain't hardly believe it myself, let alone tell and make myself the fool. And you ain't believes me when I *did* tell you."

She realized it was pointless to quibble over the issue now. She stepped toward Rafazi; the strong smell of the blood covering him caused the gurgle in her stomach to return.

"You come, try to save me from Massa's clutches," she said, "and now, y'done killed us all." Her eyes glazed over with contempt. If her child lost his father, it would be *his* fault.

Not *hers*.

It never occurred to her to be afraid of Rafazi.

"No," Irene said with glee in her voice. "Rafazi gonna make the white folk pay! *All* of them!"

"Once the sun come up and cain't nobody account for Butch, they gonna come for all of *us*!"

"No, Gertie. Ain't you seen what Rafazi done? Butch weren't no match for him!"

Gertie stared at the girl in disbelief. The dire implications of a dead white overseer in the kitchen yard of a plantation in the middle of the night seemed endless to her, but she decided to address Irene's direct argument. "There ain't but one of him, stupid girl! What he gonna do 'gainst an army of white folk wantin' revenge for one of they own?"

"Face them with an army of our own," Willie spoke up.

The words made her heart sink. *Our*. He was going to become like Rafazi. As if his mind was made up, his decision made without regard for her or their child. Rafazi was what he was, but she refused to entertain the idea of Willie, or anyone else, becoming like him. She wouldn't even dare give voice to it.

"What army? What we's gonna do 'gainst whips and guns? What we's got to fight with?"

"Me," Rafazi said plainly. "With Willie and Irene's help, I can make us all like me."

"You wants to make us bloodthirsty demons like you? 'Cause that's all you is! The livin' dead!" Gertie exclaimed.

Rafazi had no response, which confirmed the stories she had heard as a child. The Ramanga Tribe had been merely chilling folklore to Gertie, but Rafazi's existence meant the folklore was true, every bit of it.

"What you mean?"

Willie's question clouded her eyes with tears. Did he not know the sacrifice he would be asked to make? Or did he not care? She didn't know which one was worse.

"I remember the tales of Ramanga. I remember they's chose to make some of they's prey they own." Gertie returned her gaze to Rafazi. "How y'all do it, Rafazi?" she asked defiantly. "Tell them. They wants to be like you so bad, tell them how you got to be like you is. Tell them what they's gonna have to do." Rafazi's continued hesitation to speak angered her. "Tell them!"

"I was fed Ramangan Blood," he began, "then killed. I awoke immortal."

Gertie spun in anger to Willie, her eyes pleading, begging for his reason to take hold. "You forget the legend?" Gertie began softly. "Or ain't you know it? You say you ain't gonna do nothin' to take yourself 'way from me, and here you go do this here." With tears streaming down her face, she took a breath of courage. "If'n you do this here," she said, "I cain't follow you to it. I cain't bring our child into this darkness, Willie. I won't."

She hadn't realized he was holding her belly until she looked down and then took his hand in her own. She could see his anguish as he fought to return her gaze. Her wet eyes softened, and she gently cupped his cheeks with her hands, making him face her. She had to get through to him.

"You and this here child is all I got in this world, Willie. Now, I cain't 'bide you dyin', not now, not in no kinda way. You promise me we's gonna be a family. White man stole our families 'way from us. We ain't s'posed to do the same to one 'nother."

"He want to make us immortal, Gertie."

"Immortal slaves to blood mean you still a slave! He wanna snatch 'way your life and make you a murderous monster. That what you want? You seen what Rafazi done to Butch. That what you wants us all to be?" A tear fell from Willie's swollen left eye, and she smiled at him through her glassy vision, willing him to come back to her. Back to her good guidance.

"I wants freedom," Willie choked, "and I's don't know how else to gets it."

"But Willie, this here ain't freedom. You be tradin' iron for blood. You gonna go 'round killin', stealin' life for death? Ain't a lick of good can come from it. You cain't do evil and not become evil. And killin' 'bout the worst evil you can do."

"And what about all the evil they've done to us?" Rafazi asked.

"You cain't answer evil with evil!" Gertie scowled back.

"This here ain't 'bout being evil, Gertie," Willie said. "It 'bout being rid of the evil they's done put us through."

"And what if'n you cain't be rid of it? Or what if'n you all powerful determined, and it turn out to be a lie? What if'n the legend wrong? What if'n Rafazi just claimin' Ramanga, and you drink his blood and he kill you, and you just die? What become of me and our baby then?"

Willie's healthy eye grew soft, and tears now flowed from both his eyes. Gertie wiped a tear from his swollen left eye gingerly, bringing a sob from his throat. This was the Willie she knew, one of compassion and feeling. The man she had welcomed into her own body, the one who had fathered the child growing inside her now.

"Our baby," Willie murmured through his tears, "is why I gots to do this."

The crack of her hand against his cheek reverberated in the air and shocked all four slaves, including Gertie. She gritted her teeth and glared at Willie. "What you gots to do is wake up!"

"Exactly what them Barrows is gonna do if'n you keep yellin' at me!" Willie hissed.

"How I s'posed to love you if'n you gonna act like you hate me?" Gertie sobbed.

"How is I hatin' you?"

"'Cause you good and ready to believe this here nonsense and kill yourself! I cain't think of nothin' more hateful."

"You done seen what Rafazi is with your own eyes! I's ready to pay this price for freedom!"

The impassioned quiver in Willie's voice made Gertie sob again. How could such righteous devotion be so misdirected? How could he have become so enticed by this evil? How had she failed him?

No.

This was Rafazi's fault.

"I ain't blind to what this is, Gertie," Willie allowed. "I's terrified of what this here will make me, but I ain't gots no time to worry. Our child get bigger in your belly ev'ry day, and make one less day you's can run. And I done racked my mind for a place to run, a way to run to it, and I ain't found nary an answer. And, like you say, Massa gonna demand retribution for Butch, and you knows he gonna look my way for it. But now Rafazi got the strength he need to give me strength, too. Strength and speed to take us far from this here place. Take things we gonna need fast, build us a home fast, like we's always talked 'bout. With this here, it ain't just our freedom, it's our baby's, too. Strike down anyone fool enough to dare take him 'way from us. Ain't enough to gets free, we gots to stay free for our lil' one."

"So, the price for freedom," Gertie wept, "is killin'? How long you plan on payin', Willie? 'Cause if'n you do this here and rise from the dead, dead is all you gonna know. How long before you turn on your family when your belly say it's time to pay the price again?"

"I ain't never."

"How you know, Willie? You seen Rafazi lickin' Butch's blood off his fingers. Now, I done seen terrible things done by white folks, but I ain't never seen nothin' like the downright evil I seen this night. And you cain't pay for good with evil, Willie. You just cain't."

Gertie turned to Rafazi with a scowl of contempt, tears still burning in her eyes. "I don't rightly know how you done blinded these two. Maybe you bendin' they minds like the legend say, but my mind is clear. I seen you for what you is, and I blame *you* for twistin' Willie's head all 'round. Every wicked thing we's 'bout to endure is from you killin' this here white man. And look at you. All this power, you still ain't nothin' but a slave like the rest of us."

"'Cause he alone, Gertie," Irene said.

"This don't concern you, child," Gertie snarled.

"*Child*? I ain't so much younger than you."

"Now, you listen here. I's tryin' to talk some sense back into my Willie for the sake of our child! I don't need you buttin' in on why he gots to die!"

"We already dead," Irene said, her voice even. "They done already stole life from us. I threw myself in the lake to drown 'cause weren't nothin' left for me to live for. But Rafazi and Willie pull me from the water. Rafazi ain't offerin' no lone journey. He promise a new tribe where we rise up together. What we got otherwise?"

Gertie took Willie's hands and placed them against her belly again. "You promise me," she said to him, her eyes locking with his. "You promise *us*. Rafazi full of strength and speed now, he can save hisself. We's gonna find us another way."

"What other way there be, Gertie?"

"I don't rightly know, but there ain't gonna be no way if'n you die."

Willie groaned before his shoulders shook with sobs. He dropped his head, but Gertie, with a sad smile, took his face in her hands, grateful for his tears; they meant his mind had finally returned to her.

"We gots to lean on one 'nother," Gertie continued. "We's gonna find a way for us and our baby together. Long as you don't take yourself 'way from us." Gertie's breath caught with elation and relief as Willie took her in his arms and kissed her. They lingered, their lips touching, sobs of joy heaving from hers.

"Forgives me," Willie whispered into Gertie's parted lips.

A chill covered her as his arms released her. Frozen in shock, she watched him nod to Rafazi, who transformed again. With the tip of a sharp talon, the Ramangan cut a small slit across his wrist and raised it to Willie's lips.

Gertie reached for the two men. "NO!"

Suddenly, Irene's arms wrapped around her waist from behind. She beat against Irene with her fists.

"Let me go!" Gertie yelled, fighting against her in a fury, but Irene kept her at bay.

"You'll see, Gertie," Irene said softly. "This just the beginnin'."

"Get 'way!" Gertie yelled at Rafazi. "You get 'way from my Willie, you demon!"

Gertie watched Willie's right eye blink before he put his lips over Rafazi's wrist. She saw the movement in his throat as he sucked the blood and swallowed. Gertie knew she was screaming, and she knew she might be heard. Maybe she wanted to be heard. Maybe others would stop this from happening, but Irene's quick hand over her mouth took away her hope.

Hot tears ran down Gertie's face as the house slave's grip proved to be stronger than she expected, and she wailed into the dirty rag Irene held over her mouth. Time slowed for Gertie as Willie stepped back from Rafazi, a pained look on his face as he wiped excess blood from his lips.

"I know you hate me," she heard Rafazi tell her as he took hold of Willie's head, "but I promise you, he will never feel more alive."

With both hands, she yanked Irene's arm away, freeing her mouth. "Please don't kills him! Willie, you ain't gots to do this! *Please!*"

Willie's good eye met Gertie's a final time before Rafazi broke Willie's neck with a quick but mighty twist. Gertie's knees buckled, and she collapsed as the horrific crack of Willie's neck rang in her ears.

"WILLIE!"

Fifteen

TWO GIRLS AND A BOY

There was nothing but blackness. No sound, no air, no feeling. Only black stillness.

Until a rich and brilliant red swam before his eyes.

It was all Willie could see; he was fully engulfed in the red, and it was beyond beautiful. He had no idea if his eyes had been closed before or how long he had been floating in this red, but it felt like forever, as if it were all he had ever known.

He could still taste the bitter metallic flavor of blood in his mouth, but it had changed. Slowly, steadily, it had become sweeter, then smoother. The flavor became indescribable. Nothing he had ever eaten or drunk came close, and somehow, knowing it was blood made it more enticing. He could feel it expanding and multiplying in his body, nourishing him. Fortifying him.

He could no longer feel the familiar beating of his heart, but instead felt a pulsing radiating strength and vitality. It started where he knew his heart to be and surged throughout his entire being. There was more power and energy with each pulsing surge coursing through him, and yet, it was so blissful he felt he could remain in this state forever.

Soon, sounds began to seep into his idyllic consciousness. Familiar sounds. The faraway whinny of a horse, voices. Sobbing. The sobbing grew closer, and he felt a rounded weight thumping against his chest, soft but insistent. A faint impulse from deep within him seemed to urge him to reach for this weight, but he was in such a place of deep relaxation, he couldn't bring himself to move at all.

Then the weight was gone, and he could hear distant yelling. He could not make out the words, but they were filled with passion and fire. He thought the voice shouting them sounded like Gertie.

Gertie.

Every memory he had of her came rushing into his mind, including of the child growing inside her. Their child. Then more memories came crashing into his consciousness: his enslavement, his fellow slaves, the plantation . . .

Rafazi. Rafazi's plan.

His own death.

The pain in his neck, his eye, his back . . . It had all slipped away. And he was beginning to move. Willie realized his eyes had been closed all along because they now had begun to flutter, creating creaks and breaks from the beautiful, all-encompassing red of his vision. *Something* was animating him, and he felt a sensation akin to standing up, but this was much smoother, effortless. His legs did not bend; he was simply being lifted until he felt himself upright with a solidness under his feet.

He opened his eyes. Only a tint of the red he'd experienced before remained, coating his vision; despite it, he saw more clearly than he ever had before. He raised a hand to his left eye and found the swelling was gone. He took in his surroundings, reacquainting himself with them—the milk house, the kitchen yard.

The faces of Rafazi, Irene, and Gertie staring at him.

Butch's dead, mangled body.

"Your eyes . . ."

He turned toward the voice and blinked. The red tint over his vision lifted once he blinked, and his sight became even sharper. He recognized Gertie as she moved to him, and he watched her hands move about his face. The tips of her fingers tripped lightly along his healed eye. She moved behind him, and he felt her lift his shirt. The flat of her palms ran along the length and width of his once-again smooth back muscles before she turned him to face her. Her eyes fluttered with uncertainty, and he noticed her hands shake as she removed them from him.

"Y'done healed," she said, her voice thick with wonder as she backed away from him. He took a step toward her, but she yelped with fright. So, he stopped where he stood.

"It be me, Gertie," he said. She stared back at him as if his voice was foreign to her. "I's still me. Look at me."

"This ain't natural," she whispered, her sobs returning. "You ain't natural."

"Maybe I ain't, but Gertie, I ain't never felt this good!" He could feel his face beaming with a smile, but Gertie's tears remained.

"Ain't no human can survive what Rafazi done to you, but you let him do it. You chose this here over us . . ."

"Not over you, Gertie. *For* you. For our baby." He could feel the love within him radiating from where he knew his heart to be. He could feel its pulsing. Every emotion he had died with still remained.

"Stop!" Gertie cried, turning to Rafazi. "How you's doin' this? Make it stop! It ain't natural!"

"He's still Willie," Rafazi told her. "His mind, his words, his actions, they're all his own. I'm not doing anything."

"Make it stop!" Gertie fell to her knees in a heap of sobs, burying her face in her hands.

Slowly, Willie lowered himself onto his knees, still keeping a safe distance from Gertie. "Two girls and a boy," he said softly. She looked up at him, her sobs hitching. "You say, in the tall grass, after we . . . The stars was shinin' so bright, you'da thought the sun were still in the sky."

An involuntary chuckle trickled from her through a sob, and Willie allowed himself a small smile. "We's lay there, quiet, and I stroke your hair. Stayed so long we was powerful tired on the paddy in the mornin'. We ain't sleep. You look me in the eye, say, 'Two girls and a boy.' And I say, 'What you's talkin' 'bout?' And you say, 'Two girls and a boy. That's what I wants our family to be.' And I ask you why, and you say 'It's 'cause a boy could never stop lovin' his mama with two girls messin' with him all the live long day.'"

Gertie's sobs quieted, and her eyes shimmered as she took Willie in with an intensity he had never seen in her before. "Now, if'n you ask me," he continued, "that's the night the child in your belly come to be. Weren't no plantation, no work, no worry. Just Gertie and Willie, layin' in the tall grass. And right then I ask you . . ."

"'You reckon this what freedom feel like?'" Gertie whispered back.

"And you say, 'No. Freedom woulda let us sleep.'"

Gertie's body heaved with new tears, and Willie inched closer to her. "Willie . . . ?"

He nodded, and she broke down, wrapping her arms around him. She had never felt better in his arms. Her touch was so intense, it was electric to him. But her arms were slipping from his back until she was holding on to his arms with her hands, her head against his chest.

"I's tired," she sobbed. "I's so tired . . ." She had transformed their embrace into a simple bracing of her body against his, an act of function rather than emotion.

"I's sorry, Gertie." He would keep her like this for as long as she allowed it, though he was now uncertain of what she would allow anymore.

"We need to get rid of this overseer's body," he heard Rafazi interrupt. "And Willie needs to start learning how to manage his new existence."

"Let's dump him in the lake," Irene suggested.

"Wait," Gertie said as she released Willie and got to her feet. Dejected, Willie stayed on his knees. He didn't want to do anything to disturb Gertie further. His decision had cemented the wedge between them, but he remained steadfast. He loved her. He had made this decision *because* of his love for her. If anything, his transformation had deepened his love, made it more concentrated, but he did not feel the same intensity coming from her.

Not anymore.

"What you mean by what you say 'bout Willie?" she asked Rafazi.

"He needs to learn how to survive in this form, and he'll need to avoid the coming sunrise. It will end him."

"Sunrise . . ." Gertie's breath grew heavier as her eyes narrowed at Willie with resentment. "Y'done this thing, and death can *still* come for you?" She nearly growled at him before she focused her rage back on Rafazi. "When he ain't on the paddy, what I's s'posed to say to Monroe? What I's s'posed to say when he get to askin' 'bout Butch?"

"Hush now, Gertie." Willie stood but retained his safe distance. "Ain't nobody gonna 'spect you, and they already think Rafazi done run. They's gonna be lookin' for me now, but they ain't gonna find me. Not 'til I's ready."

Willie recognized Gertie's look: a bristling he had seen far too often recently, but he chose not to respond to it. What was done was done. There was nothing more important now than getting on with the business of why he'd done it. "We needs to get you back to your cabin before anybody know you's gone," he continued. "Me and Rafazi'll do the rest."

Rafazi threw Butch's huge frame over his shoulder as if it were no heavier than a bedsheet. "I'll take care of him," he told Willie. "Why don't you take Gertie back? Stretch those new legs of yours."

But Gertie took a significant step away from Willie. "I can walk on my own power."

Willie shook his head. He found it ironic that in the moment where he was feeling the best he ever had physically, he was adrift emotionally. The action he'd taken to create a new life for his family may have broken it apart.

"Wait," Irene said, her brow crinkled in concern. "What 'bout me?"

Panic coursed through Willie. The last thing he wanted Gertie to hear or deal with was Rafazi's intent for him to rebuild the Ramanga Tribe.

"After all this here y'done seen," Gertie hissed at Irene, "you still wanna *die?*"

"Maybe we all doomed no matter what we do," Irene chuckled, "but I'd rather *try*. Even if I don't got what you got."

Gertie huffed. "What I gots?"

"Willie. Now, I don't covet the man, and I know you don't abide what he done, but he come back from the dead still in love with you. He loved you 'til the moment he died and still do. I reckon I could live 'til the end of time and never find me a love anything close."

"All right, now," Willie said as moisture returned to Gertie's downcast eyes. "Gertie got her own mind, and ain't nobody gonna be bendin' it one way or 'nother. I don't even knows how to do it no how. But we needs to do what need doin'. Rafazi, you get rid of Butch, then come meet me on the other side of slave village. Irene, throw them gun pieces in the lake, and go on back to the manor, now. We gonna tell you when it's time for what come next." Irene sullenly moved to pick up the gun fragments. "And Irene? Mind yourself. I know you's powerful angry, but we gots more work to do before we's can go exactin' revenge, y'hear?"

Irene gave Willie a reluctant nod before heading toward the lake, while Rafazi scooped up Butch's squashed heart and disappeared with the dead overseer in a blur. Willie and Gertie were left to stand in silence for what seemed to him like an eternity.

"You ain't gots to wait on me," Gertie said. "I knows my way back. You and Rafazi gots plottin' to do, so y'all best get to it."

"You right." There would be no convincing her this night. So, Willie felt adrenaline fill his veins, ready to propel him forward, but her words kept him from rocketing away.

"I hate this. I hate what y'done."

"I know. But it's done. And . . ." He felt a phantom sensation of his breath catching, but there was no air within him. Sadness washed over him, and a tremble found its way into his voice. "You's gonna believe what you's gonna believe 'bout me from here on, but my promise to you be true. You and our . . . the baby gonna be free. I's gonna make it so."

"It's still our baby, Willie."

They stared at each other, and Gertie's shoulders slumped. She ran her hands over her belly with a weary sigh. "You think it's a boy or girl?"

"Don't rightly know, 'cept I's gonna love it true like I do the mama."

"Damn you, Willie . . ." Gertie wiped away her tears before holding out her hand to him. "Show me what it's like . . ." He found his smile before sweeping her up in his arms so fast it made her gasp audibly. "Don't you drop me, now."

"Never."

Without another word, he dashed off with her in a Ramangan blur of his own.

Guilt is the link to
your humanity.

Sixteen

MONSTER

Gertie squinted against the wind whipping across her face, the same wind rolling tears along her temples with its speed. Willie's speed. She felt weightless in Willie's arms as the fields went by in a flash. He had always been strong, and she had always felt safe in the embrace of his arms, but this was a new sensation altogether. She cursed the thrill it stirred within her.

Gertie was momentarily disoriented by their abrupt stop as he set her down in the grass behind slave village. The smile on his face made her turn away. It pained her to see him delight in something so sinister.

"You happy now?" she snapped.

"Ain't nothin' I say gonna make this right to you," he said, his smile gone.

"Then why y'done it? Ev'ry time I tries to steer you right, you go wrong. I say, don't run, cain't no good come from it, you run. I say, don't takes Ramangan blood and die, you takes it and die."

"You say, 'Don't do nothin' to take me 'way from you.' I's here."

Gertie gritted her teeth. "But you ain't know you's gonna be, Willie!"

"Yes, I did, Gertie. *You* ain't know. You don't know *ev'rythin'*." The forcefulness in his voice stunned her silent. "Who right and who wrong don't matter," he said, calming his tone. "In this here life, all we's know is what we ain't got. Ain't gots freedom, ain't gots family, ain't gots claim to our own lives. White folks say we ain't gots no purpose but to work they's fields. Monroe say he hate me, say he hate we's breathe the same air, like we ain't s'posed to breathe, like we ain't human."

Gertie studied him closely as he spoke. She wasn't sure why, but she was enthralled by him; and she wondered if it had anything to do with his transformation.

"Now, you take Monroe and me. He hate I's here, but why is I here? Ain't ask to be. I's happy right where they's found me before they's kill my kin and snatch me up. He want me to work. I gots to live to work, and I gots to breathe to live. Well, I did, just like he do. I gots me two eyes like he do, two hands, two arms, two legs, two feet. Just like he do. And I reckon if'n he get cut, his blood be red as mine. He eat better food, but I gots to eat to live, too. I reckon when I was 'live, we wasn't much different, him and me. More same than different. So why he hate me?" Holding up his arm, Willie pointed at it.

"This here. This here skin. I come into this here world, same as him, but his skin light, and mine dark. Our crime is bein' born with the wrong skin. You ask me, ain't no sense in somethin' so foolhardy as sayin' one skin is good and one is bad when ev'rythin' else the same."

"Willie, I's tired," Gertie sighed. None of his yammering changed the fact that he had gone against her wishes. "You been a-jibber jawin' somethin' awful. What is you tryin' to say?" The darkness in the sky was beginning to lighten, and Gertie grew concerned for her own rest as well as Rafazi's warning about Willie needing to survive the sunrise.

"Whatever or whoever done seen fit to put them in this here world done seen fit to put us in it, too. And if'n it was to works for the white folks, none of us would ever dreams of freedom. There somethin' more for us, Gertie. Rafazi show me we's can be special, too. More special. Skin ain't gots no power. Cain't make you no stronger or faster. But Ramangan blood do. Now, I knows it scare you, but Gertie, I's love you more now than I ever did and will for all time now. And I gots the power to keep any promise you ever ask of me."

"'Cept the one I ask of you to not take that demon blood." She took no pleasure in watching him defeated from her words. But she spoke the truth. No matter how flowery the words, what he'd become now was still evil. "I gots joy in my heart you rose from the dirt like y'done," she said, "but I seen you *die*. I wants to be wrong, but I's powerful afraid of what this evilness I begged you to stay clear from gonna do to you."

"It ain't evilness, Gertie."

"If'n it make you do what Rafazi done to Butch, it is."

"And Butch ain't done evil things?" She had thought Willie would raise his voice to her again, but instead, he winced, doubling over and growling in pain before he fell forward.

"Willie? Willie, what wrong?"

Propping himself on his hands and knees, he raised his head to speak, but instead of words, another growl came, and he fell over on his side. Gertie gasped helplessly as he shut his eyes tightly, covered his ears, and unleashed a frightful roar of pain. It was a sound Gertie had never heard him make before. This was it, her fear realized: Willie wasn't right, he never would be again, and there was nothing she could do to help him. Still, her heart ached for him. She got to her knees and put her hands over his.

"Willie, please," she cried. "You scarin' me somethin' awful!"

Willie's eyes opened wide, and Gertie fell back and away from him. They were red again, and his face was contorting itself into the same features as Rafazi's when he took Butch's life.

Ramangan features.

Willie opened his mouth, and his sharp teeth and fangs were wet, so wet they were dripping with fluid of some kind. A short squeal of terror escaped Gertie's throat as she instinctively placed a hand on her stomach. For the first time, she was afraid of Willie.

"Get 'way from me, Gertie." It was a low but ominous groan, like he was fighting to contain himself. Willie had disappeared, and a monster had taken his place.

"I's 'fraid this would happen!"

"I say, get 'way!" Willie roared, licking his wet fangs. Leaping backward from his position, he soared through the air until he landed several feet away, putting considerable distance between them. "I's sorry!" he whined like a wounded animal. "It's too much!"

"Too much what?"

"Blood! Too much blood!"

"He can't be here right now."

Gertie yelped in shock and found a drenched Rafazi hovering over her.

"His desire to feed is too strong," Rafazi explained. "He'll learn to control it. He's still your Willie. You'll see. Soon. I promise. But don't tell anyone anything yet."

As fast as he had appeared, Rafazi's blur disappeared in the night, taking Willie with it.

Trembling with fear, Gertie watched them disappear into the wilderness, her heart so heavy she unleashed powerful sobs she could not control. She had lost. She was alone in this world again, carrying the child of a man who no longer existed—a love snuffed out by pure evil.

"Gertie!"

She never turned at the sound of the voice, nor did she make any attempt to quell her cries. Within seconds, Derby was knelling in front of her, his hands rubbing up and down her arms. It was the second time she'd seen a look of genuine concern for her across his features. Yes, he would cast an eye in her direction; she was a woman—it seemed just about every slave woman caught the man's eye at some point.

But this was different. This, and the time on the paddy when Willie had chosen to defy Monroe. Derby's usual roguish smile was replaced with something else, something more.

Derby was known to be an arrogant sort, perhaps because of his size. He was broader than Willie. Taller, too, and he regarded himself the plantation stud, a claim supported by his considerable prowess among the slave women of the plantation. So, why was he here now?

"What you doin' out here cryin' at this hour?" His voice was warm. Comforting. But Gertie didn't answer. For as much wrong Rafazi possessed, he was right about keeping quiet. The knowledge that Ramanga did exist would tear the slaves apart. Besides, Willie had chosen an evil he could not come back from. There was nothing left but to mourn him.

So, she allowed Derby to pull her to her feet. Gertie had no feelings for the man, and she would not pretend she did, but she did need support and rest. Regardless of how she felt, she would be due on the paddy come sunrise.

Seventeen

A LESSON IN BLOOD

black bear moved across the grass in the wild, looking for a place to settle before sunrise. A nearby rustling in the trees caused the bear to look up. As the disturbance went quiet, the bear hunkered down on a large patch of grass with a lazy snort, its peace restored.

For only a moment.

A blur slammed into the bear, causing it to roll several feet before bear and blur crashed into the trunk of a huge tree several feet away from the peaceful patch of grass. The dazed bear roared at its attacker: a fully transformed Willie, who roared back at it, full of Ramangan adrenaline.

The bear swung a huge claw at Willie, knocking him down. Instantly, Willie was back on his feet, running at the now-charging bear. Baring his dripping wet teeth and fangs, Willie grabbed the animal by its front limbs, stopping it in its tracks before lunging forward and biting through the bear's fur. His teeth penetrated the animal's skin, and as he clamped down with his jaw, he heard a horrid crack before blood spurted forth. Drinking as much as he could, Willie allowed the blood to gush out over him before pushing the dead bear to the ground. Still not satiated, though, Willie hovered over the bear and continued drinking.

"Has anything ever been so delicious?"

Reluctantly, Willie looked up to find Rafazi smiling down at him. He knew he was covered in blood, his eyes glowing red. He felt his lips curl into a smile, the nectar of life still dripping from them. "Never!" he exclaimed. "I ain't never felt this way before, Rafazi! I loved killin' this here bear!"

"Sounds like you've also discovered your bite force," Rafazi observed.

"My what?"

"Your bite force. Not only are your teeth as sharp as blades, but your strength also extends to your jaw. Bite down hard enough, and you can bite through bone."

Willie's enthusiasm waned a bit as he looked himself over, replete from the blood. Even the scent gave him a sense of euphoria. The thought of drinking human blood entered his mind and sent a tingle of anticipation up his spine.

What was he becoming?

He was surprised to see Rafazi chuckling.

"Your mind is trying to understand why every other fiber of your being is craving human blood," Rafazi said.

Willie's mind was indeed spinning. The thought of killing a human being and feasting on the blood went against everything he thought he believed, and yet, though overwhelming, the thought ignited his senses. Even with the rush of the bear's blood still running through him. "I never knew there be joy in killin'."

"Try not to think too much about it. It's the hunger." Rafazi took a seat next to Willie on the massive dead bear. "It's a part of you now. When it's new, you want to kill everything in sight.

You hear the blood pumping in their veins, and you want it. You can hear blood now, can't you? You can smell it, too."

The constant thump of blood pumping through the veins of the animals in the woods echoed in Willie's ears like the blood of the slaves sleeping in their cabins had.

"I smelt Gertie's blood. Hers and the baby's," Willie whispered, his eyes welling with tears. "I ain't never want nothin' so powerful much. It smelt so powerful good . . . And I thought I's . . . I thought I's gonna . . ." Willie dropped his head and let his tears come.

"Blood is the source of everything," Rafazi explained softly, "but for us, it's more powerful and magical than any human could ever understand. It fuels our immortality and connects us to the humanity we spawned from. The blood of a human who carries deep love for you can heal and revitalize you greater than any other. It's why you desire Gertie's so. They say we can even smell it."

"Smell love?"

"Yes."

"What it smell like?"

"I wouldn't know."

"You ain't never known no love?"

Rafazi paused, and Willie searched his eyes. The elder Ramangan seemed to be deep in thought. "No," he finally said. It didn't seem plausible to Willie that someone could be in existence for seven centuries and never have known love of some form.

"My life," Rafazi sighed, "was no life. I was abandoned by my family, mistreated by the man who employed me. I had no one until . . ."

He stopped, tightening his lips as if he was keeping himself from weeping. Willie waited patiently, knowing Ramangans were capable of feeling as they did when they were humans. The raging ocean of emotion surging through him was proof enough.

"I do not know the scent," Rafazi said, clearing his throat. "But I do know Gertie's blood would be exquisite in smell and of delectable taste to you—the greatest blood you could ever experience because of her love for you. It might not seem like it now, but her love is pure and true, and for you alone, and it's in her blood. Love carried in the blood becomes tangible for a Ramangan."

"What tangible mean?"

"It means real. For a Ramangan, true love in human blood contains real power. The same is true for hate. It's carried in the blood, too. Like Monroe's."

"What 'bout Monroe?"

"Monroe hates you like Gertie loves you. These whip-crackers hate us as a whole, but they don't care about any one of us in particular. I could feed on Monroe and be fine. Might taste a bit bitter as hateful blood generally does, but Monroe's hate for you is true and pure for *you*, like Gertie's love is. It makes his blood poisonous to you."

"Well, I don't wants his blood no way! And I ain't never gonna taste Gertie's blood, no matter how good it smell."

"You never know, Willie. We're about to step into war. Anything can happen in battle, and if Monroe's blood can't be avoided, Gertie's could save you. This is why control is so important. It will help you feed without killing. We'll stay in these woods a time so I can teach you."

The thought of tasting Gertie's blood was far too unsavory a concept for Willie to dwell on, and he was thankful for the change of topic. "What all you gonna teach me?"

"How to control your strength, navigate your blur, burrow underground to escape sunlight, how to bend minds, like you saw me do with Barrow's boy, everything."

"All this here power," Willie said, "the speed, the mind bendin', and what all else more there be, how ain't none of it keep you off the plantation?"

"Regular feedings of blood are what sustain our power. Without them, we grow weak, frail. When they found me, after years of me eating nothing but vermin, I hadn't the strength to fight back or the speed to run away. All I had was the gift of their tongue. Besides that, I didn't have what you do."

"You's been 'live seven hundred years," Willie scoffed. "What I got you ain't?"

"Courage. I was turned against my will, but you *chose* the Blood, and your reason for doing so is a noble one. Choosing the Blood is a courageous act. It will make you stronger. On top of that, there was something very special about your human blood, and that's meaningful."

"Why?"

"Because sometimes, the mix of Ramangan Blood and human blood creates something extra, a power the rest of the tribe doesn't have. One woman in my old tribe could grow wings and fly like a bird; another could walk by day. They became our leaders."

"What you get special?"

"I didn't. I was among the weakest of the tribe. But your human blood, it was unlike any other I've ever come across. There's no doubt in my mind the mix of it and Ramangan Blood will create something incredibly special, powerful. And it will free us all."

Willie could feel the conviction in Rafazi's words so strongly it made him believe them. There would be no more hoping or wishing for freedom. With this new power, they would liberate all the slaves, and Rafazi was clear about it being Willie who would lead the charge—a heady thought the new Ramangan was not comfortable with.

"You ever feel guilt?" Willie asked. He realized he hadn't asked the question of Rafazi; it really was a question for his future self.

"Guilt is the link to your humanity," came Rafazi's answer.

"Don't dwell on it, but don't let go of it. It will guide you, show you the difference between the willing and the contemptible."

"The willin' and the who?"

"The contemptible are the ones we will rain down retribution upon. Slave drivers, those who stripped us from our land, chain and beat us, break apart our families, violate our women. They are pure evil, undeserving of human life. But the willing? Well, you'll come to find there are a lot of people who are drawn to our peculiarity and are more than willing to lend us a little blood when we need it. Like you did for me. Now then, you should feed again before sunlight. Animal blood only keeps you strong for two days—half the time of human blood—and only if it's a big animal like this one."

Despite the myriad questions racing through Willie's head, one answer was clear as he followed Rafazi away from the bear—there would be no turning back.

Eighteen

WHAT EVIL BREEDS

I thought Charlie would be example enough to keep you niggers in line, but apparently, he wasn't."

Sweating in the sun, Gertie stood with a small group of slaves—Tussy, Fanna, Fuddle, and Minor—in front of a ranting Monroe on the paddy. The five of them were on display for the other working slaves as the chief overseer paced in front of them, with Amos and a few other overseers lined up behind him.

"First, Ol' Shit Boy bust out of an iron cage somehow and run off," Monroe carried on, carelessly swinging his whip around. "And I thought I was bein' the best nigger-breaker I could be, tryin' to beat sense into Ol' Willie. But he done up and gone a second time, and not a single one of y'all will tell me where either one of them went to. And now, Butch done gone missin'."

Gertie bit her tongue to keep herself quiet. When Monroe pranced about like this, lecturing them, violence was sure to follow. But there had never been any cause for the brutality she and the rest of the slaves were made to endure.

Until now.

Whatever wickedness was about to befall them now was Rafazi's fault. His evil blood turned Willie away from her and their child in the night. Now, she was forced to suffer Monroe's rage for it.

"The cage gettin' broke, then Shit Boy, Willie, and Butch all disappearin'?" Monroe counted the events off with his fingers. "They all got somethin' to do with each other, and one of you Negroids know what it is, so I am *graciously* givin' y'all the chance to tell me all on your own."

Monroe got in Gertie's face first, so close his nose poked against her cheek. She held her breath so as not to smell his. "You gonna tell me where your beloved went, or do I get to beat it outta you?"

Gertie remained silent. With the mood Monroe was in, she was sure she'd be thrashed for even suggesting what Rafazi truly was, and she would be made to pay the price for explaining what had happened to Butch. Monroe would hear her account as either in protection of Willie or utter nonsense. Either way, she and her baby would be subjected to the same violence.

"Y'know, your master took away my chance the other night, but I think it's time Ol' Monroe got his cock wet." Monroe's foul breath was moist on Gertie's cheek, sickening her stomach. "I reckon I'd have a might better time fuckin' it outta you, 'less you wanna tell me what I wanna know."

"I don't rightly know where they's at," Gertie insisted. Since it wasn't a lie, she could live with saying what she did. She felt a tinge of relief as he backed away from her.

"Tussy!" Monroe's loud shout startled Gertie, and her stomach dropped as he inched closer to the older slave. "Tussy, you the nosiest Negress done ever lived. Where they go?"

"I ain't gots no clue, boss," Tussy answered plainly.

"You? *Not* know somethin'? I don't believe it." Monroe chuckled before stepping back and swinging his whip at Tussy, slashing it across her abdomen so hard blood seeped onto her work dress. Tussy fell to her knees onto the damp ground as she yelped and clutched her stomach. Instinctively, Gertie clutched hers and took a step toward Tussy.

"Don't you move a *goddamn* muscle!" Monroe barked at her, and she backed away as he hovered over the whimpering Tussy. "Try again, you black bitch!"

"I's swear, sir! I ain't gots no clue as to either one of them!"

Gertie gnashed her teeth in turmoil. She felt for Tussy, but what she knew couldn't help them. Scanning the paddy, she took in the other slaves gawking at them. She could also see that Derby never stopped working. His head down, he never needed to be reprimanded to continue working by the overseers like the others did; he didn't even take peeks at Monroe's tirade. In slave village, he may have strutted around with his bare chest, demanding the attention of all, but on the paddy, he was quiet, diligent. He wouldn't be questioned. If only Willie shared Derby's restraint!

Yes, he'd been seduced by evil, but seduction only works if one wishes it. She did not struggle to resist Derby's advances, but Willie *chose* the evil of Ramanga over her. And now, his act of evil was affecting others who had no idea of what he'd done.

"I suppose you two shitskins is as clueless as the women-folk?" Monroe turned his attention to Minor and Fuddle. With a huff, Monroe launched a wad of tobacco spittle at them and sucked on the ball in his cheek before making his way to Fanna.

"What about you, niglet? You don't know nothin' neither, do you? Hell, I ain't never even heard you talk. But we gonna find out today if you can talk." Monroe leaned in close to the young girl as she wiped the sweat from her brow. "You know my friend Amos over there? He just *dyin'* to get his hands all over you. And judgin' from the last time he touch you, you would hate every minute of it. Now, I don't know if you can talk or not, but you gonna learn. You tell me where them blackies done gone, and I'll do my level best to keep Ol' Amos away from you."

Amos was grabbing his crotch and flicking his tongue at Fanna. The whole scene brought hot tears to Gertie's eyes. Willie's choice had created this strife, and he wasn't even here to take the punishment.

"Okay. I tried." Monroe shrugged after several seconds of Fanna's silence. "Amos, take this here niglet with you and have you some fun." Monroe grabbed Fanna roughly and dragged her to Amos.

It was too much. Gertie heard the quiver in her voice as she called out for Fanna to be spared. Only a small bit of relief came to her as she heard the others call out in protest as well. They may not have been safe, but at least they were united, which was more than she could say about her and Willie.

"Well, lookie here!" Monroe exclaimed. "All the niggers wanna talk now, huh? Well, go on. Say somethin'!" The slaves fell silent once again. "Y'all don't seem to understand the seriousness of the situation. Them niggers is replaceable, but we got us a missing white man on our hands! Butch ain't the kind to up and leave his post without a word, and I don't rightly know what happened, but if I find out them two shitskin escapees even lifted a finger to hurt Ol' Butch, woo-wee! I will beat the black off each and every one of y'all, put you back in the sun, blacken y'all up again, then beat it off a second time! Now, if y'all so against Amos havin' a hard-earned break, tell me what I want to know!"

"She ain't nothin' but a lil' one, boss," Fuddle pleaded. "She don't even know what we's talkin' 'bout. She don't know nothin' 'bout nothin'."

"Don't you worry none," Amos said as he snatched Fanna away from Monroe. "She'll know plenty once I'm done with her."

Struggling against Amos, Fanna managed to break free from his grasp, only to be surrounded by the rest of the overseers.

"No!"

The girl's declaration took them all aback. It was the first word anyone had heard Fanna utter. But her voice seemed to tickle Monroe.

"Well, what do you know? It speaks!" Monroe and the rest of the overseers laughed as Gertie watched the young girl's hands ball up into fists.

"No, what, niglet?" Amos asked, towering over her.

"No . . . touch me!"

Another round of laughter led to Amos seizing Fanna's neck and squeezing before he pulled her close. But there was something haunting in Fanna's eyes. Gertie recognized the look; she had seen it in Willie's eyes, too.

Defiance.

"Or else what?" Amos growled at Fanna, who never blinked. She struggled to gather the breath to say what she wanted to say.

"*I's . . . gonna . . . fuck . . . you . . . up,*" Fanna managed to croak before Amos released her and smacked her so viciously, she was thrown off-balance, giving the overseer enough time to grab her around her waist and throw the girl over his shoulder. She flailed and cried as Amos walked off with her, a sinister grin across his face. An innocent young girl was about to pay the price for Rafazi's so-called plan. Gertie joined the chorus of voices pleading for Fanna's release.

"Shut up! Y'all shut them yaps!" Monroe raised his pistol sword in the air and fired a single shot, effectively quieting the slaves. "'Less y'all wanna share information about them runaways, keep y'all's mouths shut!"

They all averted their eyes, save for Minor, who was glaring up at Monroe. "And you best take your eye off me, boy," he directed at Minor. But Minor did not obey him. So, Monroe put the blade of his pistol sword up to Minor's neck. "You done gone deaf, boy?"

"Whatever becomes of Fanna be on your hands, boss," Minor said with flaring nostrils.

Monroe flipped the blade up and slashed it across Minor's forehead before knocking the gun barrel into his temple, sending the slave to the ground. Monroe dropped a knee in the crook of Minor's neck, blocking his air supply.

"You got somethin' else to say, boy?"

Minor pushed against Monroe while his legs thrashed about. Gertie wanted to cry out, but she bit down on her tongue to keep from doing so. She couldn't afford to have Monroe's violence visited upon her, not with the baby she was carrying. No one else said a word either. No one else but Fuddle.

"Please, boss! He cain't breathe!"

Without releasing or looking away from Minor, Monroe swung his pistol sword blade backward, slicing Fuddle's leg. Fuddle cried out in pain as he fell to the ground, cradling his bleeding appendage. It was then Gertie realized—Tussy and Fuddle nursing bloody wounds, Minor being denied oxygen, Fanna suffering from Amos's depravity—none of it was Rafazi's doing after all.

It was Willie's.

When Monroe finally stood, Minor rolled to his side and coughed like death itself had released its grasp on him. Whatever this so-called plan Rafazi had was, Gertie knew it would be the death of them all.

Somehow, she had to stop it. She had to stop Willie.

Nineteen

TALES OF RAMANGA

oddamn!"

Gertie knew Minor was imitating Monroe's angry language to express his own ire—it was how they learned this new tongue—but his furious exclamation made her flinch all the same.

Here, in the sick house as night fell, Gertie and a couple of the other slave women were helping tend to the wounds of Fuddle, Tussy—who was being uncharacteristically quiet—and the fuming Minor. Gertie remained silent too as she tended to Fuddle's injured leg.

"I's goin' soft as I can, now," Dorothy said in response to Minor's outburst. A portly woman in her fifties with a prominent bosom and skin slightly lighter than the others, Dorothy gingerly fastened a makeshift cloth bandage around Minor's head.

"Ain't you, Dorothy," Minor huffed. "It be this here god-damn place. How I's s'posed to know where Willie done run to or why Butch disappear? Monroe aim to kill me!"

"But he ain't," Gertie said bluntly, unable to stay silent any longer. "Let's just be grateful and hopes for a better day." Her words brought a deathly silence to the room. Minor's furrowed brow was directed at her, and she wished she hadn't said anything at all.

"Hope for a better day?" Minor asked. "What hope done got us? What it got po' Dorothy?"

"He ain't lyin'." Dorothy shook her head. "Massa got rid of me soon's I dried up. Wasted all my good milk on them awful chilren of his."

"Hmm mmm," Minor concurred. "And what it get Fanna? Who know what Amos puttin' her through? Po' girl ain't done a damn thing. Ain't nothin' to hope for, Gertie! None of this ain't never gonna change!"

Gertie's jaw tightened. Minor's words caused an eruption of comments in harmony with his sentiment, and like last night by the milk house, she felt alone. She knew none of them knew what she did, but the talk was escalating toward running, and she felt, once again, as if she was the only one with any sense.

"Y'all okay in here?"

Not for the first time, Gertie found a bit of comfort in Derby's unexpected presence.

"I heard yellin'," Derby said as his eyes rested on Gertie.

"Weren't nobody yellin'," Minor grumbled.

"Don't you lie, boy." Dorothy chuckled. "You's yellin' louder than Monroe."

"Well, I gots cause to yell!" Minor said. "I cain't takes me no more of this here!"

"So, what you wanna do, Minor? Run?" Dorothy challenged.

"Don't start no talk 'bout runnin' now," Gertie said firmly.

"So what if'n I do run?" Minor said, ignoring Gertie. "They ain't find Willie."

"Y'all hear me?" Gertie asked, but was once again ignored.

"It ain't been but a night or two since they run," noted Fuddle.

"And they still ain't find them!" Minor said.

"Y'all stop this here foolish talk! Y'hear?"

"But they find Charlie when he run. Look what happen to him," Dorothy countered.

"Maybe I runs faster than Ol' Charlie," Minor said. "Willie and—"

"Willie and Rafazi ain't the same as you!"

The volume of her own voice surprised Gertie, though it brought the talk of running to a halt, which was her goal. But she realized her statement would form questions in their minds, questions she wasn't ready to answer. She needed to tell them something else to keep questions at bay.

"All I mean," Gertie started, thinking as fast as she could, "ain't no good can come from runnin'. Willie run off with Charlie, they's get caught, Charlie get ate up by the hounds, and Monroe open Willie's back up. Now, he done run again, he gonna get caught again, and this time, Massa'll claim his foot. Ain't nothin' else waitin' for us out there no way." She turned to Derby, who gave her a nod of solidarity, and for a moment, she thought her speech would be enough.

"You say Willie and Rafazi ain't same as me. What you mean?" Minor asked.

"And who Rafazi?" Dorothy asked.

"Y'all ain't hear a word I say 'bout not runnin'?" Gertie cursed the crack in her voice as Tussy cocked her head at Gertie inquisitively. *Knowingly.* Tussy's eyes bore into her so deeply she averted her eyes. With just a look, Tussy had known she was pregnant, had known Willie was the father. Gertie didn't need her knowing what she knew now.

"What you mean they ain't same as me?" Minor repeated.

"She mean they's better than you," Fuddle said. Gertie

sighed but was thankful for the intrusion, especially since she didn't have an answer he could accept. "Willie stronger, for one, and faster on the paddy. He smarter, too."

"Willie ain't no stronger than me!" Minor protested. "Or faster! He done got caught first time he run!"

"Will y'all please stop talkin' 'bout runnin'?" Gertie pleaded. She could still feel Tussy's eyes on her.

"I know you's feelin' some kinda way 'cause Willie left you behind. Again." Gertie didn't appreciate Minor's snarky tone but thought it better to remain quiet. "But if'n I was him, I'da left you behind just the same, 'specially if'n you was jibber jawin' at him 'bout hope like y'done us. Ain't no hope here. Hope out *there*. Now, I don't care what none of y'all say, I's runnin'. Gertie, where they head to?"

Gertie remained defiantly silent. She'd grown tired, tired of speaking wisdom only to be ignored, tired of protecting Rafazi's evil for Willie's sake, tired of protecting *Willie's* evil. The Pangool would have been immensely displeased with her. She didn't remember Minor getting up nor did she remember raising her hand, but she felt it pushed firmly against Minor's chest, keeping him in place.

"Ain't nobody runnin'. Not tonight, not no night." It was as if her voice didn't belong to her. It had become hard, coarse, commanding—authoritative. She did not dislike the sound.

"I ain't the kind to lay hands on a woman," Minor warned her, his tone dark, "but if'n you don't get outs my way . . ."

"What you gonna do?" Derby stepped forward, pulling Minor's focus. Gertie watched Derby's hands turn into fists. Would he fight Minor on her behalf?

"Y'all stop fussin'," Fuddle whined. "Last thing we needs is to be turnin' on one 'nother."

"Ain't nobody turnin' on nobody," Minor said. "All she need to do is get outs my way."

"I ain't got no trouble with you, Minor. But you threaten

Gertie again, I'ma have to put me a hurtin' on you somethin' fierce." Derby stood nose to nose with Minor, and Gertie feared the worst.

"She know where he be."

Tussy had finally spoken, plainly and calmly, and the words gutted Gertie. Apparently, she was unable to hide the truth living on her face from Tussy.

"Willie and the other one Monroe were barkin' 'bout. She known all along." Tussy narrowed her eyes on Gertie. "But she ain't want you to go to them. She ain't wanna be nowhere near them."

The sting of tears scratched behind Gertie's eyes. She knew that once she said it, once she told the truth, there would be no turning back. Willie truly would be lost to her. He had turned evil, and she was holding life inside her. Good. For the sake of her child, she could not side with evil.

"Ain't no good can come from runnin'," Gertie whispered.

"Where they be, Gertie?" Tussy asked.

Gertie sighed, breathing through the tears she could not hold back. "Ain't where they be. It *what* they be."

"And what they be?" Tussy pressed as the whole room hung in anticipation of Gertie's next words.

"They Ramanga." The words hung in the air like the death they described. "Rafazi Ramanga, and he done made Willie Ramanga, too." All the air was sucked out of the room, and Gertie had to remind herself to breathe.

"Ramanga? They tribe was lost to the plague. Eons ago, my mamma say." The tremble in Tussy's voice was as unmistakable as the horror in Dorothy's gasp.

"Night Monroe bust up Willie's eye, he tell me Rafazi be the last one left, right in this here sick house," Gertie said slowly.

"Who Rafazi?" Tussy asked.

"The one done broke out the cage. The one Monroe call Shit Boy."

"Ramanga ain't real," Dorothy said, her voice trembling. "They just legend."

"Yes, they is real!" Tussy insisted. It was the first time Gertie had heard the self-assured woman raise her voice. "But they s'posed to be gone from the plague!"

"What plague? What Ramanga be?" Minor asked, his brow scrunched in confusion.

"You ain't never been told tales of Ramanga when you was a boy?" Fuddle asked. Minor shrugged.

"They was a mix of god and man," Tussy began, "but god and man ain't s'posed to mix, so they turn evil. They wait 'til night, then takes your blood, and leaves you dead, or makes you one of they own."

Minor's shoulders began to hunch before he started laughing in earnest. "They 'takes your blood'? Y'all get me all riled up just to be funnin' me?"

Now that she had spoken the truth, Gertie needed them all to know exactly how serious the revelation was. Handed down stories were one thing, but she had witnessed the evil of Ramanga with her own eyes.

"Now, Minor, you knows I ain't never speak a word ain't true. So, when I tell you I watch my Willie change, watch his eyes go red, his hands turn to claws, his teeth get sharp, I ain't funnin' you. I watch him turn into a monster. And Rafazi the one done it to him. Irene kick up all that fuss 'bout the milk house, so I follow after Willie that night. And when Butch come behind me, Rafazi rip his heart clean out his chest!"

The room grew still.

"Shit Boy," Tussy whispered with realization. "The night Massa had his way with you in the breedin' room, somethin' with a powerful awful smell come through the cabin, somethin' too fast to see, and when it gone, Fanna were lyin' in the cot."

"Legend say Ramanga ungodly fast," Dorothy gasped before covering her mouth, but Minor was laughing again.

"Y'all talkin' all this here mess when I's tryin' to talk 'bout being free!"

"Ain't no freedom to be had, Minor!" Gertie argued, fighting against the sobs rising within her. "I seen Rafazi kill Willie. I seen him feed Willie his blood, seen him snap Willie's neck, seen Willie fall in the dirt and die! And then he rise with the same red eyes Rafazi got, grab me up and race me back to slave village faster than you can blink a eye, and then, just as fast, turn into a monster and scream at me for blood! I seen Willie die, Minor! I seen Rafazi snatch him 'way from me and rush him into the woods. He gone, and he hungry for blood. Monroe may put the whip to you here, but you live. Run, and you runnin' straight into evil."

"So, you catch Ol' Willie dippin' his stick in Irene, and now you mad and wanna come talkin' at me with this here foolishness."

"No, Minor. I ain't mad at Willie! I's mournin' him! I done lost him to wickedness. Downright evil I's tryin' to save you from!"

Minor's eyes were cold. Not a word had gotten through to him. "I's runnin'."

"You ain't runnin'." Gertie choked back a sob at Derby's words. "Willie weren't dippin' in Irene. Gertie talk true."

"How you know?" Minor challenged.

"'Cause I were there!" Gertie blinked, but Derby gave her no time to interject. "I seen Willie with my own eyes, and it be just like she say. I hear him scream for her blood and find her on her knees, cryin' her eyes out. And he had the face of a demon. Only reason Gertie standin' front of us now 'cause the last of his human mind know her, but I reckon it gone now. He'da bled me dry, evil as he was screamin'. My kin in Togo tell me Ramanga tales, but they ain't never scare me like what I seen. I ain't want no part of what he done become, and you don't want none either. Runnin' from Monroe ain't what we's got to be worried 'bout. What we's got to be worried 'bout is what we's gonna do if'n Willie come back here hungry."

ONLY ONE WORD OCCUPIED Gertie's mind, and it screamed at her louder than Monroe ever could, so she screamed it at Derby.

"Why?"

The gentle summer breeze rustled her hair as Derby turned to face her, and in her turmoil, the sight of him distracted her. The night suited him. There was something of a majestic nature to his stance, his torso bulging with muscle, free of clothing, his taut skin, as dark and smooth as her own, glowing underneath the moon and the stars. He was a jovial sort who was not prone to involving himself in serious matters. So, why had he taken up hers?

"Why you lie?" Gertie asked him.

"It work, ain't it?" Derby chuckled. "You ain't want Minor to run, he ain't gonna run."

"He ain't wanna listen to me. Why he listen to you?"

"Don't matter none, do it? What matter is Ol' Derby got you what you want."

"No, I means why he listen to you and not me? I talk true, and you . . ."

"Lie?"

She stepped back when he came forward. Derby smiled. "I lie 'cause you needs me to, to keep Minor from runnin'. I's always gonna do what you need doin', Gertie." None of Derby's words made sense to her, nor did they answer her one-word question. "I don't know if'n Ramanga true or if'n it ain't, and I don't care none. All I care is Willie done up and left you. Don't matter why. He gone. Ain't a man 'live deserve to be called a man for leavin' a woman like you behind."

"What is you jibber jawin' 'bout now?"

"I know what y'all thinks 'bout Ol' Derby. I likes me some honeypot, and I ain't 'fraid who know it. Ain't been too particular neither. Don't mean I don't wants more. And you *is* more, Gertie."

She hadn't realized he'd taken another step toward her until she felt his hand on her cheek. Had she been aware of him moving toward her, she was sure she would have stepped back again. But his gentle words—had she gotten lost in them?

Her love for Willie was pure, but it was a lie to say they were not fraught with struggle. They clashed about running, defiance against Monroe, taking Ramangan blood. How wonderful it would have been for her words not to be challenged, her wisdom taken to heart. Derby didn't even need to believe her words to respect them, to lie for them, for *her*.

"Willie scare you somethin' awful. Ain't no woman s'posed to be 'fraid of her man. This here toil bad enough. Ain't no needin' you bein' scared of the one man you s'posed to have rest with. Now, I don't know what Willie done, and I don't care. But I tell you this here. I's glad he gone. I can be your rest now, Gertie."

Gertie's existence consisted of worrying, wondering, and working, and she felt as if she was doing all of it alone. Somehow the warmth of Derby's hand caressing her cheek soothed her. She was so tired. And now, there was a child. She was thankful she was not showing yet; she was not ready for the stress it would bring on top of everything else. There was no point in alerting Derby to the child she carried. But she found such ease in his touch.

"I ain't no hard woman," Gertie said, looking up at Derby, whose hand gently moved to the nape of her neck. His touch was firm, steady. She hated how safe it made her feel. "But ev'rythin' I say, I say true. Ramanga is true. Go on, ask Irene. She know."

"Ain't no needin' me askin' Irene nothing. I believes *you*, Gertie. I believes whatever you wants me to."

How much easier her partnership with Willie would have been if he had regarded her words with the same reverence Derby was showing her now. Gertie felt tears well in her eyes and the gentle pull of Derby's hand at the back of her neck. Her cheek fell against his chest as she felt his arms embrace her, and without thinking, she wrapped hers around his back. His words, his glorious words. She felt seen. Heard.

"I's do whatever it take to protect you, Gertie," he said, and her arms gripped him tighter.

Twenty

A POINT OF FOCUS

The deer's left eye blinked back lazily at Willie's glowing red eyes. In full Ramangan form, his fangs and teeth were lodged into the neck of the animal, feeding, as Rafazi watched closely.

"Now!"

At Rafazi's command, Willie released the deer and watched it stumble a bit as it blinked again, finding its footing. Willie's red eyes pulsed with want as Rafazi smacked the deer on its hindquarter, sending it running off into the night.

It had been an eventful twenty-four hours for Willie.

A night ago, he was human. Now, he was marveling at his own strength as Rafazi taught him to leap high into the air and flip, his arms outstretched, his hands balled into fists capable of punching through the surface of the earth and digging through the dirt and muck to burrow underground and bury himself to escape the sun. He was in awe at no longer needing air as he waited for night to fall again.

Still, though physically he was at a peak he'd never known before, mentally he was drained. Choosing death was no small feat, especially considering Gertie's view on the matter. She refused to understand his sacrifice was for her and their child. Rafazi had made good on his promise. Willie only hoped he hadn't lost Gertie in his quest to free her.

Rafazi's hand landed on Willie's back, and he turned to find the man smiling at him like a proud parent. "Good," Rafazi said. "Now, return. Focus on the man you were. Bring to mind a memory of your human life."

Willie closed his eyes and pictured Gertie. He wished to recall her smile, the smell of her skin, her touch. Instead, all he saw was the scowl on her face as she drew away from him, looking at him like he was a monster, her words playing in his head like a sad refrain.

I hate this. I hate what y'done.

Though the memory was unpleasant, it fulfilled Rafazi's requirement. In seconds, he felt his extended brow retract into his forehead. Running his fingertips along the skin on his face told him his brow had returned to its original state. His talons had transformed back into regular nails, and the red tint in his vision was gone. Running his tongue along his teeth, he felt the jagged edges had become smooth again, and the fangs had also withdrawn.

Despite returning to his human form, Willie could still feel immense strength in his body, the power in his blood. He would always be in awe of it and surmised Gertie would always be in opposition to it, until it delivered freedom to her as he had promised. It was a promise he intended to keep.

"How do you feel?" he heard Rafazi ask.

"Tired. And hungry."

"I know." Rafazi nodded. "Control takes time, but it's necessary. And you're getting better at it a lot faster than I did. Did you notice how tranquil the deer was when you bit into it?"

"Yeah," Willie said. "And my mouth gets so wet when I's 'bout to bite."

"It's our venom. We secrete a dual-purpose fluid in anticipation of the feed. It gives humans and animals a feeling of pleasant relaxation to make the bite easier to take."

Willie called to mind his first encounter with Rafazi and the euphoria his initial bite had brought.

"Taken on its own," Rafazi continued, "it has a healing effect on humans. But in battle, it makes the bite even more painful."

"Like you done Butch."

"Exactly. It depends on intent. You didn't wish the deer harm, so your venom was pleasurable."

"Deer taste different than the fox I caught back yonder. The one you makes me set free."

"For control, Willie." Rafazi chuckled. "There will be plenty more blood. But yes, deer, fox, horse, lion, they all taste different."

"You done drank lion blood?" Willie asked, surprised.

Rafazi nodded with a smile.

"What lion blood taste like?"

"Why ruin the surprise?" Rafazi laughed, and Willie shook his head. Rafazi had seven hundred years of knowledge to teach him. Willie could not fathom taking in so much information. "There are all types of blood, and they all taste different. Same with humans. It's part of what keeps things so enticing. Some have similar tastes, so you will develop favorites, as you would with food, but there's no way of knowing when you'll encounter the same flavor again with humans. Which is why we'd go after families . . ."

Rafazi stopped himself as Willie took him in with dread. He knew human blood was in his future, but he hadn't quite made peace with it, something Rafazi must have sensed. "At any rate, your sense of smell will develop to the point where you'll begin to recognize what you like. Lots of things factor into taste—what they eat, where they live. But let's focus on what you need to know now."

"Okay. What next?"

"Binding. It's part of mind bending. When I fed from you, it created a binding connection, allowing me to send my thoughts to you telepathically. It's how you could hear me in your head even though I hadn't turned you yet. But it can only go one way until the human is turned."

"So, you makes me hear you in my head, but I cain't makes you hear me?"

"Not while you were human, no. But the same binding connection is made when you do turn someone, only stronger. We share a connection now through blood because mine made you. But it takes focus to work effectively. A lot more focus than mind bending."

"I can makes you hear me in your head?"

"Yes. If we get separated in battle, we can still communicate with each other. The binding grows stronger with focus. The stronger the binding, the farther the distance we can communicate from. Could be a lifesaver if one of us gets captured."

"Captured?"

"We will be met with great force, Willie. Barrow won't take kindly to his property staging a revolt against him. Once they realize the full extent of our power, they'll be terrified, and those whip-crackers will come together like never before to snuff us out."

"That's why we's got to make more like us."

"And we will, but there may be many who feel like Gertie. We have to be prepared to be outnumbered. Having the strength of ten men is great, until it's one against twenty. Binding will make training the ones you turn easier."

The gravity of being dead was still settling within him, but now, the enormity of their undertaking was pressing on his shoulders. They would have to plan smartly, get the better of the overseers with as much stealth and speed as Ramangan power could provide. They would need a place to safeguard their people, the ones who would choose against taking the blood, like Gertie. They all deserved protection and freedom.

The manor would make for a great stronghold, he thought. If they could take it.

"Excellent idea, Willie."

He was so focused on his thoughts that Rafazi's voice surprised him. He realized the elder Ramangan had heard his thoughts.

"I knew you'd be a fast learner. Let's see how strong the connection is."

Rafazi's blur took off and left Willie standing alone in the wilderness. Immediately, he resumed his Ramangan form. Yes, he possessed power—he had taken on a full-grown bear and won—but Rafazi had far more. He had given the man his trust, his life for Ramangan blood, but left alone in the wilderness, he felt his certainty slipping. Rafazi had openly confessed his cowardice. Had his ploy all along been to run off and leave Willie with the responsibility of freeing the slaves on his own?

"Rafazi! Rafazi!" Willie called into the night. "Rafazi!" Only the crickets answered back until a voice echoed in his head.

You're not playing fair, Willie.

Willie's shoulders dropped as a wave of relief calmed his nerves. He spun around, trying to discern Rafazi's location. "Where you be?"

Wrong question.

"You cain't be too far if'n you still hear me."

Not true. Our hearing is superhuman, though it requires focus as well. Something you clearly have a hard time exercising. Stop speaking, and communicate with me with your thoughts.

Willie sighed and shut his eyes. Words rushed around in his brain, but none of them formed one single cohesive thought.

You're trying too hard.

"You say focus, I's focusin'! It ain't work!"

Think of Gertie.

Willie did so and felt a rush in his blood.

What do you feel?

It was a loaded question. His heart swelled with love; his blood boiled with his frustration. Why couldn't she understand he wasn't taking himself away from her and their baby? Why couldn't she see what he was doing was the only way for them to be free? Why did she have to fight him on every choice he made, all the time? Why didn't she trust him?

Because she's scared.

Willie's eyes shot open.

Gertie is a point of focus for you. I thought conjuring thoughts of her would get you where you needed to be.

Tears welled in Willie's eyes. Twice now, negative thoughts of Gertie had triggered the successful use of his Ramangan powers.

Focus is achieved by your strongest thoughts. As you grow stronger, focus will become natural. Your frustration with Gertie is only evidence of your love for her.

But why cain't she love me the same, he thought.

She does. Give her time. The Blood leaves little room for middle ground. It is either feared or revered.

Then she fear me, Willie thought, this time purposefully.

She does. But in time, you will prove yourself. You will fulfill your promise to her, and she will bask in the freedom you provide. She will come to know her fear is unwarranted. The sooner we return, the sooner she will come back to you. So, we must continue our training.

Though Gertie was against Ramangan power, it had filled him with purpose. He was determined to see his task through and, with the help of Rafazi, build an army to defeat . . .

Willie was slammed to the ground with massive force and lightning speed. When the shock of the attack wore off, he looked around and found nothing but trees. On alert, he got to his feet and took a crouching stance, readying himself for another strike.

It didn't make sense for Rafazi to attack him, but there was no one else who could have done so. A rustling in the distance made his eyes pulse. He focused his attention on the direction of the sound and balled his fists. He was preparing for war, one he would have to lead. He would have to fight, and fight well, if he hoped to be victorious.

Willie let out a howl of pain as he was knocked into from behind and sent face-first into the dirt. He pushed himself up off the ground and growled in anger.

"What you doin'?" he yelled out.

Do not lose your focus. Attacks can come at you in all forms. If you can stop mine, those of our enemies will be much easier to ward off. Listen. Focus. Let your senses and instincts guide you.

Willie felt the phantom feeling of releasing a breath, and though there was no air in his lungs to expel, he followed through with the action as he remembered it, which brought him a sense of calm. Closing his eyes once more, he listened intently. There were sounds all around him—the continued chirp of crickets, animals rustling through the grass, the constant beating of their hearts, the blood rushing through their veins—but nothing posing a threat.

A change in the resonance of the wind, a distant whirling, became more pronounced. The whirling got louder; it was coming from Willie's left side—no, from behind. Willie turned to find a huge boulder flying directly at him at incredible velocity, threatening to topple him. With mere inches between him and the great rock, Willie reared back and swung mightily with his right fist, smashing the stone into pebbled fragments. As they showered to the ground around him, he looked at his fist in awe—barely scratched, and the broken skin was quickly repairing itself.

"Imagine what you could do to a face." Willie turned again and found a smiling Rafazi standing next to him. "Let's continue."

"You know I don't like you in my house."

Dawn's early light streamed through the windows, and Big Jim sighed as he watched his chief overseer shift his weight from one leg to the other in front of the oversized mahogany desk the plantation owner sat behind. Monroe was out of place in his elegant study, with its floor-to-ceiling mahogany bookshelves filled with tomes Big Jim hadn't read.

Reading them was of little importance—though he did enjoy new editions of *The New Atalantis* whenever they were released. It was the possessing of the books that truly mattered. Possessing things was the theme of his life, which was why he had called Monroe here.

"Has your hearing escaped you?" Big Jim asked Monroe, reclining in his massive leather chair, puffing smoke from his red clay pipe.

"No, sir," Monroe answered shakily. "I know you don't like me in your house, boss."

"So, you know how terribly you must have performed if I'm willing to stomach your presence, don't you?"

"I suppose, boss."

"You suppose?" In moments like these, Big Jim regarded his overseer like he would a child or a dog. Or someone even worse. "You remind me of my father."

"Thank you, boss."

"He was a low-class, moronic drunk without an ounce of refinement," Big Jim snarled, and Monroe's smile faded. "Couldn't keep money or grow a crop to save his life. A pure waste of a white man. You're as bad as he was. He wouldn't have been fit to stand in this house, and neither are you, especially considering the reason I've called for you. But here we are." They were senti-ments Big Jim wished he could have said to his father's face, but Monroe made a decent stand-in.

Clarence appeared at the door of the study carrying a sil-ver tray with a bottle of brandy and two crystal glasses. Behind him stood a tall man with thinning dark hair that matched his beard.

"Boss," Clarence said, his head and neck slightly bent, "your guest done arrived."

"Let him in, Clarence."

With an eye on Monroe, Clarence stepped aside and let the balding man enter before him. "I ain't known Monroe were gonna be here, boss," Clarence said. "Shall I fetch another glass?"

"That'd be mighty white of you," Monroe said to Clarence with a quick smile, but it faded fast after a firm "no" from Big Jim.

"I only share my French imported brandy with company. Monroe is *not* company. Put the tray down and leave."

Clarence obeyed as Big Jim poured the brandy and offered his guest a glass. The balding man accepted the glass graciously, and Big Jim took a moment to enjoy the look of twisted con-fusion on the face of his chief overseer. He did so delight in the discomfort his power elicited in others.

"Look at him," Big Jim said to his guest, referring to Monroe. "And he's as dumb as he looks, too." His guest chuck-led, and Big Jim watched Monroe's face redden. "His only talent is numbers, and if he wasn't as good with them as he is, I'd rid myself of this blunderbuss. Hell, I still might."

Monroe's eyes went wide, and the owner felt a small smile form on his face. "Monroe, this is Oliver Gibbs. He is the cap-tain of the Lakeside Slave Patrol. And he's here because you, in a shocking display of cowardice and stupidity, allowed not one, but two slaves to get away on your watch. It's also come to

my attention one of my overseers has turned up missing from
his post. Also, on your watch. Clearly, you have lost control of
my plantation. Still, I do not wish to go through the work of
replacing you unless I must. Were I to do so, folks might learn
about those escaped niggers and start thinking I don't have my
plantation well in hand. So, I have called Oliver in to do what
you obviously cannot. Tonight, you will accompany a faction
of his men into the woods with a couple of my puppies and
retrieve those wayward niggers. Oliver and the men accompa-
nying you will be paid for their discretion. I assume, Oliver, this
is something I can count on?"

"Absolutely," Oliver Gibbs replied. "My men are courageous
and loyal."

"And poor," Big Jim added. "I am paying for their hunting
skills and their silence. And to ensure success, I will be adding
a little honey to the pot. These ornery, ungrateful blackies have
caused me enough embarrassment. So, I will award additional
compensation for the man who brings me their heads without
their bodies attached. Am I making myself clear?"

Oliver's face lit up, which Big Jim expected. He also expected the excitement Monroe directed toward him.

"Me too, boss?" the chief overseer asked.

"Your reward for aiding in the success of this endeavor is
keeping your job," Big Jim said. Though he took glee in watching Monroe's face fall and in crushing his spirit, he was even
happier with the confidence expressed to him by Oliver.

"Don't you worry, Mister Barrow," Oliver said. "Those niggers will be caught and are as good as dead."

Big Jim poured himself a second glass of cognac and toasted
the slave patrol captain. "Glad to hear it."

Twenty-One

To Live or Die

It was a slow slog off the paddy for Gertie as the sun slipped away to make room for the coming moon. Sleep had eluded her the night before, as it had ever since she'd witnessed the horrifying deaths of Willie and Butch. Their murders.

Though toiling for her master was nothing she looked forward to, she felt grateful for the distraction from the nightmarish images plaguing her mind. It was also a distraction from the eyes she'd felt on her all day. Everywhere she looked, there seemed to be people staring back at her.

"Word done got out."

Derby's voice made her jump, but the realization it was him—and his presence—was comforting. "I reckon Minor and Dorothy got to blabbin', but ev'rybody been a whisperin' and chatterin' all day. Even thems in the cotton fields."

"Whisperin' 'bout me?" Gertie asked.

"'Bout Ramanga."

Gertie felt her throat close up. Yes, she had taken a stand against Ramangan blood for herself and her child, and she was against anyone else taking it as well, but she didn't need the reality of Ramanga to become common knowledge. The ears listening to slave chatter were also white and came equipped with whips.

No one wanted to catch the whip for any reason, but Gertie was making an especially earnest attempt at keeping her head down for the sake of her child. She was holding out hope the Pangool would intervene and deliver her to freedom. But not knowing—or having any control over—the fate of her child weighed heavily on her, as was keeping the secrets of her pregnancy and Ramanga from Monroe.

"They's cain't!" Gertie hissed. "If'n Monroe get wind . . ."

"Ain't nobody tellin' Monroe nothin'," Derby assured her.

"Ain't nobody gots to *tell* Monroe nothin'. Ain't s'posed to be no talkin' on the paddy. If'n they's yappin' 'bout it, he gonna *hear* 'bout it."

"I reckon he gonna find out for hisself soon enough."

"What you mean?"

"Bessie done tell me she hear Monroe fixin' to head out with the paddy rollers to go hunt Ol' Willie down. Heard him say he don't care none whether Willie come back 'live or dead."

A shiver ran down Gertie's spine. His words frightened her too much. So, she found a way to lessen their power and distract herself from them.

"Bessie say, huh? Ain't she one of the ones y'done dip your stick in?"

"Why, Miss Gertie? Is you jealous?" Derby's smile flashed so bright she had to turn away to keep from smiling herself.

"Is it true, Gertie?"

A young slave woman sidled up to them, speaking in a low, conspiratorial tone. "Willie done turn Ramanga?"

"How?" an older slave scoffed, keeping pace with them. "Ramanga done been gone. Ain't no way."

"My nanabarima say Ramanga cain't die, not long as there be blood in the world," proclaimed a third slave who inserted herself into the conversation Gertie did not want to have. "When he comin' back, Gertie? He gonna make us all Ramanga?"

"All right, y'all," Derby said calmly. "We's done just got off the paddy, now. Gertie tired."

"We's all tired," said the third slave. "If'n I gots to drink me a little blood to be free, so be it!"

"Free?" Gertie asked. "You thinks Ramanga blood gonna free you? Free us? Ramanga is death! Yeah, Willie took blood and died, then got right back up a thing of pure evil. Dead s'posed to stay dead. If'n it don't, it ain't walkin' the earth for good, let alone deliverin' nobody from nothin'."

"But where he get the blood from?" the first slave asked.

"All right, I done say that's enough, now," Derby broke in, taking Gertie's arm to lead her away. But she snatched it from his grasp, fire in her eyes as she faced her interrogators.

"Don't matter where the blood come from," she hissed. "What matter is it real. And it evil. Ramanga blood took my Willie 'way. And I tells you this here: If'n Monroe do go out and find him, he gonna be one dead white man. And once Willie get a taste for blood, he gonna come back here for more. He gonna want us all to taste it, make us all like him, bind us to blood, and doom us all to death and darkness. Killin' to live ain't no kinda life. If'n y'all wants to live, y'all stay clear of him."

She was sure her public declaration would spread the rumors even faster, but she no longer cared. She was done protecting Willie and his evil choice. The slaves needed to be protected against making the same wicked choice he had made, or else they all would be truly doomed.

"You wrong 'bout this here, Gertie."

Tussy stood behind her now, Fanna clinging to her waist. The sight of the girl sent Gertie's heart lurching into her throat. When they had arrived on the paddy in the morning, they'd found Fanna sprawled out, barely conscious and beaten, with bruises all over her legs, her dress ripped, her left eye, cheek, and bottom lip all swollen.

They had rushed to her aid, but she was so traumatized, she wouldn't let anyone touch her except for Tussy, who was warned away from Fanna by Amos. The overseer slapped the poor girl roughly to bring her to full wakefulness, then worked her twice as hard as anyone else in her exhausted and assaulted state.

No one's day had been longer than Fanna's.

"How you be, Fanna?" Gertie asked, her eyes soft. She reached out for the young girl, but Fanna recoiled from her, moving behind Tussy and clutching the older woman tightly. "I knows," Gertie whispered, afraid her full voice would crack. "They hurts me, too."

"All right, now," Tussy whispered to Fanna. "Gertie don't mean no harm. You's all right."

Gertie's soft look was returned with hard eyes from Tussy.

"Tussy, please. Listen at me, now . . ."

"Hush your mouth, Gertie, y'hear?" Tussy hissed, covering Fanna's ears. "I done lied to this child. She ain't all right. She ain't never gonna be all right. Not no more. Ain't none of us ever gonna be."

"Tussy, listen at me, now . . ."

"No, you listen! Talkin' all that hope talk—you see this child? I reckon this child died a thousand times last night. Ain't no hope for her. How she gonna break free of what Amos done to her? And she ain't the only one. What 'bout me? How much longer you think I gots left to sit 'round hopin' for things to get better? Huh? Young as she is, Fanna might as well be old as me now. But you still drudgin' on, hopin' on this, hopin' on that. You ain't seen your worst day yet. You gots time. But time run out. You gonna learn. Just like I done. Lookin' at what they done to this po' child; ain't no good in this here world, Gertie. Only evil. If'n you gonna survive it, you needs to get you some evil of your own. And if'n Ol' Willie got him some to give, I's takin'."

"Tussy, you don't know what you's sayin', now . . ."

"I knows 'xactly what I's sayin', and so do you. You can scare Minor, but I tell you this here: If'n Willie come back with Monroe's blood on his tongue, I's gonna be the first to say yes to his askin', and I's takin' Fanna right 'long with me."

Gertie felt a tightness around her heart. Conflict would spread through slave village over this. She could not simply wish darkness away; she would need to make herself an active force against it. Which meant standing against Willie if he did return.

Which was exactly what she planned to do.

They've taken everything from us.
Even our names.

Twenty-Two

KWADZO OKORO

Wind whipped past Willie's ears as he moved through a vast patch of trees under the stars. With his Ramangan vision, a clear path was laid out for him that never would have been visible with his human sight. The edges of his field of vision were darkened, creating invisible blinders, and the path was bathed in a bright red light twisting and turning before him. All he had to do was follow the red in his eyes and lean in the direction it guided him toward. The red found its way through the trees, steering Willie around each trunk and branch with ease.

The speed sent pure exhilaration rushing through Willie's veins, causing him to emit a series of jubilant shouts as he moved. Nothing truly evil could make him feel this good or fill him with so much purpose. If only Gertie could *feel* what he felt!

As Willie reached the end of the patch of trees, a smiling Rafazi emerged. Willie brought himself to a stop, and his red tint faded. He felt as though he should have been out of breath after his run, but he remembered he no longer needed to breathe.

"Another phantom feeling?" Rafazi asked.

"Ain't got no air in me," Willie said, nodding. "Why I's still feel like it in me?"

"Every person is different, but generally, the human brain has a difficult time adjusting to death. It tends to cling to its known impulses. The more familiar your system becomes with Ramangan Blood, the more it will gain the trust of your organs and their new mode of functioning, and the phantom feelings will go away," the elder Ramangan explained. "That said, it should have taken much longer for you to master your blur as you have. Your blood, Willie. I can't imagine the heights you will reach with the power forged between Ramangan Blood and whatever ran through your living veins. The revolution you will lead will change the world."

The revolution he would lead. From his death sprung a new kind of life, one filled with blood, speed, and power Willie never dreamed possible. But it had just been bestowed upon him and already he was being called to lead. It was akin to bestowing a kingdom onto a child unable to speak, let alone rule. His power was immense, yes, but it alone did not a leader make. The trouble was, he had no idea what else did.

"I ain't been nothin' but a slave, Rafazi," Willie lamented. "Ain't nobody gonna listen at me. Even I gots sense enough to knows I don't talk right. Not like you. You sound like the white folks, and they's the ones in charge. Orders gonna sound right comin' out your mouth."

"What you have, I have always lacked," Rafazi said. "Courage. Instead of it, I was given cowardice."

"No, now, you's wrong as wrong can be. I seen you tear Butch apart, yank his heart clean out his chest. Kill him dead."

"Vengeance is not the same as courage. My vengeance was propelled by your presence, your courage. Vengeance is a followed impulse, a reaction. Courage is a choice. It drives you to do the thing you know is right, even in the face of opposition."

"Like Gertie not wantin' me to run," Willie said in realization.

"Or her not wanting you to take the Blood. There's what she wanted, which would have kept things the way they were, and kept her and your child in danger, and what you knew needed to be done to ensure their freedom."

Rafazi scanned the woods around them and then turned to face Willie fully. "Making hard decisions for the greater good and acting on them with purpose and sacrifice is courage. You chose to give up your human life so Gertie and your child could live theirs in peace and liberty. Gertie didn't want you to *die*. You want her to *live*. That is what makes you a leader. And when she is sitting somewhere with your child suckling at her bosom, safe, with no plantation, no paddy, no overseer, and no master, basking in the freedom *your* choice made possible, she will revere your sacrifice and respect your courage, and her ardor for you will know no bounds."

Willie felt his smile return. Rafazi had given voice to his deepest desire, and possibility flooded his senses once again.

"The thing you still need more of to be a leader is training," Rafazi said with a good-natured slap on Willie's shoulder. The two men laughed together in the moonlight, the laughter of free men.

"All right, now. What next?" Willie asked.

"Again, through the trees. But this time with surprises."

"What you mean surprises?"

"Head back through the thicket, and you will see." Rafazi's blur disappeared, and Willie refocused on the trees until his red vision returned. Once again, he went racing through the trees, allowing his Ramangan blood to steer him. He was fully unprepared for Rafazi's sudden presence in his path. As he tried to slow himself, Rafazi rushed at him, and with a solid punch, knocked Willie back, landing him on his back in a patch of grass.

"Speed is great," Rafazi said, standing over him. "But in battle, control is better. We've no way of knowing what we'll face. We move far faster, but their lack of speed can knock us off-balance, especially when we're in our blurs. You must anticipate any attack so you can adjust accordingly. Now. Again."

Rafazi helped Willie to his feet before disappearing in his blur for the second time. Though he was aware of his own strength, Willie was now acutely aware of Rafazi's. His chest stung from where Rafazi's fist had connected. While he was sure Rafazi would not do him serious harm, he was concerned with his inability to stop before his mentor's attack. As fast as his blur was, anyone could pop up out of nowhere in his path without him being able to stop. What if it was one of their own people?

What if it was Gertie?

Willie shook his head and took on his Ramangan form. His red vision pulsing, Willie raced through the trees again. He felt himself moving faster than before, more purposefully. This time, when Rafazi appeared in his path, Willie was ready. Rafazi charged at him, but Willie leapt so high he sailed over Rafazi and kept going.

Willie laughed to himself as his feet landed on the ground again; he couldn't believe how high he'd jumped. But there was barely time to analyze this as Rafazi appeared again, this time popping up from out of the ground.

Rafazi slammed two hands into Willie's abdomen, sending him sliding backward across the wet grass beneath them. Regaining his bearings, Willie ducked his head down and lunged forward, clasping his arms around Rafazi's waist, and flinging him against a tree. The elder Ramangan launched a counterstrike, delivering a violent punch into Willie's side, but Willie grabbed hold of the punching arm and used it to hurl Rafazi again, this time high into the air.

While his mentor was suspended, Willie jumped, flipping his body until his head was pointed at the ground. With his arms outstretched as he hurtled down, he punched through the surface and tunneled under the earth, pushing himself through the dirt just below the surface.

He could hear Rafazi's feet land above him, his blur chasing after him. Willie pushed and burst through the ground ahead of his mentor and threw a fist across Rafazi's face, landing the elder Ramangan on his back. But Rafazi was back on his feet immediately, and soon, the two were toe to toe, trading punches in a flurry of fists blurring against each other in a superspeed bout of fisticuffs.

While each blow hurt Willie, he was amazed at his tolerance for pain. Throwing his palm into Rafazi's neck, he made his mentor stumble back. Willie grabbed hold of his arm, rushed behind Rafazi, and twisted the arm high.

"If you were to continue to twist my arm at the shoulder, you now have the strength to break the socket and pull the arm off," Rafazi said. "It's an inventive way to extract blood. Painful for the human you're extracting it from. It could result in death."

Death. The word echoed in Willie's mind. Images of what Rafazi had done to Butch flooded his mind, as did Gertie's haunting words.

If'n it make you do what Rafazi done to Butch . . .

"You must understand," he heard Rafazi say, "staging a revolt is the same as war. People die in war. More importantly, people are killed in war. You must prepare yourself to kill, Willie."

The phantom feeling of a gasp seized Willie as he released Rafazi. Revolt and revenge sounded delicious to a mind hungry for freedom. But the truth of what it would take to achieve was beginning to hit Willie. Killing would be a part of his future. His *existence* would depend on it.

"Make no mistake, killing will change you," Rafazi continued. "There's no question about that. But not in the way it would have when you were human. It will solidify your new life. It will adjust your senses, your strength, your mind."

"But you train me to feed without killin'."

"Yes. The point of Ramangan Blood is not to kill indiscriminately. But their blood is our life. So, why not take it from those who wish us dead?" Willie turned away from Rafazi, the conflict within him rising.

"Tell me this," his mentor continued, trying to assuage him. "Do you think Butch, having witnessed my power, would have changed had I allowed him to live? Or do you think he would have tried to kill me the first chance he got? Or alerted Monroe and Big Jim and the others to what I was and come after me, after us all, with a vengeance?"

"He'da come after us."

"And do you think they would have come after us to kill us?"

Willie blinked. The answer was clear in his mind. "Yes."

"Yes. Because our lives do not matter to them. Nothing about our existence does. They've taken everything from us. Even our names."

Willie felt every fiber in his being tense. Their names. He hadn't given thought to his name in so long. His true name.

"Do you remember yours?" Rafazi's question made Willie realize he'd lost himself in thoughts of the past—his home, his family, his capture, his death. He tightened his lips. He did not trust his voice. "Do you remember when they stole it from you?"

Willie's eyes went red at Rafazi's question. No one, not even Gertie, had ever asked him about his name, his *true* name.

"They calls me runt," Willie recalled, his voice trembling. "I ain't know they's tongue when they put me up on that auction block. All's I keeps hearin' when they's pointin' at me, runt.

Runt. And they's a'chucklin' when they says it. Like I's dumb. Weren't but a boy, and I ain't know what all else they's sayin', but ev'ry time I hear that word, runt, it feel like they's slappin' my face. Then one of them comes up, say, 'C'mon, Runt.' And they's been sayin' it so much I reckon they's thinks it be my name, so I say . . ." Willie could not stop his lip from quivering. He clasped his hands tightly to keep them from shaking and looked away so Rafazi would not see his tears. "Kwadzo."

Kwadzo.

The name his father had gifted him with, the one his mother called out when it was time for his supper, the one his sister would sing teasingly whenever he got in trouble. The name of his birth.

His name.

In eighteen years, he hadn't hadn't heard it. He had had to die to hear it again, but it felt as if a shackle around his heart had fallen away. Despite having no breath, he felt as if he could breathe again.

"That man slap me so hard," Kwadzo continued, giving up trying to control the trembling in his voice. "And he keep slappin' me, and them mens was laughin', sayin' runt over and over."

"Why did they start calling you Willie?" Rafazi asked softly.

"They's sell me to Barrow, and I done grown, so he say he cain't calls me runt no more. I's too big. He say my name Willie. And this time, I knows what he sayin' 'cause I done learnt they's tongue. And I says again, 'Kwadzo.' And he get Monroe to strap me to a post and beat me 'til I say my name Willie, sayin' he need to breaks me. And I done broke."

Willie's sobs would no longer let him speak. Sinking to his knees, he released years of anguish pent up from the theft of his identity. Being forced to take possession of a name not his own was a scar of slavery like any other, one announcing to anyone hearing it his life did not belong to him. But he was not alone.

Countless others had had their identities stripped away in the same way. They needed to be reclaimed.

"You are not broken," he heard Rafazi say. "You are reborn. Leave those white men's names behind you. They were never yours. You are Kwadzo, born on a Monday."

Kwadzo.

His name was Kwadzo. He felt the pain leave his cries, only to be replaced by the joy of hearing Rafazi declare his name's meaning.

"Born on a Monday," Kwadzo repeated, looking up at Rafazi, who was pulling him to his feet.

"What is the name of your kin?" Rafazi asked.

"Okoro," Kwadzo said, and he could hear a sense of pride return to his voice.

"What is your name?"

"Kwadzo Okoro."

"Say it again."

"Kwadzo Okoro."

"You are Kwadzo Okoro. This is the name you will be called by from now on, known by, remembered by. Kwadzo Okoro. He is the one who will free his people."

Pride and purpose collided and bloomed within Kwadzo as he found his smile. Kwadzo. To him, it sounded the same as freedom.

"Thank you," Kwadzo said to Rafazi, whose only response was to grasp his shoulder, but the emotion they both felt was overwhelming. The two men embraced, solidifying their bond and resolve. "This here feeling I got, I ain't think it be mine again. But you done gives it back to me."

"No, Kwadzo," Rafazi said. "You made the choice. I just facilitated it." Kwadzo felt his brow crinkle, and Rafazi smiled. "It means I support your choice."

"Ev'rybody need choice," Kwadzo said. "Whether they wants the Blood or not. And I aims to gives it to them. Ain't no time to wait. This here power, this Blood, it will free our people." The Blood. It brought him back from the dead. It gave him back his name. It could do anything. *He* could do anything. And now, he was finally ready to.

Rafazi smiled. "Then let's go free them."

Twenty-Three

ELIXIR FROM THE GODS

Not sleeping proved unsettling for Kwadzo, as did not breathing or eating. It was a disconcerting thing to be both dead and alive. To somehow feel human but no longer be human. And yet, he looked forward to what was to come. Going into battle meant he would have his first taste of human blood. He was thrilled and, at the same time, frightened to his core.

"You smell that?" Rafazi asked. The two of them had been moving through the wilderness at a moderate pace when Rafazi pulled him behind a patch of trees.

Kwadzo closed his eyes and enhanced his sense of smell. "Blood. Lot of it. They's comin' for us." He noticed there was no tremble in his voice when he said the words. Mere moments ago, he had felt the grip of fear, but it had faded with the scent of blood in his nostrils. He opened his eyes, the red tint returning to his vision. "Why I ain't scared no more?"

"Why would you be scared of a meal delivered on a platter?"

Kwadzo returned Rafazi's smile as he felt venom begin to coat his teeth in anticipation.

"This will be your first fight, Kwadzo," his mentor cautioned. "Your first taste of human blood. It will be like nothing you've ever tasted. Animal blood cannot compare. It will also be your first taste of vengeance. The combination of the two will be exhilarating. So, don't lose your focus. Don't allow yourself to get lost in the blood. It is merely a fight, not our true purpose. And if he is with them, beware of Monroe."

Kwadzo nodded, feeling the rush of adrenaline in his bones, in his blood. Finally, he was in a position to take his revenge against Monroe, something he had imagined so many times before. He just had to avoid the man's blood. In his vengeful elation, he had involuntarily taken on his Ramangan form.

"Temper yourself, Kwadzo," Rafazi said, placing a hand on his shoulder. "You need to show these paddy rollers or whoever they've sent for us that you are a leader. Reserve the monster. Make them be the ones to earn its appearance. You are no longer their Willie. Show them the calm and focus of Kwadzo."

Unclenching his fists, Kwadzo willed his blood to settle, allowing his features to return to their human form. Leaders were composed. Their words carried weight. Physical force was reserved for those who were not civilized enough to hear reason.

Though the white folks called Kwadzo and his people savage, they weren't the ones who locked others in shackles, worked others to breaking in fields, whipped others until they bled, violated the women of others, allowed their dogs to eat others to death. He had seen it time and time again. The generation before him had lived a life of toil and suffering without intervention until they died.

That would change.

They stepped out from behind the trees into a clearing, listening to the approaching horses. "I hears them comin'. Why cain't I's see them?" Kwadzo asked.

"You can," Rafazi replied. "Just like you can hear from great distances, you can see great distances, too. Squint your eyes."

Kwadzo did so, and his eyes adjusted in such a manner he felt the sensation of movement. His sight retained its clarity even as his field of vision stretched ever forward, past trees and bushes, mile after mile, capturing everything from birds nesting in trees to critters scampering across the ground. Then he caught sight of them: a pack of four slave patrolmen on horses and two barking bloodhounds, all being led by Monroe. Kwadzo could see the wrinkles on the man's face as clearly as if he were face-to-face with him.

Suddenly, he was hit by an odor so rancid his nose scrunched up of its own accord. The stench was so foul, he felt a sour churn in his stomach, and his eyes began to water.

"You can smell Monroe's hate now, can't you?" Rafazi asked him.

"It stank somethin' powerful awful!" Willie said, running his wrist across his eyes before closing a hand over his mouth. "You cain't smell it?"

"It's not for me to smell. That hate is for you."

The strength of the smell angered him, and with a grunt, Kwadzo resumed his Ramangan form, his red eyes pulsing. Once again, Rafazi's gentle hand landed on his shoulder.

"Control," the elder Ramangan whispered to him. Kwadzo stilled his blood again and returned to his human form, but his hands were balled into fists. "This will be a golden opportunity for combat training. Remember what I've taught you. Fight the urge to get lost in the blood, and let the stench in your nostrils remind you to stay clear of Monroe's blood. Follow my lead. They'll never see us coming."

Kwadzo caught Rafazi's arm before his blur could take him away. "No. I wants them to see us. I wants to face Monroe down. Then we's do the same to Barrow. Ain't gonna be no more kowtowin'. They come to us."

"By the blood of Gamab," he heard Rafazi whisper, and the words crinkled his brow. "An old expression." Rafazi smiled. "No matter. As you said, let them come to us."

The two men nodded to each other in determination, and Kwadzo realized fear never returned to his mind. He was confident in his patience, waiting for Monroe to discover him. He did not have to wait long.

"Well, well, well! I do declare!"

Monroe's yellow and brown smile had finally reached Kwadzo and Rafazi. Though the stench of Monroe's hate ravaged Kwadzo's senses, he kept his composure, his face straight, his hard eyes fixed upon Monroe.

The overseer brought his procession to a stop in front of Kwadzo and Rafazi, whistling at the barking hounds to keep them at bay. From his perch atop the horse he rode, Monroe smirked down at them, his smile crooked, his cheek bulging. Even with the knowledge of what Monroe's blood could do to him, Kwadzo felt eerily calm. Possessing true power was a strength all its own.

"Y'know, when I sent you to help Ol' Shit Boy, this ain't what I meant," Monroe said.

"But he did help," Rafazi responded. "More than you know."

"Well, Land o' Goshen! Ain't this somethin', boys?" Monroe asked loudly of the paddy rollers with him. "Caught red-handed and still ornery! I reckon y'all thought y'all got away clean, ain't you?"

"You ain't catch us, Monroe. We's been waitin' on you." Kwadzo reveled in his measured voice and the ire it seemed to elicit in the overseer. Mouth agape and brow crinkled, Monroe gawked as if he were searching for insults he could not find.

"Who fixed your face up?" Monroe finally asked in a huff. "Y'all got some nigger-lovin' Quaker abolitionist helpin' y'all out here?"

"No, sir," Kwadzo said, then shook his head at his use of the word "sir." It had been so ingrained in him to show respect to this man who dehumanized him at every turn. "Me and Rafazi here look out for ourselves," he said.

"Do tell," said Monroe, shifting his eyes back to Rafazi.

"Just did," said Kwadzo.

"Rafazi? You mean Shit Boy?"

"Not no more."

"Not no more, huh? You as ornery as you wanna be out here, ain't you? Runnin' 'round like your life belong to you." Despite the bravado, Kwadzo saw uncertainty in Monroe's eyes. "What you got all over you, boy?"

"Blood. I mauled me a black bear some time ago so's I could drink its blood."

"Unbelievable!" In stitches, Monroe turned to the slave catcher nearest him, who was laughing along with him and all the others. "You hear the nonsense comin' out of this here nigger's mouth? Don't that beat all? This boy ain't even a full human, and he got the nerve to talk to me like he think he a white man!" The collective laughter grew louder as Monroe leaned forward on his horse. "I'll tell you this here, Willie."

"Kwadzo."

"What in the hell did you say to me, boy?"

"My name ain't Willie. My name Kwadzo Okoro. And I *ain't* no boy."

"I'ma have me a right good time breakin' your black ass for good," Monroe growled through gritted teeth, veins popping in his neck. "Hell, I reckon I'll be enjoyin' myself so much I'll end up beatin' the black right off you! You could be as bold as a white man all you like then!"

This proclamation made Monroe and the slave catchers crack up with their loudest laughter yet. Kwadzo turned to Rafazi, who simply gave him a wink. Kwadzo remained calm and silent until the laughter died off and remained so until the silence grew awkward.

"Y'done?" Kwadzo asked, prompting Rafazi to chuckle.

"My good sir," Monroe said, addressing one of the slave catchers with him, "would you be so kind as to kill this here uppity nigger? And take as long as you like doin' it."

The burly, bearded man Monroe was speaking to dismounted from his horse. Tall and wide, he crossed to Kwadzo, slowly at first, but soon, he was running. He pulled back a meaty fist and launched it forward with all the might and velocity his big body could summon.

Kwadzo didn't even flinch.

The slave catcher found his fist clamped in Kwadzo's hand, which stopped the man so abruptly, the force propelling him forward caused him to stumble and fall to his knees, his fist still in Kwadzo's grasp. While the slave catcher groaned in pain, Kwadzo kept his eyes on Monroe.

The overseer's eyes went wide as Kwadzo, with a sharp twist, ripped the bearded man's arm off. The slave catcher screamed as blood spurted from his shoulder, and Monroe and the other slave catchers looked on in horror as Kwadzo and Rafazi took on their Ramangan forms.

Kwadzo could feel Rafazi launching himself forward from his side, but his senses were overloaded by the blood, the fresh human blood. Smelling it from a distance was nothing compared to having it right in front of him for the taking. His heightened senses seemed to focus only on the accelerated pumping of the big and burly slave catcher's heart and the blood gushing from him.

Discarding the severed arm, Kwadzo raised the man to his feet by his neck before biting into him deeply. He was immediately seduced by the taste. He couldn't imagine having ever consumed anything else. The more he drank, the more he lusted, and soon, his control was gone. With nothing but the man's heartbeat and the sounds of his own greedy swallowing ringing in his ears, Kwadzo dug his talons deep into the man's large frame, releasing more of his blood.

Blood, this gorgeous red nectar. There was no way he would ever be able to get enough of it. The new Ramangan allowed himself to fall with the slave catcher's body as it toppled to the forest floor, flesh clenched in his fangs and talons. Kwadzo was drenched in the now dead man's blood, sucking it in from every wound, and it was pure bliss. Nothing he had ever experienced had brought him such satisfaction.

He couldn't stop.

He didn't want to stop.

Kwadzo, I need your help.

Rafazi's voice in his head reawakened his senses to the world around him. Monroe, the horses, the hounds—they had all vanished. Kwadzo pushed himself up from the mangled dead body of the man he had killed, the blood still dripping from him.

The man he had killed. His blood-soaked hands shook. Guilt coursed through him—but so did hunger.

He still wanted more.

A gunshot made Kwadzo turn his head toward the sound. Rafazi was surrounded by three rifle-toting slave catchers, all of whom were bloody and bruised from the elder Ramangan's attacks. Two guns were aimed at the stumbling Rafazi while the slave catcher who had fired the first shot was scrambling to pour a second round of gunpowder down the muzzle of his weapon.

The man directly in front of Rafazi fired his rifle as Rafazi slashed him across the face with his talons, tearing the man's face to shreds. The man dropped dead instantly, but the shot had weakened Rafazi more. The third man fired, and Rafazi went down, and in that second, Kwadzo felt like a slave again. The source of his salvation lay slain before him, and the residual fear from his human memory stunted his action.

"What the hell is it?" he heard the third man ask the other remaining as they stood over his mentor's body.

"A goddamn demon if you ask me! Ain't never seen nothin' like it!"

"Did we kill it?"

Their collective breath escaped them as Rafazi's eyes opened, and he uttered but one word:

"Nope."

Grabbing the barrel of one of the slave catcher's guns from his prone position, Rafazi swung it hard and launched the man screaming through the air. Kwadzo's eyes went wide as Rafazi stood, his eyes pulsing red as the lead balls shot into him pushed out from his flesh and fell to the ground.

Spurred by Rafazi's resurgence, Kwadzo ran up behind the other slave catcher, twisted his head, bit into his neck, and feasted on his second human of the night, sending a stream of blood into the night air as he drank the life from him.

Though the flavor on his tongue thrilled him, Kwadzo had learned his lesson from his first encounter with human blood, and he reluctantly pulled his fangs from the neck he was feeding on to pay attention to what Rafazi was doing.

Even with his left leg twisted horrifically from his fall, the last slave catcher Rafazi had launched across the clearing was trying to crawl to safety. But Rafazi stalked after him, grabbing the crawling man's left ankle with one hand and lifting him upside down in the air.

"Please! No! My family! Have mercy on me!" the slave catcher begged.

"And did you give mercy to the slaves you were sent to capture who begged for their freedom?" asked Rafazi. "Or did you take joy in beating them before collecting your reward? Or even ending their lives?"

"Please," the slave catcher implored, "we ain't got much. How else am I supposed to put food on the table for my little ones?"

"Maybe stop fucking your wife. This will help." Blood shot across his face as Rafazi bit into the slave catcher's leg.

Having dropped the man he had been feeding from and leaving him for dead to watch Rafazi, Kwadzo, still drenched in the blood from his latest kill, moved to the elder Ramangan submissively. He found the aroma of the last living slave catcher's blood intoxicating.

"Can I taste him?" Kwadzo asked in a desperate whisper. He lowered his gaze like a reprimanded child as Rafazi shook his head.

"You should see yourself."

Kwadzo looked down the length of his frame. He was sopping wet with blood from head to toe, and still, he wanted more. Rafazi pointed over Kwadzo's shoulder, causing the new Ramangan to turn and look at the body of the first human he had fed from and shudder.

The large man's torso was in shreds, his neck torn open, a look of pure horror in his dead eyes. A look Kwadzo was responsible for, a life he had taken without pause or regret. He recalled Gertie's words of warning.

If'n it make you do what Rafazi done to Butch, it is.

Evil.

He had become her definition of it. But even now, despite being fully sated, he shook with the want to taste the man in Rafazi's grasp.

"You failed, Kwadzo," Rafazi said flatly. "You got lost in the blood. If those whip-crackers would have had silver instead of rifles, they would've ended me."

Shame gnawed at Kwadzo, but not as badly as his need for more blood; he could not keep the red out of his eyes. With a sigh, and with the last slave catcher screaming in opposition, Rafazi tossed the man's body to Kwadzo with one hand.

"Please! Please, no! Don't kill me!" begged the slave catcher whom Kwadzo had caught with both hands.

"Ain't gots power to stop," Kwadzo said, salivating. "It's like elixir from the gods." Lifting the protesting slave catcher over his head, Kwadzo bit deep into his rib cage, ignoring the dying man's cries as he took in the cascading blood until he'd had his fill and then let go of the carcass. Once again, his hands began to shake as the reality of what he'd done set in, and he couldn't take his eyes off the red covering nearly his entire being.

"Gertie say we evil," Kwadzo said, his voice cracking. He was both horrified by his actions, and yet, the blood slaked him. "She say if'n I could do to a man what you's done to Butch, I's evil. And I did. How I's gonna face her again after what I done?"

"I promised Gertie you are still her Willie. But you must learn control. It's good this happened now. Had it happened in battle, we—"

The savage barking of a bloodhound interrupted Rafazi as the dog emerged from the bushes and charged at Kwadzo. Something deep inside him, a large leftover piece of his former self, froze at the sight. Visions of running with Charlie flashed across his mind, visions of Charlie gurgling, choking on the blood in his throat as the hounds—including this hound—ate the life from him.

The dog's jowls clamped around Kwadzo's leg. He yelled out, first in pain, then in anger. He was no longer Willie the slave. He was Kwadzo the Ramangan. If he could take the life of a man, he could do the same to this dog and avenge Charlie.

As the bloodhound dug into the flesh of his leg and lapped up the escaping blood, he punched the dog in the top of the head. The blow brought a whimper from the dog as it dislodged itself from the younger Ramangan's limb. The dog was still stumbling on its legs when Kwadzo picked it up, snapped its neck, and released it, watching it drop like a rock to the ground.

"I take it you don't like dogs."

Rafazi's voice reminded Kwadzo of the pain in his bitten leg. His moves were so fast against the slave catchers, they never got the chance to deliver a blow on him, but the dog had caught him off guard, and its bite went deep.

"Them dogs kill Charlie," he said.

"I heard rumbles about this," Rafazi said, as Kwadzo winced at the pain in his leg, though it was already healing. "You were the one who ran with him. You've been searching for freedom for some time."

"This here leg hurt somethin' awful! It ain't s'posed to hurt this bad, is it?"

"I never said Ramangans don't feel pain," Rafazi said with a chuckle. "But you'll notice the wound is already healing. I imagine your hand healed in a similar fashion after you punched that boulder into pebbles. You are immortal, yes, but immortality does not mean invincibility. There will be pain, but you will heal far faster than any human, even if you suffer a wound fatal to a human. You can even be killed, in a sense, and return again. But the sun, fire, silver, the wood of a willow tree, and, in your case, Monroe's blood—enough of any of these will end your existence. But not a dog, Kwadzo. Never a dog."

Kwadzo smoothed a hand over the blemish-free skin where a minute ago there had been a bloody wound. Yet another Ramangan miracle.

"While you were gorging yourself, Monroe raced away on his horse and with the other dog," Rafazi told him. "I imagine he'll report what he saw directly to Barrow. This could make our goal a bit harder to achieve."

"Monroe don't matter," Kwadzo said. "We needs to get back and make our case . . ." A new scent entered his nostrils, one of fresh blood, robbing him of his focus despite the amount of blood he had already consumed. "I smell more blood."

The whizz of an arrow sounded through the air, and seconds later, the projectile flew past them both, lodging itself into the trunk of a tree inches from where Kwadzo stood. His eyes flashed red, as did Rafazi's, and they peered into the woods, searching through the trees, ready for whatever or whoever was coming next.

Twenty-Four

THE NATIVE

T his carnage of ours will leave an impression on anyone who sees it," Rafazi said. "Five dead white men will be missed. They will see it as an act of war."

"You think they the one's shot the arrow?" Kwadzo asked, keeping his eyes on the woods as a dizziness buzzed in his head.

"No," said Rafazi, "but I do think a better use of our time would be not waiting around to find out. We have more pressing matters."

"We's ain't gonna be waitin' long," Kwadzo said just as a wave of weakness overtook him. He felt his legs give out underneath him. He was tilting toward the tree beside him, the same one the arrow was embedded in, but he could not raise his arm fast enough to brace himself, so his shoulder and side slammed against the trunk, and the red tint left his eyes. His sight went fuzzy, his thoughts murky. He opened his mouth to speak but could form no words. A sinking sense took hold as he felt himself slipping away. Losing the fight against his closing eyes, he saw nothing but black.

The black gave way to red, the same brilliant hue he'd experienced before Ramangan Blood reawakened him. Again, he was engulfed in it. The same feelings of utter bliss consumed him, but now there was something new. The dizziness lifted, and his mind felt clear, energized, ignited. There was a new alertness within his consciousness now.

Kwadzo had never considered himself an intelligent man, but an acute sense of knowledge was surging through him. The last sentence he had spoken ran though his head over and over; it no longer made sense. His brain reworked and rewrote it until he felt speech was possible again. His eyes darted open, their red tint and his consciousness having returned, and he stood straight up.

"I don't think we'll be waiting long," Kwadzo said, looking to Rafazi with a bit of confusion.

"You okay?" asked Rafazi.

"Yeah. Yes," Kwadzo corrected himself. "I said something I could have worded better." The sound of his voice seemed foreign to him. His speech had become clear, clean, concise—the way the Barrows spoke.

The way Rafazi spoke.

"I speak like you now," Kwadzo observed as he felt himself revert to his human form. He hadn't meant to. Perhaps it was because his calm was returning. "Like the white folks. How am I speaking like them?"

"We don't speak like the white folks," Rafazi said with a smile as he also returned to his human form. "We speak through the knowledge of the Blood. Consuming human blood strengthens the body and the mind. A stronger mind speaks strongly and clearly in any language. No matter the tongue you're exposed to, over time, you will master it as well as your mother tongue. The longer the exposure, the easier and more quickly you will master it. The clarity of language will also help you find the words you need. The adjustments the Blood makes can overwhelm the senses sometimes."

"So, that's why you sound the way you do."

"Over the centuries, I've learned many languages. *Je parle français*—"

"*Êtes-vous allé en France?*"

The two Ramangans blinked at each other in shock.

"You responded to me in French," Rafazi said. "How much French have you heard?"

"None. I'd never heard the tongue until you spoke it, but somehow, I knew what you said."

"And how to answer. *Nihongo go wakarimasu ka?*"

"*Nihongowa nan desu ka?*"

"So, it's safe to say this is also the first time you've heard Japanese?"

"I don't even know what Japanese is, Rafazi."

Rafazi cracked up with laughter. "There is no way this is supposed to happen this fast, especially for languages you've only heard one sentence of! This is incredible!"

"Man-blood demons."

The new voice broke through their mirth and shifted their focus to the young man emerging from the trees, his bow and arrow at the ready. No older than twenty-five, his long black hair was fashioned in a ponytail hanging down the length of his back. His skin was darker than the whites but not nearly as dark as Kwadzo's or Rafazi's. His chest was bare, and long, wide straps of animal hide hung from his waist, partially concealing the front and back of his bottom half.

Throughout his years in captivity, Kwadzo had heard tales of the people the white folks called Indians. They were described as savage and deplorable, similar to how his own people were viewed. Some were forced into enslavement while others were slaughtered mercilessly. Some fought back against the white

folk, which told Kwadzo they were fighting *for* something—
something the white folk wanted for themselves, which meant
it belonged to these people first.

Kwadzo could hear how fast the young man's blood was racing. The scent emanating from him was even more desirable
than the blood he'd already guzzled. The young man's blood
smelled sweeter, cleaner. Richer. And Kwadzo wanted it. He pictured himself tearing the man open at the chest and devouring
him whole. He fought back the curl his lips wanted to form at
the thought, fought against the crimson his eyes wanted to flash.

The young man moved closer cautiously. Though the smell
of the archer's blood made venom fill his mouth, Kwadzo knew
the man was undeserving of his bloodlust. Besides, his fright
was warranted if he had seen Kwadzo and Rafazi's display of
violence against the paddy rollers, and it did not need to be
exacerbated.

Only a few feet remained between them and the tip of the
young man's drawn arrow. The quiver in his cheeks was apparent, and Kwadzo took pity on him.

"What was it you called us?" he asked the man.

"Man-blood demons," the young archer repeated as he
looked past them to take in the dead bodies left in their wake.
"Watch you kill. Drink white man blood." The young man
aimed his arrow directly at Kwadzo, the shaking of his hands
becoming more pronounced.

"You speak the white man's language?" Kwadzo asked, lifting
his hands in the air. The young man lowered his aim a bit but
held his ground.

"Must. Only way to know lies," he responded.

"And now you wish to kill us?" Rafazi asked.

"Must protect my people," the young man said.

"And who are your people? The Indians?" Kwadzo asked.

"White man call us Indian. They wrong. We native to this
land."

"You were born here. This is your home," Kwadzo said in realization. The young man nodded.

"White man call land New World," he said. "This land, my people here for centuries."

"We wish you no harm. I understand the need to protect your people." Kwadzo looked with soft eyes at the young man, whose shaking lessened, and his weapon dropped even lower.

"White man has no honor. War over land and bring shame to Great Spirit with power. But your power greater. Ancestors speak of bad spirit, skin-walker, demon, but none born of man."

"We are not bad," Kwadzo tried to reassure him. "We possess the Blood of Ramanga. From the Gold Coast of Africa. The Kingdom of Ghana. I chose to become this way to free our people from the white man."

"You free your people, then go?"

"We have nothing to go back to. We won't go anywhere. We will conquer the white man and take over," said Rafazi.

"You claim land for your people. Like white man." The young man again raised his bow, his hands surer this time. But Rafazi let a small chuckle escape his throat.

"You have seen what we can do. What could you do against us?" The young man lowered his bow once more at Rafazi's response. "This land, it belongs to your people?" Rafazi asked.

"Land belongs to no one. My people sworn to protect it, like ancestors did. We live in peace, white man come, bring fire sticks, kill our people, force us from land."

"Our stories are not so different," Kwadzo said. "The land I once called home was across the sea. The white men who took me from it burned my village to the ground and killed my family. We want the freedom to make new lives for ourselves here without the white man's oppression. When we take down the plantation from the white man, our two peoples can find a way to share this land in peace. Respect and care for it like your people do, and protect your people from any who would rise against you, the same as we would for our own people." Kwadzo extended a hand toward the young man, who took a step back from him. Kwadzo withdrew his hand and held it up again. "My name is Kwadzo. This is Rafazi. What do they call you?"

"Nez."

"I mean you no harm, Nez. I simply wish to make this vow, and you can tell your people they have nothing to fear from us."

Nez nodded and smiled in response. And that was good enough for Kwadzo.

Twenty-Five

A SIMPLE SOLUTION

In his large and luxurious parlor room, Big Jim was having a jovial night in the company of men of high station, largely consisting of other wealthy landowners. And in the Province of Carolina, Big Jim was the wealthiest. Officials appointed by the Crown, like Governor Abraham Collins, knew the true power lay with the landowners. And as an official of the Crown, it was the governor's duty to elect council members to handle the affairs of townships. Big Jim used his considerable wealth and influence with the governor to ensure those put in positions of authority would in turn succumb to *his* authority.

In effect, he *was* the council.

As such, especially in Lakeside, things were done his way. And tonight, his way was a night of revelry in his parlor room. Women, of course, were not allowed to attend these affairs, and no woman was allowed in Big Jim's parlor unless she was there to serve, or, if he so deemed, service. Once the festivities began, the door to the room was locked, and Clarence was given specific instructions not to allow anyone entry unless he was given word to do so by Big Jim himself.

Ale, cider, brandy and wine flowed freely, served by a select number of house slaves, including Irene. They were chosen by Big Jim for their physical charms. Of course, if any of the men wished for a dance to the music being played on the clavichord by the white indentured servant of one of Big Jim's guests, the house slaves would be required to oblige.

With his third glass of brandy so far this night in hand, Big Jim took a long drag on his pipe and allowed himself to relax. His concerns about his runaway slaves would soon be gone. Monroe's presence with them notwithstanding, Big Jim had every confidence the men of the slave patrol would teach those runaway niggers a lesson they would not forget. And he would have their heads severed and hung in slave village as a warning, in case any more of the slaves were thinking of stealing from him.

So, tonight, he took it upon himself to celebrate his impending win. Across the room, he watched Irene bend to serve ale to one of his guests. The shape of her curved bottom lightened his mood. She'd suffered his cold shoulder long enough. He would grace her with a visit to her room later. Yes, it was a jovial night indeed.

"'Tis a fine night for ale and song," Oliver said, plopping down at the foot of the chaise longue upholstered in lush red velvet Big Jim was reclining in. The plantation owner had designed the room's décor around the chaise longue—all dark reds and woods. He'd gone to painstaking lengths to have the room just as he wanted it, so he did not appreciate Oliver spilling ale from his mug onto his imported Persian rug in his drunken state.

"Mind your mug, Oliver." Big Jim sniffed. "Anita!"

A young woman with half a decade's worth of years on Irene

weaved her way through the throng of guests and slaves to heed Big Jim's call.

"Yes, Massa?" she asked with a smile. Where Irene's prettiness came across as naïve, Anita's was more wanton. The fullness of her lips elicited lewd thoughts, and her smile was downright lascivious. Her hair was a wide and wild black bush atop her head. She was a shade or two darker than Irene in complexion but was much more robust in frame.

The raggedy dress she wore clung to her feminine form tightly, and the voluptuousness of her shape caused Oliver to look up at her slack-jawed. While Big Jim preferred women of a slenderer variety, like Irene, he appreciated Anita's appeal. He had stumbled upon her in his son's bedchamber once, her breasts exposed while she vigorously stroked young Thomas's burgeoning manhood. Even the boy had found it difficult to look the slave in her eyes.

"Clean up that ale before it soaks through," Big Jim said to her breasts.

"Yes, Massa," Anita said, pulling out a small rag from an apron tied around her waist. Kneeling and bending to blot up Oliver's mess caused the top of her dress to gape, exposing the swaying décolletage the garment contained.

"How does such curvaceousness come to be wasted on one so inferior?" Oliver asked Big Jim, his eyes remaining on Anita.

"I don't know," Big Jim said. "Personally, I prefer a much less hearty stock."

"But the girth of a woman speaks to her station."

"Yes, it does. And I enjoy the pleasures one can exact from those *below* his station. I find them to be limitless. Although I did indulge in a slave with a plumper rump and found it to be a pleasing experience. A field slave," Big Jim whispered.

"Land o' Goshen, man!" exclaimed Oliver. "You'll rot your cock off!"

"I've had a smashing time, but I must be off."

Big Jim and Oliver both regarded Robert Callowhill approaching them with confusion. Of all those in attendance, he was the only one whose mind seemed to be elsewhere.

"I do you the graciousness of inviting you to my home, and this is how you honor it?" Big Jim snapped.

"I do appreciate your kindness, James," Robert said, "but my wife . . ."

The simple mention of Robert's wife caused Big Jim and Oliver to fall into hysterics.

"Your wife?" Big Jim asked incredulously. "You act as if the woman is in control of you, Robert."

"I would never let something as inconsequential as a wife come between me and merriment. And there is much merriment to be had," Oliver said, scooping Anita up and placing her on his lap. She let out a squeal when he cupped her breasts, crudely hoisting them about. "Does your wife have these, Robert?"

"Nevertheless," Robert continued as though the slave patrol captain had not spoken, "she becomes easily agitated. She is, of course, looking forward to Charity's upcoming soirée."

"Do you honestly think there will be any fun to be had at Charity's stuffy soirée?" Big Jim challenged. "Have any of them ever been fun? Why do you think I built this room, established these nights, and forbade her from both?"

"Surely, she can hear the revelry," Robert countered.

"No woman dictates my actions. Besides, it's a twelve-thousand-square-foot manor," Big Jim said. "There's plenty of house *not* to hear in."

Big Jim and Oliver's laughter was cut short by a banging on the door of the room that grabbed their attention. Clarence jumped at the sound. "Clarence!"

"Yes, sir, Massa, sir." Clarence stumbled up.

"You know what I want!" Big Jim hollered across the room.

"Yes, sir. Forgives me for bein' skittish. Just my nigger nature, I guess." Clarence then hollered at the closed door. "Get, now!

You go on away from here, whoever you is! If you ain't already in here, Massa don't wants you in here!"

"Clarence!" a voice called from the other side of the door. "You open this door!"

"I ain't got but one Massa, and he say don't open this door for nobody!"

"Boss? This here's Monroe. I know it's y'all's council meetin' night, but you gotta let me in. Please, boss! Somethin' awful happened out there in them woods!"

"Impossible," Oliver called out to Monroe. "I gave you my best men."

"And they all dead!"

The clavichord music stopped, and the room fell silent. Big Jim's cheeks went red with embarrassment, but Monroe's declaration left him momentarily stunned.

"Will y'all please let me in? I don't think Madam Barrow is takin' too kindly to me standin' out here yellin' like this. She glarin' at me somethin' awful."

"Perhaps it would be wise to let the man in."

Big Jim winced at the sound of Elder Easton's voice. Because of the man's quiet nature, he'd forgotten about his presence. The preeminent minister of Lakeside, Elder was tall with dark, imposing eyes. His voice always carried an ominous tone and his words even more gloom when he peered over his glasses to deliver them, like he was doing to Big Jim now.

"It would be far more prudent to have your overseer give his account in the privacy of the room than in the presence of a woman. Like niggers, women's minds are feeble, which is why they are prone to such gossip. It's best she not hear what she cannot understand, especially with him speaking of death."

"Perhaps you are right, Minister Easton." A wordless nod instructed Clarence to open the door and let Monroe in. Big Jim saw his wife peeking through the door before Clarence muttered an apology to her and shut it. Monroe was panting and perspiring, but apart from the look of stupor on his face, the overseer seemed unharmed.

"Just as I suspected," Big Jim said, closing in on Monroe. "Not a scratch on you. How is it you somehow escaped death when the others apparently could not?"

"Because they aren't dead!" Oliver yelled. "He's lying!"

"I ain't lyin'! You ain't seen what I seen. If you did, you'da run straight away, too!"

"So once again, cowardice rules your actions," Big Jim growled. "Two runaway niggers miraculously killed four slave catchers while you turned tail and fled."

"Ain't like what you think, boss. You ain't seen what I seen!" Monroe maintained. "They weren't human!"

Big Jim was fuming. It was bad enough his guests had become privy to this information. If word of his runaway problem were to spread beyond this room, more than his business would suffer. His good name and reputation were on the line. And it was Monroe's fault.

"To what do you imply when you say, 'they weren't human'?" The question was posed by Doc Farkus, a meek and timid man, the advance of his years showing in the thin white mop of hair left on his head. A trusted and respected council member, he oversaw all medical matters in Lakeside and trained his students to mend sickly slaves when it was warranted. Big Jim found him strange, but he'd served the community well for many years.

"Doc Farkus raises a pertinent question," Minister Easton said. "Perhaps we should hear Monroe's full account."

"Very well," Big Jim huffed. "Talk. And I urge you to speak the truth."

"Boss, I swear I tell you true, I ain't never seen nothin' like it! I'm tellin' y'all these ain't no normal niggers," Monroe whined. "Them niggers done turned into vampyres!"

For nearly an entire minute, the room was silent. The utter lunacy of Monroe's declaration boggled Big Jim's mind. It was pathetic the lengths to which he would go to, to absolve himself of responsibility for this negligence, and this excuse was beyond asinine.

It was also hilarious.

The first burst of laughter escaped Big Jim by surprise, but he could not stop the next one. Soon, he was laughing in earnest, and most of his guests were doing so right along with him. The laughter became so raucous, Big Jim struggled to catch his breath.

"I can see y'all don't believe me," Monroe continued as the laughter grew louder. "But y'all will when the sun come up, and them men ain't come back. Y'all will believe me when the rest of Mister Gibbs's men go searchin' for them and find their dead bodies!"

The conviction in Monroe's words never wavered. And with the laughter dying down, Big Jim's anger at his overseer's preposterous assertions resurfaced.

"How dare you come up with this outlandish story and use old country nonsense to try and support it," Big Jim seethed. "There's no such thing as vampyres. Those were the tired old tales of bored and stupid old women."

"Begging your pardon, James," Doc Farkus said, "but your overseer's account may not be as far-fetched as you might think." With this simple acknowledgment, Doc Farkus had everyone's attention. "Back in Hungary, my nagyanya told us tales of creatures, once human, who lurked the night in search of blood, but we paid them no mind. Then, as a young man, I encountered one. She was strong and fast, inhumanly so. She, too, was from the darkest depths of Africa; the color of her skin left no doubt. And yet, she carried an air of intelligence I've not seen the slaves possess. Her clothing and demeanor indicated wealth. She spoke my native tongue and revealed her human self to me. And I dare say, for an incredibly dark-skinned woman, she was quite beautiful."

"Did she attack you?" Minister Easton asked. "Take your blood?" Big Jim was astounded at the intensity of interest in Doc Farkus's story. Were the men starting to believe him? Were they starting to believe Monroe?

"She did take my blood, but she did not attack me," Doc Farkus recalled. "She was charming and simply asked for it, assuring me I would leave the experience with my life intact. Being a man of science, of course, I agreed in exchange for information. I wanted to see if she would truly bite into my flesh, ingest my blood. She took on a monstrous form, and her teeth grew sharp and jagged."

"That's right!" Monroe hollered in validation. "That's what I seen!"

"She made a point of making her bite gentle," Doc Farkus continued, "and I experienced a pleasurable phenomenon after the initial breaking of the skin. I watched her swallow, simply fascinated. Afterward, she was quite candid, especially about her vulnerability. An embedment of silver would end her existence, she said; otherwise, she would live forever. Claimed to be approaching fifteen hundred years, though she appeared to be no older than thirty or so. When I questioned her about the past, she seemed to have a detailed knowledge of history. She was the most cultured African I had ever known."

"Yeah, well, Willie and Shit Boy ain't cultured. They just monsters!" Monroe insisted.

None of this was helping Big Jim get to the root of the problem, a problem caused by a mere slave. And now, Monroe's ludicrous claims were being given credence by Doc Farkus, turning the tide of the room to his overseer's way of thinking about these two runaways. But it was all conjecture. Big Jim needed to get to the truth.

"The only way we're going to know what happened is if we find out what happened," Big Jim sighed. "Oliver, Monroe will take you back into the woods . . ."

"No, sir!" Monroe interjected. "You can fire me if you need to, boss, but I ain't goin' back into them woods. No way, no how!"

"If I may be so bold as to offer an alternative, James."

Minister Easton was already staring down at Big Jim again. Of course, Big Jim knew the church was rife with needed repairs the minister couldn't afford, but Elder's standing among the residents of Lakeside was such that he possessed the power to protect or destroy Big Jim's reputation with one sermon.

"Please, Minister," Big Jim said stiffly.

"The Devil's influence cannot be underestimated, James."

"I don't disagree, Minister Easton. But don't you find this all to be—"

Minister Easton raised his hand in silence, and Big Jim tightened his lips. "The Lord is not the only one who works in mysterious ways. Slaves are simpleminded to be sure, but simple minds are fertile soil for Satan's seeds. Let us not forget about the savagery of the Indians living in those woods. I've seen their rituals, which look downright demonic to me. Who knows what influence they may have had on your runaways if they crossed paths?"

"Are you saying you believe Monroe's gibberish?"

"I cannot pretend to know what voodoo wickedness these slave niggers brought with them on our ships, and I don't suppose any of them in here with us would be inclined to tell us. But suppose it is true? Suppose we are dealing with the Devil's wickedness right under our noses? Would it not be wise to take spiritual precautions regardless? We seek the Lord's protection against the vile, and if there is nothing to fear, we've only grown closer to God."

Elder adjusted his glasses and cleared his throat but kept his eyes on Big Jim, whose bluster had weakened a bit under the good minister's stare. "Now, James, I know you to be a man of the Lord, though I have not seen you or your family in His house as of late."

Big Jim fought the urge to roll his eyes. *Here it comes*, he thought. "This I regret, Minister," Big Jim said measuredly. "There has been much to attend to lately. As you can imagine."

"I'm sure. But as many in our community depend on you and the health of your business, so too could the Lord's house benefit. As you may or may not know, the roof is in need of repair, and the wood of my pulpit has seen better days."

"I'm sure it has, Minister."

"Here, then, is my humble suggestion. A more Christ-like solution, if you will."

"Can't wait to hear it."

"Some of the plantation owners bring their slaves to church one Sunday a month to hear the Lord's good words, but we have none scheduled for this coming Sunday, just two days from now. Why not bring your slaves? They can sit on the floor in the back, naturally, and I will preach to them after the regular service and instill proper Christian values into them, counter whatever demonic influence has taken root. This way, the town will see you have your slaves well in hand, and when the men of the slave patrol do retrieve your runaways, they will be made to understand the punishment they receive is handed down from on high."

The minister glanced at the slaves in the room once before turning his gaze back to Barrow. "You may even want to reward the less troublesome slaves with this spiritual treat as opposed to your ornerier ones. Show the troublemakers they have to earn God's grace and start minding you and their overseers. Or maybe even bring a few of the troublemakers, as hearing the Word of the Lord might loosen their lips as to where your runaways are hiding. Put the fear of God into those niggers, and you'll never have to worry about them again."

"Meanwhile, I can gather up resources of silver if it turns out Monroe is correct about them being vampyres," Doc Farkus offered. "I believe our blacksmith is knowledgeable in working with silver. Perhaps they could be captured, restrained, muzzled; I could examine them. Discover the science behind what they are and what they are capable of. Perhaps the secret to our longevity lies in their blood."

"Another excellent idea," Minister Easton agreed with a rare smile. "If these truly are vampyres, knowing more about them will give us control of them. And if they rebel, we'll have the means with which to kill them."

"Quite right," Doc Farkus said with a gleeful giggle. "I shall tell the blacksmith straight away."

With a sigh, Big Jim nodded to Clarence, who let Doc Farkus out. Robert was all too quick to follow. Big Jim didn't like any of this, but all things considered, he had little choice left.

"Then I'll be seeing you at church," he said to Minister Easton, who responded with a raise of his glass.

"This is an occasion of mirth and merriment," the minister declared. "Let us have music!"

The playing of the clavichord resumed, but Big Jim's jovial mood had passed.

I don't rightly know
how to love a killer.

Twenty-Six

Before Daybreak

Time was growing short for Irene and Anita as they raced across the Barrow property under the moonlight. Big Jim had become so perturbed by the whole business of Monroe's claims, he had rushed all his guests out of the manor as soon as it had seemed proper. He had been barking at the house slaves to set about cleaning the parlor room when he was confronted by, and thrust into an argument with, his wife.

This all created the perfect storm of chaos for Irene to rally a few slaves like Anita she was sure would be open to Rafazi's promise but who were staying behind to keep Clarence occupied while she and Anita took off. Of course, Irene knew Monroe's account meant the revolution had already begun, which meant Willie and Rafazi would be coming back, which meant she would be turned.

"How you knows they gonna be there?" Anita asked as they ran past the pantry house. Anita was never one to take part in

ridiculing Irene for her predicament with Big Jim like some
of the other house slaves did. Irene suspected it was because,
though Big Jim never fancied Anita, he was aware many of his
friends did. The poor woman was being groped and prodded
every time Irene saw her—and some of the slave men were as
bad as the white men. The dalliances Anita had shared with
Derby didn't do her reputation any favors either.

"'Cause they done killed white men," Irene said, stopping at
the cookhouse to catch her breath. "Ain't no comin' back from
that. But Rafazi say they can't survive sunlight, so we gotta
hurry!"

"Shit Boy is a Ramanga?" Anita chuckled. "He ain't but a lil'
thing."

"He ain't seem so little when he rip Butch's heart clean out
his chest. And his name Rafazi."

"Who named Rafazi?

Irene spun with a yelp of surprise to find Rosana stepping
out of the cookhouse. Of the three women, Rosana's skin was
the darkest, but she was still several shades lighter than the bulk
of the field slaves. Tall, stout, and probably in her fourth decade,
Rosana wore a patch over her right eye to hide the injury she
had suffered from Thomas's malicious sense of humor, the reason she had come to be called Ol' Patchy.

"Rosana!" Irene gasped. "You scared the life outta me! What
you doin' out here this time of night?"

"Damn room Massa got us all crammed in get too hot,"
Rosana huffed. "But I s'pose you wouldn't know nothin' 'bout
that, now, would you?" Irene ignored the slight. "I come sleep in
the cookhouse when it get to be too much. Where y'all runnin'
off to?"

"Slave village," Anita said with a lilt of excitement in her
voice. "Irene say Willie and Shit Boy is turned Ramanga, they
done killed Butch, and now they gonna come back to free us!"

"You say Ramanga?" Rosana asked.

Irene nodded. "Shit Boy's true name Rafazi, and I seen him turn with my own eyes. They plannin' a revolt, and they gonna turn me. But we gots to get to slave village before . . ."

"Daybreak." Rosana's face was filled with awe, but her eyes were wide with fear, her mouth agape, her nostrils flaring. "'Cause they's cain't survive the sun."

"You know 'bout Ramanga?" Irene asked.

"My kin in Mali taught us to fear the gods," Rosana said quietly. "The god of life, death, and renewal be the great Gamab. My kin say the Ramanga Tribe his descendants, say he made them with his blood."

"They's gods?" Anita asked enthusiastically.

Irene's breath caught. Rafazi had promised Willie would turn her. Would she become a goddess?

"Will he turn me, too?"

Irene was taken aback by Rosana's sudden request. "This ain't for the weak of heart, now, Rosana."

"I ain't weak! I's sick of this here place. Works us like dogs and treats us worse. And I gots me a headache where my eye used to be ev'ry day thanks to Massa's nasty boy. If'n what you say is true, I want every part of it. No matter what I gots to do."

Irene could only smile. "Well, c'mon then!"

SLEEP ELUDED GERTIE FOR the third straight night. Not that the days were any better. She had forced herself through her exhaustion to work even harder on the paddy. Anything to distract herself from the nightmarish visions she could not shake during her waking hours. With blood permeating her thoughts when she was awake, she didn't dare sleep for fear of what she would see in her dreams.

In these quiet moments at night, lying restlessly in her cot, when there was no one to plead her case to, she tried to remember the father of her child with fondness, but his grave decision vexed her to no end. He professed his love for her and their baby. So, why weren't they enough for him to take comfort in? How had she failed him?

Or had he wanted to become a killer all along?

She ran a hand over her belly. *I don't mean to think ill of your daddy*, she thought. She turned on her side, her fists, stomach, and heart in knots. She still ached for Willie, his touch, his love. But as much as her heart ached with desire for him, it also ached from his betrayal and abandonment. There was nothing she could rely on now besides her convictions.

And yet, a part of her, one deep in the pit of her broken heart, held out hope he would come to his senses—as much as a dead man could—and come to understand the folly of his ways.

"Gertie?"

Her eyes darted open. Her breath caught in her throat as she looked upon the vision in front of her.

Willie.

She could only see his face, but it was normal again. The face of the man she loved, smiling warmly at her. And, for a moment, all her questions, all her convictions disappeared. She was simply happy to see him alive and returned to her. Just as she hoped.

"I thought I's never gonna see you again," she sighed dreamily.

"Impossible. My thoughts never left you."

There was something different about him, something new. In place of his tempered rage was composure, a quiet confidence. His eyes were full of determination, purpose. He even sounded different.

"You different," she breathed, placing her palm against his cheek. His skin was warm. Real.

"I know. My speech. I sound like the white folks to you."

It was true, but there was more to it. "But somethin' else, too. Likes you clear of mind."

"I *am* clear of mind, Gertie. I'm in control of who and what I am. I'm clearer than I've ever been. And the point I'm clearest on is you. I know we've had our differences, but they don't matter to me. All I want is to love you and our child as deeply as I can."

His words coated her heart like honey. "There you go again, just a-jibber jawin'." But she couldn't stop herself from smiling. She touched his lips with her fingers, but she hesitated to kiss him. As much as she wanted to believe what was happening was real, she could not shake the things she'd seen, the things she knew, the things she didn't know. Two nights he had been gone. She did not know if human blood had passed through his lips, and she was afraid to ask. She began to wonder what state his clothing would be in if he were to stand from his kneeling position. She was terrified it was covered in blood.

"I've reclaimed my true name," he said rather abruptly. Gertie didn't know what he meant, so she didn't know how to respond. The bravado in his voice when he said the words, however, sobered her. The loving haze she had felt when she first saw him was beginning to fade.

"Ain't seen you in two nights," she ventured, steeling herself. It wasn't a question she wanted to ask, but she had to. "What y'done since you's been gone, Willie?"

He smiled, but she noticed he'd winced when she'd said his name. "You'll find out," he said. "Come out behind the breeding rooms, quick, before daybreak. It's finally time, Gertie."

Before she could ask him what it was time for, he was gone in a flash, and the wrong kind of ache returned to her heart.

Twenty-Seven

TOO HIGH A PRICE

A large group of slaves had gathered behind the breeding rooms by the time Gertie arrived. Nearly all the field slaves—both rice and cotton—were present, along with Irene and a couple other house slaves. They murmured incessantly as they gawked at Rafazi and Willie, and Gertie felt her stomach sink at the sight of them. They were covered in dried blood. Willie had tasted blood.

He had killed.

She had felt so warm in his presence when he first returned, so hopeful. But it was a mirage, a dream. A lie. Her Willie was still being driven by Ramangan blood and Rafazi's disastrous plan. She watched the two of them, standing before the slaves as if they were on display on the auction block, making themselves a spectacle.

"You looks mad enough to spit," Derby whispered to her. His voice was soaked in the smirk he was wearing. But she didn't respond. She didn't want to miss a word Willie was going to say. "Don't you worry none," Derby continued. "I's been tellin' folks to stay 'way from whatever Ol' Willie gonna tell them. He ain't gonna snatch nobody up this night, I's gonna make sure of it."

Gertie turned to him with a sigh. He stood straighter, flexing his bare chest muscles, which were directly level with her eyes. He was showing off as much as she was sure Willie was about to. It didn't impress her. "I know you gots designs on me, Derby," she said, "but I gots too much else to be worried 'bout."

"Ain't none of your worry somethin' I cain't lighten the load of?" Derby asked, running a hand across her hair. She wondered if Willie could see what was happening, if he would still be inclined to do something about it if he did.

Gertie tightened her jaw. She thought of telling Derby about the baby, but she wasn't sure if it would make him leave her alone or dig in his heels. "I 'preciate you's takin' my side in all this here, but it cain't be nothin' else. Y'hear me?"

"Mm hm. You say what you say now, but it don't takes long for womenfolk to lean on Ol' Derby." He smiled as he slipped away to lose himself in the crowd.

"Y'all hush now!" Tussy called out, causing Gertie to turn away from where Derby had been standing, and the murmurs died down. "If them overseers get wind of us, we's done for!"

"Tussy's right," Willie began. He seemed nervous to Gertie. "We don't have much time. But if you all take what Rafazi and I say to heart, we'll have all the time in the world. First, I want to apologize to all of you who work on the paddy. Knowing Monroe as I do, I'm sure my absence, combined with Rafazi's, and the broken cage probably brought you trouble meant for me. I'm truly sorry, and I am here to make it right. Once and for all."

"Time's a'wastin'!" someone in the crowd called out. "Is you Ramanga or ain't you, Willie?"

The murmurs rose again and grew more insistent, but this time, Willie simply raised his hand for quiet and got it. Gertie wondered if he'd placed them under a Ramangan spell she was somehow immune to.

"Willie is dead. He should have never existed," he said, bringing a lump to Gertie's throat. "It was nothing more than a name given to me against my will by the man who called himself my master because he didn't want to pronounce my real name, Kwadzo. So, I killed Willie and resurrected Kwadzo. And the one who made it possible is the man beside me. Some of you may have known him as Shit Boy, but his name is Rafazi, and he was the last surviving member of the Ramanga Tribe."

Gertie was wiping away hot tears of anger. Her true name was not Gertie, and she could not remember the last time she'd heard the name of her birth spoken aloud. But dwelling on that would do as much good as dwelling on the family that death took from her. The past can never be changed.

Gertie was the name given to her in this New World. It was the name Willie whispered to her in the throes of their passion, sending shivers down her spine. The name he knew her by, just as she had known and fallen in love with him as Willie. His name had meaning for her, as she had hoped hers had meaning for him. It was the name of his life here, the one she knew, the one she was a part of. Kwadzo was the name of his death.

She would have no issue standing against Kwadzo.

"I'm not the only one who was taken from. They've taken from all of us—our home, our families, our dignity, our freedom. But Ramangan Blood can give it all back to us."

The mumbling among the slaves returned. Gertie steeled herself. She could not, would not, allow Kwadzo to hand out death sentences. She started making her way through the crowd until Derby caught sight of her and made a path for her.

"You comes back here, talkin' fancy like the white folks talk, talkin' 'bout Ramanga savin' us all, but we's know good and well

Ramanga ain't nothin' but evil," she spoke up once she got to the front.

A considerable faction of the slaves chimed up in agreement with Gertie. She kept her eyes on Kwadzo, who seemed shell-shocked under her gaze—so much so it made her heart lurch. She had to remind herself: This was not her Willie; this was Willie's killer.

"The last time some of you saw Kwadzo, when you knew him as Willie, his eye was swollen shut, and his back was ripped up from Monroe's whip," Rafazi said, then turned to Kwazdo and added, "Show them now."

Kwadzo pulled off his blood-stained shirt and spun slowly so everyone could see his fully mended back. Gasps rose through the crowd. "My sight is sharper, and I am faster and stronger than I've ever been," he told them. "I'm stronger than any white man who has ever put me on a ship, worked me in a field, or whipped me where I stood."

He stopped to look around at the gathered crowd. "Yes, we did run from this place, but we've come back to take vengeance, to give purpose to the Blood. To get justice for every wrong done to us. To take back everything they took from us and claim what should be ours. *We* are the ones who make this plantation what it is. *We* are the ones who built that manor we aren't allowed to enter. *We* are the reason Barrow is as rich as he is. And while *he* eats the pork and beef we prepare for him, he serves *us* mush in the troughs like animals!"

Heads began to nod. Small exclamations of agreement rose, and the sounds of encouragement spurred Kwadzo on. "They destroyed all we knew and brought us here to this land. So be it. What I want for us now is to stake our own claim, make our own way. I want us to take down this man who makes us call him 'Master,' and end his reign over us!"

The murmurs of excitement were growing within a smaller faction of those gathered, but Derby was moving through the bigger group, whispering as he went, reminding them of the truth, just as he said he would, and for this, she was grateful. She could not allow Kwadzo's rhetoric to take hold. She had to protect them from the evil he had become.

"All that fancy talk make y'all forget what Willie say?" Gertie asked, turning to face the gathered slaves, her back to Kwadzo.

"Willie was my plantation name," he said in a low voice, as if she'd offended him. "My name is Kwadzo."

"He say he done killed Willie," she continued, purposefully ignoring him. "And he ain't lyin'. I seen him do it. I was there. I seen him drink Rafazi's blood and then let Rafazi crack his neck and kill him. When Willie come to, eyes red, his whole face done turn evil! Y'all remember them stories 'bout Ramanga? Well, he right 'bout them bein' true. The *worst* parts be true. Look at they's clothes. That's blood they gots on them! They feeds on blood. Ain't nothin' more evil!"

"They ain't evil!"

Gertie could feel her nostrils flare as Irene defended them. "Child, hush!" she spat.

"I done told you before I ain't no child!" Irene snapped back. "You done spoke your piece, now I gots to say what I gots to say." Gertie's jaw tightened. If Irene's pretty face started swaying the men, Gertie would have to fight twice as hard.

"I was there, too," Irene began. "And the only reason I was is 'cause Willie, I mean, Kwadzo, save my life. I threw myself in the lake after Barrow threaten to kill me."

"By crushin' you underneath him?" one of the menfolk called out. A smattering of snickers followed, and Gertie saw Irene's eyes change. They narrowed under her furrowed brow, and with her arm outstretched and her finger thrust forward, she turned slowly, accusatorily, at the crowd.

"Y'all gonna listen at Gertie when she talk, but I's just a high yellow whore to y'all, right? Y'all think I like that fat old man climbin' on me? Huh? Y'all think I ain't retching the second he leave me be? Y'all think 'cause I got this here light skin, I got it better. Better how? It ain't light enough for the white folks and ain't dark enough for y'all, so what's better? If all y'all hate me, where I belong?" She stopped to let her words sink in.

"Y'all think us in the house got it better? It's worse! They feel like yellin' or beatin' on somebody, we's right there. Barrow feel like gettin' his cock wet, what I's s'posed to do? Best I can hope for is he do what he do quick and don't leave a child in my belly. That's all the life I got. Ain't no house slave got it no better. And we's just as deservin' of freedom as anybody else! Now, I don't know 'bout y'all, but I's ready to let it be and fight for a new life. A free one."

Her argument gained the smaller faction a few more members.

"You ain't say a untrue word, Irene," Gertie said softly. "I ain't wish what they done to us on nobody, but it ain't 'bout them. It 'bout findin' good in the life we been givin'. Bein' good is all we got. I ain't sayin' I don't wants freedom; ain't a slave 'live that don't. But if'n we do this here, do the same to them, it don't make us no better."

"Then what we s'posed to do, Gertie?" Minor stepped forward and asked.

"I don't rightly know," she admitted. "But not this here."

"Gertie right. Freedom ain't freedom if'n you gots to become a dead thing to live," Derby said. "Don't nobody wish on Irene what she done suffered, but Gertie tryin' to tell y'all it ain't worth givin' up life."

Rafazi began to chuckle, and they all stared at him. "Forgive me, I forget how young you all are. I've existed on this earth for more than seven centuries. I remember what your ancestors were like before they turned against one another for the gold of the white man, before outsiders grew bold enough to invade our land as if it were their own, taking what they wanted without consequence. I remember the pride and strength of our people. But people have limitations. Ramangans have far less. And if we band together, we can—"

"We can what?" Gertie interrupted him. "Die?"

"How we know you's Ramanga anyway?" Derby challenged. "You don't look like much to me." Sounds of agreement from the larger group, which Gertie now stood in front of, rose.

"So, you doubt me, do you?" Rafazi asked as his eyes went red to the sound of gasps. "Do you doubt this?"

Before anyone could blink, Rafazi and Derby were gone. It was Derby's screams that drew their eyes upward where Rafazi was perched on the wide, thick branch of a nearby tree, several feet above the ground, holding Derby by the neck.

With his arm outstretched, Rafazi, now a monstrous sight, held Derby's considerable weight in one hand with ease while Derby dangled in the air, his feet kicking for purchase that wasn't there, his arms wrapped desperately around Rafazi's forearm, begging not to be dropped.

Amid the slaves' frightened murmurs, the small group standing with Irene, which included Tussy and Fanna, looked on with small smiles. The sight of elation on the young girl's face at such malice troubled Gertie deeply. She had already been through more than any child should even know about. If this wickedness took hold, it would destroy her.

Breath escaped Gertie's lungs as Rafazi released Derby, allowing him to fall toward the ground. In moments, the Ramangan became a blur, racing down the tree trunk until the blur overtook Derby, grabbed him, and plunged them both into the earth, only to explode back up to the surface several feet away.

Though his disposition was calm, Rafazi's visage remained frightful, and his red eyes pulsed. He let go of Derby, who was shaking in fright, covered in dirt, and coughing up still more. Gertie rushed to his aid as Derby fell to his knees.

"Thank you kindly, Rafazi," Gertie said to him before turning to the others, who were looking on in shock. "There. Now y'all see what monsters they is, what they wants us to be. If'n we do this here, it gonna get *us* killed is what it gonna do!"

"This power is our chance to be free, Gertie. Why can't you see that?" Kwadzo sounded like Willie with his plea, but Gertie refused to be deceived.

"'Cause it ain't *freedom*," Gertie said, her voice rising with indignation as she rose to her feet. "You gots to kill to live now. That's evil. And cain't no *good* come from *evil.*"

"That man rose from the dead still lovin' you," Irene snapped, "and this how you act?"

"If'n he *loved me*, he wouldn't never have died!" Gertie avoided Kwadzo's eyes, even though she could feel them on her. She feared one look from him would break her.

"Y'all done gone 'round in the same circle for long enough, now," Tussy sighed. "You 'bout run outta night, so if'n you gots you a scheme, you best get to it."

Gertie could no longer avoid him. It seemed a hopeless ploy to say anything more, but something deep in her heart was telling her to try. "Just let me say this here," she said, finally facing him again, before she lost her nerve, before sobs took hold of her. "Y'done made your choice. You change your name, what you is, and you cain't change none of it back. But you cain't ask nobody else to be what you is. It ain't natural. It ain't right."

The tiniest of voices cried out from within Gertie as she looked upon the monster who was once her Willie. *Come back,* the voice whispered, but it was dying. Then, his eyes, the last part of him she still recognized, changed. For the shortest of moments, they flashed red, and when they were human again, they were cold, hard, the eyes of a monster. Willie was truly gone. She was grateful when he looked away from her and took in the gathered throng. She didn't think she would have been able to take his look much longer. Maybe, never again.

"Gertie's right," he said softly, his voice so much like Willie's her heart tightened with grief. "I chose darkness. I did it so I could live in the light. So Gertie could; so we all could. She wants to do good, be good, but the truth is, our good is not recognized in this world, not by these white folks. They call us black, the color of evil to them. Now, whether black has always been evil to them, or it's become evil because of what they think of us, it doesn't matter. They've decided our fates for us based on their beliefs and built a world where we cannot win. There is no reward for being good, not for us."

"Vengeance ain't no better," Gertie whispered, choking back a sob.

"I'm not after vengeance, Gertie. I want retribution. We were put on this earth, same as them, but they have all the say, decide when they can take a life, violate the woman I love, the mother of my child?"

Gertie's eyes shot up at this Kwadzo. She heard his voice crack, saw his body tremble. She could see he hadn't meant to reveal the knowledge of the child inside her, but this, too, was another thing he could not take back. "What gives them the right? Every good we do here is met with evil. So maybe it takes evil to defeat evil."

Gertie didn't know when her hands went to her belly, but when she hung her head, unable to stop the flow of her tears, she saw them clasped around the last thing she had left in this world.

"Tussy asked what our plan is, and it's a simple one," Kwadzo continued. "This land we work, the manor we built, we should benefit from our sweat. Barrow will not give us what is ours, so we will take it. We can't all take the Blood, and we shouldn't. But this fight is a fight for all of us. Our people need to continue on in the natural way, and those of us with the Blood will protect our people, our humans, for all time.

"We won't force anyone. Doing so would make us as bad as

the white man. But those who are willing can join Rafazi and me in the Blood. We will train you in your new power and build a Ramangan force to push Barrow out. The manor will become our stronghold against any opposition.

"Some of you have heard about the peoples who were here before the white man brought us here. This land, all the land where plantations stand across the colonies, is stolen land. So, together with the Native peoples, we will care for and nurture it and build lives for ourselves. Free lives without oppression.

"Make no mistake, this *will* be war. Once they feel our power, they will strike back to kill. Those who take the Blood must be prepared to answer back in kind. Daylight approaches, so you must choose now."

"Well, it 'bout time you got 'round to askin'!" Tussy exclaimed. "Yes, sir!"

Gertie called out to her, but Tussy stood firm as she took her place by Kwadzo's side. "Don't you come at me with that evil talk, Gertie! This here Ramanga no more evil than the evil we lives with now. Might as well be dead. Not a one of them would think twice 'bout killin' any of us. Why should we? And blood cain't taste no worse than the mush Massa give us."

"Once you're turned, it will be the best thing to ever coat your tongue," a smiling Rafazi said to Tussy. It turned Gertie's stomach. Irene and more slaves from the smaller faction voiced their accord and joined Kwadzo and Rafazi, as did Minor.

"Y'all can turns me, too," he grumbled. "And I's takin' back my name like Kwadzo done!"

"What is your true name?" Rafazi asked, putting an arm around his shoulder.

"Ekow," Minor revealed with a choke of sadness. "Ekow Tetteh."

"Ekow Tetteh," Rafazi repeated. "Born on a Thursday."

"Like 'Willie,' we will kill 'Minor' so Ekow can be resurrected," Kwadzo said.

"Good." Ekow nodded.

As choices were made, two groups among them became clear, so clear they stood separate from one another. The lion's share of them remained behind Gertie while those who had chosen Ramanga stood behind Kwadzo. Only Fanna stood between the two groups, unaligned.

"Don't you dare," Gertie hissed at Kwadzo, holding out her hand to Fanna. "Come on, child. You ain't gots to worry 'bout none of this here foolishness."

But Fanna didn't move. She stared back at Gertie for what felt to her like an eternity, her eyes growing harder every second.

And then she turned to face *him*.

"Is I too young?"

Fanna's question burned a hole through Gertie's heart. Her eyes shifted up to him, and her head turned determinedly from side to side. Her ears burned from the one word howling inside her head.

Yes.

But she wouldn't dare speak it. Instead, she would let "Kwadzo" show his true nature. If he said yes, it would prove humanity still resided in him—and with it, hope. But if he said no, it would be evidence of his monstrosity no one would be able to deny.

"You weren't too young to be stolen."

All heads turned to Rafazi, who moved to the girl, kneeling to face her. "Weren't too young to work, to beat, to violate. And he did violate you, didn't he?" Fanna nodded as tears escaped her eyes. "Do you want revenge?"

"What revenge?" Fanna asked.

"It means you want to punish him for what he did to you."

"Fuck him up?"

"Fuck him up, indeed." Rafazi stood and extended a hand to Fanna. With a last look to Gertie, she took his hand and followed him behind Kwadzo.

"She will be protected by all of us," Kwadzo promised. Gertie knew the words were directed at her, but she never saw him speak them because her head was hanging in defeat, her mind and heart exhausted. "Us fussing the way we've been, Gertie? It's happening because of their *hate*. They've been ruling over us with hate for nearly a hundred years. One hundred years of hate, raining down on us day after day, after day. We turn against each other and end up making it easier for them to tear us apart. They've been doing it to our people since they brought us to these shores. Hope keeps us waiting for them to change, but they are never going to. *We* have to change *them*. We have to change our own fate. What I am now will."

"Show me." Gertie had grown so weak, she could barely hear her own voice.

"Show you?"

"Show me what you truly is!" She raised her head and threw the words at him through gritted teeth, in a burst of anger-fueled energy. "Show them *all!*"

Kwadzo complied and took on his Ramangan form amid gasps of shock. Rafazi was not as known to the slaves as her Willie had been. For them to see him become this Kwadzo, this monster, would reveal the evil he was without doubt. "Now answer me this here. Would you ask your child to be what you is? Would you ask your own flesh to die like y'done? Drink blood like y'done?"

He looked down at himself, the stained blood on his clothing, the talons extending from his fingertips, but he would not look at her.

"I cain't," she cried, no longer able to control the waves of sorrow swelling within her, barely capable of forming her words. "I cain't . . . our baby . . ."

He reached out to her, but she backed away. "Y'done tasted blood, Willie. You's a killer, now. I don't rightly know how to love a killer. And if'n you kill Fanna, you gonna have a child's blood on your hands."

"I will keep her safe, Gertie."

"How she gonna be safe? You 'bout to kill her."

Gertie felt Derby's dusty arm go around her as she turned her back on Kwadzo. Though she walked away with the bulk of the slave population, she felt defeated. She had lost Fanna and Willie. Her sobbing never abated.

There was nothing more she could do.

Welcome to the Blood.

Twenty-Eight

TWENTY-THREE

Kwadzo helped Rafazi pull the last of those who had chosen the Blood to her feet, making her the twenty-second. Twenty-two out of nearly three hundred remained with him.

There were more before he had begun offering his blood to them to drink. The sight of it proved too much for eight who chose not to take his blood. When Rafazi explained the dangers of sunlight and silver and the burrowing underground until nightfall required of all who were turned, seventeen more decided against the Blood. Once Tussy's neck was cracked—the first of them Kwadzo turned—and she dropped to her death, eleven more ran back to slave village.

Kwadzo remembered the feeling: the fear he had felt when the first of his neck bones cracked, the tranquility he had felt when he was floating in the Red, the rush of relief when he realized only his human life had come to an end, not his existence. Soon, those who remained would be seduced by blood.

Then, they would be made killers.

Just like Gertie said.

He didn't know if these twenty-two would be enough, but they did seem earnest, especially Tussy and Irene, both of whom were now discovering the power of their blurs. They were rushing through the trees, shouting in joy as Rafazi encouraged them to embrace their newfound speed and freedom.

"As you may have noticed, the time it takes to awaken from the Blood varies from person to person," Rafazi was telling those who had awakened amid the rush of Tussy and Irene's blurs zipping through the wilderness. "For some, it's immediate. Others can take days. Likewise, some Ramangan abilities can manifest at different times depending on the person as well."

Three remained in the Red: Juba, the last one they'd pulled from the ground; Rufus, a sickly, elderly man when he was alive; and Fanna, whose current state conjured up all of Gertie's words against him over and over in his head.

Evil.

Wicked.

Killer.

There was no love in the words she had spoken. Everything he had done, this choice he had made, was for her and their child, and in the end, he'd lost her for it. He'd watched Derby put an arm around her as she walked away, and she never moved away from him, never shrugged his arm off her shoulders. Despite her assurances to the contrary, he had been replaced.

There was no denying he'd become a killer now. But he was also the one who had made a vow to free and protect his people along with the land and the Native peoples it had been taken from. A vow to free and protect Gertie and their child. She could not take the biological fact of their baby growing inside her away from him, dead or not.

If she had truly turned her back on him, he decided to view it as a liberty. There was no longer any need for him to reckon his actions with her beliefs. He would exact justice how he saw fit. Kill as he saw fit. No matter what she thought of his decision, he'd made it for a reason. And he would fulfill his promise, regardless.

She could do good.

He would do *right*.

A loud, dull thud and a groan of pain pulled Kwadzo from his thoughts and his gaze to the trunk of a nearby tree where Tussy lay prone in the grass, rubbing her forehead. "I's fine," she croaked while a few chuckled at her predicament, including Rafazi, who moved to help her to her feet. "I's doin' fine 'til . . ."

"You started thinking about how to make it through," Rafazi surmised, and Tussy nodded. He turned his attention to the group. "You can and must always trust your Ramangan vision. It will never fail you. We will guide you all through it, but know this: The actions of fighting, hunting, and the use of your speed will come to you naturally. You are all predatory creatures now, ingrained with the instinct to use your power to feed. What we are here to do is help you harness it. Control it. Right, Kwadzo?"

Kwadzo blinked. There were twenty-two of them, all of whom had taken his blood. He was responsible for their existence and would be leading them into what would most assuredly become war, one in which he had no true idea of what they would face.

Kwadzo had only been a Ramangan for a few days himself, and he knew so little, yet he was expected to be their leader. There was not enough time to teach them what they needed to know, but it didn't matter. Their people were suffering. They needed to act—and fast. They needed to win. But first, they needed to know they could.

"It's true," Kwadzo said. "We are all dead, and as dead men and women, Barrow owns us no more. Our disappearance from the house, the fields, and the paddy in this great a number will not go unnoticed. And you can be sure Monroe and the rest of those whip-crackers will make those left behind pay for our absence. So, we owe them the plantation and their freedom."

"You will be amazed at what you are capable of," Rafazi added. "Taking the plantation and the manor is just the start. With the power running through your veins, our veins, we can be more than free. We can rule the world!"

It was a heady thought to be certain. But amid the murmurs of excitement from the nineteen gathered, Kwadzo knew it was folly to focus on anything other than this first victory.

"If you plannin' on attackin', you should wait 'til after Missus's soirée start," said one of the former house slaves he'd heard Irene call Rosana. "She havin' it tomorrow night. We's been workin' our fingers to the bone for it."

"Monroe ran back and told Barrow what y'all done in the woods," Irene added. "One of them white men he was entertainin' said he knew 'bout your kind and sent word to the blacksmith to make them swords of silver."

"Silver?" Rafazi asked. "But they don't have them yet?"

Irene shook her head, and Kwadzo filled with urgency.

"Then the perfect time to strike is tomorrow night, like Rosana suggested. Before they get those swords," Kwadzo said. "Barrow is sure to invite upstanding Lakeside citizens."

"You mean other slave owners," Rafazi said. "Doesn't give us much time."

"We can't take too much time either. Besides, their defenses will be down; they'll never expect us. We'll take the manor and cut the head off Lakeside's proverbial snake."

"Provera . . . what? What word you say, Kwadzo?" Ekow asked.

"You'll learn soon enough," Kwadzo assured him before zeroing in on the former house slaves. "We'll give you three a little different lesson tonight. We're going to teach you a little mind bending because I'm going to need you to go back to the manor."

"What? No, Kwadzo! I wanna stay out here with you!" Irene said, and Rosana and the third former house slave, whom Kwadzo had heard Irene refer to as Anita, vocally concurred.

"It's to avoid suspicion."

"But what if'n they already knows we gone?" Anita asked.

"Then you'll bend their minds," Rafazi said. "We'll teach you. Just like I did with Barrow's boy. You remember, Irene."

"Rafazi made him forget takin' his blood," Irene told the other two, smiling.

"You drank from Massa's boy?" Anita asked Rafazi with wide-eyed shock.

"It was an eventful night," said Rafazi with a wink.

"Above all else, remember: Stay inside once you get back. Avoid the sun, flame, and silver at all costs. We'll also teach you how to communicate with your mind, which is how I will communicate with you before we strike. So don't attack until you hear from me," Kwadzo said, staring at Irene.

"What you lookin' at me for?"

"Because I know you want to tear Barrow limb from limb, and it will be difficult not to with the power you now have. But we will lose the element of surprise if you do. We have no idea what kind of chain reaction this could set off. And since there will only be three of you there of the Blood, I don't want any of you, or any of our humans, put in unnecessary danger."

"Then I'll turn more." The mischievous curve in Irene's smile amused Kwadzo, and he relented, but remained firm.

"Turn those you find willing, but they will become your responsibility, like you are mine. And the same rules apply. Agreed?"

Irene's nod was sufficient for Kwadzo, who watched resolve creep across the nineteen faces before him. Gertie's words, which minutes ago were screams in his head, became whispers, albeit persistent ones. There was only one night to ready them for battle. To ready himself.

It will be enough, he heard Rafazi say in his head, giving him a smile full of determination. *It will have to be.*

And so it would.

"There are some basics you will need to know—" A growl of pain escaped Ekow as he doubled over and fell to the ground, halting Kwadzo's words.

"I's so powerful hungry!" Ekow said, his eyes pulsing red.

"I know," Kwadzo said, understandingly. "It's the hunger for blood, and it's natural for us. It will affect all of you soon enough. We'll need to hunt animals, but in the meantime . . ." Kwadzo took on his Ramangan form, which triggered Ekow to do the same. He sliced a talon across his wrist and offered the rising blood to Ekow. But in a flurry of speed, Rafazi pushed Ekow away and clasped a hand over Kwadzo's bleeding wrist.

"No," said Rafazi gravely. "A Ramangan's blood is toxic to another Ramangan. It creates a heinous deformity one can never come back from." Making sure everyone was listening, he continued, "This is paramount: We do not feed on our people, we do not share the Blood outside of our own people, and above all, we do not feed on each other. No matter what."

"But I's hungry," Ekow whined just as a nearby rustling spun Kwadzo's head toward a nearby grouping of tall bushes. All those awakened—now including Juba—were looking in the same direction, eyes red and pulsing.

"You can come out," Kwadzo called toward the bushes as he stepped toward them. Into the clearing stepped a short, skinny man. The darkness of his skin told Kwadzo he worked on the paddy, and its smoothness spoke to his youth.

Though he meant to exhibit control, Kwadzo felt himself unable to revert to his human form or clear the red from his eyes. The smell of the young man's blood was utterly enchanting, and Kwadzo wanted nothing more than to drain him dry.

He couldn't imagine what the aroma was doing to the others behind him who were experiencing the scent of human blood for the first time.

Have they all turned? Kwadzo asked Rafazi in his mind.

Except Rufus and Fanna.

Why does some blood smell so much better than others? Kwadzo asked.

What you smell is fear, Rafazi answered back. *Nothing smells sweeter, except for love.*

Kwadzo turned to see Rafazi in his Ramangan form along with all the others.

As strong as the scent is, there is no doubt in his mind he's about to die, he heard Rafazi say.

"He smell good!" Ekow barked out. "It's suppertime, y'all!"

"Stay back! Have you forgotten Rafazi's words already? We don't feed on our people!" Kwadzo growled back, even as Ekow was inching himself forward. The scent grew even stronger as the young man visibly shook, but Ekow followed his Maker's cue and backed away. Kwadzo closed his eyes and willed himself back to his human form.

"Willie?" the young man muttered.

"Kwadzo. And you have nothing to fear." The young man nodded but refrained from stepping forward. "What is the name they have given you?"

"Bitty," he said. "On account I's so small, I reckon."

"Have you come to join us?"

"I don't rightly know," Bitty admitted. "I's scared of what y'all is, but I don't wants no more of livin' under Massa's rules."

"So, make a choice, boy," Rafazi said, retaining his Ramangan form.

"Easy, Rafazi," Kwadzo urged.

"If he doesn't intend to take the Blood, what is he doing out here?"

"What does it matter? He is one of our people. I swore his protection. Even if he chooses against the Blood, maybe he can help us convince the others we are not what Gertie says we are."

This caused Rafazi to take on his human form. "So, she is the weight I sense within you." All eyes were on Kwadzo now, and he stiffened. The drama of him and Gertie had played out for all the slaves to see. It didn't seem befitting of a leader to him, nor would Rafazi's bringing it up again.

"It is her love for you which fuels her opposition," Rafazi continued, to Kwadzo's embarrassment. "Every great change is madness until the change is made. But we've only one night, Kwadzo. We need you here. Now."

Looking out at the newly turned, he saw Rufus and Fanna had awoken and taken their Ramangan forms. Like the others, their eyes pulsed red. His blood had made them all, which meant he could *feel* them all—feel the rush of their blood, the hunger in it, the power in it. And right now, they were a powder keg waiting for Bitty's blood to light their collective fuse.

"This is Bitty," Kwadzo told the group. "He may still be undecided about the Blood, but his is off-limits."

Fanna let loose with a growl and launched herself forward, her blur forming around her.

"I said stop!" The command came out of Kwadzo like the roar of a lion. Fierce, direct, and so authoritative it not only stopped Fanna, but it also caused her to revert to her human form. They all had, except for Rafazi, who was once again smiling at him. Did he, Kwadzo, have the power to control their transfigurations? Did Rafazi carry such control over him?

"I know full well the pain of the hunger, and our first order of business will be to get you fed," Kwadzo told them as discomfort began to cloud more of their faces. "We may no longer be human, but we are *not* savages. Bitty is one of our own, so he will not be touched. He smells as good as he does because he's afraid. The greater the fear, the stronger it presents in the blood for us. Love and hate are also carried in the blood, and both offer unique scents and tastes for us."

"You smell love in Gertie's blood?" Irene asked. "What love smell like?"

"Indescribable," Kwadzo answered without hesitation. "As sweet as Bitty's smells, it would be bitter in comparison."

"I reckon she ain't smell so good after all that fussin' and fightin'," Ekow said, wincing in hunger pains.

"If'n Gertie don't loves you no more, I reckon I can," Juba offered with a flirty giggle. Despite the desirable nature of her frame, it was a comment Kwadzo felt was best left ignored.

"The intensity of emotions affects the scent of the blood," Rafazi said, taking his place next to Kwadzo and coming to his rescue. "What Kwadzo smells from Gertie is reserved for his nostrils alone. Regular love and hate do not present in the blood, not in a general sense. But true love, love held expressly and specifically for you, will be the best blood you could ever smell or taste. It could even heal you were you in need of it. The opposite is true of hate. The blood of someone who hates you directly—"

"You mean the way Monroe hate Ol' Willie?" Rufus observed. "I mean, Kwadzo?"

"Precisely. Monroe's blood would just be blood to us, but to Kwadzo, it could prove lethal, especially if he were to ingest it."

"Can we gets fed now?" Anita groused. "My stomach grumblin' somethin' awful."

Just then, a second rustling caught Kwadzo's attention.

"You heard it, too?" Rafazi asked. "More paddy rollers?"

Kwadzo shook his head. This disturbance was different than Bitty's, who remained standing away from the new Ramanga Tribe. This was more than a mere stalker in the woods. There was a distinct rumbling in his blood, but he was sure it had nothing to do with the twenty-two. The rumbling grew, and he sensed it getting stronger, closer. Then, through the shrubbery in the distance, two glowing dots of red eyes stared back at him. In a sense, he knew what it was—knew it was something of his blood, of his making—but exactly *what* eluded him.

Allowing the red to return to his eyes caused the ones in the brush to pulse and move closer until crumpled fur and floppy ears pushed through.

"One of Massa's hounds," Kwadzo heard Rufus say. He regarded the old man with a smile. The Blood had not returned his youth, but there was no doubt to the vibrancy it gave him. His once-slumped over shoulders now were straight, his empty mouth was filled with teeth, and the sprouts of hair age had spared on his head had grown full again.

Kwadzo knew all too well what the Blood did to humans, but he never dreamed animals could reap the same benefits. The bloodhound scampered forward to Kwadzo, docile in his presence, affectionate even. It whined, as if in apology, as it moved its tongue over the place where it had bit Kwadzo before he had ended its mortal life.

"By the blood of Gamab," Rafazi gasped. "You had killed that hound."

"Right after it bit me."

"And drank your blood."

Kwadzo chuckled in disbelief. He trained his red eyes on the bloodhound's and their eyes pulsed in unison. "Show yourself to me."

The red in the dog's eyes intensified, and its jowls seemed to double in size as it opened its mouth wide. Huge white fangs bookended now sharper, more jagged teeth. The muscles on its frame expanded and bulged, and Kwadzo could feel the wind created by its mighty tail whipping back and forth. The hound let out a bark at least three times as loud as it had when it was alive, then reared up and licked Kwadzo's cheek.

"Have you ever seen anything like this before in an animal?" Kwadzo asked Rafazi.

"I have not, but it may be the greatest thing I've ever seen in seven centuries!"

The power of Ramangan Blood, it seemed, knew no bounds.

"You're my hound now," Kwadzo said to the dog, "and I'm going to name you Charlie." Charlie released a series of happy barks.

By the looks of things, Kwadzo's army had increased to twenty-three.

Twenty-Nine

THERE WILL BE WAR

Gertie couldn't breathe.

Fifty-some slaves left with the one who called himself Kwadzo in the dead of night to become creatures of evil. Now, she and the remaining slaves were left in the lurch. The water her face was submerged in was tepid thanks to the morning sun. She tried to push back against the crushing pressure of the fingers pressing down on the back of her head. She could hear warbled voices above her and the muffled yelling of Monroe as he held her head underwater.

The chief overseer had been on a warpath ever since the number of slaves who had shown up for work had decreased, and Monroe's panic had led to the least productive day she had ever seen on the paddy. It was the first time she'd seen the overseers work harder than the slaves. Questionings were followed by threats, followed by beatings, followed by even more beatings. It also seemed vital to Monroe that Barrow not find out about the missing slaves.

None of the slaves lied. No one knew where the missing ones were—not truly. Monroe and his men were exhausted from the bruises they had spent the day inflicting. Still, she preferred this act of violence to the invasion of his hands she had suffered a few hours earlier. He had dragged her into the cotton fields, the edges of the boils stabbing into her back as he had hovered over her, mauling her breasts, slapping her buttocks, jamming his fingers inside her, his putrid tongue hanging out of his mouth as she did her level best to keep it from entering her own. Never had she been so happy to hear Amos's voice than when he had called out to Monroe, the urgency of his tone removing the chief overseer from her.

Now, this new injustice threatened to take her life. If she died, at least her death would be a natural one. In that regard, perhaps Kwadzo was right. Maybe the only path to true freedom was death.

Weakness set in. Gertie felt her instinctual movements of survival slowing. Then the warbled voices grew clearer, louder, as oxygen became available. She sucked it in so deep into her lungs, she coughed from the sudden excess of it.

"That clear your mind some?" The stink of Monroe's breath cut through the freshness of the water she'd been submerged in, and Gertie fought against the urge to vomit. "Where are they?"

In truth, she still felt it wise to refrain from sharing anything about Ramanga with the overseer, and the others seemed to be of like mind. Besides, she needed to conserve her breath, both for her and for the baby. Her face smacked against the wet paddy as Monroe released his grip on her.

Bracing herself on her hands and knees, she looked around at the brutality on display. Welts and scraps abounded on all the slaves in sight, along with swollen eyes, busted lips, bloody limbs. She heard Fuddle cry out as he stumbled and fell from what she was sure was a broken leg. The left side of Derby's handsome face bulged with bruises, and blood dripped from his mouth. Abuse of this nature was not new, but this heightened level would continue to affect those who had chosen to stay until those who chose to leave returned.

And then, it would get worse.

"If you ain't gonna talk, then get your fat ass back to work." Monroe's words followed a kick in her rump, and Gertie fell face-first on the paddy again. Derby helped pull her to her feet and led her away.

"I's get her workin', boss," Derby said, as Monroe huffed and spit, tonguing the ball of tobacco in his cheek while he converged with the other overseers.

It was clear Derby's ordeal with Rafazi had left him rattled. Instead of taking the opportunity to make a romantic overture toward her—something she had been sure was coming after her public spurning of Kwadzo—he remained silent, a pillow of human flesh. He'd even covered his torso with a shirt.

"They gonna keep beatin' on us like this here 'til we tells somethin' new," he said.

"What we's got to tell, Derby?"

"We's can tell what they be."

Despite herself and the situation, Gertie chuckled. "They's just beat us harder and longer, and I cain't takes much more."

"On account of the baby."

Perhaps it was the knowledge of another man's baby in her belly that caused Derby to pull back on his pursuit of her. It was for the best. With their fates being uncertain, the fate of the child's was even more so. Still, hearing him mention the baby set off a wave of disappointment in her she could not explain.

"You say doin' good is all we gots," Derby continued as he got her settled next to him on the paddy. "Well, tellin' Monroe what they is, is 'bout as good as you gonna get. You tell him 'bout Ramanga and 'bout your child, Willie's child, ain't no way you ain't gettin' looked on with favor."

"If'n Monroe ever find out 'bout this baby, Barrow'll take it 'way from me sure as I's standin'," Gertie said.

"Ain't gonna matter none no how. Barrow gonna send Monroe into them woods to kill Willie dead for good."

The idea chilled her blood. Yes, she was opposed to Kwadzo in every way—what he was, what he stood for. But she could not abide being the catalyst for his permanent demise.

In her mind, Kwadzo and Willie were two separate people, two separate species, but in her heart, she knew Willie was still there, underneath the monster. If the monster died, so would Willie. The monster's existence provided her with a place to direct her anger. Were the monster to be snuffed out, Willie would go with it, and with no guarantee of their baby's fate, she would be truly alone in the world again.

"Don't you say nothin', y'hear?" Gertie's instruction was met with an affirmative nod by Derby, who resumed his work on their section of the paddy. After a beat, she asked, "I's s'posin' this here baby in me done made me ugly to you now, ain't it?"

"Ain't nothin' ugly 'bout you, Gertie," Derby said. "But this here evil you's talk 'bout, I done felt it. When Rafazi drag me through the ground, I thought I's gonna die, thought I *were* dead. They's gonna come back here, Gertie. They's gonna come back here, and there gonna be war on this here plantation. Folks is gonna die, and I don't wants to be one of them."

Neither did she.

"Monroe!"

They both jumped at the sound of Barrow's voice. Sitting high on a steed, he looked over the paddy from a bit of distance. Gertie figured he had no interest in getting dirt on his shoes.

"Seeing your master don't mean stop workin'!" Monroe barked with an arbitrary crack of his whip before he rushed to Barrow. "Mornin', boss. You shouldn't be out here on the Lord's Day like this."

"Seems slight," Barrow said, his eyes narrowing as he surveyed the paddy.

"Pardon, boss?"

"Slight. As in fewer slaves working on the paddy. Why are there fewer slaves working the paddy, Monroe?"

Panic struck in the eyes of the overseer as Monroe scrambled. "No, boss, ain't fewer. No, sir. It only look that way 'cause we been reassignin' them."

"Reassigning them." It was clear from Barrow's tone he didn't believe Monroe.

"Yeah, them damn cotton niggers been gettin' lazy as all get out. So, I sent some of them paddy niggers over yonder to get the work done. Orders got to be filled, and these niggers ain't got no Lord no way, so workin' double duty ain't gonna do them no harm."

Barrow's eyes stayed on the paddy while Monroe spoke. It was a serviceable lie the chief overseer had settled on. The cotton fields were far enough away from the paddy that Barrow would need to ride across the land to confirm Monroe's word. But he was wearing finery. He was going somewhere off the plantation. He wouldn't have the time.

"Well," he sighed after a long while, "maybe therein lies the problem."

"Pardon, boss?"

"The niggers are indeed without the Lord. Exposure to the wisdom of the Good Book could prove beneficial."

Gertie felt a shiver run through her as Barrow's eyes settled on her. It was as much of an invasion as his physical assault of her had been.

"Put some horses on the old wooden wagon and fill it up with as many slaves as it'll fit. I'll be taking them to church. The good Minister Easton has agreed to preach to them. Perhaps a sermon will get their memories working again."

Gertie gasped when the plantation owner pointed at her. "Make sure *she* comes. Oliver's men went out into the woods and instead of finding Willie, they found four dead white men, bodies torn up viciously, likely from a wild animal attack."

"Weren't no animals, boss," Monroe insisted, a quake in his voice. "I tell you true, them niggers done turned into vampyres!"

Four dead white men. It must have been their blood Kwadzo and Rafazi had been covered in.

"I built this land into a business the whole town benefits from," Barrow growled. "My plantation is my legacy, and it will not be tarnished by two goddamn runaway niggers! Now, this is the last time you will speak this vampyre twaddle of yours. Am I making myself clear?"

"Yes, boss."

"Make sure Gertie is in that wagon. I suspect her memory is in need of the Lord the most," Barrow said, "and will be the most useful."

"Yes, sir, Boss. And Boss?" Monroe asked meekly. "Can I go to church, too?"

"No, you imbecile. You just told me how lazy the cotton slaves were being. You're my chief overseer. Who's going to keep them in line if you're gone?" Snapping his heels into the horse's sides, Barrow took off toward the manor.

"Well, you heard your master," Monroe snarled, stalking up to Gertie. "Get your fat ass up!"

Thirty

THE FEAR OF GOD

It was hot. Working on the paddy in the heat was one thing, but this somehow felt worse. Gertie and a large group of slaves from the Barrow Plantation had been packed tightly together in a huge wooden wagon pulled by two horses.

Confined in this space, the stink and stickiness of their combined sweat was nearly unbearable, a feeling compounded by the rough ride—the slaves knocked into each other roughly with every bump the wagon's wheels rolled over.

Gertie shifted her shoulders, trying to unsuccessfully free a hand to wipe the sweat accumulating on her brow. She sucked her teeth and winced at a sharp prick in her hand. She was sure she'd gotten a splinter for her effort instead. The wagon was following behind an elegant horse-drawn carriage containing the Barrows.

Slaves were never allowed to leave the plantation, so this trip was particularly troubling. Destruction was on the horizon, and there would be no peaceful resolution, no matter how many supplications she offered to the Pangool of her homeland. She was starting to think perhaps the New World was too far away for them to hear her. Here, being good had not brought her peace nor delivered Willie from evil, but it had brought life into this fiendish existence of diminishing hope, which was a new misery all its own for her.

The wagon drew closer to a building with a lofty narrow top to it much higher than any of the other buildings around it. At the top was a piece of wood with a shorter piece, which crossed the longer one near its top.

Gertie saw a huge group of white folks walking into the building, dressed in their finest clothes—finely embroidered doublets and coats and three-point hats on the men, and long linen gowns exposing intricately designed petticoats, lace ties, and coifs for the women.

The white folks glared at the wagon full of slaves with expressions varying from curiosity to downright disgust. Gertie felt movement against her shoulder she discovered to be Clarence, who was eagerly smiling and waving at the white folks.

The Barrow family exited their carriage, and while the mistress and her children made their way toward the building, Big Jim approached the wagon. He kept wiping at his brow and glancing toward the white folks still outside the building.

He seem nervous, Gertie thought.

"Now y'all listen up," he said in a voice louder than necessary. "Y'all wait here until everyone's gone inside. Then you will get out of this wagon peacefully, or you'll have the slave patrol to answer to, do you understand? Now, they are going to walk you in, and you will sit on the floor and keep quiet. Once us white brethren get our grace, the good minister will preach to you. You mind him when he's talking, and keep your traps shut!" Big Jim nodded to a line of men standing outside the building holding rifles. One of them moved to the back of the wagon and released the hatch there so the slaves could disembark.

As they did, Gertie could feel the hatred coming off the whites as strong and hot as the heat. Looking out at them, she recognized the people Barrow was standing with now. They were from the lunch he had made her help serve. She caught sight of the awful redheaded girl who had so easily spilled blind abhorrence for her people from her youthful lips. She thought of the child growing in her belly. Children inherit things from their parents. She wondered who her child would favor more, herself or Willie. The thought made her shudder.

Gertie noticed a man standing with the girl and her parents who had not been at the lunch: a bearded, muscular redheaded man who looked much more like the girl than her own father. Then, the redheaded girl tugged at Big Jim's coat and pointed directly at Gertie.

"Mister Barrow," she squealed, "please tell your niggers to quit staring at me!"

Her complaint turned the unfamiliar redheaded man's eyes toward the lot of them. The girl's father stood in his way, but he was easily pushed aside as the redheaded man made his way up to the slaves. The freckles in his face glistened ominously in the sun, his chest heaving with the weight of his anger.

"Ain't a one of y'all fit to cast eyes on this little girl," he growled. "She is a child of light, and y'all ain't nothin' but dirt walkin' upright. Any one of you catches her sight again, I will pluck your eyes out myself."

Dirt walking upright. The words rang in Gertie's mind as she followed her master's instruction to be peaceful, but her hands balled into fists. She had heard the same three words spoken by the redheaded girl at the Barrow luncheon.

One hundred years of hate, Kwadzo had said. Something about the way the young redheaded girl had pointed at her stirred up a similar feeling.

Spotting the back of Derby's head ahead of her in the crowd of slaves being ushered forward at gunpoint, Gertie slipped up to him and grabbed his arm. "What you make of all this here?" she hissed up at him.

"Don't make no difference," he muttered back. "We's here."

"He don't seem right, Barrow. Like he gots worry."

"You shiftless niggers."

Gertie winced at the sound of Clarence's voice behind them. "Always talkin' mess you don't know nothin' about. Massa ain't got no worries 'cept that ungrateful nigger you done loved up on. That's right, y'all field niggers don't never stop chin-waggin', so I know Willie put that baby in your belly."

"You don't know what you's talkin' 'bout, Clarence," said Gertie through gritted teeth.

"I know that baby ain't yours or his. It's Massa's. And he gonna whip you good when he find out you ain't tell him 'bout it."

"Will you hush up, Clarence?" Gertie pleaded. "Cain't you see somethin' else goin' on here? Somethin' ain't right 'bout this here. What is this here place? Why Massa brung us here?"

"Why, you ungrateful . . . This here is the grace of Massa's Lord shinin' down 'pon us," Clarence admonished them. "I hear him tell them men at the manor. He want us to have his God's glory, and I reckon he givin' it 'cause he tired of you triflin' field niggers not tellin' him where Shit Boy and Willie done run to. He done brung y'all here to set y'all straight. If'n I was y'all, I pay attention in there so y'all don't get designs on runnin'. Somethin' in them woods is killin' good white men. It ain't gonna think twice 'bout killin' no wayward runaway slave niggers."

Derby was about to say something in response, but Gertie stopped him, shaking her head. It amazed her how different the experiences of bondage could be from slave to slave. Good white men, Clarence said. She could not deny the idea that there could be good white men, good white folks. Surely the virtue of goodness could not have been confined to her home village. But she had yet to come across any white persons in the New World who displayed goodness. As much as she was against what Kwadzo and Rafazi were, she was sure the men they had killed in the woods were not good. But there was no reasoning with Clarence, whose head she realized was lurching forward from the force of the butt of a paddy roller's rifle.

"Y'all quit gabbin' and hush up!"

"Yes, boss. Sorry, boss," Clarence said, his voice labored from pain. He smiled his compliance then covered his mouth to keep himself from making any more noise in pain as the slaves entered the building. They were all kept in the back and made to sit on the floor in the hot building.

Gertie watched some of the white women using fans to cool themselves as a tall man with glasses rambled on in the front of the room. She mimicked their motion with her own hands, but it didn't do her any good. She could still feel sweat dripping from her skin and pooling underneath her, and, like the rest of the slaves, she could do nothing but sit in it.

The tall man seemed to go on talking for an eternity. Nothing he said made any sense to her. There was much mentioned about someone he called "Christ," and how it was imperative they consider this "Christ's" virtues—kindness, patience, temperance, love—before any action they took so those virtues could be emulated.

She didn't know what temperance was, but she had never seen the Barrows display any of the other virtues mentioned, so she assumed they ignored it as well. Unless temperance meant to torture, violate, and assault. The longer the tall man spoke, the angrier she felt, though she would not allow herself to admit or acknowledge this. But the feeling only festered with his every word.

When, at long last, he stopped talking, the white folks moved toward the exit, walking past the slaves as if they didn't exist. They had to part to make room for the white folks to leave. One woman stepped on Gertie's hand, seeming to linger, putting her weight on the foot on Gertie's hand, before moving on. The pain was agonizing, but Derby's quick palm over her mouth kept Gertie from crying out.

"Not here, not 'round all these white folk," he whispered as she suffered quietly through her pain. Once the white people were gone, the tall man, flanked on either side by paddy rollers and their rifles, came and stood before them. Clarence raised his hand, searching their faces like a child seeking approval.

"Boss, I reckon we's can get up off this here floor and sit on them benches?" he asked.

"No, you can't," a paddy roller answered. "Keep your black ass where it is and shut up."

Gertie's jaw tightened as Clarence obeyed, and the tall man looked down over his glasses at them all. He held a thick, black book to his chest and sighed. Gertie was amazed the man had more words within him to speak.

"Slaves of the Barrow Plantation," he began, "I have spoken with your master, and it seems there is some confusion as to how you all need to behave. Now, I speak for God, and I am here to clarify things for you all. Despite whatever voodoo practices you were familiar with back in the jungle, you must abandon them and follow the word of the Good Book."

The tall man tapped his book. "Now, the Good Book says y'all must be good niggers. You must mind your master, your mistress, and your overseers. Do not steal, do not talk back, do not run away. And if you hear of another slave wanting to run away, you tell your overseer directly.

"Do not lie about anything. Keep your mind on your work, and do not go talking among yourselves. If you've time to talk, you've time to work, which is all you need to concern yourselves with. When your superior tells you to do something, be it your master, your mistress, your overseer, or any upstanding white man or woman, you run and do it. No matter what." He kept that hard gaze on them. "Yours is not to question. Y'all are to do what you're told to do when you're told to do it and be grateful for it. Because whatever you get from your master and mistress is all you are ever going to get in this world. There is nothing else that awaits you. Niggers are all you are. And niggers, like animals, have no claim to anything.

"The fact of the matter is, none of you have souls. You are not fully human like us good, white Christian folk, you see. So, there is nothing awaiting you when you die. The promise of heaven simply does not exist for any of you. When you die, you get thrown in a hole and will be no more. So, do what I tell you so you don't spend what time you do have getting whipped and shackled. Be good niggers. Or else."

The tall man readjusted his glasses, the paddy rollers yelled out to them all to make way for him, and he walked past them without a second glance.

Gertie struggled to breathe.

None of this made sense.

Being brought to this building, hearing white folks given instruction they did not follow, the vile words about them from a man they had never seen. Nothing was new. The overseers reminded them how insignificant they were every chance they got. The only purpose it served was igniting her anger. She called to mind Barrow's demeanor when they first arrived.

Nervous. Like he had worry.

Something else was afoot, and she was certain it had something to do with what happened in those woods, with Kwadzo.

Once they were all loaded back into the wagon, Barrow spoke with a small circle of men by the building's entrance, while Charity strolled the length of the wagon. Gertie thought the look on her face was a strange one: Her eyes were reduced to slits, her lips were slightly parted, and her chest heaved with her heavy breathing as she stopped in front of Derby and seemed to shudder at the sight of the man.

"My, my, the heat is sweltering," she said to Derby. He threw a quick look at Gertie, who could only shrug before he refocused his eyes on their master's wife. "Perhaps you should remove your shirt."

Fright clouded Derby's face, and anger began to stir in Gertie once again. The mistress looked toward the building where her husband was still otherwise occupied, then back at Derby. "Take off your shirt!" The order rushed out of her mouth with a heated gasp.

Fear flashed across Derby's eyes before he pulled the fabric from his body. Charity Barrow gawked at the man's muscularity, devouring his form with her eyes even as his shoulders slumped in shame.

"I trust the good minister gave y'all instruction from the Good Book," they heard Barrow say from a distance.

Charity slipped away from the wagon quickly as her husband approached it. He moved to Gertie, standing before her.

"Yes, sir," Gertie said. She assumed her acknowledgment would be enough, but he remained in front of her, staring her down, seeming to demand more from her. "But truth be told, he ain't say nothin' we ain't heard from the overseers." She surprised herself with her forward language, but she didn't regret it. A part of her felt good about the assertive nature she was exhibiting.

"You heard where Willie is?" Big Jim leaned against the wagon, getting closer to Gertie's face. It was a move meant to intimidate, but today, it didn't.

"Ain't seen him in days. Don't rightly know where he be."

"And you don't know of any kind of slave hideout in the woods I don't know about, someplace you niggers whisper about when you get to plotting about running away with my property?"

His tone grew more aggressive with each word, giving the slaves around her pause. Of course, none of them dared say anything, especially about the other slaves who had left with Kwadzo and Rafazi. They all knew they would bear the brunt of the punishment if he learned of their absence. But despite all of that, for some reason, Gertie remained unfazed.

"Don't rightly know."

Gertie knew her tone was abrupt; she could hear it as she spoke. What she couldn't seem to do was stop it. Big Jim sneered. She could tell his patience was already wearing thin. The problem was, so was hers.

"Well, allow me to educate you. Willie and the other one? I own them. Like I own you. And they ran from my plantation without my say-so, and running is stealing." Big Jim stepped back and yelled out his vitriol at all the slaves in the wagon. "Y'all understand? Your lives are *not* your own, they're mine! I own every last one of you, and you will do what I say when I say to do it, or you will get the whip! You will tell me what I want to know, or you will get the whip!"

His face had gone red with anger, spittle hung from his bottom lip, and the veins in his neck bulged. Barrow was putting on a show, Gertie thought. There would be no reason for him to do so if he wasn't worried about something. Or afraid of something.

Or someone.

Gertie was starting to lose her fear of this man who called himself her master.

"I'm not asking you," Big Jim growled at her, targeting her again. "You know what I want to know, and you are going to tell it to me, or so help me God, you will regret it immensely. Now, where are they?"

He was barking like a rabid dog, but his eyes were wide. His nostrils were flaring. His hands were shaking fists. He was rocking back and forth on the balls of his feet.

He was scared.

"You don't wants to know where they is," Gertie realized, straightening her back and raising her head. "You wants to know how to stop them. 'Cause you 'fraid what happen to them men in the woods might happen to you if'n you don't."

Gertie recognized the anger making her speak these words must have been the same kind Willie must have felt in order for him to have taken Rafazi's blood. For the briefest of moments, she imagined *herself* filled with Ramangan blood, strong enough to punch a hole right through Barrow's white face with a mighty black roar. But, in reality, her field of vision filled with Big Jim's fat face scrunched in fury as his meaty fist hurtled toward her.

The last thing she saw was the ruby in Barrow's ring before everything went black.

IT WAS THE DULL ringing in her head, followed by a sharp ache, that awakened Gertie. She felt a piercing sting in her upper cheek, and her nose throbbed in pain.

And then she remembered—it was where Big Jim had punched her.

She opened her eyes to pitch blackness. Her breathing increased with her panic. She shifted her body, but the clank of metal stopped her movement.

Letting out a slow breath, she tried to calm herself and moved again. She yelped at a sharp pain in her ankle, and the metal clanked louder. There was an ache in her shoulders, but she could not move them. She shook her entire frame in frustration, and the clanking rattled in her ears. She could feel the iron cutting into her wrists and ankles from cuffs binding her. She bit her lip as her chin banged into a hunk of metal, another cuff around her neck. She felt intolerable heat on her skin, the ache in her bent legs.

She had been put in the hot box.

She had been encased in metal, placed under the hot afternoon sun, and left to bake. She could feel the pull of her skin against the metal with every movement, telling her she'd been stripped naked. She panted, and the air grew sparse. With her throat parched by heat and fright, she attempted to control her breathing. She gathered as much saliva in her mouth as she could, then swallowed to coat her throat.

"Help! Help me! Help!" Gertie called out in a hoarse voice, but there seemed to be no one to hear her. Even in the darkness, she could still see the look in Big Jim's eyes when he had punched her. It was full of murderous intent. If she died here, he would have succeeded in killing her and Willie's child.

There was no one who could save her. Not Derby. Not Willie.

No one except *him*.

He had risen from the ground speaking of love in his dead heart for her. She did not believe a dead heart could love, could be anything but unnatural evil. But maybe evil had not driven his decision. Maybe what she felt so intensely today, he had felt for days, weeks, months.

Years.

It dawned on her that her goodness had not kept her out of this box, had not spared her from humiliation, violation, violence. Despite her objections to his method, maybe he was right. Maybe he still loved her. Maybe, because he was Ramanga, he would hear her call. And maybe he would answer it.

She swallowed another collection of saliva.

"KWADZO . . . !"

Thirty-One

THE BURDEN OF RESTRAINT

The sound of Charity Barrow's clapping echoed through the manor. She was a frantic mess in anticipation of her soirée. She'd been calling out "Chop, chop!" and barking orders at the house slaves ever since she'd returned from church, and Irene was sick of it—of her.

It was even more frustrating because she now possessed the power to mutilate Charity Barrow. She could rip the woman's head from her body, yank her heart out, or drink her fill of Charity's blood. But she had to wait.

Kwadzo had guided her, Rosana, and Anita through the hunting of two moose from which the three women had fed. But though satiated, Irene was hungry for human blood. Watching Charity Barrow yell at the slaves over the table placements in the dining room, she could smell the woman's blood, and it caused Irene's venom to drip in her mouth.

However, she was duty bound to restrain herself. Kwadzo

had a plan, and she was a vital part of it. She just had to wait until nightfall. She would taste Charity's blood soon enough.

"No, you imbecile! How many times must I explain to you how to set a table? And where are the utensils?" Charity aimed her second angry question directly at Irene, which presented a problem. Avoid the sun, flame, and *silver* at all costs, Kwadzo had warned. The utensils meant to be set out were made of silver.

Besides Anita, two others worked to set the table with Irene, both of whom she had turned. She, Anita, and Rosana had returned minutes before dawn. Irene bent Clarence's mind, telling him through red eyes they had awoken early to get things ready for the mistress's soirée.

But the other house slaves knew better. When Irene showed them what she was and told them what was coming, her words were met with more excitement than she had anticipated. In all, she had turned five of the house slaves.

When Clarence came to them with an invitation to go to church, Irene bent Clarence's mind once again, telling him they had to stay back to prepare for the soirée. It was a believable lie, but by then, the sun had fully risen, which meant she could not steal a hog or two to temper the hunger of those she'd turned.

And they were hungry.

"And why are you all standing there glaring at me?" Charity Barrow snarled. "I declare, I have never known a more ignorant, lazy set of slave niggers in all my life!" One of the house slaves emitted a low growl, her lips shaping in a small snarl. Charity zeroed in on her. "Did you just *growl* at me?"

"Don't mind her," Irene said, positioning herself between the house slave and Charity. "She ain't mean no disrespect. She ain't feelin' so good this afternoon, is all."

"I don't care about her or her feelings," Charity snapped, grabbing the skin on Irene's arm and twisting. The pain was as Irene remembered it. Ramangan Blood, it seemed, did not alleviate pain, but knowing the power she held within made it harder for her to keep her promise to Kwadzo. "Now, y'all do what I tell you to do when I tell you to do it, or I'll get Monroe in here with his whip. Am I making myself clear?"

Fighting the urge to wince from the pinch, Irene stared back at Charity with hard eyes. She thought of how easy it would be to bite the woman's nose off and drink straight from the hole in her face. "Yes, ma'am."

"Good. Now, go get the silver."

The crash of porcelain shifted their focus to the other end of the table where the other of Irene's making, Polly, was doubled over, holding her stomach. Irene heard Charity gasp when the young woman looked up, her eyes red and pulsing. They shone even brighter against her tawny-brown skin and her abundance of black hair fashioned into several large, round tufts atop her head.

"I's powerful hungry," Polly said, producing so much venom that a thick strand of it dripped from her bottom lip. "And she smell *good.*"

Before Irene could react, Rosana's blur brought her into the room. "Don't you worry none, Missus," Rosana said, straightening the hungry Polly and covering her eyes with a palm. "I's give her some cornmeal right quick, and she be good as new."

"How did . . . Patchy, where did . . . Where did you come from?" Charity stammered. "You're supposed to be in the cookhouse. Cooking."

"Yes, ma'am," Rosana said. "I will, ma'am. Let me go on and get this here girl fed so's she can do her work."

"I'll come, too," Irene said, moving toward the door before Charity could grab her arm again. She wondered if Charity would address what she'd seen or dismiss it from her mind.

"Where are you going?"

"To get the silver, like you done ask me to." Irene soaked her tone in honey. The weakness of her remaining progeny was apparent, but at least Anita was left in the room. *"Watch her,"* Irene whispered to Anita before following Rosana out. Glancing back at Charity, she saw the woman wore a startled and confused look on her face, and Irene couldn't resist giving her an vague taste of what was to come.

"She right 'bout one thing, Missus," Irene called. "You sure do smell good."

"Barrow done put Gertie in the hot box!"

Rosana's words tore through Irene like a knife. It was true she didn't see eye to eye with the woman, but she knew what Gertie meant to Kwadzo. And thanks to the gift of his blood, Kwadzo meant everything to Irene.

"Clarence tell me," Rosana said. Polly was still slumped in her grasp. "Say Massa ask Gertie where Willie be—"

"Kwadzo," Irene corrected her.

"Well, Massa ask, and she talk back, say Massa was 'fraid of him, so Massa punch her, and when they gets back from wherever they's went to, Massa put her in the hot box."

Kwadzo had given Irene responsibility and on her watch, Gertie had been put in the hot box. If he returned to discover Gertie and the child inside her dead, he could hold Irene personally responsible.

"Clarence ask Massa to let her out?" Irene asked.

"He Clarence." Rosana scoffed, clicking her tongue against her teeth and rolling her eyes. Kwadzo had instructed her to keep wearing her patch to avoid suspicion, but the Ramangan Blood had healed her scar and restored her eye. Because of this, the covering had become a nuisance. "You know he ain't ask," she said, vigorously rubbing a palm against her irritated eye before putting the patch back in place. "Say she deserve it for talkin' back."

Irene's brow crinkled in thought. She had to get Gertie out.

"What are you dirty niggers doing in here loafing when you're supposed to be working? And what's wrong with that one's face?"

Irene hadn't thought they'd be discovered so soon in the keeping room at the back of the manor, but Virginia's voice startled Irene and Rosana, neither of whom had noticed Polly was in her Ramangan form. Moving faster than either Irene or Rosana could anticipate, Polly blurred forward and plunged her teeth into Virginia's neck. The Barrow girl opened her mouth to scream, but Irene was on her, covering her mouth to muffle the sound. Polly's eyes became so bright they seemed to sparkle.

"She smell like her momma." Polly exhaled as she pulled away from Virginia, the white girl's blood dripping from her lips. She ducked her head for another taste, but Rosana pulled her away. "I wants me some more!"

Holding Virginia as tight and close as she was, Irene couldn't help but be overwhelmed at the scent of the girl's blood. This was exactly what they weren't supposed to do, but Irene was having a hard time focusing on anything other than the nectar spilling out of Virginia. What was done was done, but Irene couldn't help but be envious. Her progeny had tasted human blood before her.

It hardly seemed fair.

Rosana was succeeding in keeping Polly away from Virginia, but Rosana's exposed eye had gone red, and she shook with hunger. "It smell so good," Rosana moaned. "What we gonna do?"

Keeping Virginia's mouth covered, Irene moved to face her. She allowed her eyes to go red and found her focus. "You ain't gonna scream," Irene said, her voice low and smooth. "You gonna raise your sleeves and hold out your arms for us to taste your blood." An eternity seemed to pass as Irene stared into Virginia's eyes.

"What in tarnation is taking so long, Irene?"

Charity's impatient call from the other room did not help matters.

"We be done in a minute, don't worry none, missus." Charity's huff and the sound of her retreating steps provided a modicum of relief, but Irene worried Anita and her other sire would smell Virginia's blood and react, worried Charity would barge in, worried she had stopped the revolt before it could even begin.

But then, Virginia pushed up the sleeves of her dress and held out her arms. Irene could hear the quickened pace of the human's heart pushing the blood through her system. It was the sweetest scent she had ever smelled.

"Don't bite deep, and don't take too long," Irene told Rosana. "Polly, grab some cloths from the cabinet so's we can dress her wounds." Polly's eyes were glazed over, venom dripping from her lips. "Polly!" Irene's pointed hiss brought Polly back to her senses.

"I's sorry, Irene," Polly said, following Irene's instruction as Rosana took one of Virginia's arms in her hands.

"Control yourself, now," Irene reminded Rosana. She nodded before she and Irene both bit into Virginia's arms. A rush of euphoria surged through Irene as the blood—the human blood—hit her tongue. Left to her own devices, she would have devoured the white girl whole. The incredible flavor seemed to clear her mind immediately, creating a sharp focus. As good as the blood tasted, though, she knew there would be much, much more to come if they heeded Kwadzo's words.

"All right, now." Irene pulled away, and Rosana followed suit.

"Y'all hear that?" Polly's question silenced them all, and Irene's hearing sharpened. Despite the clarity of her hearing, she could hear voices but not their words. Monroe's and someone else's. A familiar tone she couldn't place coming from outside.

"Monroe talkin' to Derby," Polly whispered, returning to her human form.

"Dress the girl's wounds," Irene instructed.

"What y'all in here doin'?" The three Ramangans turned to find yet another house slave before them, a human girl who'd chosen to not be turned but was supportive of the cause. "Is y'all killin' the Barrows already? Miss Charity send me in here to find out what keepin' you from fetchin' her silver."

"You fetch it for me. And not a word about what you've seen here," Irene told the girl before turning to Rosana and Polly. "Take Virginia to her bedchamber and get her ready for tonight. Make sure she wears a scarf."

Irene noted the clarity in her speech as she bent Virginia's mind again. "You will not remember what happened here. You will be kind to Rosana and Polly and agreeable to everything they do." Virginia nodded silently.

"What are you going to do?" Rosana asked her.

"Figure out how to get Gertie out of that hot box."

Thirty-Two

BEST LAID PLANS

The heat was excruciating.

Having lived the entirety of her human years in the Province of Carolina, Irene was no stranger to the intensity of the sun's rays during the month of August. But standing in the archway of the manor's back door with Ramangan Blood running through her veins, the sun felt as if it was made of death. Though the awning over the back porch protected her from it, she was mindful to step back from the slivers of sunlight shining through the porch beams.

She could hear Monroe talking to Derby, but the words were still hard to make out clearly. Remembering Kwadzo's training, she squinted, and her eyes went red, as did her vision as it stretched out before her. In the distance, she could see Derby and Monroe standing in front of one of the overseer houses with another field slave she didn't recognize. A slave having a conversation with an overseer was alarming enough, but for a slave to be standing in spitting distance from an overseer house—it simply was not done.

Derby had aligned himself with Gertie in opposition of Kwadzo and Rafazi. Perhaps he was trying to convince Monroe to release her from the hot box. She had to get closer. Considering it had no door, the washhouse would be ideal. It was just a few feet from where Monore and Derby stood, and Irene knew it would also be empty. The problem was all the sunlight between it and the back porch. She knew she was faster than any human could see. Maybe if she was swift enough . . .

The heat was torturous as she launched her blur across the yard. Irene fought to keep from crying out. She felt empathy for everything ever put into the brick ovens in the cookhouse. She could hear her skin sizzling, smell the singeing of her hair. If she stopped, Irene knew she'd perish.

To survive, she pushed herself forward faster, speeding such that she was unable to stop of her own volition. Aiming herself to go through the doorway of the washhouse, she was stopped by her crashing into the wash boiler. Thankfully, the water it held was no longer heated. A pile of tablecloths and bedcovers fell over her, aiding in her cooling down. Streams of smoke rose from her skin and head as she smoothed her hands over her hair. She could feel the torched ends of it growing back under her fingers and could not help but chuckle at the miracle she'd become.

"What in tarnation was that?"

Monroe's words were as clear as a bell now. Moving to the wall and keeping herself hidden, Irene closed her eyes and focused her hearing.

"I don't rightly know," she heard Derby say, "but you gots to hear this here, boss. Go on, Bitty. Tell him like y'done told me."

"I don't need to hear no slave's jibber jabber," said Monroe. "Is they vampyres or ain't they?"

"I don't rightly know, sir," Bitty admitted.

Irene remembered Bitty as the one who had stumbled upon them in the wilderness. The one whose blood had smelled so delectable. He must have run back after the others had burrowed themselves underground to avoid the sunrise. No wonder he had been so fearful last night; he was spying for Gertie and Derby!

"But I do what Derby tells me and follow them out to the woods," Bitty continued.

What Derby told him to do. Maybe Gertie didn't know what Derby was up to, Irene thought.

"But did they say they's vampyres?" Monroe whined.

Irene didn't know what the word meant, but it seemed of grave importance to the chief overseer.

"Did they's faces turn evil? Did they drink your blood?"

"No, sir," Bitty said. "When I say no, they ain't force me, but they's talked 'bout my blood. One of them charge at me for it, but Ol' Willie stop her, say I's off-limits. But they's faces was evil. They's even had them a evil dog out there with them."

"That's where that hound went to. I knew it!" Monroe's voice filled with vindication while Irene's fists tightened. All the posturing Derby did on Gertie's behalf, yet he hadn't once asked about her release from the hot box. Derby never once made any mention of Gertie.

"They say they's from the Ramanga Tribe," she heard Derby say.

"What voodoo nonsense you say?" Monroe asked.

"It be the tribe they of," Derby explained.

"Shit, I don't care 'bout that," Monroe huffed. "They're vampyres!"

"Folks was scared when they's come back," Derby said. "But now, on account of what happen after them that run with Willie . . ."

"What? What happen?" Monroe asked sternly.

"Well, sir, you beat up on us a might bad," Derby said.

"Y'all stubborn niggers deserved it for not tellin' me the truth of what happened!"

"Well, sir, Ol' Derby here tellin' you true now. Folks been talkin' 'mong theyselves. They done seen twenty-two of them that run done stayed gone, and now more say if'n Willie comes back, they's gonna have them a change of heart."

Irene leaned her head forward. The voices had gone silent, but the pressure of the blood rushing through their veins had increased. The sound of it pounded in her ears as loudly as the accelerated beating of their hearts. The scent of fear wafted across her nostrils.

"And Ol' Willie gots them all riled up, too," Bitty added. "Say they's gonna free ev'ry slave on the plantation and take it from Massa."

Damn right, Irene thought. A smile grew on her face as she heard one of the hearts beat even faster. She was sure it was Monroe's. But it didn't matter. There would be nothing he or anyone else could do against Ramangan power. They were all going to die tonight, and she couldn't wait.

"Tell him 'bout his blood." Derby's words wiped the smile from Irene's face. He wouldn't. He couldn't . . .

"Oh yeah, they says your blood can kill Ol' Willie." She wanted to race to Bitty and rip his throat out. "Says the hate you gots for Willie be in your blood and can kills him."

Gertie may have opposed Kwadzo, but being a party to his demise was too insidious, even for her. This was all Derby. The betrayal had to be reported to Kwadzo, but she couldn't deliver two pieces of bad news to him. She had to find a way to get Gertie released first. Even if Gertie had a hand in this treachery, which Irene no longer believed she did, Kwadzo would forgive her. But if Irene allowed Gertie to perish without at least trying to free her, Irene was sure he would be far less forgiving of her.

Shushing the squealing hogs as she rushed in through the manor's back door did Irene no good. Their collective hooves scraping across the floor made a hideous sound. She was sure they were frightened by being scooped up and blurred across the yard at a ferocious pace, but there were still newly turned ones who hadn't fed, and she couldn't risk another incident like the one with Virginia in the keeping room.

Irene hoped Charity had not found out about her daughter being fed on, but if she did, Irene would simply remove the thought from her mind when she bent it to get Charity to convince Big Jim to release Gertie. With the exception of the pigs, she found the house to be uncommonly quiet. Until it wasn't.

"What in the good white Lord is this here?"

Clarence stomping toward her was better than Charity doing so, but he presented problems of his own. "What is them filthy hogs doin' in Massa's house stankin' up the place before Missus's soirée? He gonna tan your hide for this when he get back, and you just a'itchin' for it, ain't you?"

"Clarence . . ."

"I don't understands you, girl. We's in here tryin' to do ev'rythin' Miss Charity need done for her soirée, but you and them you's say had to stay back ain't done nothin'! And I ask Miss Charity, I say, Miss Charity, is you ask them gals what Massa offer to take to his Lord's house, to stays back and help ready things? And you know what she say? Guess what she say."

"Clarence, we don't have time for this. We have got to get Gertie out of that hot box!"

"No! That's what she say," Clarence carried on, ignoring her. "She say she ain't say no such thing. Which mean you ain't do nothin' while we's gone but lie. Lie, lie, lie! And no, Gertie ain't gettin' out that box, no way, no how. What she 'spect was gonna happen, talkin' at Massa like she done?"

He would go on and on and on if she let him. So, she grasped his arms, stared into his eyes, and pulsed her own red, just as she'd done before. "Clarence, I'm going to need you to shut up."

"All right then." His compliance was immediate.

"Now, where is Charity?"

"Upstairs in the master bedchamber, decidin' on a gown with the seamstresses."

"And where is Barrow?"

"Meetin' the man in charge of the paddy rollers so's they can gets them a posse to go after Willie and that Shit Boy."

"What about everybody else? Virigina, Thomas, where are they? Have you seen Anita or Polly or Rosana?"

"Who Rosana?"

"Ol' Patchy," Irene said, rolling her eyes.

"What she doin' in the house?" Clarence asked, his eyes still glazed over. "She been up in here all day long when she s'posed to be in the cookhouse cookin'."

"Have you seen any blood, Clarence?"

"Blood?"

"Yes, blood. Have you seen any anywhere? On anyone's clothes? On their lips?" A crash from upstairs sent her eyes looking upward. There was no telling what the newly turned had gotten up to without supervision. "Forget we spoke," Irene told Clarence. "Forget I asked you anything about blood, and if anyone comes for any of these hogs, ignore what they do to them."

"All right then."

Irene released him and ran up the stairs in her blur. She followed the scent of blood into one of the bedchambers and found Virginia, nude atop a bed with her limbs spread out on the large bedcover, while Polly and another house slave Irene had turned bit into her fleshy flanks. There were bite marks about her shoulders, stomach, and thighs, and a cloth stuffed into her mouth prevented her from screaming. The girl's eyes were wide with fright.

"What are you doing?" Irene growled, her eyes red and pulsing with anger. Polly and her accomplice looked up; their faces were covered in blood.

"But she tastes so good," Polly whined. "And we're so hungry!"

"You were supposed to be getting her ready for the soirée! Who knows how much blood you've taken from her!"

"What's the difference?" Polly asked with a shrug. "We're taking over anyway, right? We're just getting a head start." She giggled until Irene blurred at her, grabbing her by the neck and slamming her against the wall.

"You stupid girl," Irene hissed. "You and your hunger will keep Gertie in the hot box and ruin Kwadzo's plan."

"Kwadzo's plan doesn't start until tonight. We're here, and there's nothing they can do to stop us. There's nothing *you* can do to stop me." Polly thrust her knees forward, slamming them into Irene's middle, knocking Irene back and freeing herself. As Irene stumbled back, Polly rushed at her, wrapping her arms around Irene's neck and throwing her to the ground. Irene got to her feet quickly, and the two women faced each other. Before Polly could move again, Irene lunged forward and plunged a fist into Polly's chest.

The crunch of bone echoed in the room as Irene opened her hand inside Polly's chest cavity and took hold of her heart. Polly groaned and twisted in pain as her Maker squeezed the organ. Irene had no idea if snatching Polly's heart from her chest would end her existence, as it would were she human, but she figured squeezing down on it would send the hurtful message she intended.

"I made you," Irene breathed. "I can end you. Don't make me." Polly nodded, wincing in painful defeat. "Clean this, and her, up, like I told you to. If you two are still hungry when the work is done, there are hogs downstairs. When you're done with them, get rid of their bodies." Irene punctuated her point by squeezing Polly's heart once more before retracting her hand, leaving the new Ramangan doubled over, suffering through her skin and bones healing themselves. Irene moved to Virginia, removed the cloth from her mouth, and found the girl paralyzed with fear.

"You niggers are crazed!" the Barrow daughter whispered tearfully. Polly's argument was not without merit. Nothing would have satisfied Irene more than taking Virginia's life. But Kwadzo had essentially entrusted her with her own group of Ramangans in preparation of the revolt. He had saved her life, given her hope, and made her a powerful immortal. She owed him her unwavering loyalty.

"You will forget everything that happened in this room," she said, staring her red pulsing eyes into Virginia's, swallowing back her ire and hunger, all for the greater good. "You will have no fear, and you will enjoy the soirée to the fullest." With her eyes glazed over, Virginia nodded, just as a yelp sounded from outside the room.

Irene sped from the room to the hallway and found Thomas standing behind Anita, humping roughly against her bottom as his hands groped at her breasts. Anita's protests for him to unhand her were ignored as the boy began pulling down the front of her dress. Anita then grabbed Thomas's wrists and dropped to one knee as she slung the boy over her head, landing him on the floor with a thud. She hovered over Thomas and took on her Ramangan form, causing him to quiver and scream out. Irene rushed to him and quickly knelt to cover his mouth as he wet the front of his breeches.

"This child done put his hands on me for the last time," Anita snarled. "I's 'bout to tear them from his wrists!"

"I'll help." Behind Irene stood Rosana, her patch gone, also in her Ramangan form.

"What is wrong with you two?" Irene asked furiously. "Has the Blood relieved you of all sense and patience? Do you know how dangerous it is using your powers in the open like this before the revolt? We'll be found out! I know the boy is insufferable, but Kwadzo is depending on the element of surprise." She removed her hand from Thomas's mouth.

"You niggers are going to get it from my daddy when he finds you!" he yelled before Irene silenced him with a harsh slap to the mouth. Once again, her eyes went red as she stared into the eyes of the Barrow boy.

"You had an accident," Irene said to him. "You will get dressed for the soirée and forget what's happened here. And you will not put your hands on Anita under any circumstances. Do you understand?" Thomas nodded with glazed-over eyes.

"Change the boy from his soiled breeches, clean him up, get him dressed, and behave yourself," she then ordered Anita, who nodded, pulled the boy to his feet, and moved him down the hallway.

"You behave yourself, too," Irene told a smiling Rosana, whose face was once again human and was putting her patch back on over her eye.

"You like being in charge, don't you?"

Irene's only response to this was a small smile of her own. "I've got to get Gertie out. Kwadzo can't come back to find her dead."

"Hogs! Why are there hogs in my house?" Charity's wail from downstairs was unmistakable. Panic covered Irene and Rosana's faces.

"Clarence said she was with the seamstresses in her bedchamber," Irene said.

"She was earlier, but I did just see her downstairs in the salon room checking the cleaning work of the girls there," Rosana said. "She damn near caught me using my speed."

Irene zoomed away down the staircase and to the first floor

before slowing herself to a human pace as she reached the archway of the keeping room where Clarence stood, two hogs still at his feet while the rest scampered out the manor's open back door. Behind him in her elegant undergarments was Charity, swatting him about the head and shoulders, railing at him.

"I'm afraid the hogs are my doing, Mistress," Irene spoke up. Charity, her face red with rage, turned to her.

"Why would your stupid, stupid mind think it was a good idea to bring hogs into this house when it is being prepared for my soirée? It's bad enough those nigger seamstresses have no clue about elegance; I have to put up with this, too?" Charity barked.

"I shall remove them. But I must ask a favor first."

Charity broke out in laughter. "A favor? Has my husband's cock finally driven you insane? What makes you think you can ask me for anything?" With her pinching fingers, Charity reached for Irene's arm, but before she could latch onto skin, Irene grabbed Charity's hand and bent it back at the wrist to the point of breaking. This day had been trying enough. She would not suffer Charity's cruelty on top of it all.

Not anymore.

Irene flashed her eyes red at Clarence, an action that made Charity gasp. "Stay put, Clarence."

He remained obedient to Irene's command while Charity cried out in pain and fell to her knees as Irene held the pressure on her wrist.

"I could spare you the memory of this," said Irene plainly as Charity whimpered in her hold. "Wipe your mind clean of any cause for concern. I realize now you don't deserve such pleasantry. So, no tricks. I will command you showing you my true face, and you will obey."

Irene knew if she applied just a bit more pressure, Charity's wrist would break. But the woman, despite her obvious pain, seemed ignorant of her position.

"Release me this instant! I command you!" she demanded, pulling and slapping at Irene's forearm with her free hand, her eyes watering, her skin beet red. It seemed she still saw herself as superior to Irene, to every slave.

Irene decided it was time for her to see what power truly looked like.

She watched Charity's eyes bulge as she began to take on her Ramangan form. Wishing to bring the woman to terror, Irene felt herself slowing her transformation, controlling it, elongating the stretch of her brow, raising the red in her eyes from dull to bright. Charity's breath hitched with each change in Irene's appearance, and by the time her transition was complete, Charity's mouth was slack. She trembled uncontrollably, and the fear within her blood was intoxicating.

"Now you see who has control of your life," Irene asserted, licking her wet, jagged teeth before turning to Clarence. "Take those two hogs back outside." While he did as he was told, Irene returned her focus to Charity.

"I am far more powerful than you can ever imagine. I will taste your blood, and if it is half as good as it smells, I will relieve you of it entirely. But for now, I need you to convince your husband to release Gertie from the hot box. You will do this without revealing why you are asking, or I will tear the still-beating heart from your chest, and the last thing you will see is me devouring it. Or perhaps I will simply inform your husband you have been fucking a nigger under his nose. I'm sure being hung would be less painful than death by my hand. Have I made myself clear?"

Charity's frightful tears rolled down her cheeks. "What evil are you?"

"You don't ever wish to find out."

Thirty-Three

BRING ON THE NIGHT

harity paced the grand foyer in her perfectly tailored gown, her hair styled in an elegant updo, exquisite diamond earrings dangling from her ears. In anticipation of what she was about to do, she couldn't help her furrowing brow or the wringing of her hands. She stopped, looking up to the top of the curved double staircase where Irene stood on the balcony, watching.

The smell of Charity's blood had only grown more delectable. Irene knew this was not just from the fear she instilled in Charity. She knew with great certainty the woman was also terrified of confronting her husband. Irene flashed her red eyes at the woman, warning her she was not to deviate from her task. She watched Charity's shoulders hunch at the action and heard her gasp. Nothing more was needed. Irene had seen to it everything necessary for the soirée was taken care of, even directing Clarence as he was still under the influence of her mind bending.

"Dear heart!" Charity blurted a little too loudly as Barrow walked in through the manor's front doors. He regarded her affectionate greeting with pause.

"Well," he drawled, taking her in while running a hand over his crotch. "It has been some time since the sight of you has raised my cock. Perhaps you would like to please your husband by hitching up your skirts and bending over."

Charity placed firm hands against his advancing abdomen. "Perhaps you could earn the pleasure by granting your loving wife a favor." With an exasperated sigh, Big Jim stepped back, placing his hands on his considerable hips. Charity continued, "Though her mouth demanded punishment, perhaps it would be prudent to remove the slave girl from the hot box."

The laughter Big Jim barked out at the suggestion threatened to bring the walls of the manor crashing down, his head thrown back, his fat belly hefting with each exaltation. Charity shrunk before him. Irene knew exactly how she felt.

"You still haven't found the runaways," Charity tried again. "Perhaps now, after suffering the consequence of defying you, she will be forthcoming."

"I am not taking that black hump out of the box, Charity. Quite frankly, I'm a bit shocked to hear you ask such a thing. Since when do you have compassion toward slaves?"

"This is not compassion, James," Charity said, her voice rising with the level of her unease. "This is survival!"

"What in tarnation are you talking about?"

Charity turned as if she was going to look up at Irene but stopped herself, thinking better of it. The fear in her blood cranked up again as she grabbed Barrow's arm.

"These slaves are dangerous, James! They are not human! And they will . . ."

Irene felt the heat rise in her own blood. Perhaps she should have bent the woman's mind after all.

"All right, all right, that's enough!" Big Jim cut her off dismissively. "I will have Monroe's head for spreading his nonsense to your ears. I told him never to utter his gibberish again, and then he does. To my wife, no less!"

"But it wasn't . . ."

"Shh, Charity, hush now. This is all above your comprehension, but rest assured, there is no cause for concern. I've met with Oliver Gibbs again. The slave patrol's best men will go after those ungrateful uppity niggers at sunset tomorrow once silver swords have been acquired and deal with them accordingly. All you need to concern yourself with is the soirée. And my cock."

Barrow was groping his crotch again, his eyes slits of lewd intent aimed at his wife, which caused Irene to roll her own eyes. She considered rushing out to free Gertie from the hot box herself, but no one was supposed to know of her power yet. Charity was the only one who'd been exposed to it who hadn't been mind-bent to forget, which Irene realized now was a mistake. Barrow's disregard for the woman had protected the revolt this time, but if she continued to open her mouth, eventually someone would listen.

It was a relief to hear Barrow's plan of attack would come one night too late, but Kwadzo still had to be told about Gertie before he returned. If he launched his revolt without knowing, Gertie would certainly perish, and Irene was sure he would gut her next. There was also the matter of Derby's duplicity. Kwadzo knew what Monroe's blood could do to him, but thanks to Bitty, Monroe now knew it, too. She knew she was supposed to await his word, but he had to be told about all of it.

So, amid Barrow's groans and Charity's whining about being discovered as they rutted below, Irene found a quiet corner on the second level of the manor. She closed her eyes and focused her mind on Kwadzo, willing her thoughts to him. It was the best she could do, and she hoped it would be enough.

KWADZO. BITTY WAS SENT to us in the woods by Derby. He ran back and told Monroe everything he heard. Now Monroe knows what his blood can do to you. And Barrow put Gertie in the hot box. I tried to get her out without alerting him of the plan, but I failed. You have to save her before it's too late. Forgive me.

Kwadzo's eyes went red as Irene's words rushed through his head. He was already prepared to stay clear of Monroe's blood, but he was determined to repay the man's cruelty, just as he would make Barrow pay for every single act of his viciousness, especially the malice he had inflicted on Gertie. Apparently, defiling her and humiliating her wasn't enough, now he threatened her very life, and whether he knew it or not, the life of their child. Kwadzo would see his blood for it.

Even though she stood against him, considered him evil, a killer, and refuted the love they felt for each other, the love he felt for her still prevailed. She was still Gertie. Her feelings for him may have changed, but not his. His love had grown deeper and stronger in death. He would save her and grant her the opportunity to live free in any manner she wished. Even if it was no longer with him. The soil blanketing him and the others as they lay underground was cooling. It wouldn't be long now. Night would fall.

And so would Barrow.

Thirty-four

CHARITY'S SOIRÉE

It was an elegant affair in every way, especially the food and the wine. All of Lakeside's elite were in attendance: fellow landowners and their wives; merchants; shopkeepers; the governor and his young wife; military officials and other royalists; Minister Easton, of course; Doc Farkus; and Oliver Gibbs, the captain of the slave patrol, and his wife. There were even a few well-regarded artisans in attendance. So many people. Too many people.

Big Jim hated having a manor full of people. There was music, which he supposed was festive, but Big Jim was already bored. He had a different idea about what constituted fun than Charity did. For instance, him buggering his wife less than an hour ago over the high oak chest Charity now stood in front of—talking to David Mitchell and his old, ugly wife—had been fun.

Until of course, her whining and complaints of pain and timing. Her unwillingness to give herself over to depravity was the true cause of their marital woes. He was wealthy, powerful. The simple things an ordinary man found pleasurable could not satisfy a man of his supreme stature. Damn Charity and this confounded soirée! He was so bored he could spit.

"A fine evening you've put together here, Mister Barrow."

Big Jim rolled his eyes at the sound of Anna Callowhill's voice behind him, and he was met with further annoyance when he turned and saw who she was with. He expected Robert, who looked as browbeaten as any man who allowed his wife's words to carry weight should. Who he did not expect was Penelope, all pigtails and toothy grins, and the muscular man with a beard and hair as red as Penelope's he'd met at church earlier that day, Robert's overseer.

"Thank you for the kind invite." Anna smiled. "I hope you don't mind that we brought Penelope and Samuel along."

Big Jim hadn't bothered to remember the name of the mere overseer, even if it was told to him. It carried no importance.

"Forgive her, James," Robert muttered. "I told her you didn't allow your own overseers in your house, let alone one of a guest. I was also clear that, with the exception of your own, this was not an affair for children."

"I will not have my Penelope looked after by some Negress mammy while I am not there," Anna retorted. "Besides, Penelope is thirteen years old and quite poised. Mister Barrow saw the evidence of that at the luncheon he so generously invited us to. Surely, he would make an exception in this case." Anna's eyes seemed full of fury toward Robert but full of adoration for this overseer. "And I thought Samuel had proven his mettle after having dressed down his slaves at church."

Big Jim felt his annoyance turn into amusement as he watched the woman's words stir Robert's growing frustration.

"Something else he had no right to do," Robert huffed. "You do not address another man's slaves, especially when you have none of your own. They are not your responsibility. James, forgive me for allowing such disrespect. Samuel, leave this place at once."

"His slaves were disrespecting Miss Penelope," Samuel said in calm defiance of his boss. "You would have your daughter made to feel unsafe in favor of filthy niggers?"

"She was in no danger! James had his slaves well in hand!"

This exchange had just made his wife's event far more interesting. And young Penelope's resemblance to Samuel—in light of how much she looked like her mother—was not lost on Big Jim either. It had all given him a change of heart.

"Well, now, I have said before, these slave niggers are savage and unpredictable," Big Jim said, knowingly stirring the pot. "Even in the surest of hands, one's slaves could act out. I daresay your overseer acted prudently, Robert."

"Thank you, Mister Barrow," Samuel said, and Big Jim choked back a chuckle at the sight of Robert rolling his eyes. "Oliver recruited me to join the band of men going after your runaways tomorrow night, and I am happy to take my place among them." Robert looked as if his head would burst any second.

"Good man," Big Jim said, unable to keep the amusement from his voice. "I daresay you've stumbled upon an opportunity a simple man like you will never have again, Samuel. Please, eat. Drink. You shall earn it come sunset tomorrow. It's but a night, right, Robert?"

The man only grunted, yanking a glass of wine from a tray carried by an oddly silent Clarence, and walked off. The slave usually never passed up an opportunity to kowtow, but it was a gift to be free from his incessant blathering this night. Between the nigger's silence, the drama brewing with the Callowhills, and his trusty glass of brandy, Big Jim surmised he might survive the event yet.

I'll be the one writing
the history and I don't
even know your name.

Thirty-Five

SHOW HIM TO ME

Kwadzo raced through the woods at a fever pitch in full Ramangan form, rage fueling him forward. The thought of Gertie and his child—their child—in the hot box made him want to devour the entirety of Lakeside whole.

"Kwadzo!" Without stopping, he turned to find Rafazi's blur leading the new Ramangans several paces behind him. "What was the point of building our army if you're going to leave us all behind?"

"Our own kind have betrayed us! Irene sent me a message. Bitty was sent to us by Derby to gather information. Now, Monroe knows the power of his blood."

"Derby's treachery can't be that much of a surprise. And you are prepared for Monroe. Surely, the man won't simply bleed himself dry . . ."

"Barrow put Gertie in the hot box!"

Rafazi pushed his blur harder to move side by side with Kwadzo.

"Irene tried to get Gertie out without revealing herself but couldn't. I am going to paint the manor walls with Barrow's blood!"

Kwadzo pushed forward, but Rafazi caught hold of his arm and forcefully slammed him up against a tree, stopping him, just as the rest of the Ramangans caught up.

"Release me," Kwadzo said with steely calm.

"I will. But first, I want you to listen. Pay attention to your surroundings."

Kwadzo focused. Familiar voices sounded in the distance, voices he recognized, including Monroe's.

"Now, I want you to think," Rafazi said. "Derby sent that boy Bitty to betray us. Do you think this was Derby's doing alone? Or might Derby have been doing Monroe's bidding? Or even Barrow's? You hear those voices, don't you? If we take a moment or two to listen in, we might be able to discover whether they've set a trap for us."

His rage aside, Kwadzo could not deny the prudence in Rafazi's words. So, he turned his ear toward the voices, retrained his focus, and listened.

"They're in there, drinkin' their fine wine like they ain't gotta care in the world," he heard Monroe say, his words slurred with drink. "And you know what? They don't. Butch weren't one of them. He was one of us. And them goddamn vampyre niggers took him! But they don't care.

"Here we are, good, solid white men, the ones who keep this plantation going, keep them lazy niggers from slackin', and what do we get for it? Do they invite us to their fancy gatherin'? Hell, Ol' Barrow told me point-blank he don't even like me bein' in his house! They ain't got a lick of respect for us. They don't care 'bout Ol' Butch . . ."

Monroe's whimpering stopped his words, and Kwadzo turned to Rafazi. "It would seem there is little cause for concern."

"And now we know," agreed Rafazi. "We'll take care of the riffraff and await your word. Go save Gertie. But give them a good scare first. Just a touch of seasoning for the rest of us."

With a nod acknowledging Rafazi's wink, Kwadzo blurred toward the overseers. Horses grazed next to the overseer house they were all gathered in front of, a crackling open fire before the men, bottles of whiskey in their hands. The closer he got, the more agitated the horses became, neighing and bucking.

And then horror covered the overseers' faces as Kwadzo slowed his approach just enough for them to see him in his blur. He wanted to slash Monroe across his ignorant face as he passed, but he was unsure how much damage the man's blood would do to his hand and talons. Instead, he released as vicious a growl as he could muster as he shot past them. Embers from their fire floated in his wake, and their yelps and squeals at his escaping presence filled his ears, but he paid them no mind. Gertie had to be saved.

Collecting a bucket of water from the well in the kitchen yard, Kwadzo rushed to the back of Barrow Manor where, on the ground, sat a locked metal box far too small to hold an adult. Ripping the lid off it revealed an unconscious Gertie, chained and contorted unnaturally, forced to fit into this inhumane torture chamber.

With hot tears in his red eyes, Kwadzo broke away the chains binding her to the box and poured the water in to cool it. Then, being careful of the skin pressed against the metal, he gently lifted her out. He ripped the cuffs away, cautious of her wrists and ankles, and used the same mix of tenderness and force to break the collar around her neck until he was holding her limp body in his arms.

Crying out in anguish, Kwadzo delivered a furious kick to the box, sending it several feet away. Her cheek and eye were bruised so deeply they both were a purplish hue, and her swollen nose bore a callous imprint of some kind. Her wrists, ankles, and neck were bloody and bruised from the cuffs. Knowing Gertie's trauma would be fresh when she awoke, Kwadzo reverted to his human form.

"Gertie?" he whimpered, holding her closer when she did not respond. "Gertie? Gertie, come on, now. I'm here."

He shook her gently but desperately.

"Gertie, wake up . . . Your Willie is here, Gertie . . . Please!"

She remained limp in his arms.

"No! No, no, no!" His blur carried her to the lake. He held her in the water and splashed some on her face. She had to wake up. She *had* to. If he lost her now, he feared he truly would become the bloodthirsty, evil monster she believed him to be. Without her and their child, there would be no need to be anything else. He ran a hand over her stomach and thought of his still unborn child. "Please help me wake your mama!"

Maybe her body temperature had to cool first, he thought, so he dipped her under the water for a few seconds before pulling her up again, repeating the action as gently as he could until she moaned, and her eyes fluttered open. An involuntary panic set in as they went wide, and she began to flail about, taking in big gulps of air. Kwadzo supported her back and legs, keeping her afloat, allowing her to work through her disorientation.

"It's okay, Gertie, don't worry, I'm here now." Grabbing his arms, she pulled herself up, shaking as she stared back into his eyes. "Don't be afraid, Gertie. It's me. You're safe now. I'm sorry." His voice cracked as he pulled off his dirty shirt and helped Gertie put it on over her nakedness. "I can't seem to stop bringing you misery, can I?"

Gertie blinked slowly, her eyes rolling before they focused on him again. "Willie?"

"Yes, I'm here."

"He . . . he tried to kill our baby," she whimpered. Kwadzo shut his eyes, but his tears still escaped them. "In the black, I called . . ." Her head lolled back, and Kwadzo supported it. "It were so powerful hot . . . But I called to you . . . in the dark . . . to saves me . . . and here you be."

"I will always be here for you, Gertie. I can love you from afar if you need, but please, let me love you. If you can't, you can't, but . . ."

"Two . . ." she whispered, then cleared her throat. "Two girls . . . and a boy . . ." Kwadzo could no longer hold back his sobs, but she held her fingers to his lips. "I called to you . . ."

"I know, and your Willie is here . . ."

"Not Willie," Gertie said. "*Kwadzo.*"

His name. His true name spoken from Gertie's lips as her fingers lightly caressed his lips.

"I were good," whispered Gertie, "and I spoke true. And he still try to kill me. Kill this here child inside me. He don't care 'bout no good I done."

"No, Gertie," Kwadzo sniffled. "He doesn't."

"And that's why you become Kwadzo. Ain't it?"

"Yes."

"Then show me."

"Show you?"

"Show him to me. You's wearin' Willie's face. I wants to see Kwadzo."

Kwadzo's head was spinning. She had been so diametrically opposed to anything Ramangan, but she also had been through so much. No good could come from upsetting her in any way. But the scent of her glorious blood carried no fear.

"Gertie, I don't think . . ."

"Hush now," she whispered, her fingers still pressed against his lips. "Show him to me. Go on, now."

Slowly, Kwadzo allowed his features to morph, licking away the venom coating his teeth. He felt her fingers abandon his lips and trace over the ridges of his brow, the visible veins in his face. Gertie's skin, seen through the red hue in his eyes, made her all the more beautiful to him. And then, her gentle fingers returned to his lips.

"You save me, Kwadzo," she said, "and I thanks you. And I thanks you for bringin' Willie back to me from time to time." She fell silent, and Kwadzo basked in her affection. "These here lips, they done known blood?"

"Yes."

"But there weren't no good in the men you took it from?"

"No. There wasn't."

"Ain't but two things in this here world. Good and evil. Evil like hidin', playin' like it good. But I reckons good can hides, too. It hidin' in you, ain't it?" Kwadzo opened his mouth to speak, but Gertie's shaking head silenced him. "You gots more blood to taste this here night, ain't you?"

"I do."

"And once y'done taste it, we's gonna be free." He nodded. "Then I reckons I best gives you a message for Willie now, Kwadzo. You tell him I's sorry and gives him this here."

Gertie pulled Kwadzo close enough to kiss, and kiss him she did. Not the Willie she grieved. *Him.* Kwadzo. In his true form. On his lips, allowing her tongue to dance with his, sliding along his jagged teeth.

Gertie had returned to him with her full heart, and he would savor this unexpected pleasure, one he never thought he would experience again. Despite the task set before him, Kwadzo felt her lips leave his far too soon.

"I don't needs me no lovin' from afar," Gertie whispered to him, bringing his hand to her belly. "You gives me this gift when you's human. I gots to honor that. I gots to raise this here child as a human, so I cain't never be what you is. But I ain't gots no intention of doin' it alone. So, you go make this here world better for our child, then you come back to me, y'hear? You promise me."

"I promise."

Thirty-Six

THE CRIMSON CRUSADE

Though he couldn't identify the individual sounds over the chatter of Charity's guests, the confounded music, and the smacking of lips as people ate the food, there was some sort of commotion happening outside the room, perhaps all the way outside.

Something was going on with some of his slaves as well. Some of them seemed listless, like Clarence. Others seemed to be staring at him expectantly, like Irene.

When her eyes weren't on him, the girl was downright jumpy, moving through the crush of guests awkwardly. He watched as she nearly spilled a platter of food on some woman, probably someone's wife. Big Jim's eyebrows rose in surprise when the woman slapped Irene for her near mishap. Irene glared back at the woman, immediately igniting the ire of everyone close to the scene. Big Jim sipped his drink and grinned. The slave's obstinance would get her whatever retribution was coming her way, and as bored as he was again, he was thankful for the entertainment.

"What in tarnation do you think you're looking at, girl?" the woman barked at Irene, whose frown slowly became a smile.

"A dead woman," Irene retorted, causing everyone nearby to close in on her. But before the show could begin, the doors of the grand room burst open, and Monroe and Amos rushed in, splattered with blood and short of breath, their faces flush with panic.

"What the hell are you two doing in my goddamn house?" Big Jim growled, marching up to them, livid.

"They here, boss," Monroe huffed. "Them vampyre niggers is here, and they comin' for the house!"

"It's true," Amos added. "A whole gaggle of them came and took Barnaby and Cletus. Me and Monroe barely got away on horses."

"Boss, I know you ain't believe me before, but you need to now. We gotta barricade the doors and keep everybody safe!" Monroe insisted.

"James!" Charity called out to him from across the room. Looking in her direction, he noticed smiles on several of the slaves' faces but ignored them.

"How dare you come into my home, spouting your non-sense, and embarrassing me in front of my guests. This goes beyond the pale, Monroe. You're fired. I want you off my property tonight," Big Jim growled. "I warned you against this twaddle, and I will entertain it no longer. Now, get out!"

Before Monroe could protest, the freshly severed human head of a man, blood still dripping from the neck, sailed over the overseers' heads and into the grand room, landing with a thud and rolling to the middle of the floor. The eyes in the head were open wide in terror, as was the mouth. The shock of the sight rendered Big Jim and all his guests speechless.

"Now?" he heard Irene ask. The sound of her voice startled him, and when he looked in her direction, he saw Irene and five more of his slaves had transformed into something grotesque. Their brows were engorged and extended, the veins in their faces could be seen, and their eyes glowed red. He had never seen anything so vile, so monstrous. He could conjure no words for this sight either, so, he stared until he was shocked by another familiar voice.

"Yes, Irene. Now."

Big Jim turned toward the doors again, and there he stood. Willie. His face had the same hideous features, as did the horde of slaves behind him. The only one who looked normal was the slave girl at his side, Gertie. One of his bloodhounds was with the slaves, too.

Words of fury rushed into Big Jim's head, but a bloodcurdling scream sounded, keeping him from voicing them. Jerking his head back in Irene's direction, he found her covered in the blood of the woman who had slapped her; the woman lay dead on the floor, her throat ripped out and still within Irene's clutches.

Big Jim stared daggers at Willie. He was unsure where Monroe and Amos had disappeared to, but as pandemonium began to rise in the grand room, he was sure of one thing.

"You niggers die tonight!" Big Jim hollered at Willie, who only smiled.

"We shall see."

"THE TIME HAS COME," Kwadzo called out to those behind him. "Move fast, strike hard, avoid the silver, and keep moving. Don't get lost in the blood. This night, we take back our freedom!"

Screams of fright accompanied the frantic scampering of Barrow's guests in all directions. There were three other sets of double doors besides the ones Kwadzo and his legion of

Ramangans stood in front of in this massive room just beyond the manor's grand foyer, each set leading to a different area of the house. Guests rushed through each doorway, shoving the working slaves—and each other—out of the way.

"Kill the niggers!" he heard Big Jim shout. "Kill every last one of them!" The call sent the braver men running toward Kwadzo and his crew with villainous intent in their eyes.

"It's suppertime, y'all!" Ekow called in response, and Kwadzo felt Gertie shudder against him as his Ramangans, led by Rafazi, charged Barrow's guests, their blurs whizzing around the room and through the doorways.

Her vulnerability came to the forefront of his mind. In the melee, he also caught sight of Big Jim using the crowd to try and cover his escape through a pair of doors. Monroe and Amos had run off as soon as he had tossed their fellow over-seer's head into the room, and he would find them both soon enough. Right now, he had to get Gertie to safety. Scooping her up in his arms, Kwadzo rushed Gertie to Irene in his blur.

"Irene," Kwadzo called out over the bedlam. "Where do you reckon the safest place in this house is?"

"The basement," Irene replied as a platter sailed past her while the clash of the fight and screams of pain and terror sounded.

"Fine. Take Gertie there now, make sure she's secure, then return to the fight."

"Wait, now," came Gertie's weak protest as he set her down and shielded her from a man running toward them. "What I's s'posed to do in the basement while y'all up here fightin'?"

"This isn't just fighting, Gertie. This will be war," Kwadzo told her before spinning on the attacking man, slamming his fist into the man's face and dropping him instantly. "You are carrying the future of our people in your belly. The single best thing you can do is stay alive."

"Come back to me," she whispered and nodded to him as she took Irene's hand and was whisked away in her blur.

The blurs of the Ramangans created a hazy view, as did the red mist from the blood spurting forth from their winning attacks, but Barrow was nowhere to be found. Kwadzo blurred himself through the doors he had seen the man escape through and found himself in an even bigger space.

Here, men had obtained weapons: swords, guns, daggers, even tools they'd taken from the hearths around the house. Roughly half the Ramangans he had turned in the woods were fighting here, and the white folk they battled against were not letting up, though their attacks were less than effective.

They swung swords and the bayonets of rifles too slow to load, wildly missing their intended targets due to the Ramangans' speed. Kwadzo assumed these men were fighting in defense of Big Jim, who was missing from this large room as well.

A shot rang out, and Kwadzo watched Rafazi fall to his knees, blood seeping from his midsection. Another white man saw this and ran at Rafazi's back with his sword at the ready. Kwadzo launched himself through the air and sailed into the advancing man. He tackled him to the ground, crushed the man's neck, and fed on his blood.

"Bye, bye, blackie!" Behind Kwadzo, another white man ran at him swinging a cat-o'-nine-tails. Reaching back, Kwadzo caught all nine lashes of the whip in his hand, then yanked hard, pulling the attacking man within his grasp. With his free hand, Kwadzo thrust his arm into the man's chest, grabbing his heart. The man's eyes went wide with horror as Kwadzo squeezed, crushing the heart inside the chest cavity. The man released his last breath, dying on his feet before sliding off the Ramangan's arm.

IRENE COULD FEEL GERTIE'S arms tighten around her as she raced through the grand room. She carried the woman on her back as she blurred through the fight. The weapons closet here had already been opened. She slowed as calls for silver came from two white men standing on a table: one aged and meek-looking, the other bespectacled and tall. They were guarded by two more white men, both of whom held rifles taken from the weapons closet.

"Irene!" she heard Gertie squeal, and to her left, a white man charged at her with the bayonet of his rifle pointed at her. Before she could react, Kwadzo's bloodhound pounced on the man, knocking him to the ground and tearing through the back of his clothing and into his flesh. Irene moved closer, and the dog turned to her, its snout dripping with blood. It barked once at Irene in acknowledgment before jumping back into the fray.

"Massa's hound," Gertie whispered. "But he twice as big and he . . ."

"He's not Barrow's anymore." Irene smiled. "He's one of us. Kwadzo made him; named him Charlie."

Reaching the weapons closet, Irene found it empty save for a few daggers, a pistol, and a small suede pouch. Irene grabbed the pistol and pouch, then blurred out of the grand room and down a hallway toward a side door just as another white man with a sword rounded a corner in the hallway, saw her, and ran at her.

"Die, you demon nigger!"

With a pivot, Irene avoided the blade, caught the man by his neck, and slammed him into the wall beside the side door. With Gertie clutching her tighter than ever, Irene dug her sharp talons into the small of the man's back. As he howled in pain, Irene seized a string of bones in her hand. The hideous cracking of breaking bones and ripping flesh rattled in her ears as she tore the man's spine out of his back, splattering herself and Gertie with blood in the process. The screams ended as death took him, and Irene rushed through the side door, shutting it behind her.

They descended the stairs into the pitch black of the cellar. Irene heard Gertie gasp as the red in her eyes cast a faint, dark crimson hue that guided their way. Spotting an oil lantern, Irene turned it on and set it on a nearby crate. Gertie climbed off her back, and Irene reverted her eyes, along with the rest of herself, to her human form. As Gertie looked around at the various items stored in this utility basement—mill sacks, threshing racks, sickles, gathering baskets—Irene set about readying the pistol.

"We're going to fight our hardest," Irene said as she placed the pistol in Gertie's hands, along with the suede pouch, which had a short strap. "But there's no telling what may happen. If any of them come into this basement, protect yourself."

Gertie's fluster was apparent and understandable. She was fighting to catch her breath, and her face was splattered with blood. Irene could hear the accelerated pumping of her heart, could smell the fear in her blood; she could hear and smell the blood of the child Gertie carried. There was no way to ease Gertie's mind completely, and there was no time to even if she could.

"I know how hard this must be for you," Irene said softly. "I know you didn't want this for Kwadzo, for any of us."

"I ain't know . . ." Gertie was shaking. Finding a rag, Irene gently wiped the blood from Gertie's face.

"It's not wrong to fight them, Gertie. They've wronged us horribly. They've got swords, whips, knives, guns, and they don't hesitate to use any of them against us. But now, thanks to Rafazi and Kwadzo, we have the Blood."

"What it like? Reach in a man, pull his bones clean out his back. How it feel? Havin' all that power?"

"Exciting. Scary, intoxicating, empowering. It feels like a lot of different things all at once." Gertie looked down at the gun as the sounds of battle crashed above. "You could feel it, too," she added.

"No, I's too 'fraid to die," Gertie admitted with a sad chuckle. "'Sides, it'd be killin' this here child inside me. Ain't a doubt in my mind that man meant to kill you and me, but I cain't sees myself killin'. Ain't in me."

"Pressed hard enough, it's in all of us." Irene had said the words as gingerly as she could, but she meant them. There was nothing left to be said save for instructions. "The gun is already loaded with one shot. Just pull the trigger if you need to. There are lead balls, gunpowder, and a short ramrod in the pouch. Drop a little powder in the barrel, then a ball, then use the ramrod to shove it all the way down. Then, pull back the hammer, pour a bit more powder in the little pan in front of it, and you'll be ready for a second shot."

"I's gonna need to shoot this here thing more than one time?"

"Hopefully, you'll never have to shoot it at all."

"I ain't always been kind to you," Gertie said with labored breath. "I talks 'bout good all the time, and I reckons you been good to me this whole time. I thanks you."

Irene smiled and gave a nod of appreciation before turning and once again taking on her Ramangan form, but Gertie's hand on her arm stopped her from blurring away.

"You watch out for him, y'hear?"

"I owe him as much. He saved my life, then gave me life eternal."

Dashing back up the stairs, Irene found the combat had escalated. Both those she had turned in the house and the humans who had refused the Blood were being attacked by Barrow's guests with the weapons they'd found.

Irene rushed to a white man thrusting a sword into a human house slave. Diving for his feet, she pulled him to the floor before crawling up his body, slashing away at his flesh as she went, until she got to his neck and bit into it, drinking deeply.

"Irene . . ." The weak voice of the fallen human slave bleeding beside the man called to her. "Save me," the slave woman said with a struggle, coughing up blood. Irene examined the wound left from the attack on her, the blood pooling beneath her. Death was imminent.

"I know of only one way to do so," Irene told her, "and you did not wish it."

"I do now," the slave woman said. Irene quickly cut her wrist, and the woman clamped down on it, extracting as much blood as she could before life left her body. Irene stood up and immediately felt a familiar pinch on her arm. Turning, she found Charity and Virginia, their faces full of fury, but she could smell the fear in their blood.

"I demand you save us from this horridness immediately!" Charity yelled.

"You stupid savage slave niggers!" Virginia shouted. "You ruined our home! You ruin everything!"

"I don't care if you are a demon," Charity said. "You still *belong* to us, and you will put an end to this foolishness once and for all!"

With a knowing smile, Irene thrust her hands forward, straight into the midsections of the Barrow women. They cried out in agony; terror covered their faces as she blurred them against a wall and wrapped her hands around their innards.

"I warned you how painful death by my hand would be," Irene said. "Did you forget?"

"Why?" Charity managed to croak out, tears running down her cheeks.

"Because it wasn't enough for you to be the worst kind of human being. You raised your children to be as wicked as you, and they would have raised theirs to be the same, as would their children's children. Your bloodline will be a blight on this world no more."

"Blight? Who taught you that word?" were the last words Charity Barrow ever uttered as Irene ripped the entrails from both her and her daughter. Lifting Charity's to her lips, Irene tasted the woman's blood, then shrugged.

"I've had better," she said, dropping the viscera and blurring herself back into the battle.

Standing back-to-back with Rafazi, Kwadzo fed on the latest man to rush at him bayonet-first. He heard shots ring out before he felt Rafazi slump against him.

Throwing the now dead man he'd been feeding from in the path of even more who ran at him, he reached behind himself, grabbed hold of Rafazi's shoulders, and flipped himself back, up, and over his Maker, landing in front of the man who had shot Rafazi. Kwadzo slashed his talons across the man's face, shredding skin and muscle before turning his attention to Rafazi, who had fallen to his knees.

"Silver?" asked Kwadzo.

"Just a close blast of lead," the elder Ramangan groaned. "I will heal." As Kwadzo pulled Rafazi to his feet, a blood-drenched Tussy blurred up to them.

"I can't find Fanna!"

Kwadzo's heart sank. Though he needed to find Barrow, worry for the young girl overtook his objective. He was concerned she would be seen as an easy target for the attacking men, who seemed to have discovered the dangerous effect silver had on the Ramangans.

He'd seen three of his twenty-three go down from attacks

from sharp silver objects—silver eating utensils, porringer handles, and candelabras were all wielded as weapons against them, and the Ramangans were outnumbered.

Superspeed was a blessing, yes, but it also made things, people, easy to miss. He needed to make sure Fanna was safe.

"Go. Find her," said Rafazi before he blurred back into the battle, zipping between three advancing men and creating a shower of blood amid them.

Kwadzo followed Tussy's blur back out to the grand foyer, up one side of the double staircase, and down a corridor less populated than the rooms downstairs. A few of Barrow's guests were running along it, presumably looking for safety. None of them presented a threat, so Kwadzo and Tussy blew right past them, looking through the rooms they passed for Fanna.

An anguished wail stopped them both. Following the sound, they arrived at a doorway without a door—it had been ripped from its hinges. Amos was backing away from Fanna, her eyes red and pulsing, her teeth and fangs dripping with venom.

"You best back up, girl, 'less you wanna get hurt. You think I'm afraid of you?" Amos asked, his voice shaking, betraying him.

"Yeah, you 'fraid. You gonna die 'fraid."

There was no evidence of blood or battle on her. Her speech had not changed. She must have used her blur to avoid the fight and seek out her tormentor, saving all her rage for him. Kwadzo stepped toward them, but Tussy's hand on his shoulder stopped him.

"Uh-uh. You want Barrow? This vengeance is hers to get."

Amos hadn't even noticed them in the doorway. His terrified eyes were on Fanna, who seemed surprisingly methodical in her menacing stance, appearing like a lioness who had cornered her prey. And the cowering zebra's time had grown short.

"I'm warnin' you, girl," Amos said, taking another step back toward the bed, which sat in the center of the large room. "You may be a demon, but you ain't but a lil' demon. Won't take me a second to put you over my knee again. Or maybe I'll sit you on my cock like I done, show you what's what again. You can't have forgotten how good I feel, loud as you was screamin'."

Fanna smiled right through his empty taunts before closing the distance between them with her blur. When she stopped, her arm was extended forward, her hand in a fist, and Amos was sailing through the air. He landed hard on the bed, his eyes wide in surprise.

"I say I's fuck you up," Fanna growled at Amos as he scrambled off the bed, grabbing the whip holstered on his belt. Once again, Kwadzo moved to step in, and once again, Tussy stopped him.

"No, sir," she said. "She's got him right where she wants him."

"I'll kill you, you little bitch!" Amos yelled as he swung his whip, but the youngest Ramangan ducked, easily avoiding the attack. He raised his leg to kick Fanna, but she caught the limb. With a sinister howl, she tore the leg from Amos's body, and his blood spurted all over her. Amos fell back on the bed, squealing in violent agony as Fanna held the leg like a giant turkey drumstick and sank her wet fangs into the bloody flesh at the end of the severed thigh.

As her eyes crossed, Kwadzo was certain this was Fanna's first taste of human blood. Amos never stopped screaming as Fanna moaned in satisfaction. Then, she began beating him with his own detached leg. After a few hits, she discarded it, pounced on the overseer who had so viciously stripped her of her innocence, bared her wet fangs, and bit into his neck. Hard. She drank deeply as Amos tried to push her off, but between her strength and the blood draining from his hip and neck, the overseer was no match for her.

The bedsheets were soaked red with his blood by the time Fanna sat up from feeding on Amos to attack him with her talons. Shrieking in rage, she slashed her claws across his face and chest, shredding his clothes, skin, and flesh, moving down the length of his body until she got to his groin. Ignoring Amos's dying pleas for mercy, she wrapped a hand around his limp member and ripped it mercilessly from his body, blood spilling from the newly created orifice.

The expiring overseer shook uncontrollably on the brink of his death as Fanna resumed drinking his blood until she was drenched in it, satiated. As his last breath left him, Fanna beat her fists against Amos's carcass hard, then harder and more insistently, until she was sobbing. Her cries became wails of anguish, and Kwadzo and Tussy finally went to her, gently pulling her off the dead overseer and holding her as she wept.

"You're finally free now, child," Tussy said, and the words seemed to abate Fanna's cries. She looked up at Kwadzo sorrowfully.

"I's sorry," she sniffled.

"After what he did, he earned every moment of the death you gave him."

Fanna wrapped tight and unexpected arms around Kwadzo, like a daughter taking comfort in her father. Tussy nodded and smiled.

"Told you she would be all right."

"The fight rages on. I must get back to it," he said, hugging the young girl back, a warmth within his heart growing for her. With her abuser slain, he began to feel an ease emanating from Fanna as she beheld her new freedom. It was his wish for all his people to feel the same. This was what they were fighting for. "Take all the time you need."

"Don't need more time," Fanna said, rising to her feet.

Kwadzo marveled at her resilience.

"Hell, you heard the girl! There are a lot more evil men in this house who need killing, and like Ekow said, it's suppertime!" Tussy exclaimed, and the three of them blurred out of the room, leaving Amos to rot.

Racing through the main floor of the manor, Kwadzo found the battle had taken a different shape. The men the Ramangans fought against now were more skilled. The Ramangans were individually more powerful than their opponents, but they did not have the same technique as the white men they fought. One night of training, no matter how intense, was not enough to prepare for battle.

And still, Barrow was nowhere in sight.

"Our people possess force, but our foes attack with precision and experience," Rafazi reported, blurring up to him amid the fight before leading him into another room, one closed off from the rest of the house and smaller in size compared to the other rooms on this level. Kwadzo clocked several lanterns and candles around this room. "Their swords are not silver, but they still slow us."

Have they figured out fire? Kwadzo asked Rafazi telepathically.

Not yet, came the answer as they both blurred into the crush of the fight.

In the corner of the room, Tussy fought with a vengeful vigor in her eyes. She struck swiftly and with strength, as if she'd had the Blood for many years. She avoided the blade of a heavyset bald man she was fighting, who had overextended himself with his failed attack. Tussy grabbed hold of the man's head and used her bite force to sink her teeth into his bald dome.

She hungrily drank the blood shooting out from his cranium while he shrieked in suffering. Kwadzo snapped the neck of a man rushing for him as he watched a redheaded man run up behind Tussy, holding a large lantern at full flame high above his head.

Time seemed to slow for Kwadzo, and he heard himself cry out in warning as the redheaded man slammed the lantern on Tussy's head.

She was immediately set ablaze.

Tussy screamed as the fire took hold, and her burning, twisting figure was such a spectacle, it momentarily paused the fighting in the room. The flames flashed back and forth from orange to red as they quickly consumed her. It was as if she'd been doused in grain alcohol.

"Tussy!" Kwadzo yelled, launching himself toward her, only to be pulled back by Rafazi.

I'm sorry, brother, he heard Rafazi say in his mind. *It's too late. The flames have already claimed her.*

"TUSSY!"

Fanna's cry broke Kwadzo's heart, but he caught her as she attempted to race past him.

"It's too late, Fanna."

She sobbed in his arms, and Kwadzo felt the sting of his own tears as Tussy fell to the floor in a heap. She, and the clothing she wore, burned hot until the flames faded, the brightness slowly diminishing until there was nothing but a hefty pile of burnt ash.

Tussy was no more.

"What are y'all waiting for?" the redheaded man shouted as he grabbed another lantern. "Burn them all!"

A renewed battle cry went up from the white folk as they all grabbed lanterns and candles and chased after the Ramangans, who all blurred out of the room and scattered throughout the house. Seeing the speed with which the fire had extinguished Tussy put a fright into all of them, Kwadzo included. But they could not simply give up. A new plan of attack was needed.

"This is usually the time when I would make my escape," he heard Rafazi say as Kwadzo looked around and found he,

Rafazi, and Fanna had made it to a very small room at the edge of the manor.

"We need a new vantage point of attack," Kwadzo said.

"We need to put out the flames. Leave them in complete darkness."

"Gather whoever you can and get to the well."

With a nod, Rafazi and Fanna blurred away through the door leading out of the back of the manor. Kwadzo needed to regroup, but he hadn't the time.

"I reckon you're the nigger responsible for all this fuss."

The redheaded man, the one who had set fire to Tussy, stepped into the small room holding a lantern in his hand. Up close, Kwadzo could see he was a beefy sort, tall and bearded. Kwadzo's Ramangan form seemed to have no effect on the man, even when he pulsed his red eyes.

"That supposed to scare me?" the redheaded man scoffed. "'Cause you don't. I ain't *never* gonna be afraid of no nigger, ever. Not even a demon nigger."

Kwadzo could hear the man's words, but his eyes were on the high flame burning inside the lantern. The man also carried a fire poker, but Kwadzo was certain it wasn't silver. The stench of the man's blood was foul, but not as rancid as Monroe's, and he did not detect fear in the man's blood.

"Demon or no, you gonna die tonight," the redheaded man said as he ran at Kwadzo, leading with the lantern. The man swung the lantern at Kwadzo, who leapt high to avoid the flame. His trajectory sent him sailing over the man's head, and Kwadzo kicked him in the forehead as he went over. The man fell hard enough to drop the fire poker and the lantern, shattering its glass. The mechanism which held the oil cracked, seeping out as the flame burned itself out. The imminent threat gone, Kwadzo spun around, kicked the fire poker out of reach, and stood over the man menacingly.

"Kill me now," the redheaded man groaned, "and I die a hero."

"I'll be the one writing the history," the Ramangan said as he kneeled, "and I don't even know your name."

Faster than Kwadzo could anticipate, the redheaded man snatched a dagger from his belt and swiped its blade up, slicing Kwadzo across the neck, causing the Ramangan to straighten and stumble back, clutching his throat in shock. A sharp, intense burning sensation spread from the cut, a new kind of pain, one that became more pronounced as it lingered. The wound bled; it wasn't healing.

Kwadzo didn't know when the redheaded man had gotten back on his feet—the searing pain clouded his mind—but he could see the man charging at him with a rage-filled expression, slamming into him while delivering a second swipe of the blade to Kwadzo's already severed jugular.

The force of the attack sent the two of them stumbling back, out of the back door, over the back porch and onto the grass behind the manor. Flat on his back, Kwadzo struggled to speak, only to hear the gurgling of his precious Ramangan Blood as it escaped him. The intensity of the pain was beyond horrendous.

The feeling surging through him now was death.

Immortality does not mean invincibility. Rafazi's words rang in his mind. What he couldn't make sense of was how such a small blade had caused this defeat.

Silver.

It was the only explanation. The blade of the redheaded man's dagger. There was no way he could have known the blade was silver, but the thought offered no consolation. The strikes of silver kept his healing power at bay, allowing blood to escape his throat at an alarming rate, causing his very essence to slip away.

And in the end, it had all been for naught.

He cursed himself for not listening to Gertie.

Gertie.

He would never set eyes on her again, nor meet his child. Overwhelmed with profound grief, his eyes shifted up to the twinkling stars in the night sky, his final earthly image before endless black overtook him.

Thirty-Seven

THE GOOD IN EVIL

olled into a ball, knees to her chin with her arms wrapped around them, Gertie shuddered with every new battle sound that rang out above her. Every shudder made her look to the pistol on the floor next to her. The weapon had been cold and heavy in her hands. She had no intention of using it, and she wondered how long it would take Kwadzo to come back for her.

Kwadzo. Kwadzo. Kwadzo.

She couldn't stop repeating his name in her head. The name of the one who had saved her and Willie's child inside her. She understood now. Willie wasn't gone; he hadn't left her. He lived inside Kwadzo, and Kwadzo only existed because of her Willie, who had made the ultimate sacrifice to save her life and the life of their unborn child. In spite of all her righteous indignation, her claims of correct and proper thinking, the edicts she chastised Willie for not following.

And still, miraculously, he had returned from the dead with his love for her intact and was leading the fight for the freedom of their people. She realized now how wrong she'd been. Good was not finite, and neither was evil. Kwadzo had taken the power considered to be evil for centuries and transformed it.

She suspected even the supreme Roog would have approved.

As a series of gunshot blasts shook the basement ceiling, Gertie noticed the battle was escalating, and thoughts of Kwadzo perishing in battle entered her mind. The consequence of his death, a final death, would crush her, but now, after all he had accomplished, it would also led to the destruction of his people. Their people. She couldn't sit idly by and not fight for him. She couldn't let him die again. Maybe, even as she hid in the cellar, he needed her.

With newfound purpose, Gertie took the pistol in her hand and found the weight of it somehow less than before. Yes, this would be her defying Kwadzo's wishes, but he had defied hers for her own good. She understood now. There was fight in her. She would fight for her people, for her child.

For Kwadzo.

Thirty-Eight

RETURN FROM THE RED

It was all too familiar—the brilliant, rich red filling his eyes, the pulsing in his heart, the surge of vitality rushing to his throat, slowly but surely healing the wound the silver blade had left. He was at peace until an unseen, mystical force sat him up and opened his eyes just as it had the first time he died. His vision went red.

And he could smell blood.

It seemed immortality did not prevent the ultimate torment of death. As his senses returned in full force, hunger gnawed at his insides, and he searched the various scents emanating from the open door he'd fallen through until the one he'd smelled last became clear to him.

He got up slowly, his strength quickly returning as he moved across the back porch, into the small room and back into the manor. Kwadzo narrowed his eyes, focusing until he caught sight of a shock of red hair bobbing in the next room over—a serving room from the looks of it, a room lit by candles set in elaborate candelabras where cooked foods were plated to be served—shoving his silver-bladed dagger into a house slave, who cried out in agony.

It was a human cry, for Kwadzo did not feel the loss in his Blood as he did when a fellow Ramangan perished—but he felt it in his heart, a heart that demanded bloody vengeance.

Dashing forward, Kwadzo blurred through the crush of people still engaged in combat. Multiple dead bodies, both light and dark of skin, were scattered across the floor. He felt his heart seize up with a burning sensation twice, telling him two more of the Blood had perished by fire somewhere in this house. Every being lost, be it human or Ramangan, was one too many. He needed to find Big Jim and end this. But the monster in him demanded one more pound of flesh first.

Speeding toward the redheaded man, Kwadzo slammed both fists into his back, sending him flying into the wall. Kwadzo heard the crunch of the man's nose breaking before he fell hard on his back.

"I killed you," the redheaded man groaned up at Kwadzo, his nose contorted and bleeding.

"Unfortunately for you, I was already dead."

From his prone position, the redheaded man brandished his dagger once again, and Kwadzo skipped back from it, remaining cautious as the redheaded man got to his feet.

"Whatever evil you are, holy silver strikes fear in your heart."

Kwadzo never took his eyes off the blade. All he had to do was snatch the dagger away. Surely a cut to the hand would do far less damage than the cut to his throat had. The redheaded man laughed as he lunged for Kwadzo, making the Ramangan hop out of his path. "Killin' you the first time was easy. I'ma enjoy the second time."

The man charged Kwadzo, who planted himself in the man's path and grabbed the dagger's blade. Kwadzo's skin sizzled against the blade, and his eyes pulsed as he let out a growl of pain. It was a pain he had prepared for and was able to endure, at least for the moment. The redheaded man pulled at the dagger, but Kwadzo kept his grip firm on the blade, and with his free hand, he grasped his adversary's neck, pulling him in close. Kwadzo twisted the dagger from the man's grip and hurled it away. The silver blade took a chunk of Kwadzo's sizzling skin from his palm with it.

"There is a fundamental difference between us, though not the one you think," Kwadzo said through gritted teeth. "A Ramangan can rise from a killing, but a dead human *stays dead.*"

Finally, the sweet aroma of fright entered his nostrils, and Kwadzo smiled before stabbing his jagged teeth and fangs harshly into the neck of the redheaded man, who unleashed a ghastly screech.

A thrill ran through him at the terror in the man's blood. He didn't know if it was because the man had previously bested him, or if it was the wealth of fear his blood now possessed, but Kwadzo lost all thoughts of Big Jim, the battle, his mission. He lost himself in this man's blood, savoring every drop as he sucked the life out of the screaming man.

With a quick and strong twist, he separated the man's hand from his forearm at the wrist and shoved the stump in the redheaded man's mouth to quiet him. Kwadzo then lifted the man at the waist, fangs still in his neck, tilted him up and back, and continued guzzling the man's blood even as it washed over him, drinking his fill until the man's body went limp in his grip.

Dropping the carcass to the floor, Kwadzo closed his eyes, humming his satisfaction. Checking the wound from the silver blade on his hand, he was relieved to find it was small and healing. The wound at his throat had now fully mended. Now that the monster had gotten its moment, the guilt set in. He had lost himself in the Blood again. How long had he abandoned the fight for his own satiation?

"SAMUEL!"

Sobbing followed the shriek of a woman who rushed into the room with a young girl, no older than Fanna. The woman fell to her knees at the corpse of the redheaded man, holding his face in her hands while the young girl—with hair the same color as the man's—looked on, sobbing uncontrollably.

"Mister Knudsen! No!" the young girl cried.

Neither of them even acknowledged Kwadzo, who hesitated in attacking them. Their grief seemed genuine, and indiscriminate murder was not his purpose, though he had no reason to believe they did not carry in themselves the same hate as the man they grieved.

"Get up! Get up, the both of you, this instant!" a white man shouted as he rushed into the room as if he'd been in pursuit of the woman and girl. He didn't seem to notice Kwadzo either. "How dare you embarrass and defy me when James was good enough to hide us from harm!"

"Samuel was fighting the good fight." The woman spun on him tearfully. "The way a *man* should! I could not sit and watch you cower any longer!"

"I will not have my family crying over a goddamn overseer!" He grabbed the woman's arm, but she yanked it away, glaring up at him, her eyes narrow with rage.

"*Your* family? How blind *are* you, Robert?"

"Mother?" the young girl sniffled.

"Look upon him, child," the woman said, pulling the girl closer to the dead man. "Do you not see your face in his? Mister Knudsen is the man who sired you. He is your true father."

The white man looked gut-punched, and a familiar scent entered Kwadzo's nostrils. The redheaded young girl looked up and finally noticed the Ramangan.

"You killed him, didn't you?" Kwadzo could tell the young girl's words were directed at him, but they were not his concern. Instead, he stayed focused on the familiar odor and found it was coming from the man who had chased after the woman and young girl. It was faint, but it was Big Jim's scent. Ignoring the girl, he moved to the man.

"I smell Barrow on you," Kwadzo growled, grabbing the man's neck. "You've been in close quarters with him. Where does he cower?"

The man's heart was beating extraordinarily fast. "I do not agree with this!" he cried. "Your people suffer unjustly!" Whether the man's words of kindness were out of fear or sincerity didn't matter to Kwadzo. As long as they led him to Barrow.

"I knew it!" the woman grumbled. "I knew you harbored affinity for these savages!"

"Nigger lover!" the girl yelled at the man, her little hands balled into fists. "It should be you lying dead on the floor! And you"—she faced Kwadzo again—"you killed my daddy! I hate you filthy fucking niggers!"

This display of hatred was disrupted by water flying into the room, splashing the lit candles of one of the elaborate candelabras and putting their flames out. Fanna followed shortly after holding an empty bucket. Her arrival and the sudden reduction of light in the room brought the noise of their pointless blather to a stop.

Before she could utter a single word, another white man, bloody from the battle and wielding a spiked club, swung it hard into Fanna's back. She growled in pain before turning and slamming her bucket into the white man's head. As he stumbled back from her attack, Fanna kicked him in the knee so hard the bones within audibly cracked. Crying out in a painful howl as he fell, Fanna pounced on him, ready to feed.

"You get your filthy nigger body off him!"

The enraged young redheaded girl dove at Fanna, pulling at her leg in a feeble attempt to remove her from the hobbled white man as her mother screamed and cried.

When Fanna remained unfazed from the assault, the young white girl bit down on Fanna's leg so hard her teeth pierced the young immortal's skin, sending a rush of blood into the young white girl's mouth.

Ramangan Blood.

The compounded actions happened in such quick succession Kwadzo could only look on, his eyes wide in shock. Never in his imaginings of this battle did he envision a white person ingesting Ramangan Blood. The white folks were violent and savage enough as humans. If they were to take hold of Ramangan power, he feared the entire world would be decimated. He needed to find Big Jim, but he also could not let the white girl die. There was only enough time to put his effort behind one endeavor.

Before he could move, however, Fanna gave a swift and strong back thrust of her leg as she fed on the injured white man, dislodging the redheaded girl and sending her flying backward in front of a group of white men who had just entered the space, fighting two Ramangans.

A bloodcurdling scream escaped the mother as her daughter was trampled in the melee. He was too late. Fanna's blood would turn the girl, and she would feel her progeny soon enough. It was now a worry for another time. There was no other choice but to focus on Big Jim.

"There are hidden rooms behind the walls of this house," the man named Robert whispered as Kwadzo turned back to him, tightening his grip.

"From which one did you crawl out of?"

"I'm not sure. I chased after my whore wife and her bastard child thinking they were my own. We ran through a darkened corridor until a door opened, but I do not know how to get back."

"Then point me toward this door."

Thirty-Nine

ONE UPPITY SLAVE

ig Jim sat back in his thick leather chair, sipped his
brandy, and sighed. The sounds of the battle shook the
walls of this large, hidden sitting room. He was ac-
commodating a small group of the guests here, the most elite
in attendance.

And Clarence.

He hadn't stopped whimpering since. Clarence was a spectacle in front of his other guests, his torn shirt and jacket removed
and bunched up over his chest wounds at Big Jim's command,
to keep him from bleeding all over the floor. He preferred it
when the slave was quiet, but Clarence had sustained his
wounds by placing himself between his master and one of those
black demons before it moved on to another attack. Big Jim
couldn't take the chance of leaving him exposed in his current
condition. Clarence knew where the secret room was. He would
have bled and begged at the door and led those hellish creatures
right to Big Jim's hiding place. Clarence's presence here was far

from ideal, but at least he hadn't lost his gratefulness like the rebellious niggers beyond the wall had.

Like Willie.

He was the cause of this! There had to be a way to stop him. To restore the natural order.

To kill him dead.

Lord only knew the unholy damage those ungrateful slaves were doing to his house. And after all he'd done for them!

"Do you reckon Robert will be all right?" Oliver asked Big Jim, who simply rolled his eyes.

"The man deserves whatever befalls him," Big Jim scoffed. "I offer him and his family shelter from the madness of the demon niggers run amok, and my kindness is repaid with his women running off after his overseer?"

"Are you not concerned for *your* wife and daughter, James?" Governor Collins asked, his young wife sitting by his side, her mouth in a tight line.

"Should I have risked my own life searching among those demons for them, Governor?" Big Jim asked. "One must think of the greater good in dire situations. I saved my boy, but you saw what's out there. What more could I have done?"

"What are we sitting here for, Daddy?" Thomas interrupted, clinging to a rifle nearly as long as he was tall. "We should be out there killing those niggers!"

"The boy makes a good point," agreed Oliver.

"And do you know *how* to kill them?" Big Jim asked.

"With silver, of course," Doc Farkus said.

"Then by all means, Doctor, have at it! Save us all! Something I would love to see, considering you planned for silver swords to be delivered *tomorrow*!"

"How was I to know what these creatures had planned?"

"There is no use laying blame for this at anyone's feet," Minister Elder Easton interjected, standing to look down at them all over his glasses. "Speculation is the work of fools. What's done is done. It is no one's wish, and I do not intend to be crass, but should Madam Barrow and the lovely Virginia perish tonight, it shall be the least of our worries. Though I doubt this evil iteration of nigger will be smart enough to discover us, should their violence persist, they'll be emboldened to move on to the next plantation and the next."

The hidden door to the secret room rattled, setting everyone on edge. Oliver, Thomas, and Big Jim readied the guns they had managed to bring into the room, and Big Jim patted his vest, making sure the blade he had grabbed from a weapons closet was still there in case the guns didn't do the trick and one of those demons got too close for comfort.

The door creaked open and in stepped Monroe, carrying a long broadsword, the blade of which was dripping blood onto the floor. He was sweating and chewing on his ball of tobacco with a gritty smile. The confident swagger his former overseer was adapting did nothing to lower Big Jim's blood pressure.

"Well, how do, y'all?" Monroe said, shutting the door behind him. "Things done got a might unseemly out there. Good thing I had my sword with me. Got me a good swipe of one of them *vampyres* on my way in. Blade went clean through him. Or her. I can't tell with their faces all muddled up with evil."

"How in the hell do you know about this room?" Big Jim shouted.

"Boss, I've worked for you a long time. I make it my business to know things. Like when I told you your slaves turned into vampyres. I suspect you done seen for yourself I was right. Shame you ain't listen to me in the first place."

"Listen to you? This is all *your* fault, Monroe! It was your job to keep those goddamn slaves in line, not let them turn into revolting hell demons to come and destroy my house! You got good white men killed, you dolt, which is why I fired you!"

"I suppose you right, *James*. Don't reckon I have any obligation here no more. Guess I'll just take my trusty *silver* sword here and be on my way."

"Silver, did you say?" Doc Farkus's question halted Monroe's exit.

"Why, yes, Doc, I did. See, when I came here and tried to warn y'all 'bout what was comin', and y'all chose not to believe me, and I was summarily dismissed from my employ right when poor Ol' Barnaby's head come flyin' through the door—"

Big Jim rolled his eyes. Monroe had become downright insufferable. "Will you get on with it?"

"Well, I hightailed it out in all the commotion to do the one thing any man of valor would do in this situation—"

"You went to the blacksmith." Doc Farkus's guess took the wind right out of Monroe's sails. Big Jim chuckled, grateful for the peg he'd been knocked down from.

"Yes, I went to the blacksmith! I was 'bout to . . . Dammit, Doc, I was gonna . . . Had me a whole thing I was doin' . . ."

"So, you went to the blacksmith and brought back one of the swords he was making for tomorrow night's hunt. Good for you, Monroe. Fat lot of good it's doing you in here where there aren't any demon niggers!" Big Jim barked to a now-pouting Monroe.

"Vampyres!"

"Regardless! A real man, armed as you are, would be out *there*, fighting the good fight! Instead, you're in here prancing around like a peacock. What a useless clod you are. You're as useless as tits on a boar!"

"Useless, huh? Well, if push come to shove, and I lose this here sword, I'm still the only shot you got of survivin'."

"How?"

"My blood can *kill* Willie!" Monroe's declaration brought a collective gasp of shock from everyone in the room, which brought back the man's bravado. "Them vampyre niggers went off with Willie and had themselves a meetin' in the woods. Now, not all them slaves is in league with Ol' Willie, and some of them that ain't sent them a spy out there. Turns out if you hate a vampyre nigger, your blood can kill them."

"Well, we all hate niggers." Big Jim's jibe was followed by murmurs of agreement.

"No, see, you hate niggers, sure. But one nigger ain't no different than the next to you. But me? I hate *Willie*. Hate him with a passion. Always have. And that hate is in my blood. Blood we can make him drink and kill him with."

If this was all true, it would give Monroe the chance to be the hero, the savior. *His* savior. Big Jim shuddered at the thought.

"Now, this here's what I'm proposin'," Monroe continued, as if he were suddenly in charge. "We go out there, boss, me, and you. All's I gotta do is cut myself on the arm here a little bit, nothing deep now, just enough to draw blood. Now, Ol' Willie know my blood can kill him and sure ain't gonna wanna die. That's all the threat he gonna need to stand down, and—"

Monroe was interrupted by a rumble outside the walls that had become deafening, as if some massive force was pushing them in, slamming against them, louder and louder, until large cracks began to form.

In minutes, the front wall of the secret room came tumbling down, creating a massive crater in the room. On the other side was darkness—save for a hovering red glow that slowly got brighter.

In seconds, they stood before the hidden white folk. A dozen slave niggers with snarling demon faces and blood on their lips. Behind them were more of Barrow's slaves, but they still looked normal. And leading them all was Willie.

This filthy, ungrateful, uppity nigger, a mongrel Big Jim had given purpose to, was now standing in front of him as if he had every right to. Willie didn't have a demon face like the rest, but he was a demon just the same. Big Jim could feel his teeth chattering with anger.

They'd torn down his goddamn wall!

"So, this is where you've been hiding," Willie observed drily, looking around the room. "Creative little coward, aren't you? Well, not exactly little."

Dropping his pistol, Big Jim snatched the rifle in his son's hands and fired a shot into Willie, knocking him onto his back; Thomas picked up the pistol his father had dropped. The red in the eyes of the rest of the demon slaves intensified, threatening to overtake the warm glow the lanterns in the room gave off.

"You niggers got five seconds to get the hell out of my house, or I will put you all down!" Big Jim yelled. Confusingly, it had no effect. "What are y'all waiting for? I gave y'all a direct order to get out of my house, and not a one of you has moved a muscle! Did y'all forget who your master is?"

And then, like some ungodly creature, Willie rose to his feet, as if by some unseen power, and the rest of the demon slaves began to growl. Holding a palm to his chest, Big Jim watched horrified as the lead he'd fired into Willie's flesh pushed itself out from his body and dropped into Willie's waiting hand.

He nearly dropped his rifle when Willie crushed the ball of lead in his fist, then transformed into a demon like the rest. Demon Willie smirked, holding up his hand and causing the growling to stop. How did his uppity slave gain so much power?

"They have no need for a master," Willie declared. "They are free."

They were *not* free. They would *never* be free. They belonged to *him*, and they *always* would.

"The hell you say! Kill them!" Big Jim shouted to the men with him.

Oliver and Thomas leveled their weapons and started firing into the group of demon slaves when what looked to Big Jim like two frightfully fast ghosts emerged from the pack. And as fast as they had appeared, they'd returned to the pack. Oliver lay dead with his throat torn out, and Thomas was howling in pain beside him, missing one of his eyes.

"Hurts to have your eye taken, doesn't it, boy?" a female demon slave said, rolling the boy's eyeball between her fingers as Thomas held a hand over his bloody eye socket. "Now you know how it felt when you did it to me."

"At least I'm not a filthy nigger!" Thomas screamed. Using her demon speed, the slave was back in front of him, plucking the remaining eye from his boy's head faster than Big Jim could blink. And then she slammed her fist into Thomas's face so hard it smashed inward; Big Jim could do nothing as he watched his son fall dead.

"You'll be next, fat man," she told Big Jim, while he, and everyone else left alive in the room, stood petrified.

"No, slave. You are."

The words came out smooth and sinister from Monroe as he plunged his sword into the female demon's side until its tip came out her other end. He sliced upward and held the entirety of the silver blade in place as she bled and quaked from the silver embedded in her. The blade quickly overcame her. Her eyes went black as coal, and her skin turned gray and lifeless. Her body began to disintegrate slowly, falling away from the sword until there was nothing left but dust underneath the clothes she had worn.

"Get behind me, boss!" Monroe shouted as Willie, and the rest of the demons, rushed toward them.

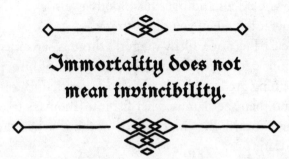

Immortality does not
mean invincibility.

Forty

LOVE VERSUS HATE

There was no time to mourn his fallen sister. The familiar reek of Monroe's blood turned Kwadzo's insides. Before him stood his two greatest adversaries, but one of them could be his undoing if he wasn't careful.

The overseer was standing cocksure before him. Monroe knew the threat he posed, the dust of the destroyed Ramangan spurring him on.

"You been missin' my love taps, boy?" Monroe smirked, waving the broadsword in Kwadzo's face.

While his fellow Ramangans raced around doling out punishment to the others in the room, Kwadzo lunged at Monroe, talons first, with a wild swing of his arm. He could feel himself pulling back, relying on his human capability, cautious of Monroe's blood. But while he hesitated, Monroe was emboldened, slicing his broadsword deep across Kwadzo's side. A sharp, intense burning sensation erupted, one that was all too familiar.

Silver.

"Stings, don't it?" Monroe hissed, his smile the epitome of evil. "Pure silver, vampyre. A gift from the Old Country!"

The short blade of a dagger had been enough to return Kwadzo to the Red, and here Monroe wielded an entire broadsword of the poison metal. A rage ignited in his blood matching the pain he was suffering, and he released a loud and vengeful roar. Once again, he sounded like a lion, and it filled him with resolve. Kwadzo could defeat Monroe and his sword and settle the score with Big Jim, who cowered behind his overseer like a scared child.

Kwadzo watched through a haze of pain as a wicked smirk crossed Big Jim's face while his left hand went to Monroe's forehead, a move that furrowed the overseer's brow.

"Boss?"

Then Big Jim's right hand emerged holding a short, stout, and thick blade. Faster than Kwadzo believed possible, Big Jim swiped his blade across Monroe's throat, then his chest, then his abdomen.

And then, he started over again.

Monroe's blood gushed out and over Kwadzo as Big Jim kept cutting. The skin on the Ramangan's hands and face sizzled where the blood landed. Another slice sent a stream of Monroe's blood spurting into Kwadzo's eyes, and an agony so fierce seized him, he did not know if he could bear it.

This pain was silver thirtyfold.

Through his foggy vision, Kwadzo could see Monroe's dead eyes close in on him before he felt the wet, dead weight of the man on him. He was powerless to stop Monroe's fall, and he fell to his back, Monroe's body on top of him and the overseer's blood spreading everywhere.

The effect was paralyzing. Kwadzo could not close his mouth in time, and the blood draining from Monroe's severed neck oozed into it, seeping into his system. Having no breath meant he could not cough the blood up, which meant it flowed directly into his organs.

It was like swallowing death.

"You thought you was gonna lead you a revolution? Against me?" he could hear Big Jim shout at him. "Not a chance! Always knew you niggers weren't human. But you'll die, just like anything else."

Momentarily clearing his vision, Kwadzo caught sight of Big Jim hovering over him, the silver sword high above his head, ready to deliver the killing blow. The immense pain seizing him intensified, and Kwadzo began to shake uncontrollably. He could feel himself perishing with a deep sense of dread, of permanency. He thought of Tussy. Charlie. Rafazi.

Gertie.

And then a blur slammed into Big Jim. It knocked the sword from the plantation owner's grasp, but now it was falling blade-first toward Kwadzo, whose vision was still clear enough to see it and panic. Instinctively, he stopped the silver blade with his hands before it could pierce Monroe's dead body atop him and drive into his own and roared in pain from the burning of his palms against the poisonous metal.

Kwadzo turned on his side, Monroe's body rolling off him, to let go of the blade, but the skin of his palms stuck to it, peeling away in the process. In his agony, he caught sight of his savior— Charlie. The bloodhound, in Ramangan form, hovered over Big Jim, growling, his fangs inches away from the man's face.

"You stupid mutt! You're *my* dog! You're supposed to be helping *me!*" But as Charlie viciously barked and snapped at his former owner, Kwadzo's vision clouded again. He heard voices, familiar voices, leaning in close to him, voices filled with concern, anguish, defeat. He could hear Charlie whining, feel his large, flat tongue licking against his cheek.

"I'm already dead," Kwadzo told them blindly, weakly. "The fight must be won . . . with or without me . . . Our freedom . . ."

"He needs blood!" someone shouted as Kwadzo's eyes fluttered, flashes of red and black appearing behind his eyelids, calling him home. He thought of his mother, his sister, his father.

"KWADZO!"

He smelled her blood, even sweeter than he remembered it, before she even called his name.

Gertie.

Finding the strength to open his eyes, he saw her, a pistol in her hand, falling to her knees beside him, her eyes shimmering with tears. He could see Rafazi next to her, but sensed the room was empty save for his people and dead bodies. The scent of Big Jim was gone.

"What happen to him?" Gertie asked Rafazi tearfully.

"He needs blood."

"Then give him Monroe's blood! What is you waitin' on? He dead right there!"

"Monroe's blood is what did this to him, Gertie! He needs *your* blood. Monroe hated him like you love him. Made his blood poison."

"And mine?"

"The only thing that can save him."

Heavy sobs escaped Gertie, and Kwadzo could feel his own tears welling.

"You smell it, don't you?" Rafazi asked, leaning in close to him. "Her love. Take it."

Despite his weakened condition, Kwadzo felt his eyes pulse with anger. Reaching out, he grabbed Rafazi's arm as hard as he could, and the effort sent searing pain ripping through him.

"I told you, I will never feed from her!" Kwadzo groaned, even though his venom began to secrete. "I'm so weak, and her blood—I could kill her!"

Rafazi's arm slipped from his grasp seconds before small, soft hands enclosed one of Kwadzo's.

"Hush now," he heard Gertie say. He could not stop his tears at the sound of sweetness in her voice. "This here Ramangan Blood come into our lives, and you ain't listen to a word I say. So, now, you listen at me when I say this here: I is full of love for you. Our love done made life inside me. We's belong to each other. Now you takes what you need from me, Kwadzo, and you keeps your promise." Kwadzo felt Gertie cradle his blood-soaked torso in her arms. His vision cleared again briefly enough for him to see her smile. "Go on, now."

Closing his eyes before they went hazy again, Kwadzo pierced the skin of Gertie's neck. She gasped, then moaned as she pulled his head closer, urging his fangs, teeth, and venom deeper into her flesh until the rush of blood crossed his lips. Gertie's blood. He lost himself in the smell and taste of her. The supreme love she had for him, and he her, manifested as aroma, and now, taste.

The more he drank, the more strength welled within him. He could feel Gertie's blood mixing with Monroe's in his system, combatting it, conquering it. He fought against the two hands pulling at his head. Finally opening his eyes, he found his vision was clearer than it had ever been, his pain gone, his flesh healed, the full measure of his senses returned.

And Gertie's unconscious body.

"No, no . . . What did I do? What did I DO?"

The slowness of her heartbeat and the smell of smoke filled his senses at the same time. A blur rushed into the room, revealing itself to be Irene. "Barrow's set fire to the manor!" she yelled, alarming everyone. All but Kwadzo. Something new burned inside him, something stronger.

"Get our people clear of this house! Now!" Kwadzo ordered, placing Gertie's body in Rafazi's arms, telling him separately, "Do all you can to wake her, but do *not* turn her. Make sure our people are safe from Barrow in slave village as well."

"You speak like you plan to stay."

"I must. There is no way or time to explain it, Rafazi, but by the blood of Gamab, I will save this house."

By the blood of Gamab. He had heard Rafazi use the expression, but he had never understood it until now. Something deep inside his core was changing, adapting. Expanding.

"By the blood of Gamab." Rafazi nodded with sudden assured reverence before blurring out of the room with Gertie and the others.

"What about them?"

He turned to find a Ramangan standing before two people: Clarence wounded and shirtless, and a slight white man with thinning, white hair.

"They were the last two left before you . . ." The young Ramangan let her words trail off.

"I could be of use to you," the white man said with a tremble. "I am a physician. Given the chance, I could possibly ascertain why silver affects you so, perhaps even provide you with protection against its effects."

Killing was not Kwadzo's true intention. Fairness was. Justice was.

"Clarence is a pain, but he's one of us, I guess," the young Ramangan said as Kwadzo looked at his injuries.

"Can you manage them both?"

"Yes, sir! I'm Polly, by the way. Irene turned me."

"Take them with the others. And welcome to the Blood, Polly."

With a smile, Polly hoisted the two men over her shoulders and disappeared in her blur. Kwadzo stepped through the hole in the wall back into the main house, which was alight with flame.

The fire was spreading quickly, and Kwadzo could sense it had been lit in multiple areas from the outside. His vision went from red to orange, not from the flames per se, but *because* of them. The orange vision was not simply a reflection of the fire, it was his own.

Something inside him was drawing him to the flames, telling him to rush directly into them. And yet, he did not fear the action. Something was rumbling through Kwadzo now, and possibility vibrated in his veins.

A bark sounded behind him, and he found Charlie waiting patiently in the hidden room. "I thought you went with Rafazi!" The flames had risen so high, the dog had no chance to jump and escape them. "All right. But you need to stay close." Charlie blurred right up to him. "On the count of three." Charlie let loose with three deliberate barks, and, together, they raced off into the flames.

Forty-One

BY THE BLOOD OF GAMAB

The flames engulfed Kwadzo, devouring his clothing, burning his flesh, but somehow, he was able to bear it. He also couldn't stop.

His blur was moving him at a velocity he had never experienced, one almost out of his control. He could hear Charlie's whining; the dog was floating in his blur since Kwadzo was moving so fast his blur had expanded beyond him. The dog's hair was singeing off but not at the rate Kwadzo was burning. It was as if being in his blur somehow protected Charlie.

The Blood boiled within his veins as his orange vision led him up the manor's stairs and through the flames burning in the bedchambers and auxiliary rooms. His legs continued to propel him as fire burned through his entire being.

He was naked now, and the hair on his head had also burned away. He was burning so intensely he thought he might explode, and he ventured a look behind him. The areas he had raced through were free of flames, but he was still aflame, his orange vision sparkling bright.

He was *absorbing* the flames.

He could feel the fire flowing through his internal system, and yet, he was surviving it. There was an overwhelming sense his body would not allow him to stop until it had consumed the flames entirely.

And before long, he realized he had as his movement came to an abrupt halt.

There, in the middle of a charred room, Kwadzo seized up in a pain indescribably fierce. He hollered in anguish as the last of the flames covering his naked body sank into his being. Lurching up, he found a full-length, soot-streaked mirror and marveled at the sight of himself.

Bright orange and red cracks were etched into his skin, as if he had veins of lava bursting through his flesh. Flames danced upon his scalp in place of his hair, and his eyes had become brightly burning balls of fire flickering in his sockets.

Slowly, the cracks disappeared, and the fire on his head sank into his head. He winced at the itchy feeling of follicles pushing strands of his hair up through his scalp until the head of hair with which he was familiar returned. The fire in his eyes died down, and involuntarily, Kwadzo watched himself revert to his human form: nude, undamaged by the fire—and feeling stronger than ever.

Charlie emerged from behind a burnt desk, shaking his body as dogs do. And though he wasn't in Ramangan form either, his fur restored itself as he shook.

"I did it, Charlie."

As the hound barked cheerfully, Kwadzo took in the room, obliterated by the fire, save for a small corner where he spotted a partly singed tablecloth. He wrapped it around his bottom half and used shredded rope he had found to tie the tablecloth at his waist. A piece of metal on the ground cooled his foot as he stepped on it. In wonderment, Kwadzo placed his other foot on what he realized was the silver sword. There was no pain. Surmising his hunt for rope had brought him back to the hidden room from where he'd started, he picked up the weapon by its blade.

Nothing.

You survived!

Rafazi's voice in his head brought Kwadzo immediate comfort.

I told you, you are special. I knew it the moment your blood touched my lips.

"Rafazi! I hear you still! You can hear me?"

Any words directed at me you speak aloud sound in your mind first. Have you forgotten? If we are communicating mentally, I will hear the words meant for me.

What of our people? Gertie?

All safe. Can you not feel your brothers and sisters of the Blood?

Kwadzo closed his eyes and focused on those he had turned. Ekow. Irene. Fanna. All the others. He could feel the wholeness of them. He could also feel the loss of those who had perished. He could feel the absence of Tussy. But there was no way he could feel Gertie, a mortal.

She lives.

Kwadzo felt the phantom sensation of releasing a sigh of relief.

You are stronger now. More powerful. I can feel it.

So can I. What of Barrow?

Last we saw the whip-cracker, he was standing at the front of the house, watching it burn, with his lackeys. Show them the man who walked through fire and lived.

Kwadzo looked down at an expectant Charlie, who was already wagging his tail.

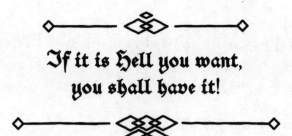

If it is Hell you want,
you shall have it!

Forty-Two

OF BLOOD AND FIRE

A collective gasp rose as Kwadzo and Charlie the bloodhound stepped out onto the front porch of the manor, which was charred and blackened by fire. The small group of white faces staring back at him were covered in shock, none more so than Big Jim himself.

"You should be dead," he said to Kwadzo. "You're a monster. A goddamn monster from Hell itself."

"Monsters come in many forms," Kwadzo said. "I'm looking at one right now."

No sooner had he said the words than the group's ire was ignited. Wicked frowns on angry faces shouting malicious insults and wrathful threats. Their vitriol was such it set Charlie barking angrily back at them.

Kwadzo could only shake his head. Here he stood without so much as a scratch, but in the face of an undeniably powerful, supernatural African force far beyond their comprehension, white colonial opinion only saw the African. And because he was African, they deemed it unnecessary for him, or the miracle he'd performed, to be taken seriously.

But no matter.

"Henceforth, let it be known," Kwadzo called out over their shouting, "this house, this land, and all it contains belong to me and my people now."

"Are you out of your cotton-picking mind?" Big Jim yelled.

"I will explain in terms you will understand. When your ancestors came to this land, it was not yours. So, you waged war against a people who did not wish it and won. In your victory, you claimed their land as your own. The same has happened here. You were engaged in my Crimson Crusade for your crimes against those you unjustly oppressed and were defeated. To the vanquisher goes the bounty."

Their angry objections rose once more.

"I will see you hang, boy! And once you're dead, I'll chop you up so every plantation can hang a piece of you up for every slave to see as a warning while your black ass burns in Hell!" Big Jim bellowed before firing a shot at the Ramangan with his rifle.

A handful of the surviving white men also raised the guns they had managed to escape the fire with and followed suit. Each bullet that struck revealed a glowing orange and red crack in Kwadzo's skin.

Big Jim's mouth gaped, and he dropped his gun as Kwadzo's eyes once again turned into flickering balls of fire. Charlie whined, cowering behind Kwadzo as the immortal felt the fire his body had consumed begin to churn within him. The small, lead spheres he'd been attacked with rolled in his core, the flames bubbling through him carrying them with great force.

They were searching for an escape.

Kwadzo's vision returned to its fiery orange tint as he took on his Ramangan form. His skin felt incredibly hot, yet the heat felt natural to him. His vocal cords shook so hard he wondered if they would be able to withstand the volume he was about to speak in, his voice rumbling forth from deep inside him.

"If it is Hell you want, you shall have it!" The words boomed out of him, and with a thundering roar, a thick stream of fire and lead blew forth from his mouth at his attackers. Kwadzo's fire spread like a billowing blanket, and the white citizens of Lakeside let loose a symphony of terrified screams as they sought to escape his flames.

They ran for their lives.

Stepping off the porch with a powerful calm, Kwadzo directed his fire with precision at each of the fleeing colonists in blasting balls, burning them one by one. This was his special power. The one Rafazi prophesied he would have. It wasn't withstanding the fire, or even absorbing it.

He could control the flames within.

Soon, only Big Jim was left, huffing vigorously as he pushed his heavy body forward. In seconds, Barrow fell flat on his belly from the exertion, his heart beating erratically. Kwadzo leaped over to him, turning himself in the air so he could land facing Barrow, feeling the fire inside die down.

"Help! Somebody save me," Big Jim sniveled.

"Why would you deserve saving, James?" Kwadzo's voice was deathly calm. "You engineered human misery. You took freedom from people, forced labor upon them without compensation, and orchestrated their torture for sport. And if their dignity demanded better for themselves, you made them pay with their lives."

"I've done nothing wrong," Barrow said, struggling up to his knees before a blur slammed into him, rolling him several feet before stopping and revealing itself to be Irene. Her eyes filling with rageful tears, she slashed away at the man with her talons, leaving him a bloody, squealing mess.

"That pain you feel?" Irene seethed at him. "That's how I felt every time you put your hands on me! I hate you, Barrow! I

HATE YOU!" Overcome with sobs, Irene broke down over her former tormentor.

Kwadzo stood back, giving her space for her vengeful anguish. A gentle hand landed on his shoulder, and he turned to find Rafazi smiling at him. Despite Irene's present distress, the two men shared their quiet victory. They had conquered their master.

"It's time to finish this," Rafazi said, nodding toward Irene. Gently, Kwadzo moved the sobbing Irene from Big Jim's bloody frame. Taking the man's right hand, he removed the gold and ruby ring and placed it on his own finger. "To the vanquisher, the spoils."

"You can't do this to me," Big Jim whined and coughed, spitting up blood. "I am a white man! I will not have everything snatched away from me by some n . . ."

Kwadzo stomped through Barrow's torso, breaking the bones of his chest cavity and smashing his heart, killing him instantly. "That will be enough of *that* word."

FLANKED BY RAFAZI AND Irene, Kwadzo, in his human form, entered slave village to thunderous applause, applause that only got louder when he held up James Barrow's severed head in front of them all.

Out of the corner of his eye, Kwadzo caught sight of Derby and Clarence sitting together on a stoop with downtrodden faces, but he quickly dismissed them from his mind.

"There is much to say," he called out, and the gathered crowd quieted to hear him. "And there will be much to do. But brothers and sisters, on this night, you stand as free people!"

The cheering returned tenfold. Soon, they were chanting his name in jubilation.

"Kwadzo! Kwadzo! Kwadzo!"

The immortal smiled at their fervor, but his smile grew at the sight of Gertie exiting a cabin with the help of Fanna.

Handing the head off to Rafazi, he moved into the open arms of Gertie, hugging her close before slipping a hand to her belly.

"Are you truly okay?" he asked her. "The baby? I thought I . . ."

"Hush now. We's fine. Rafazi gives me a drop of his venom," she said, her features scrunching in disgust at the memory. "I reckon he was tryin' to spit in my mouth, but he say it make me feel better, and he ain't lie. Feels me even better now. You done kept your promise."

"Thanks to your blood."

Gertie's nose crinkled. "This ol' Ramanga makes you do nasty stuff. You really likes drinkin' blood?"

"I do," he chuckled.

"What mine taste like?"

"Love."

"Love gots a taste?"

"And a smell."

"What love smell like?"

Kwadzo thought for a moment, reveling in the warmth of her, of their unborn child. He knew she would never take the Blood. One day, he would be without her. But this night, and for many more to come, she would be alive and free, and so, too, would be their love. It was then the true answer to her question came to him.

"You."

"Get on outta here, you," she giggled. "Now, show me Kwadzo." Once he took on his Ramangan form, Gertie pulled him close and kissed him deeply. This passionate kiss, unrestrained and in front of everyone, told him she had truly accepted him. Before long, Kwadzo felt a short arm go halfway around his waist. Fanna was hugging him and Gertie, and for the first time in a long while, Kwadzo felt the embrace of family.

Forty-Three

BLOOD RISING

hief Great Oak lead tribe many years. Has seen much devastation at hands of white man. Never see them driven away by slaves."

Only a night ago, Rafazi had been feasting on the blood of those who oppressed both Africans and the peoples native to the New World. Now, he stood next to Kwadzo, his first and only progeny, basking in the defeat of the whip-crackers. In front of a Native longhouse were Nez, the warriors of his tribe, and their chieftain, Chief Great Oak. The man was elderly, but Rafazi saw the wisdom of extended years in his eyes, something Rafazi could relate to.

"We are slaves no more," Kwadzo informed Nez. "The white man who wrongly claimed this land as his own is dead."

From behind his back, Rafazi revealed the severed head of James Barrow. "Proof he is no longer a threat to any of us." He presented the head to the chieftain, who looked deep into its eyes before giving it to Nez.

"It was not this man, but his father who was aided by British forces in driving us from the land," Chief Great Oak said in his tribe's language. "But the son was far more ruthless. He was disease in human form who brought great destruction to both our peoples and this land."

Rafazi had been of Ramangan Blood for over seven hundred years. Languages had been easily discernable for him for a solid three hundred. He suspected Nez would offer a translation for Kwadzo's benefit, but knew the young native was in for a surprise.

"Our homes were burned, and our families killed before we were brought here on ships against our will," Kwadzo responded to the chieftain in his own tongue, and Rafazi beamed with pride.

Nez, the chief, and the tribal warriors looked at Kwadzo in surprise as he continued, "We are the only ones we have left to lean on now. But I made a promise to Nez and a vow to my people to share this land in harmony and protect it from any and all who would do it harm. I'm sure Nez has told you what we are and what we can do, so I offer our protection to your people should the white folks try to attack you again.

"However, I ask for patience, as this victory did not come without loss. We must mourn and bury our dead. We must repair the destruction it took to conquer Barrow. Then, our peoples can come together for the good of the land and ourselves."

Kwadzo, his progeny, his brother. If only She could see this miracle of his Blood. If only She could see *him* and what the two of them had accomplished together.

"My people will help," the chieftain said, and Kwadzo nodded. After a quick look to Nez, Chief Great Oak stepped forward, his hand extended. With a smile, Kwadzo shook it.

PERHAPS THERE IS A *way our might can serve this earth*, Rafazi's Maker had mused to him three centuries ago, before he had hidden himself underground like a coward from a plague that reduced the mighty tribe of Ramanga to one.

Him.

And yet, from his cowardice sprang forth the rebirth of Ramanga. He was the father of a new tribe. One with purpose and vision, led by a brave man, forged by *his* Blood. Her hope had been brought to fruition by his Blood. He hoped, somehow, he'd made Her proud.

In the week since Kwadzo's Crimson Crusade, as he'd taken to calling it, much had already changed. Nez and his people had taken up residence on the land, building longhouses faster than they could have on their own with the help of Ramanagan power. With human Africans and the Native people working the fields during the day and Ramangans working at night, the crops were flourishing.

No one was haughty enough to rule out retaliation, so tribal warriors stood guard around the plantation's perimeter until sundown, then Ramangans took over the watch. Though more had been turned to handle the duty, the majority of Africans remained human. As Gertie did, as Kwadzo's child would.

Part of Kwadzo's plan was to keep the plantation business going, and doing so in a fair manner. And though Nez's people were knowledgeable in that regard, Rafazi suspected a white emissary would be needed to conduct business with the colonists.

The white doctor Kwadzo had seen fit to keep alive was joined in his duties by his wife, who had not attended the Barrow soirée. It did not take much conversing with her to realize she disliked the whip-crackers almost as much as they all did.

The couple saw to the health of everyone, Africans as well as the Native people—at least those who were open to their help—but they were most interested in Ramangan Blood: the workings of it, the power it possessed, the process of being turned. As far as Rafazi was concerned, they hadn't proven themselves to be beyond skullduggery, but so far, things were going well.

More than a few African—as well as Indigenous—women had caught Rafazi's eye. He had yet to indulge himself, but with freedom, he was beginning to feel like his old Epicurean self again and was already looking forward to the pleasures to be had in this New World.

But first, order had to be restored, and that began with the manor. Though there was still a ways to go, full rooms had been renovated, like the one he now sat in. Sanded dark oak shelves designed for books lined the walls, a long cherry wood table had been constructed, and a set of leather chairs had been refurbished. Kwadzo had chosen the room to use for council meetings.

The council consisted of the most trusted among those of the Blood: Kwadzo, himself, Irene, Fanna, and Ekow. Since she was not of the Blood, Gertie could not be a member of the council, but it didn't stop her from attending meetings.

The task of the council was to oversee the goings-on of this new plantation, its restoration work, and the path forward. As they were still mourning Tussy and the others lost in the crusade, the surviving seamstresses provided the council members with red knitted cotton clothing, according to the Akan Ghanian custom most of them were familiar with.

"We've plenty of crops to sell," Ekow was saying at their current meeting. "Trouble is how to sell them. These white folk won't do business with the Natives any sooner than they would with us."

"Perhaps the next plantation we take will have an overseer fit to take on the task for us," Rafazi suggested.

"Next plantation? We done just got free. You wants to start another war already, Rafazi?" Gertie asked.

"Not another war, Gertie." Kwadzo's voice seemed to calm her. "The Crimson Crusade was the first battle of the same war, one we have to keep fighting."

"I almost lose you in this first one!"

"This was one plantation in one province. There are others, other townships, other provinces, other colonies. Not to mention all the Native peoples of this land whose lives have been shattered by the colonists. How can we truly claim this freedom when our people remain in bondage all through this land?"

Gertie's face softened, and she held Kwadzo's cheek in her palm.

"The greatest good," she hummed with a nod. "Roog would demand as much."

"And with your support, I cannot fail." Gertie kissed him and Rafazi smiled, shaking his head at the sentimentality between them. "Then it is settled," Kwadzo decided. "We press on with the crops hand in hand with Nez and his people, fortify this plantation, and find a way to make it profitable for both our peoples. The sooner, the better. We will commit ourselves to freeing every so-called slave on every plantation in all the colonies. By the blood of Gamab."

The salutation was repeated in unison by all present before Fanna jumped to her feet.

"Wait!" she said. "We have to rename the plantation. It can't be the Barrow Plantation anymore."

"What name would you suggest, little one?" Kwadzo asked, and the child beamed at the endearing term, like a daughter would at her father.

"What about . . . the Crimson Plantation?" The name brought smiles to all those present.

"All in favor?" Kwadzo asked. All hands went up, and Fanna jumped and clapped for joy like the free child she was. "The Crimson Plantation it is."

Rafazi basked in what he'd created as his eyes caught Kwadzo's. And neither one of them could wipe the smiles off their faces.

Epilogue

BRING HER BACK TO ME

Anna Callowhill carried two bouquets of flowers through the Lakeside cemetery, a tearful mess.

All was lost to her. She had returned to an empty house after the murders of her sweet Samuel and her darling Penelope. She cursed Robert Callowhill for ever being born! How she found herself the wife of a coward and a nigger lover she would never know.

"Dear sweet Penelope," she wept, setting the first bouquet of flowers at her daughter's grave. A child lost in the dawn of life at the hand of wayward demon slaves. "I hate you niggers!" she cried out. "Please, Lord, bring her back to me . . ."

Leaning forward, Anna was unable to stop her whimpering until her air was cut off by the tight hold on her throat of a small hand far stronger than it should have been for its size. It had emerged from the dirt covering Penelope's grave, and Anna could feel the grip tighten. Gasping for air, Anna fought to free herself, but it was no use.

As the arm that held the hand forced its way from the ground, a full shock of red ringlets shot up from the dirt, and soon, Anna's precious Penelope's face came into view. She had been reborn a monster, her visage the same as that of those who had killed her: her brow engorged and extended, the veins in her face visible, and her mouth filled with sharp, jagged teeth framed by sharper fangs. When the girl opened her eyes, they were a bright pulsing red.

"Penelope?" Anna managed to croak out.

"Mother," Penelope said, running her tongue along those fangs, dripping with a clear, viscous liquid. "You smell . . . delicious . . ."

Discussion Questions

1. One of the recurring themes of the book is revenge. Willie/Kwadzo, in a desperate situation, makes an even more desperate choice to exact retribution. What would it take for you to act on the thought of revenge? What action against you do you believe would constitute just cause for retaliation?

2. Throughout much of the book, Willie/Kwadzo is at odds with Gertie regarding his actions toward gaining freedom, and it takes its toll on their relationship. Have you ever been in a relationship where someone you loved made a decision that went against your moral code? How did you handle it? Was it a deal-breaker?

3. The horror element in the book is twofold: There is the horror of the violence the Ramangans display against the colonizers, and there is the brutal horror of slavery. Which did you find to be more chilling, and why?

4. In the taking of Ramangan Blood, the slaves of the Barrow Plantation go from dominated to superhumanly powerful almost instantaneously, yet their desires remain human. Were you to obtain superhuman power overnight, how difficult do you think it would be to maintain your humanity? What rules would you set for yourself?

5. Irene is caught in a unique situation as a mixed-race woman where she is not accepted by either the African slaves or the

white colonists. Have you ever felt ostracized by two separate groups even though you were a part of both? How did that make you feel?

6. In the book, Willie/Kwadzo makes the ultimate sacrifice to do what he believes is best for Gertie and their unborn child by giving up his human life. Is there anything you believe is worth dying for? If so, what is it?

7. The slaves of the Barrow Plantation are presented with the choice of becoming powerful immortals. Arguments are made against Ramangan Blood by Gertie and for it by Irene. If you had been one of the slaves on the plantation, would you have been Team Gertie or Team Irene and why?

8. Another major theme in the book is the age-old one of good versus evil. The Ramanga Tribe has a history of evil, but Kwadzo uses their power for good, while Gertie believes they can be nothing more than evil. Do you think there is any circumstance in which doing something bad can lead to a greater good?

9. If given the chance to become an immortal vampire, would you take it? Why or why not?

10. One of the more moving moments in the book is when Willie reclaims his true name, Kwadzo. How important is identity to you? How do you define it?

11. Willie/Kwadzo had to go from being a slave to becoming a leader in a very short period of time. How do you think he handled it? Have you ever had to unexpectedly step into a leadership role without being prepared for it? How did you handle it?

12. Was there a scene or character that stuck with you more than any other?

13. Do you find this book to be controversial? If so, why?

14. Willie/Kwadzo makes a vow to share the land with the Indigenous peoples once James Barrow has been conquered, thereby paving the way for them to find liberty from the colonists and create their own agency. After all this time, why do you think Native Americans are still denied a powerful voice in this country?

15. Spoiler alert! In the end, the entire Barrow family dies. If it were up to you, would any of them have been spared? If so, why?

16. In what ways do you think the history we know would have changed after the events of the book? What other historical atrocities could have been prevented with Ramangan power? If you had the power to change history, what would you change?

© Markus Redmond 2025

ACKNOWLEDGMENTS

I would like to thank everyone who saw this book on a shelf or on a website or mentioned in an article or list and chose to pull the trigger on it. This can, at times, be a difficult book, and I truly appreciate all the readers who decided to take this bloody ride. I hope you not only enjoyed the rise of the Ramangans, but that you will be ready for book two of the Blood Saga series in 2026!

Writing a book is a solo journey in many ways. Getting a book to the point where it sits in your hands as it does now requires a community. Mine began with Lacie Waldon, my very first published author friend. I knew nothing of publishing when I met her, and she became an invaluable source of knowledge and encouragement. She believed I would get published and gave me advice that led me to adjust my query. Those adjustments got the attention of Jennifer Chevais, my incredible agent. From day one, she not only got this book, but respected it, nurtured it, protected it, fought for it. She even fought for the title.

A title that got the interest of Leticia Gomez, the editorial director of the Dafina imprint at Kensington. I could not have asked for a better home or a better guardian for this story. Leticia got exactly what I wanted to do with this book and took a stand for it, championed it, and the support it garnered still astounds me. From the publisher, Jackie Dinas, to the senior communications manager, Michelle Addo-Chajet, to the art director, Kristine Mills, the brilliant mind behind this book's astonishing cover, to the amazing production team responsible for making the interior of this book so stunning led by

Cassandra Farrin and Leah Marsh, everyone was ready to spill blood with me. It was the best industry introduction I could have hoped for.

A quick aside . . . you may have noticed that so far, I have only mentioned women in these acknowledgments. Yes, the team that diligently worked to bring this book into existence was nearly all female and each one a badass. My work has never been in better hands.

There were early readers whose encouragement gave me life. Among them were Angela Hayes, Allison McBee, Leila Hayward, Jon Matthews, Ginger Teague (who hated vampires until she met the Ramangans), Chloe Faith, an editorial assistant who provided emotional insight as a mixed raced woman of color who connected with Irene early on, my longtime friend Vernita Irvin, Ph.D., who not only cheered me on but kept my historical research on point, and friend and mentor David Greenwalt, he of *Buffy the Vampire Slayer*, *Angel*, and *Grimm* fame, the man who gave me my very first on-camera job as an actor, who called *Blood Slaves* "the American *Game of Thrones*." High praise, indeed. A heartfelt thanks to each and every one of you.

Thanks are also due to those who helped protect this book. George Francisco, a dear friend whose interest in my succeeding led him to introducing me to Daffodil Tyminski, whose legal guidance was crucial and deeply appreciated. Sam Hiyate, the CEO of my agency, The Rights Factory, who gave his unwavering support to the agents handling this book (and me), the aforementioned Jennifer Chevais and Karmen Wells, who aided in my broader vision for this book and beyond. Jules Stewart, who encouraged me to stand my ground and never waver, not just with the book but as an artist and a person as well.

There were the good folks at Burn Fitness in Santa Monica who got wind of what I was doing and would ask how things were going while wishing me and my words well; and one in particular, Eric V. Larson, Ph.D., who acknowledged upon learning the plot of the book that it was not a story about slavery but a story about a slave, as is mentioned at the beginning of the book. I couldn't have said it better myself. A heartfelt thank you to all.

My stepson Jeremy, who may or may not remember telling me stories about a "vampire of doom" when he was just a little guy. His imaginings inspire me still. Thanks, Bubba.

There were also the authors who befriended me in the 2025 Debut Author Discord. To be able to engage with other authors who were in the same boat, going through all the same firsts was a gift, but special mention must be made of my new friend Shalini Abeysekara. Not only did she shout all over social media about *Blood Slaves*, but she also created its first pieces of fan art. By the way, treat yourself to her book, *This Monster of Mine*. It's incredible.

As you can imagine, writing this book could get rather intense, so joyful outlets were necessary. During the writing of this book, those came in the forms of Singaporean television and large doses of K-pop. Special thanks to the magic created by Jeanette Aw, Rui En, Pierre Png, He Ying Ying, Brandon Wong, Chen Li Ping, Chantelle Ng, Desmond Tan, Elvin Ng, Shaun Chen, Jesseca Liu, Jeremy Chan, Cynthia Koh, Lin Mei Jiao, Rebecca Lim, Romeo Tan, and the Ah Jie, Zoe Tay. You all and many others helped pull me out of the darkness with your extraordinary talent when I needed it.

The music of Mamamoo, 4Minute, Stray Kids, Zico, Sistar, 2Yoon, Twice, CLC, NCT 127, Dreamcatcher, Nmixx, Alice, EXO, and Red Velvet also provided respite. The leader of Red Velvet also provided inspiration; she and Irene share the same name.

I also took comfort in every successful Black person, no matter the field. Every Black person I saw smile, laugh, and walk with confidence. Each instance is a statement.

And lastly, I wish to pay special acknowledgment to my wife, Isis Heuser. I met Isis when we were both fifteen years old in high school. She was way out of my league then and still is now. We reconnected as adults, and she has been loving me on purpose ever since. She has supported me through every failure, cried with me, laughed with me, and believed in me when I was incapable of doing so. She opened her heart to me, closed it around me, and never let go. At every turn, every pivot, she has been there, right beside me saying, "Go." In fact, if it were not for her, this book might not have ever come into existence. As I stated in my author's note, the murder of George Floyd stoked a different kind of anger in me, one I told her about. I expressed my distress at a system of justice that would see George Floyd dead and Kyle Rittenhouse alive and releasing a book. I was attempting to write a very different vampire book at the time that wasn't coming together, and she said, "It's too bad your vampires can't go back in time and fix everything from the get-go."

The next day, *Blood Slaves* came to me. Her comment was the catalyst. So, thank you, Isis.

I love you.